FORTUNE'S FOOL

The sequel to The Horse is Never Wrong

Mary Pagones

ISBN: 1512125350
ISBN 13: 9781512125351
Library of Congress Control Number: 2015907807
CreateSpace Independent Publishing Platform
North Charleston, South Carolina

To anyone who ever "accidentally" acquired an animal

O, I am fortune's fool!

-ROMEO, *ROMEO & JULIET* (I.III.138)

1

YOU CAN TELL THE REST OF THE WORLD TO GO TO HELL, SIMON

I'm having what I hope will be my last conversation on gravity, mass, and centripetal force. I already got an A on my physics final and a 4 on the AP Physics exam, so I know I've passed the class. Physics is the one A I've gotten in high school. All that remains is presenting my final project. In a few days, the only gravitational force I'll need to care about is whatever keeps me securely anchored in a horse's saddle.

I like my instructor, Mr. Shackleton, all right. He isn't one of those annoying teachers, the ones who assign pointless books and busy work, so I kind of make an effort, more than I usually do. I actually found physics really interesting. It came easily to me, and if I didn't have so much else buzzing around and distracting my brain right now, I might dwell more carefully on each and every number and word. My mind is roaming outside. It's that brief period in June when the skies are still overcast and it is even somewhat cool in the shade. Perfect riding weather. Almost New England weather, from what I can remember from growing up there and the vacations I used to spend in Massachusetts over the summer at my grandmother's house, when she was still alive. It's nice enough to ride every day but just cool enough that I don't break a sweat beforehand.

At least my teacher asks his students to present the projects personally to him rather than standing in front of the class. That's another advantage of having a socially awkward science dork as an instructor. I hate speaking in public, even though the guys in my physics class aren't total idiots like most of the kids at my school. I don't mind being watched when I'm on course at a horse show. But in class it's different and I'd just rather not be seen. I mean, I'm speaking in public when I am teaching a riding lesson, sure. I'll do it out of necessity; I'm not phobic or anything. But when a stupid teacher tries to make me present something in front of a class of people who hate me enough already and are looking for more fodder to make fun of, forget it. I have as much contempt for that kind of teacher as for the ones who make a big deal about not giving homework the day of the prom.

Mr. Shackleton was always really cool about assigning labs and letting us try stuff out so we didn't have to sit behind a desk all period. I hate sitting at a desk for hours a day, especially since I'm left-handed and my school doesn't have enough desks for lefties in most rooms. I always have to bend over in a weird, cramped way, and then my teachers say that they can't read my handwriting.

"Adequate, O'Shaughnessy," Mr. Shackleton pronounces when I'm done. I smile because that designation means 'pretty good,' even an 'excellent' in his lingo. There is a long and uncomfortable pause.

"Simon, there is something I've wanted to talk to you about for a long time."

I flinch a bit.

"You never asked me for a recommendation for college. And I've heard from your guidance counselor that you didn't even apply to college."

"No, Mr. Shackleton, I'm not going to college."

He looks shocked, like I've done something obscene. I think about how I'm going to explain this to him. You see, for the past two years I've been working at a show barn in my area. Most of the time I exercise the horses that need work, which can range from a twenty-year-old former Grand Prix jumper with arthritis to a hyperkinetic green baby that crashes through a course like it was tripping out on acid. I'll also ride some of the horses in the show ring: everything from some girl's fancy, imported horse from Europe who she swears is trying to kill her to a hunter that won't get blissed out on the latest supplement enough for his middle-aged weekend rider to handle him. I did win quite a few nicely-colored ribbons last season and got to go to some prominent events.

The weird thing about the horse world is that horses don't know how much money you make or the fact that their nameplates say "Owned and Loved By" with a name other than yours. Every now and then you'll find one that won't go right for its owner, no matter how much the kid's parents have paid for training. And they give up and try to sell it or at least have someone who doesn't believe he can break a leg or a neck—even if he tried—to do the dirty work. That's part of how I got the resume that is going to allow me to be a working student up in Vermont for Daniel McAllister, the legendary event rider. I sent in my resume and a few good training videos, and Vermont's where I'm going, not to college to be locked into a closet of a dorm room with books and a bunch of students who couldn't put on a saddle right if their lives depended upon it.

When he was young, Mr. McAllister won just about every award and competition there is in eventing and showjumping—except for the Olympics. Now he runs a training and breeding operation up in Vermont, in an area where most people would think is the middle of nowhere. Even he—mainly because he lacks sufficient financial backing, despite all of his connections and everything—isn't currently sending mounts to the Olympics, Rolex, Jersey Fresh, or wherever every couple of years, which is pretty amazing. He's still poor enough to have to give clinics to half-assed ammies rocking Beginner Novice and Novice levels in eventing. But he is perhaps the most respected voice in the eventing world, and that's all I care about.

The working student position is pretty much slave labor in exchange for the ability to ride his horses and learn from him for a year. That's a fair trade as far as I'm concerned. I've done mostly jumpers, so getting this at all without pages and pages of a resume in eventing is pretty amazing. I have qualified just barely enough to make myself useful up to Preliminary level but that's about it. That sounds really good, but there are kids not even old to drive already competing at Advanced level internationally.

I know it's wrong, but sometimes I find myself Googling those really rich junior kids on mounts that cost hundreds of thousands of dollars and ogling their rides like my brother does porn. Watch guys on YouTube who are in their teens racking up points at CCI-starred events. I realize I'm luckier than most to be around horses even though I'm not loaded. Still, it's hard not to want what you can't have.

I used to want to be some great rider, now I don't care. I'd just like my own mount. I used to own my own horse. But she injured herself and had to be put down. I never found another quite like her, so I don't own anything now. My brother and I share a horse (sort of) but he mostly rides at another barn (definitely not a show barn), the place where my mom works. His horse is nice but isn't going to set the world on fire, or even my heart. Like I once heard a very famous trainer say, you're not going to win the Indy 500 with a Honda, and Sean's Camera Shy is a Honda. Safe, reliable, built like a tank, and quiet enough for a child to ride. My brother can let Cam sit while he is away at college for months and get on him during his vacations and Cam'll be the same horse. I guess that's good for some people, but there is part of me that has always had contempt for animals that have nothing inside of them worth being tamed.

I explain to Mr. Shackleton how it's a great honor that I've been selected to be a working student for a year and my housing, board, training, lessons—even boarding for a horse if I get another one—will all be paid for and this will be a way to get my foothold in the industry as a professional. Somehow, this makes him more, rather than less, horrified.

"You're going to be cleaning stables for a living?"

"Yeah, but also riding."

"From this," he asks as he gestures around the classroom, "to shoveling horse shit?" Mr. Shackleton often curses when there are no administrators around with ears to hear, one of the things which always endeared him to me even though he's the kind of pasty, out-of-shape teacher with a bad haircut and shirts from Walmart that most of the other students like to make fun of. He's not fat, but that's pretty much all you can say about him. I don't expect him to get it. You either get horses or you don't, and that's all there is to know. "Look, I know you're very fond of horses and your mother encourages you but let me speak to you as if you were my son, as if I had a son. Your mother should have been taking you around to colleges to get you excited about the prospect of higher learning. If you had put in a reasonable effort in high school, an application to a school like MIT or at least Carnegie Mellon wouldn't have been out of the question. Even now—have you considered Rutgers for engineering?"

The idea of being in a classroom for more than four minutes more, much less four years in New Jersey, makes me feel like I'm choking, smothering, just hearing him say it. Like I said, the guy isn't a total jerk. But I know if I don't act now while I'm still young and dumb and fearless, I might never end up doing what I want to do.

"Have you ever been to MIT? It's a beautiful place." And Mr. Shackleton goes on about how he went to a science teachers conference there recently and how pristine and serene it was, and what a great city Boston is to go to school in, and I kind of glaze over. The truth is, I've had a conversation like this before. My guidance counselor called me into her office when I took the PSAT as a junior.

"What is THIS?" she said, referring to my scores. I was confused, because they were pretty good, even better than my smart friend Heather's because she totally blew the math. Actually, my math was perfect and both of my verbal sections were still in the ninety-ninth percentile (kind of ironic, since I talk as little as possible in school; the barn is a different story). My counselor was really upset about it, given that I pretty much have straight Bs and Cs in everything except for math and math-y science classes that don't require too much reading and memorization. Apparently, colleges don't like it when you have really bad grades and really high standardized test scores because it indicates you're not trying in school. Which I guess makes the tests accurate in some way, because I didn't try *at all* in school!

"What kind of a student gets an A-minus in calculus as a junior," said my counselor, her nose wrinkling up underneath her little pair of wire-rimmed glasses like a rabbit, "and a D-plus in health?"

"Oh, it's very easy, if you don't turn in any homework," I said, cheerfully.

So I won some kind of national semifinalist recognition or something, and they took a picture for the trophy case of me and the other kids from the high school that qualified. Basically the photo was two smiling and neatly dressed skinny Asian girls and a chubby Indian guy and me, me wearing my Killers T-shirt and my hands stuffed in my sweatshirt kind of glaring at the camera. They wouldn't let me pull up my hoodie for the photo because they said it would look like a mug shot.

It wasn't the first time I'd been called into the guidance office, though. Once I was sent down because my history teacher accused me of drawing pictures in class while she was lecturing and I was not taking notes in proper outline format. I explained that I don't take notes like normal people and it wasn't doodling. I prefer to draw pictures rather than write in words. And I reconstructed the whole lecture, explaining what the pictures meant, and they still yelled at me, saying that I should take notes in words like everyone else. Which is pretty dumb, because shouldn't the notes be how I remember things, not how the teacher does?

I also got accused of cheating when I just wrote the answers down in my calculus class, even though I was the only person who got all of the right answers, so I obviously wasn't copying. It's so dumb to write it all out when I can do the work in my head. I use all of these examples not to show you that I'm smart, by the way (I know plenty of smart people who really suck at school), but rather to explain to you why school is just dumb and I'm done with it.

Even as I walk down the hall right now, I see people hugging who never got along during the year; I hear girls crying who could barely make it to school the required number of days. They're all so stupid, loving something just because they're leaving it.

But then again, I sometimes feel as if I've always had this odd, double consciousness, even when I've been happy during my high school years. I remember on a couple of occasions, sitting in a diner with my brother at midnight or cleaning tack with some of the barn kids to prepare for a horse show, suddenly realizing how quickly it will all be over. High school, I mean. I'd be there, talking like a normal person, but another part of my brain would coolly pronounce: *730 days and none of us will be here like this, for better or for worse, it will all be over.* Or *520 days,* or however many more days until the end of this period of our lives. I know I'm not the first person to feel this way or think like this, that time's a-wasting, but if so why do people always act so surprised when life moves quickly? Maybe that's why so many of them get left behind at a jump and I don't.

Before he lets me go, Shackleton says something weird. "With a science degree, O'Shaughnessy, you have an objective skill, and if you're good at it, you can tell the rest of the world to go to hell about everything else."

This is the one thing that he says that makes sense to me; and for a second I lift up my eyes from the floor, where they have been for most of our conversation, and I feel like we understand each other for a brief stab of a second. But that's how I feel about riding, too, I think, and my eyes drop down again.

I finish talking to Mr. Shackleton and head out to the parking lot to drive to the barn. On my way, I pass my English teacher, who is talking to the principal. I try to slip by without saying anything, but I hear her mutter when she thinks I'm out of earshot, "...good riddance to the younger O'Shaughnessy kid; thank goodness there aren't any more where they came from. I don't know who was worse, the older one or the younger one. The older one was louder and more obnoxious, but the younger one was more insolent when he talked. Which was hardly ever. Just glared at me most of the time."

"Oh, the younger one was definitely worse, remember how his freshman year..."

"Yes, yes, you're right, now I remember..." Laughter.

I thought if I stood up for myself my freshman year, it wouldn't be so bad, but people's memories are short, so of course it was still bad year after year. Soon I realized that to fight for any type of respect was pointless. I watch the kids signing yearbooks, all sitting cozy on the bench in front of the high school. Suddenly, remembering how I have a copy of the yearbook in my own book bag, I take mine out and throw it in the trash. It makes a wonderful, satisfying sound when it hits the tin can.

At least there are one or two people at my barn who will understand and appreciate how awesome it is that I got such a good working student position. My truck (a hand-me-down from my brother) sputters and wheezes, but at least it starts. I know that it's not as determined to make it to Vermont as I am and its days are numbered, but I don't care—only a few more days of the old life until I walk into the new.

2

FORTUNE

Ever since I've been able to drive, I've been working at Angel Heart Equestrian Center. I used to ride at a small barn near my house where my mom still teaches. I sometimes miss the casualness of the old place and seeing my brother's horse every day despite his faults.

I know Sean likes college, but the idea of making horses into something you do on vacation, only when you have the time, is profoundly abhorrent to me, like the reversal of all that is right in the world. Of course, most civilians (non-riders) would say I have my priorities screwed up.

I honestly think Angel Heart is probably nicer than my house (and I spend more effort keeping it clean, that's for sure). The barn is all blonde, lacquered wood; its horses have to wear the same monogrammed blankets and fly sheets; there's a heated wash stall; and training board is more than what some people pay for a small apartment per month. Of course I am part of that training board, which means regularly exercising and teaching the horses of the boarders during the week so they can breeze in and ride their animals and not die on the weekends when they horse show. I swear, some of the riders spend more time online shopping SmartPak for new boots during downtime at work than they do on the backs of their horses.

Riding is only a small part of the duties of any working student, especially a high school kid like myself. The job also includes feeding and watering, helping with mucking out, blanketing, braiding before shows, and all the other activities that make the barn run seamlessly. Most of the boarders are unaware of the behind-the-scenes action necessary for their horses to be ready for them at a moment's notice, and some of them even pay to have their beasts tacked up before they ride. It cracks me up to see leggy teenage girls who can competently jump more than four feet, who could give you a rundown on the merits of Horze (yes, it is pronounced like you think it should be) versus Ariat breeches, but who can't bridle their own ponies, much less take apart said bridle to clean it. They barely even notice me: I'm just part of the scenery.

There are a couple of other barn slaves who are nice, and that makes it bearable when I'm not riding and the few older riders go out of their way to say it's pretty cool I'm going to be a working student for a year for a guy like Daniel McAllister. But even then, it's not like I'm training with Beezie Madden or a big hunter rider. People only dabble in eventing here.

I suppose now is as good a place as any to explain what exactly it is that I do and want to do. Eventing isn't like those horse shows you see in the movies where little girls wear blue ribbons on their braids as they go over eight tiny fences with their fat ponies. It's three competitions in one: dressage, cross-country, and stadium jumping. There are levels from Beginner Novice, with little baby fences all the way up to Advanced level, and after the lower levels you have to get national qualifying results (NQRs) at the previous level before you can move up and compete. I've gone to exactly nine events in my entire life, each time on a different horse, but I was lucky enough to rack up the correct points and qualifications so I can do Preliminary level if I have the opportunity. Provided I can get a horse to perform at that level. It requires much more skill than just jumping big.

At Daniel's, I know I'll most likely be jumping puddles at the lower levels ninety percent of the time with some of his baby green horses, not winning anything spectacular and that's fine with me, as long as I'm riding. Again, when I was a dumb little kid, I used to jaw on and on about how I was going to make it to the Olympics someday. But now my ambitions are somewhat more modest: avoid the Box of the office cubicle at all costs and hope the only suit jacket I ever wear is for a horse show, not to go to the office every day like most of the older ammies at my barn.

Today, I'm just riding a liver chestnut named Whisky Z over some gymnastics. Alcohol names are always popular for horses, and why that's so, you be the judge. He's the kind of ride I like—forward and responsive, even though probably not the best mount for his owner, a thirty-something lawyer who is usually too busy to get in the saddle more than once or twice a week when she isn't tallying up nine million billable hours, whatever that means. I use the large outdoor arena to set up the course I have in mind, and we're almost alone (I got out earlier from school than the younger kids), except for the big grey that is being worked in draw reins in the smaller paddock beside us.

As I pop through the combination, I watch the grey. He's huge, over 17h, and pale enough that I'm guessing he can't be super-young (greys tend to fade with age). The purpose of draw reins is to get him into a frame, but they seem to have more of an effect upon his wild, wandering eyes than on his actual head carriage. His head is artificially positioned where it should be, but as a result he's very heavy on his forehand and I can see that the owner (I'm assuming whoever is riding him is the owner since I haven't seen anyone else on him) is frustrated.

I'm not saying the use of draw reins is always unjustified—maybe occasionally in some very specific circumstances—but it's clear that this is just not an occasional use of a gadget, just from reading the horse's body. I notice that the horse's neck has the telltale bulging lower muscles from being in draw reins on a more-than-occasional basis. I consider saying something but remember that criticizing someone's riding, except in a lesson, is totally pointless.

Whisky is in a good mood, and I have no problems completing the exercise with him—he gets his strides right, he doesn't rush, he is careful—but the more I watch the grey, the more I feel a kind of choking and constraining sensation around my own throat.

When I am untacking Whisky, I ask one of the girls about the big gelding. "Oh, don't worry about him, he's on his way out. No one's really clear what his story is. He's useless at dressage—flat as a board, can't get him in frame. And they've bitted him up twice, and he still kind of crashes around cross-country. His last few appearances were at the lower levels and complete disasters. He jumps clear but scares the bejezus out of his rider. They sold him as an eventing *prospect*, actually. Pretty useless."

"Eventing *prospect*? Well, that's usually translated into 'can sort of jump but has no brakes,'" I note. "That should have warned her."

It's gotten warm, so I hose Whisky in the outdoor wash stall. The owner just left the grey for the grooms to untack, I presume, since I see one of the full-time stable hands letting him out now. He's in one of the far paddocks that's also set up for jumping. It does double-duty as a cross-country practice arena as well as turnout. He's turned out alone, near a big field of other geldings that he'll likely be out with regularly—once he's done with quarantine—if he stays long enough, of course.

Finally free, the grey begins to gallop, kicking up his heels and snorting and bucking. He's a different animal without a rider on his back.

And then, I see the oddest thing—as he runs, he actually turns and pops over one of the jumps, athletically and easily. Although I've ridden a fair number of horses that loved jumping and seemed to look forward to it when I rode them, I've rarely seen a horse free-jump willingly, except when on a lunge line or in a chute. And it's a pretty big jump.

The truth is, I like his style.

When I've finally finished with Whisky, I go straight to the barn manager. "How much is he?"

"Who?" she asks, still watching the group lesson that's beginning to warm up in the indoor. The arena still needs to be set up for the lesson by the staff, and I can tell she is upset.

"The grey, the big grey," I say.

"Why? Are you interested? I thought you were leaving us soon."

"I am."

"A couple of thousand—the owner is pretty motivated and taking a loss on what she originally paid for him. Horses like him are what happen when people are looking for bargains. She's going to be looking at a new one in Maryland."

3

THE FOOL

"**M**a, I just kind of accidentally bought a horse so I'll need the trailer when we go up to Daniel's."

"What?"

It's not as bad as it sounds. I have money saved up from the tiny salary Angel Heart gives me (well below minimum if you work out the hours I spend there), tips from grateful owners, birthday and holiday money, and a few years of general frugality. I haven't owned my own horse since freshman year so I figure I owe myself this one.

I've only owned three horses in my life: my first (pretty fancy) pony, when mom was still married to my dad and we had more serious money; the second, a pony we got a year or two after the divorce, which Sean and I shared at first and which bucked him off repeatedly, making it clear that we required different mounts; and Damsel in Distress, the Thoroughbred I owned for about two years who died. I've been looking for a horse ever since but never found one that I liked, was suitable, within my budget, or whatever.

"Remember, free board is included as part of my working student arrangement," I say. "Not having a horse would be like turning down a gift."

"Free board or an additional $500 a month on top of your stipend. Unless you found something really suitable, I was hoping you would take the $500 a month," says my mother. "You'll be sitting on plenty of different horses all day, you don't need your own. Certainly not someone's rejected gelding."

I run down his stats: the horse's show name is Fortune's Fool (most horses have weird, stupid phrases as show names, so I don't give much thought to that). He's 17.2h, nine years old, and had three or four owners in the past few years and those are just the ones people know about. Breeding indeterminate, training indeterminate.

It's also true Fortune is a gelding (my mother and I prefer mares or stallions but you can't find a place to board the latter). And his muscles all wrong from bad training. These are all facts I acknowledge.

However this is also a fact: "I've already bought him so there is no point in arguing."

"Without even getting a vet to examine him first for a PPE? Are you out of your mind, Simon?" Pre-purchase exam? *Pfft*—what's the point if I already know what I'm doing?

"Like I said, it was an accident." I am bringing the check tomorrow. I am literally shaking with excitement about riding him.

My brother is home from college and by now he has recovered from the semester—from finals and running his brains out (running cross-country and track, for his scholarship, not running his brain in the classroom). He runs even during the off-season to keep in shape, to keep his mind and body fit, he says. Although sometimes I dispute that he has any brains at all, that brother of mine. Sean usually sleeps for a week after arriving home.

Sean and I are meeting in the middle this year, only briefly. My working studentship begins only a few days after graduation. I am told I can leave Fortune at Angel Heart until I go.

The first day I ride Fortune, it's raining, so I take him around the indoor. He goes over everything but I have to practically crash him into the wall to stop him. I find this totally hilarious.

"Yup, buddy, the wall is still there," I say.

"Simon, you're a nut," says one of the hunter girls, watching me from the door. "You're completely certifiable."

Gradually, after assessing him, I force him to come to the first fence at a trot, canter over the second and then come to a halt. Halting at the wall, of course, but better than crashing.

I think the girl is being unfair, personally. Even after an hour I've seen progress—we get over a course with something resembling regular strides and perhaps more importantly, we actually stop at the end of it all. Success! Although I know some riders would say the real success is neither of us have demolished one another or the arena.

Deep down, I'm also impressed at how effortlessly he can clear the low 1.15m course in the indoor that day. It hardly feels like jumping at all.

"I'm in love," I say to my audience at the end. A bunch of the girls have stopped what they're doing to gawk, even the ones who usually look right through me.

As I'm untacking, one of the hunter princess trainers comes up to me. "You're a good rider, Simon," she says, and I brace myself. "But you're dangerously undisciplined. That's the worst possible horse for you to get."

Yeah, whatever.

"You think you're so good you don't need to take lessons but…"

Can't afford yours, hunter princess, I think.

She goes on, "The type of riding I saw in the arena just now is unacceptable on these premises. What if a beginner or a timid rider was in there?"

"I wouldn't have ridden a new horse at all with a beginner or a little kid in there. I'm not mean or stupid."

"What if a prospective new client had seen that, first thing walking into the barn?"

"I'm leaving soon, so you don't need to lecture me." Hunter princess, I'm already gone.

I ask Sean if he wants to try Fortune out before I leave for Vermont. When I show him the picture of the horse on my phone, I can see from the expression on his face that the answer is "no." Not his type. But truthfully, the horse isn't my type either, as Sean points out. "No Thoroughbred? I thought that's what you were looking for?"

"This was an impulse buy," I explain.

My mother doesn't want to go look at the horse either. She keeps saying it's a mistake and goes on about the fact a vet hasn't even seen him (although he jumps sound). But then again, she thinks not going to college and being a working student are a mistake. In all honesty, my mother's attitude kind of frustrates me. I understand why Sean doesn't get why I want to become a working student. As soon as he graduated, he stuffed his saddle and boots in a closet and hardly gave a thought to either all summer, leaving his whole suburban New Jersey cowboy image (he rode mostly Western) in the dust.

But my mom should get it, given that she worked as a professional rider, at least until she divorced my dad. Instead, she tells me I'd be smarter to get a degree in business or something and then I'd be able to afford a really nice horse—I should make big bucks doing something in IT or on Wall Street like my brother is planning to do. "The people who have the money control everything in the horse world, not the trainers," she tells me. "You're setting yourself up for failure, but I can only let you make your own mistakes." Mom's been saying that to both of us since we were little kids, sometimes during the occasional visit to the ER. Usually to Sean though, even though he rode less than I did. Actually, the kids he played soccer and stuff with banged him up good more than any horse. I've always managed to land on my feet.

I kind of know she is right on one hand about the money. But on the other hand, what's the point in having money if I don't know I'm the best I can be at riding? There is so much I don't know. I can't learn that in a classroom or just doing horses as a college activity.

I ride Fortune over the cross-country jumps alone in the morning, before the other horses have been turned out and while Hunter Princess trainer and her ilk are still sleeping. He is still dying to rush everything but trusts me enough to regulate himself. I like the fact he doesn't spook at any of the shadows in the early, cloud-covered dawn. The muscles of his body do sort of hang together oddly, but that will change with time and conditioning, I'm sure. They also told me he'd bite and kick when I tacked him up, and although he put his ears back and thought about it, he didn't. I fed him a couple of treats and he tolerated everything, with just some bared teeth and foot stamping.

Where I'm going in Vermont, they have miles of trails rather than the small, contained and manicured brush in the parks near the barn. The trails near our barn in New Jersey have gotten smaller and smaller over the years as they have built more and more houses. They have even been lobbying to pass a law that riders should have to pick up after their horses. My mother calls it the disease of suburban sprawl.

My friend Heather is the only one of my friends from the old barn who will look at Fortune. She's just finished her first year of college and still rides over the summer and breaks with my mom as well as on her college (IHSA—Intercollegiate Horse Shows Association) team. Heather is very smart although she's the kind of annoying smart person who talks about how she is going to fail whatever for HOURS before she gets like an A-minus on a test or paper.

"He's *so* cool-looking," she says. But even though on her college team she rides strange horses all of the time, she's afraid to get on him. "He's named after a quote from *Romeo and Juliet*, you know."

"I didn't know but I won't hold it against him." I make a face. I don't press the issue though because if you start to talk about Shakespeare with Heather (or pretty much any book by someone dead), you'll be there all day. If it wasn't for Heather I doubt I would have passed English in high school at all—I actually like reading, especially sci-fi and fantasy and horse books and well, all horse books are fantasy books, so no difference. But I hate all the stupid questions teachers ask about what you're reading and my thoughts are never the same thoughts that you're supposed to have about the books they require. I mean, why do I have to read crap like *Romeo and Juliet* because they say it's a classic and because it's really old? So is the *Dragonriders of Pern*, a classic, I mean, and I could totally ace a test on that book. I never even made it through *Hamlet* my senior year because it was pretty obvious when Prince Hamlet got a chance to stab his uncle in the back and didn't that Shakespeare was really padding out the whole thing. No one's that stupid in real life, only in books.

Heather dated my brother briefly in high school but despite that lapse of judgment, I feel glad that at least someone likes my new horse. (My brother dated one annoying girl, some runner on the cross-country team, for forever, and then he passed through a blur of girls of varying hair colors, Heather being the only one who mattered because she's my friend not because she dated Sean.).

Fortune, *Romeo and Juliet* will never have anything to do with my love life, not now, not ever, of that I have been sure for a long time. I'd never give up everything for love.

4

LOVE AT FIRST SIGHT

My mother drives Fortune and me to Daniel's barn in our rickety trailer. The drive is over five hours and she reminds me several times along the way that I could have bought my own car with the money I spent on the big, clumsy horse and because of Fortune I'll have to get around by bicycle, foot, or hitching rides instead. No public transportation where we are going, what my brother calls "cow-tipping, sheep-shagging" country.

Halfway through, we swap seats, to give Mom a rest.

"For $4,000, I couldn't have bought anything but a total POS car," I point out. Mom doesn't like it when her kids curse (even though we do it all the time) but POS (piece of shit) is okay to say.

"So a POS horse is better?" she says.

I glare at the road before me, determined to enjoy the driving for as long as it lasts.

My mother opens up and grows more genial and accommodating when we get to the farm. Daniel has heard of my mother and he greets her like this: "Bridget O' Shaughnessy. You—almost—beat me riding Enigmatic that day—I still remember it, I still don't know how I won. You were just a kid and I was riding a friend's horse in that hunter derby—arrogant bastard that I was I thought it would be easy to go slumming in the hunters but you gave me a real run for my money." I wonder if is because of my mother, not my own past performance, that he accepted me as his student.

Daniel walks with a slight hitch, the result of a riding accident he had a couple of years ago. I know he's got a new, artificial hip now (he calls it his "bionic" hip) but he says he busted up enough other stuff on that side of his body to the point that those parts don't quite work as well together anymore, despite the surgery. He must be approaching, if not over, seventy and he still rides and competes regularly, often on green horses he is bringing up the levels. He still has a better position than most professional riders half his age. He tells me to call him Daniel, not Mr. McAllister like I have been, which makes me like him and further reinforces my conviction in that I made the right decision to avoid more schooling of the conventional, book-bound kind.

Daniel also notes there are two other working students: Megan and Cynthia. I meet Megan's horse before I meet Megan. When I go in to check to make sure that Fortune's stall is set up, I notice that Megan has already bedded down her pony Maggie May in the barn (the name tag with the legend "Owned and Loved by Meg D" is nailed on the door). She put a stall guard up but Maggie May is so tiny the pony's already managed to slip out of the stall and is wandering around the barn aisle, looking for grain.

The bigger horses are snorting and whinnying but Maggie seems unperturbed. I put her back in her stall and close the door. I like Maggie already even though she is too small for me to ride without looking ridiculous. She looks like she is part mustang (the odd, muscular, sparkplug neck and rough mane give her away) and something else. Welsh pony maybe, I assume because of her color. Grey like Fortune, only darker and more dappled. I'm also pleased to see Megan's carefully cleaned and sober tack already stowed away on a rack with her name on it. She looks responsible and that is important to me when it comes to horses (although not much else).

Speaking of mustangs, Megan and her boyfriend arrive soon afterward in a powder blue, perfectly restored 1997 Ford Mustang. For a second I regret my decision to buy Fortune and not to get a car.

I introduce myself. "Hi, I'm Simon and I want to steal this car."

Megan laughs. "Sorry, but it's not mine, it belongs to Ricky," she says, gesturing to the guy driving the vehicle I assume is her boy-friend. "He's been fixing it up for months."

When she gets out of the car, I notice that Megan is about 4'11 and probably ninety-five pounds. That explains the pony and also partially why she was selected—I am guessing that the farm needs a "pony jock" and based upon Megan's no-nonsense attitude and size she seems perfect. Just about every farm, no matter how prestigious, is at least somewhat dependent upon young, horse-crazy girls who want to ride, so there is always a need for ponies. (Even though I've always been of the opinion that while ponies are closer to the ground, temperament-wise they're also closer to hell).

Ricky is kind of chubby, an unshaven guy with a goatee, already-thinning hair, and a black T-shirt with the name of some metal band I've vaguely heard of but don't really listen to. I'm kind of surprised that a girl as attractive as Megan has him in tow, but maybe it's the car. I kind of pet the car, like it's a real mustang.

"Hopefully Ricky won't crash it when the ice comes in the winter 'cause it is rear wheel drive even though I told him not to buy it for that reason as his only car," Megan says.

"Nag, nag, Megs," says Ricky, cheerfully.

Fortune seems to like his stall. Despite his bull-in-a-China-shop behavior under saddle when I rode him last, he is relatively quiet on the ground today with me, only a slight grumpy nip I manage to dodge and gently whack him for. He doesn't seem to be anxious, but then again I am sure he has been passed around a fair amount recently and is desensitized to newness. He eats his hay and I pat him and give him carrots and look for Daniel to see if I can turn Fortune out in a paddock alone to stretch while the horse is still under quarantine.

That's when I see the pink luggage. Megan and I look across at one another and begin to laugh simultaneously. Pink folding travel saddle rack; pink saddle cover with a floral design; pink boot bags with the same floral design, and various other mysterious pink bags with the monogram CJT.

"Who owns *that?*" she says.

"Well, don't look at me," I say.

"I'm guessing it belongs to the other girl," says Megan.

"I'm guessing it belongs to someone about to get assassinated by George Morris."

The third working student arrives but only briefly, to move her pink things to the tack room, but I recognize her instantly. The horse world is small. It's Cynthia Jackson. She's this really skinny, perfect-looking blonde girl. When I saw her ride she did mostly hunters and equitation. Only in the latter did I compete against her, of course. I only bothered with the hunters when trying to show off a really expensive sale horse or something like that, since hunters bore me senseless.

Now that I think about it, I vaguely remember reading in my newsfeed about her switching to eventing. It was one of those articles that read like something from a celebrity fan site, about how Cynthia Jackson loved foxhunting in her native Virginia and was hoping to find more success in a sport that "mirrored her childlike passion" or whatever language they like to use to describe such things and people outside of my circle.

I remember Cynthia (or "Cindy" as most people called her) for her perfect, poised position. She has that butt-sticking-up, elbows-crooked look that some judges seem to really like for hunters. Her leg was long and skinny enough to do decent in equitation but the complicated courses and having to change horses would sometimes flummox her.

I guess most normal people would know Cindy for her father, though, not for her hands and seat. He's one of those talking heads on television. He has his own cable news show where he basically gets people on to disagree with him and shouts at them about how our country is being destroyed. I haven't seen it much, only when Sean or Heather come home from college and they basically put it on so they can yell back at him. I'd like to see the brand of Cynthia Jackson's saddle beneath all that floral crap. I want to do a mental *Price Is Right* in my mind to guess how much it costs.

The time when I'm going to have to say good-bye to my mother is approaching. This is the first time we've really been away from one another; it was bad enough having to say good-bye to Sean the first time he left for school. But I'm feeling less homesick than I expected. I know I've made the right choice because the air smells like air out here and I've already noticed that things aren't as close together as they are in New Jersey, choking me. It kind of vaguely reminds me of where I lived when I was really young, when we had our own property. I hope mom sees it that way, too.

The night is quiet but I go to bed listening to The Killer's "All These Things That I've Done," which is my favorite song in the world, my psych-up song before I compete but also my comfort song. I sleep well. I decide to avoid listening to the Smiths or the Cure too much until I settle in more.

I know it's not really true, but there is a part of me that believes that Brandon Flowers, the lead singer and the songwriter of the Killers anticipated what I would be going through at so many moments of my life and wrote this song, just for me. I consider myself mostly punk and New Wave but the Killers are kind of British-influenced even though as a band they kind of defy all categorization. They are just purely great.

5

TWENTY POINTS

Daniel's farm isn't huge but it's big enough that there is enough to do so I can't get homesick. It's very easy to fall into a routine and the rituals and rhythms of barn work have always comforted me. No matter how confusing everything else might be, there are always stalls to muck out, horses to be exercised, feed buckets to be prepared and the occasional minor crisis to keep things interesting.

I've decided that I like Megan. She's an efficient worker and she generally lets me control the music played in the barn during the morning shift, which is pretty much my minimum standard for liking anyone. Cynthia, on the other hand, is something else.

Cynthia definitely falls into the tradition of those long, leggy girls who throw the reins of their sweaty beast to whoever is nearby, walk off, and text their boyfriend. However, money aside, riding-wise, I'd say she's good but not good enough and clearly this working student experience is supposed to fill the gap. Yeah, I complain about money but that is only, always, just part of the story. You need money but you also have to be able to ride and Cindy conveys more of the illusion of good riding than anything else. At least she seems nice. She's seen me compete before and remembered me from a few national events I rode in, even though we largely competed in different divisions.

The one good thing about my jack-of-all-trades, spotty resume is that I've seen a lot of different people ride and different horses, and I can usually tell pretty quickly who knows what they are doing and who will be my competition. I'm not too worried about Cindy. I'm worried about the people from outside the barn I'll be up against soon.

Megan has to room with Cynthia, so her criticisms are far more scathing. One of the privileges of being male is that, since there are only two apartments for the working students, I get a room to myself, although honestly the walls are so thin I can still hear almost everything that is said next door and also in the barn (which I guess is the point). After the first day, when we're alone together, Megan rattles off all the different brands that Cynthia has of various shampoos, civilian clothes, makeup, and the brand as well as the circumference of Cynthia's twenty-two-inch waist breeches. (Megan, although petite, apparently wears a larger size.) I know there is open jealousy in Megan's contempt but I'm more amused than anything by all the names because it's not like Cynthia is the best young rider, just probably one of the richest, thanks to her father the talking head. It's more the talented people who also have enough bank and backing to be competing on an international level at my age that I would be jealous of, if I were jealous.

Truthfully, I am not sure precisely what my ideal future life would be at this point because my most ambitious goals are far too lofty to articulate aloud and probably are not very realistic so I won't even admit them to myself. I keep saying as long as I can make money riding horses, somehow, and ride everything that comes my way I'm hoping it will all work out in the end. I've already passed the cutoff for any "Great Riders Under Eighteen" list and at this rate I'm not going to be eligible for any "Best of Under Twenty-Five" awards, either. I should be riding regularly at Intermediate, really Advanced in my estimation. Certainly, when I projected myself into the future as a kid, I was at this time. Money, a lack of consistent riding at a specific discipline, too many different horses, not the right horses, all 'good' excuses, but also all bullshit because in riding there are no excuses.

I just need to learn to do what I can, even if I never make it to the shiny cover of a magazine. Life, I remind myself, is so different from actually riding. In life, the person who cares the least, not the most, always wins, and if I don't care about stuff like money and titles and sponsors at least it won't hurt me deep in my core if they never come. There's always going to be a bunch of people who don't like me for no reason, or for reasons I can't change, anyway, and wouldn't want to if I could.

The first day of our lessons, Daniel sets up a course of several fences: a pretty standard oxer, vertical and so forth. Megan is on one of the school horses because Maggie is too small for the heights we'll be jumping. The first thing Daniel says is that although Megan will be schooling the ponies at the farm she really needs to get herself a different horse to ride if she is to be competitive once she leaves at the end of her working studentship.

Cynthia is on Blood Money, the horse which I saw her compete on throughout the past season when I was on my assortment of borrowed mounts. Blood is a 16h blood bay warmblood, docile and very finely built with a scopey jump. Blood actually looks more like a Thoroughbred than anything, and that's the greatest compliment I can give a warmblood. I don't think she could miss a distance if she tried. I actually like this mare, even though I was kind of hoping I wouldn't.

Eventually, after warming up over a few practice jumps, Daniel raises the course to 1.0m. We talk pacing and distances and counting strides. "On a cross-country course, it's not fair to just be a passenger, especially on a green horse."

Seeing strides has always come easily to me. I suppose this is where my mom's hunter princess training does help me out—ever since I could canter ground poles, she made me count aloud so I could spot a four, five, or six line, even before I could read.

Then Daniel raises things higher after we all jump clean. We count the distances aloud. Fortune clears everything easily.

"That wasn't terrible," says Daniel, and I know that he is, however slightly, impressed not that my horse jumped it but that we did so with relatively little drama. I know that my position isn't as pretty as Cynthia's by a longshot but it is stable and reasonably decent. Of course, people at my first, old barn where my mother worked used to praise it to the skies but even when I was a dumb little kid I knew I wasn't as perfect as they said I was. All of the fancy hunter princesses at my last barn thought my 'get it over and done with' jumper attitude made me look like a cowboy.

I'm still nervous—not about the riding itself but about being judged. I've ridden for as long as I can remember but I haven't had the amount of formal coaching the others have. Though Megan doesn't exactly ooze privilege, I know she graduated with an equine studies degree from a reasonably prestigious college and must have gotten some sort of regular advice there. I've had a pretty spotty background and I know that I've maxed out at what I can do myself. When I was a kid, truthfully I sort of liked the fact that other than my mother coaching me here and there I was left alone to do what I pleased, but now I'm starting to realize there is only so far I can go alone.

Megan and I are slightly relieved that Cynthia is there as a decoy for Daniel's wit: I gather that Daniel is not all that crazy about Cynthia's over-arched back or what he calls her "praying mantis humping a tree branch" position. Cynthia's cheeks flush when he says that and I snigger. But all it means is that she pushes her hands really high up the horse and leans on the neck and sticks her butt up really high in the air.

Then he has us switch horses and lowers the fences to their original positions. He puts me on Blood. I've ridden enough sale horses to be ready for almost anything and Blood is a fairly uncomplicated ride. Her mouth feels soft in my hands, like holding two baby birds between my fingers, and I barely have to touch her to set her up right over the fences.

Cynthia is white-knuckled after Fortune attacks the first jump. He probably feels as if he has nothing on his back. He cuts the next one a stride short and I grit my teeth as I see her pulling on his mouth. She nearly falls off at the oxer, pitching over his shoulder. Daniel makes her do it again. I can tell she wants to complain but she doesn't. The praying mantis thing doesn't work quite so well with my horse. You really have to hold him tight with your core muscles, I've learned. Megan tries riding him next and does even less well. Some tiny women ride big horses just fine but I know Megan hasn't learned how to use her small body mass effectively, maybe because she's used to riding ponies. I feel bad for Megan, not for Cynthia, because with all the sparkly hunter princess awards (middling as though they might be) she should be better. Don't get me wrong, there are plenty of kids with money who use it to their advantage and could ride a donkey if they had to. Cynthia is fine piloting her own horse over the jumps but I can immediately see that she is, well, beatable.

By now I'm feeling pretty confident—and then we start doing some dressage. We trade back our horses.

Cynthia proceeds through the test effortlessly. I admit that Blood Money looks pretty great as we run through a test—fluid and supple, perfectly in frame. There is also a part of me that feels, however, "Well, she would be good at *dressage* of all things." I don't have quite as much contempt for eventing dressage as I do "regular" dressage but I'm still not crazy about it. I also know that particularly after all

29

the traveling he's done recently, Fortune isn't going to be stellar, and I prepare myself for Daniel's reaction.

"What the hell was that O'Shaughnessy?"

"Um, a dressage test?"

"You couldn't get that horse on the bit if it was painted neon. Let me guess, you're one of those riders who thinks 'dressage is boring' and 'I can make up a shitty dressage score cross-country.' Typical male."

Wow, I never realized I communicated so effectively on horseback.

"Well, you can't. If you don't get high marks you're dead in the water even before the jumping begins. There are no shortcuts. Your lack of preparation for this phase shows."

Megan actually fares the best but then again, she is riding one of the schoolmasters who can literally do the moves in its sleep. I notice at one point she is giving a slightly incorrect aid with her inside leg and the horse just ignores her and does what it is supposed to do. After we finish in the arena, Daniel takes us on a tour of the cross-country course in the back of the property.

After we finish, I hose off Fortune. It's not as hot here as it was back at home but it's hot enough. With no one on his back, Fortune has his usual, cowed, defensive expression and eyes me warily. "It's okay, buddy," I say, "you didn't do anything wrong; it was just my crappy riding he didn't like." I know I'll have to change when we're done because I'm soaked as much as he is. We match, both of us are sort of faded and stained and water-logged and funny-looking.

Cindy walks by, a little too close to Fortune and he suddenly kicks out at her, surprising even me. She glares at me, as if I've trained him to do this. "He recently came from a bad situation," I explain, but she doesn't seem to understand. I doubt she's dealt with many horses with a history like Fortune's.

I'm not particularly hurt by Daniel's criticism of my riding because I know it's true. Right now, Fortune couldn't get in a collected frame if our collective life depended on it. And I haven't been very demanding that he do so. I've been having far too much fun. I've always been bad about doing things I don't want to do. Fortunately, I like a few things (like jumping and physics) and find a few other things easy (like barn chores and I suppose math and drawing at school) so I've been able to get by on the strength of those talents, even convincing some people that I'm a hard worker through a carefully-constructed illusion. I knew even before I embarked on my working studentship I'd never be able to fool Daniel. Later during the night I hear Cynthia crying about what was said to her and Megan half-heartedly trying to comfort her.

I've always liked trainers that don't bullshit you when you're trying to half-ass something. With riding, you can't trick anyone into thinking you are better or worse than you really are for very long. Maybe some people can do it with the right horse, under the right circumstances, in cherry-picked classes, if they get their trainer to hop on the beast beforehand like Cindy. But I know that in eventing there is no way, even at a relatively low level, that you can fool people for too long, and certainly not the horse.

Within a week, the farm's routine of letting horses out and taking them in, feeding, mucking, watering, clipping, pulling, and checking becomes so natural it feels less like chores and more like breathing. Truthfully, on the few occasions in my life when I wasn't so confined by the demands of horses I felt more lost and anxious than when I was busy every moment of the day. There isn't much to get me in trouble around us, anyway, especially without a car. It's all farmland, farmland, and untouched green and mountains.

The local store sells fertilized chicken eggs to hatch as well as regular eggs; tractor parts and shavings; and the frozen pizza,

Mountain Dew, Pop-Tarts, cereal, ramen, candy bars, and peanut butter I stock my tiny room and refrigerator with. Basically, stuff I can eat quickly before doing barn chores in the morning or before falling asleep at night. All three of us share a quasi-kitchen with a microwave. Fortunately, I have a separate bathroom. Megan complains that Cynthia never cleans up after herself and that the sink is full of blonde hair and her roommate's stinky, perfumed creams and stuff. "What does she think I am, the maid?" grouses Megan, forgetting that Cynthia *is* used to having a maid.

The general store is pretty much the only sign of life nearby other than a diner-style family restaurant and a Dairy Queen (which is only open during the summer months). As well as groceries and feed the little store also sells gas and organic dog and cat treats made by a local. This being Vermont, on the front of the door of the store there are hand written tear-off advertisements for raw milk; a notice that a cooperatively-run Waldorf nursery school is opening up; and ads for second-hand farm equipment and tack. But the remoteness of the rural area doesn't bother me too much. I prefer just having one tiny store versus strip malls and mega-malls, like it was back home in Jersey.

I have few complaints. Well, after the first day I quickly learned Cynthia can't clean a stall to save her life—she throws out approximately seventeen billion dollars (a slight exaggeration) worth of still-useable shavings, can barely navigate a full wheelbarrow without tipping it over, and is excruciatingly slow, to boot. I have to redo all the tack she attempts to clean or prevent her from using the wrong kind of soap or polish. But I'm used to that.

For whatever reason, Daniel has me teaching some of the better little kids and teens that take lessons at the farm. My littlest ones aren't really little—Megan is given that unenviable task—most of mine are around middle-school age. I was surprised that so many little kids evented rather than doing hunters and equitation but then again, it's not as unusual in this part of the country. Just more open space out here in general. I'm kind of envious of them and the ones that are farm kids are actually good riders and pretty polite. Some of them even call me "Mister," which I find really funny.

I could do without the little kids hanging around afterward, asking questions and trying to help. Of course, I was also annoyed by the children at the last hunter-jumper barn I worked at who never wanted to help and whose parents would buy them expensive ponies and horses that had to be LUD (lunged until dead) so they could ride them at shows and get pretty blue ribbons to match their pretty blue bows. I never thought such people deserved horses and I still don't. I don't mind the older teens of course and there are even one or two guys. Unfortunately they don't linger long, just leave with their moms or their girlfriends, with whatever female is sustaining their interest in my sport.

What I would really prefer is just to be left alone for most of the morning to work and listen to music. Working the babies as well as our own horses is where the fun really starts. I'm especially fond of one off-the-track-Thoroughbred (OTTB) mare named Trouble Me Not (Trouble) who has a lovely, springy jump—when she isn't looking down at the jumps, afraid that they are going to kill her. My first real horse was an OTTB so I know not to pull back to slow them down and not to expect too much in the way of lead changes or a collected trot right away.

The best part of the location is that it is in the genuine country where you can hack out. I haven't lived near such wide, meandering places to gallop since I was a kid and my mom and dad were still married and owned a kind of mini farmlet. My brother Sean and I would take our ponies off-property and speed to what seemed like the edge of the world when we were no older than the lesson kids whose legs barely go past the saddle and who timidly ask permission to go over a crossrail.

I've always had a good sense of direction and never get lost and after a couple of weeks of being able to gallop around without much of an agenda or a plan Fortune starts to give up the "oh shit, what did I do" and the "screw you, I'd give you the finger if I didn't have hooves" expressions he has worn the majority of the time since I bought him. He still moves like a rusty slinky when we're trying to do dressage, of course. Even at stadium he's not brilliant and crisp in his turns like he should be. Uncomplicated forward motion is what he excels at. He never refuses anything, even some odd-looking stuff I've jumped him over while hacking, like an enormous felled tree with a dead deer slung over it which some hunter must have forgotten for some reason. I'm not looking forward to the first show where I have to subject Fortune to a dressage test in public.

My brother is in Boston right now, doing some sort of internship for his finance major, wearing a monkey suit during the day and sharing an apartment with some of the guys from the program. Sometimes he calls me at 11 p.m., midnight, 1 a.m., when he's just getting in from drinking at a party or going out with his new girlfriend-of-the-week. "I can't believe you're sleeping. What are you, ten?" he asks.

Cynthia periodically leaves the barn on weekends when she isn't on night duty. A car arrives on Friday, takes her to the airport so she can visit her father in Virginia, and then whisks her back the following Monday morning. This leaves Megan and me to cover for her because she knows we have nowhere else to go. Megan sometimes sees her boyfriend. I, of course, have nothing better to do than watch the animals and play with Fortune during my off-hours. Cynthia returns

Monday morning, slightly hung over from partying, just in time to let out the horses she is responsible for, often still sucking down a massive Green Mountain coffee from the airport.

One Monday I'm so tired myself I hardly notice what Cindy is doing—she's just a buzzing blonde fly around me. I have Neon Trees cranked up high enough to keep me moving until the Mountain Dew kicks in and the first of my two brown sugar-frosted Pop-Tarts hits my bloodstream with some energizing glucose. Gotta love '80s-ish sounding music to get you going in the AM.

Suddenly, I do a double take and ask myself, did I just see what I saw? Which was Cynthia putting two horses in the same paddock that Daniel expressly told us not to turn out together. I hear snorting and pawing. They're already circling one another and giving each other death stares.

It's been a long time since I've been at a barn with stallions, but my mother had one growing up so unlike some people who assume they're explosions waiting to happen or fire-breathing monsters, I don't have a lot of fear. I'm mostly annoyed.

I use a lead rope to slap Daniel's slate-grey stallion away and clip the rope to the halter of the misplaced, ornery chestnut gelding. I lead him out of the paddock and back to his field, where he is supposed to be—alone. Then I tackle Cynthia.

"What the hell was that?" I try to contain myself and focus on the immediate problem. Ignore everything else. Just focus.

"It was a mistake," she says. She gives me that pretty rich girl stare and bats her eyelashes. "Thank you *so* much for helping me, I am *so* sorry." Cynthia may be from down south, but she's been around the country or the world (for all I know) enough that her accent usually has a kind of generic, flat, bored, toneless quality that grates on me much more than a southern drawl would.

"You have to stop screwing up. Just stop it," I say.

I go to eat the second half of my breakfast, which I've left on a tack box, but I realize that Maggie has already let herself out and is eating my last Pop-Tart. She cocks her little pony head and I swear, almost grins at me as she licks her lips. This hasn't been a good morning.

Later Megan tells me, "It's just because Cindy's paying to be here that she thinks she can do whatever she wants. It's because you and I are on scholarship." I'm surprised to learn that some people actually pay to be working students; Cynthia is one of them. Megan is here for free and in exchange for Maggie's board and lessons but she has no stipend like me (she's using money she saved while in college to be here). Learning this makes me slightly intimidated, as if I have to justify my existence in the world even more.

It's not a good day for Cynthia overall. We're responsible for schooling the green beans over fences and Cynthia goes careering over Trouble's shoulder, hitting the ground with a smack. I'm pretty sure I know why Daniel picked Trouble for her to ride today—once again, her position may look pretty over fences but perched upon the neck of a horse that is still figuring things out, she's teetering on the brink of disaster.

Secretly, I take a picture of her and send it to Sean later on. I want to tell someone what's going on in my lessons, what I'm learning, even though I know he doesn't really care.

"He calls that 'praying mantis arms' or, like one of the trainers at Angel Heart used to say with less delicacy, the 'monkey fucking a football two-point'" I laugh. I know Sean's at work although I'm calling him on my phone anyway but I really don't consider what he does at a spreadsheet work anymore than he considers what I do riding and scrubbing water buckets to be serious work. He has to hang up because his boss is there but messages me back on Facebook:

only u would look at that girl and see a praying mantis or a monkey

Surely not only me? I try explain what I'm referring to:

her riding dumbass not her ass ass

After a couple of sessions as well as the fact that Cynthia's seat sucks despite the brand of her breeches, I note that it has become clear that I alone will be riding Fortune. Even Megan is slightly scared of him. I've never understood why people find big, powerful jumpers to be frightening. Yes, he can feel out of control, but I'd rather have a horse that will pick up his knees and jump the world than a nasty little dirty stopper or a lazy schoolie that knocks against a solid fence and risks taking both horse and rider down. People are weird in terms of what they are afraid of when it comes to horses. Fortune does nip occasionally but not at me anymore and only really got Megan enough to leave a dent on her arm, not break the skin. Cynthia is quicker and able to dodge him more expertly.

I will also say this for Cindy: at least Cynthia does care about her horse and doesn't blame Blood Money for her crappy rides or complain like the whiny kids at my last barn. In fact, she was kind of freaking out the first few days when Blood apparently wasn't used to so much turnout and the mare just stood by the gate, whinnying to be let in her stall, little black muzzle quivering and trembling.

"Don't be so needy," I said and gave the mare a gentle slap on the rear with a lead rope. "Go play."

"I think I should let her in," said Cynthia. "She wants her stall."

"She's gotta get used to the schedule. Adapt or die. It's nature's way. Like they say on Shark Week."

"Shark Week?"

"On TV? Oh, never mind." How is it possible for a girl to be a college graduate and not to have heard of Shark Week? I'm baffled.

There is also the usual annoying boarder weirdness at the barn—people who complain about the perfectly fine hay, people who spend nine million hours blocking the aisle with their horses on crossties while they text on their phones, and my personal favorite, the college student who fed an enormous apple—whole—to a lesson horse and nearly choked it. I had to spend all night with the big, greedy liver chestnut as the chunks slowly slid down his throat. You never, never give a whole apple like that to a horse. *Of course* it was a college student; it takes an especially fake smart person to do a dumb thing like that. Even a stupid child at least asks permission when giving treats.

I'm vaguely made aware from time to time of a small liberal arts college located near the barn. Some of the students take riding lessons. Enough of them take classes over the summer that they are still A Presence in the area well after June, when by all rights things should go back to the locals. I see these students when I go into town and sometimes I ride by the school when I'm hacking Fortune. Often the kids have large black art portfolios that mark them as college students like hideous signs. I know better than to ride through the campus and kick up its precious turf. There is a sign on the college grass that reads: Please Don't Tread On Me. I Am Growing. Well, excuse me, oh sensitive plants.

I've heard it said that town-gown relations are, to put it politely, strained. Like, one day, I go to pick up feed and supplies from the tractor supply store. There are two of *them*—students—shopping for groceries. The boy has a mullet and thick Clark Kent classes worn "ironically" and the girl is wearing nothing but overalls like that '80s rock video. She has hair streaked with green and blue dye and what appears to be a candy necklace wrapped around her wrist.

The students talk to one another, then on their cellphones, and barely acknowledge the guy who owns the place who is patiently waiting as he rings them up. They take forever to pay as the girl fumbles through all the pockets of her overalls, giggling about nothing as she talks to her boyfriend. She eventually takes some dollar bills out of her shoe, which I think is totally grosser than the worst, urine-soaked stall I cleaned that morning. Sean and I have pretty crappy manners in some ways but mom would have slapped us across the head if we behaved like that, even as little kids. Probably that's the reason both of us were pretty fast runners from an early age.

Before the college kids walk out, I can feel the students' attention slip to me—my work boots and my flannel and my baseball cap. I know that I even smell different. Although the horse scent barely registers in my nostrils, I realize it is there like a blind person knows that most people can see things he cannot. And I know there is hay lining my pockets and in my pants cuffs. The college kids smell like incense and soap, since they've also apparently just taken showers although it is almost noon. The boy whispers something to the girl, he gazes at my manure-encrusted boots, and they laugh. I can feel the hate and contempt of the students exuding from the farmers and the locals in the store. The kids are unaware or even proud of the effect their performance has had upon their audience.

The owner helps me load the feed into the back of the farm's truck—he's an old guy but strong. After we're done we can still see the kids in the distance. "You know what they say?" he says, cheerfully, nodding in the direction of the boy and the girl. The boy now has his arm around the girl's bare shoulders. "Ten points for a deer, twenty points for a queer." And as if on cue, the couple narrowly gets missed by a dark green SUV as they jaywalk, but still they go giggling and zig-zagging like drunk people across the street, knowing the world will take care of them.

I'm not sure where I fit in into the "they" of the old guy's phrase. The fact that the couple is obviously heterosexual makes the store owner's meaning even more confusing. Still, it is clear that no matter how you interpret his statement, I'm not the one left alive and behind the wheel.

6

TWENTY POINTS (REVISITED)

The thing is, for me, given that pretty much ninety-five percent of all recreational riders I teach and work with are female (and sometimes it *feels* like the other five percent ride Western although truthfully there are a fair amount of straight guys who ride as eventers), I'm currently in a situation that can be summed up as "water, water everywhere, but not a drop to drink." It always makes me wonder why my brother didn't stick with serious riding longer. God knows he had enough teenage girls following him around the barn, offering to clean his tack, muck his stalls and be his slave for the day, but the male heterosexual mind can sometimes be just as impenetrable as the female variety, even the mind of my own brother.

When I complain about my lack of a social life to Sean, he isn't sympathetic. "If you hadn't bought the horse, you could have bought a car and driven down to Boston on weekends, and we could have hung out. It's not that far."

He's right, I guess. Although hanging out with Sean would mean talking to his date while the three of us sat uncomfortably side-by-side while watching TV together. The decision to buy Fortune feels inevitable and necessary, like oxygen. I will just have to suck it up, buttercup.

Ironically, Megan and her boyfriend go shooting at his house after I return from the feed store (although they are not in pursuit of deer or anything else apparently labeled "prey for points" in this area). They ask me to come along after I unload and lock up the grain. I'm kind of not crazy about being a third wheel but Megan and Ricky are a reasonably cool couple and don't make you feel weird about being there—they don't make out half the time or make eyes at one another while I sit in the back seat of the Mustang (once again, I'm thinking of you, Sean). I love the fact that Megan considers shooting stuff to be a romantic date. Apparently, Ricky likes to go hunting and he practices in his backyard. They line up Coke and beer cans and aim and fire.

I know this is kind of a redneck thing to do (if they have rednecks in Vermont) but it feels oddly satisfying. It takes a bit of getting used to, especially since I'm a lefty, but I get the hang of it and the gun feels important and weighty in my hand. Megan's much better at it than either of us. Ricky says he's in trouble and laughs as she slams down can after can.

Megan has a plan. After being a working student for a year she's going to go to nursing school and teach riding on the side, hopefully get a bigger horse, use Maggie for lessons, and move up the levels that way. It's a very sensible plan, I guess, although I can't imagine relegating riding to such a tiny, neatly-boxed component of my life. I'll have to figure out something else. To be honest, it really kind of surprised me when she said, telling me about her future, "I'm good, but I know I'm not good enough to make it as a professional, not to live the kind of life that Ricky and I want to live." It seemed so defeatist—how would you know, I mean? How would you know if you didn't try? And isn't it better to be okay at riding than really good at something else, because what else is like riding?

When I shoot, I always hit the targets but I waste quite a bit of ammunition in the process. My energy isn't focused or direct enough.

I just want to hurt things this afternoon. "Imagine you were aiming for a heart," says Megan, the future nurse, "make it quick and painless."

The next time I'm at the general store, this time buying my groceries for the week, I see two different college kids playing Frisbee on the lawn. The disk flutters to my feet as I exit. I pick it up. Before I can throw it back, one of the boys comes over to me. He has tattoos covering his arms to the point there is more visible ink than skin. "Thanks," he says.

"What does this mean?" I ask, pointing to the unpronounceable word on the front of the Frisbee.

"That's the name of our Ultimate Frisbee team: Nietzsche Factor."

"Ultimate Frisbee is a competitive college sport?"

"Sure is. During the school year the team even travels. We take our name from the great German philosopher Frederick Nietzsche's philosophy of the superman—a person who rises above the conventional morality of the day to do extraordinary things." He grins. "Like a Frisbee."

Despite the fact he has enough tattoos on him that it's slightly distracting from his face, I notice that the guy is kind of cute. He's built like a surfer dude and has a nice tan. Weird hippy tats and piercings aside, he looks like he works out. He has short bleached blonde hair and sort of puppy dog brown eyes. He's doesn't have that wan, underfed look that some of the other students do. And I'm getting signals. Not that gaydar is like riding a bike, exactly. I'm always slightly worried that mine isn't very good from lack of use. Again, this is an inevitable result of being obsessed with a female-dominated sport.

We chat and he establish that his name is Chris and that he is a comparative literature major and music minor who plays the oboe and he invites me to a party at the school tomorrow night.

"I bet you don't get out much, farm boy," Chris says. As he grins I notice that he has a silver stud in his tongue to match the massive amount of silver jewelry he has loaded on his neck as well as his silver pinky rings. I try to edit out the body piercings in my mind, like mental photoshopping. I mean, I know I'm into punk and alternative music so I should be more open to tats and body art, but to be honest they gross me out. They're very distracting and I can't help wondering what that would feel like, to be shot with a steel rod in such a sensitive area. It seems unsanitary and this is coming from someone who has spent half of his life ankle deep in manure with a slice of pizza in his hand. But yes, reservations aside, I'm definitely getting major signals.

"I do alright," I say. I pull my ancient, tattered Red Sox baseball cap more securely over my face and make my expression a blank. I'm usually a terrible liar, partially because I spend so much time with animals who you can't lie to, and because I usually see no reason to lie in general. But I can make myself empty on the surface to hide the truth if I absolutely have to, like when I'm playing a game of poker or flirting.

The next night, since I don't have to be there for bed checks (Megan is on duty), after evening feed and turnout, I bike over to the college, to the address Chris gave me. It's a large, frat house-style place. At least, based on the movies I've seen, it's what I imagine a frat house looks like, although thank God Sean's not in a fraternity or anything dumb like that. Chris said it is called a special interest house at his school. There are letters on a rainbow flag outside—LGBT—and the person at the door asks me if I have ID. I don't have a student ID or even a fake ID. I've never had problems scoring a few beers when necessary and my mother always let Sean and me drink a small amount of Guinness or wine or even whisky, depending on the occasion. Booze has never been a big deal for me, I can take it or leave it. But Chris sees me, talks to the guy at the door, and they let me in.

Although I assumed for rather obvious reasons that mainly gay guys would be at the special interest house, it's more of a student party, I guess. The room is packed with people of varying sexual orientations and genders. There is an unpleasant odor in the room which I vaguely recognize as pot from the times I've visited my brother at his college dorm. I've never smoked it and smelling it secondhand is nauseating enough. It's very warm outside but none of the windows are open. The stench, combined with the smell of body odor, is overpowering. I was self-conscious of smelling like horse (despite having showered) but now I don't feel bad at all about the smell that is part of me.

There is an odd, luridly-colored punch the texture of a slushee in a big bowl in the corner. I need to be up by 5:30 a.m. tomorrow to do checks, turnout, and feed, so I refuse a cup, even when offered it despite my lack of ID. Everyone else is sipping punch or beer from bright red plastic cups and I hear snatches of conversation:

"So, I have to read *Discipline and Punishment* yet again this summer— I mean, in how many classes do they require you to read that? I'm like, Foucault's bitch."

"Have to be in the language lab for a quiz by 10 a.m.—ugh—so I guess I better study when I get home—"

"I'm taking Orgo this summer so I can really focus on it and not be distracted by other classes—"

"Does Javanese Gamelan count for any of the art distribution requirements? I have to check. I'm taking that in the fall."

All of them might as well be speaking Chinese as far as I'm concerned. (Hell, maybe some of them do, even though they are mostly white, once again, this being Vermont.) Although the students look very different from one another—different streaks of brightly-colored hair, different kinds of lumpy silver or plastic jewelry, different torn and stained thrift shop T-shirts, and a few of the girls and even two of the guys have Pocahontas-style braids—they also kind of all look the same. One of them has a T-shirt on that reads, "Straight but Not Narrow." Just in case anyone was confused, I guess. I'm not going to even tease out the implications of that one.

Chris and I talk but I can hardly hear him above the music, which is some kind of dispiriting disco from the 1970s. (I don't see how people can find the Smiths depressing versus disco). The conversation is sort of negligible anyway, since we go up to his room soon enough and start making out. The whole experience is like a weird combination of a college tour from hell and a hookup. I sense I am regarded as a curiosity, someone being 'rescued' briefly from the clutches of the rural town. Which is not how I feel at all, although maybe I should.

Again, I do have to do the mental photoshopping about the tongue piercing, which still kind of grosses me out. And some other piercings not immediately obvious on first glance.

I feel uncomfortably innocent and naïve, somehow, compared to Chris and everyone else at the party. It's funny, because technically I'm living alone, like a quasi-adult. I gather that Chris just finished his freshman year but Chris goes on about all the guys he met while at band camp in high school (who knew that school bands were such dens of iniquity) over the summers and how "incestuous" the gay community is at his college. I don't know, maybe they have more time on their hands because they are only responsible for themselves.

I leave because I have to get up early and I'm worried I won't have everything as it should be in the morning if I'm functioning on fumes. I'm also sort of bored despite the refreshing momentary release from the enforced celibacy—just the knowledge that I can actually find another guy, no matter what the circumstances, is a kind of relief—though I still feel unsatisfied. The air is heavy and humid as I pedal away. The movement feels easy although I've worked more than twelve, thirteen hours all day. I've grown stronger even in the few short weeks I've been here and while I'm not running my brains out like Sean during his cross-country practices, I can walk, bike, and ride for far more miles than I ever could before I came to this place with wide open spaces.

But once I'm home, I know I can't sleep. I'm so wound up I take Fortune for a canter. Both of our conditioning has improved. He eases into a gallop without any effort and as clumsy and as stiff as he is within the confines of a dressage ring, his stride opens up easily now. He didn't bare his teeth at me or get tense when I tacked him up, either.

Daniel often talks about how eventing used to be much more about galloping and distances when the sport was a three-day affair with several additional phases and much longer courses. "Horses had to be fit back then," he says, "and you could make up a bad dressage test by being bold and forward over fences." I kind of think that Fortune was born at the wrong time, in terms of being able to excel at his sport. But sometimes I think I was born at the wrong time as well because I sure as hell don't fit in anywhere here and now. I don't fit in anywhere.

The next day, the tractor breaks down with a minor problem and I manage to fix it, having dealt with even more unreliable farm equipment at my last barn. For a few minutes, in Daniel's eyes I am competent. "Nice job, Shaughnessy," he says. I saved him money since I'm free versus a professional repair guy so that merits a great deal of praise.

We also get a delivery of hay. The guys that bring it always take off their shirts when they throw it from the truck to the ground. I can't help watching them with my head tilted down but my eyes cast up as

I work beside them. One of them is about my age, a very tall rangy kid with a chest that's almost too muscular for his narrow hips and skinny legs. His stomach looks like it is nothing but ribs and sinew. Seriously, a twelve-pack. He has blue eyes and dark curly hair that needs to be cut and looks kind of perfect so most of the time I just mumble if I need to say anything to him at all.

Today, when the hot guy first walked in to tell me the hay was there, I was hosing off the feed buckets and I accidently hit him with the spray, as I turned in surprise at his presence. I apologized but he said, "Nah that felt good." I contemplated teasing him and spraying him harder for real for one brief second, but I knew not to and tried not to watch him as he turned and went. I looked up at my horse, his big head hanging over the stall. He seemed to be gazing at me, impassively and without judgment, as if he knew what I was thinking.

Megan and Cynthia help out, passing the hay from the ground in a line, bale by bale, to the storage barn.

Eventually, I decide to take off my own shirt. I mean, it's improbable that the guy will notice, but it's worth a try.

Megan wolf-whistles at me. "I wish I was a guy and I could do that," she says.

"You could," says the cute guy.

"No thanks, I get enough hayseeds in my bra as it is," giggles Megan.

I know I'm going to regret taking off my shirt because I have no sunblock on my back and my skin doesn't tan—it doesn't even burn like a normal pale person's but goes straight to spontaneous human combustion mode.

I mean, it's probably hopeless because he made that comment to Megan about taking off her shirt, right? It's so unfair though. Why is it in my world that the hot guys who deliver the hay aren't gay versus the weird guys with body piercing who smoke pot? It can't be that way for everyone, everywhere. I guess I just have to accept that I was born under an unlucky star.

Perched on the hay mountain, I'm so numbed out by the motion and so careful about where I'm keeping my eyes, I'm not even conscious that someone has been watching me for a long time. I turn around and see Dr. Max, the vet, staring at me. Max is actually his first, not his last name, but everyone calls him Dr. Max so I do as well.

"Um, I'm looking for Daniel," says Dr. Max. He blinks behind his wire-rimmed glasses. He's wearing a plain T-shirt and jeans rather than the scrubs he puts on when he's about to do something more involved.

I lead him to the barn where the breeding horses are. As well as training and lessons, Daniel has two mares that were injured awhile back who he's kept to breed, although we're not really a breeding facility. The vet is coming by to see if the mares are ready to "take"— i.e. to be artificially inseminated. Dr. Max takes out a portable ultrasound as we wait for Daniel.

I like the doctor. Like every person involved with horses, I've known my fair share of vets. He's young for a vet and is fit and strong enough to perform most of the tasks he needs to do on his own. He even takes a lesson every other week or so and can ride and jump competently, so I can understand why he decided to work with horses, which isn't true of lots of vets.

Daniel moves slowly in the morning on the ground—although no matter how early I see him in the saddle, he still rides fine. He is visibly limping and asks me to hold one of the more nervous broodmares as Dr. Max puts on a plastic glove and takes out his equipment. I feel kind of comforted by the fact that Daniel doesn't look like a guy in his seventies—he's muscular, thin, and wiry and even his hair is only streaked with grey. His dark eyes look more piercing and sharp than most people's my age. I hope I'm that way, after twenty, forty, fifty-plus years.

"Lucky I don't have to pass a soundness exam, eh, O'Shaughnessy? If you had any sense I'd make you reconsider your future career. You don't want end up looking like me in the end."

I shrug. "I don't know—kinda like money, with health, it's not like you can take it with you. Might as well spend it while you still have it, right?"

Dr. Max says it's too early for the mares and he'll be back in a few days. "I'm pretty creaky myself in the mornings these days, Daniel," he adds.

"You're still a kid, Max."

"I wish. I've been kicked around a few times myself, in various ways, over the years," says the doctor.

Today, we're preparing some of the younger horses for the upcoming schooling show, as well as my own horse. Megan is riding one of the green ponies, a little grey Welsh cob named Remarkable (Mark for short).

"Simon, can you read my test for me?"

"You don't have it memorized yet?"

"Who has time to study here? Don't tell me you have your tests memorized?"

"All of them. I have a photographic memory."

"Whatever."

"No shit, I do."

"You would, wouldn't you, just to be annoying?"

I read: "A enter working trot. C track left. Yup, this is really hard to remember." Megan tracks left and without missing a beat gives me the finger as she passes me.

"That's not a recognized USEA move, Megan. The dressage gods will punish you for the disrespect shown to your reader. E circle left 20m." At the end of the test when she halts and salutes, I smile and give the finger back to her.

When we run through it again, I say her test without looking at the paper, even though I don't need to know it and I'm riding in other divisions. I get all the movements right, even though the wording is off in one or two places.

"You're a total shit, Simon," says Megan.

I ride Trouble without a mistake in silence. When I compete on Trouble we'll be riding in a division with stadium heights even below what she can manage schooling at home. We're trying not to fry her brain. Megan doesn't bitch during the test but when I work Fortune after Trouble she does make little comments like, "That's an interesting bend," (i.e., noting my horse's lack thereof).

By then, we've had enough of flatwork and we go over some fences on the cross-country course of the farm to clear our own brains. It amazes me how "correct" Fortune feels when jumping—even in the little time we've spent on the farm, he's better in the arena, collected and engaged when approaching the fence, springy in the back when going over—and how still utterly disinterested he is as soon as we halt and salute at X.

Cynthia practices on her own. I'm not sure if she is still embarrassed by Daniel's comments, doesn't like us, or it is a competitive thing.

"She's just so fucking fake happy all the time—or hung over," says Megan of her roommate. "I hate people who are super-happy all the time."

"You have a cold, black soul, Megan," I say. She gives me a look that is a more subtle, visual equivalent of giving me the finger.

Despite the fact that this area's remoteness clearly means that I'm destined to die a virgin with only sad, half-assed hookups on my sexual resume—like one of the more unfortunate and doomed female characters in my beloved sci-fi and fantasy novels—I feel more at home in Vermont than I ever have anywhere else. I love the hills, the way they make even the most ordinary territory feel extraordinary when I'm riding. Whenever I have a few hours to myself I like to take Fortune up into places with hardly any trails at all, just the endless green whose beauty slightly stupefies me still, long after it really has any right to do so.

There is a place on a high hill where I can take off Fortune's bridle, loosen his girth and let him graze, and lie back myself and stare at the mountains in the far distance. On clear day especially it reminds me of when I was a kid and used to ride my pony in the woods in search of the end of the world or, I don't know, the Death Star, Avalon, or the Starship Enterprise, or some fantastical place not here on earth. The name of the place changed depending on my mood and age but its remoteness was constant.

I still like to pull my hooded sweatshirt over my ears, plug in my iPod buds and listen to the chomping of grass and my favorite Killers songs. I listen and stare at what is ahead of me and feel as if I am in another world with the horse, high above every possible thing that could wall either of us in, forever. At times I am tempted to try to get lost, despite my better instincts, to say to hell with it all, even the joys of competition, and fantasize about occupying an abandoned farmhouse in an even more remote location than this. There I can be alone, really alone with just my horse to keep me company. Everything else feels fake and a lie except the motion of riding out into pure space.

7

POKER STRAIGHT

Megan and Ricky drive down to Boston one weekend and offer to let me come along so I can meet up with Sean. Heather also decides to ride up from New Jersey. It's a kind of mini-reunion for the three of us.

Our drive in the Mustang is long enough that Ricky actually allows me to touch the wheel of his precious vehicle so he can sleep in the back seat.

"Jesus, you drive fast," says Megan.

"I've never gotten a ticket," I say.

"That's like saying you're not a thief because you've never been arrested even though you've stolen shit. I can tell you're from New Jersey." She means the "people have to get the fuck out of the way" attitude, I guess. She says the name of the state like it's an insult. "For some reason I thought you were from around here, originally."

"I am—I moved to Jersey when I was younger. Understandable—it's the Red Sox hat. I was born in Massachusetts and I've never gone native in terms of my sports allegiances."

"Just keep your eyes on the road. Oh my God, we're all gonna die."

"I'm half-halting this thing, Megs, but it's not working," I say. "Kind of like when you ride Fortune."

"You're such an asshole, Simon."

I actually do have a habit of unconsciously half-halting when I'm driving, tightening my abs to collect the horse but still applying leg to create impulsion, although it obviously has a different effect on an automobile.

Anyway, we don't die. I've never required much sleep, so eventually Megan passes out from weariness and stops complaining and I get to speed most of the way into the city. I even manage to find us parking although I do have to drive the wrong way on one or two one-way streets. It's early enough that it doesn't matter.

I meet up with Sean and Heather at Fenway, since Sean has gotten tickets through his employer. I don't remember the last time we saw an actual baseball game together, live—it has been years. Every job has its perks, I guess. Mine is riding half-broken horses.

"Jesus, do they not feed you," I say, seeing him. Sean has always been slightly heavier and more muscular than me but now he has that cadaverous, runner's face, exaggerated by his newly-buzzed hair.

"I'm in training for the season. We have a new coach. He's done ultras, Ironmen, everything. Between work and logging the miles I hardly have time to eat," he says. "What have you been doing, pumping iron?"

"You look great Simon," says Heather, and hugs me. Heather looks the same—she always looks the same, which is what is so comforting about Heather. Even the same type of clothes. Same kind of hesitating, nerdy way of talking. I pause a moment. I always feel slightly inadequate when she is holding me.

"You can't wear that Yankees T-shirt," I say, pushing her away, playfully.

"I may be sitting with you guys but I am not rooting for a Boston team," says Heather.

"I've already told her that we can't promise she'll be safe, wearing that," says Sean.

"Nope. You can't rely on us to defend your honor," I agree.

"I already knew that," she says, rolling her eyes.

We take our seats.

"Heather, the only reason you are a Yankees fan is because you think Derek Jeter is cute," I point out. "You know nothing about baseball."

"That isn't a good reason?" she says.

"I'd do him, but that doesn't affect my sports allegiances," I say. "I think it's pretty clear from the current Red Sox roster that physical attractiveness has very little effect upon my sports affiliations."

"Whoa, this conversation is already getting too weird," says Sean.

"What are you going to do when Jeter retires, Heather? Lust after C. C. Sabathia?"

"Ha. Ha. You won't be laughing so much when the game begins."

Of course, the Red Sox lose—purely to spite me and Sean, I'm convinced.

We wander around the city together, looking for a place to eat. I don't say this out loud but even being in my favorite city in the world with my brother makes me feel slightly claustrophobic after a certain point. It's like I can feel its grid hemming me in. I know my brother likes it here; he says there is always something to do and he's never bored but I've always found cities to be depressing and lonely. When you're out by yourself in nature you know there is something always with you and aware of you, even if it's just a bunch of deer being watchful of your presence. In a city, you can be in a crowd of people with no one taking notice of you or worse, judging the hell out of you based on how you look and sound. I always feel like I've forgotten how I see myself when I'm in a crowd; at least it's not so bad now, since I'm with people I know. Still, I am awkward and alien and somehow my work boots and clothes are the wrong uniform.

At one point, without thinking, as we walk by a stone railing I leap up and balance on the flat surface beside the balcony, walking step by step, just to feel free and focused hanging in air and away from the crush of strange people and the smell of nasty dirt and cars and sweat. Here, however briefly, I am alone because I know no one will dare follow me.

"Simon, don't do that. You're making me nervous with the drop," says Heather. But I know that as long as I don't think it's possible to fall, I won't, something I can't explain to Heather. It took Heather years to move up in her jumping, an inch every month practically, like a patient snail. I have no patience with myself, no patience with any human beings, only patience with horses.

Heather leaves us in the evening to check out some art film. She tries to persuade me to come with her—"it's a documentary about music, Simon, you'd like it"—but I explain I need to go back to Sean's place. Sean and his roommate (one of his fellow cross-country teammates during the year, who is even more thin and drawn than Sean from running, except for his freakishly muscular thighs) host a weekly poker game for all of the interns. When we arrive the room is already filled with the type of bland, preppy rich guys Sean used to hang out with when he was on the high school soccer team. I talk about the game we just saw with some of them, but most of them are intent upon complaining about work, even though it is their day off.

The boys speak a kind of language I don't really understand—dividends, options, performance metrics—and I know that the language I speak of distances, bending and softening, collection and extension would be just as incomprehensible to them. So I don't say much, which is probably for the best. I just identify myself as Sean's brother. They're all in khaki shorts, loafers and sneakers without socks, and polo shirts and most of them just kind of look at me kind of askance because I've obviously just come from a barn.

I guess I'm never satisfied—the college guys at the campus back home (because I think of Vermont now as my home) aren't preppy enough while these guys are way too preppy for me. I'm relieved when we start to play the game. I think, next to riding (and breathing), I've been playing cards longer than anything else I've done in my life. My mom taught us how to play when we were really, really young although it didn't seem to stick as well with Sean as it did with me.

By the end of the evening I've won nearly a grand, am about halfway through a single bottle of Sam Adams, and lost the little respect I had for everyone in the room, even one of the cute guys in a plaid shirt who sits with his legs a little bit wider than he should wearing such baggy shorts. His shirt is slightly open at the bottom to reveal washboard abs that are apparently unaffected by all the beer he's been drinking. I think these guys are pretty lame in terms of their poker skills because basically what they're learning to do is gamble with other people's money all day—right—and they can't even bluff their way through a halfway decent amateur round of poker with someone rusty like me. Well, at least you're cute, I think, my face hard and impassive as I keep one eye on plaid shirt as he leans back in his chair.

Weirdly enough, from what I gather from the back-and-forth, the other interns seem to respect Sean, or at least Sean is considered to be doing a pretty good job at his internship. All of his bosses and the clients like him, and they have given him extra stuff to do. Or at least the other interns say he's a good bullshitter, which I gather is a compliment coming from them. But that's not the same thing as being good at poker, as his losing hand after hand proves time and time again. Kind of like with riding, charm can't buy you a good trip around the course.

"Well, now my friends hate me," says Sean, after they leave, as I start to count my winnings. Sean's roommate leaves with them to go out drinking.

"It's not my fault if they don't know how to play. And you should know me better, that I play to win," I say. I give Sean two hundred of the thousand, which is what he lost and then some.

He refuses at first. "What is that for?"

"For letting me play—I wouldn't have won anything if it weren't for you." He's not like most of them, whose parents are bankrolling their internships and entertainment on a weekly basis. But finally he takes it.

"How is mom?" I ask. I've talked to my mother on the phone but Sean has seen her more recently and that's a better gauge of how she is.

"She still thinks you've made a colossal mistake and are making the same error that she did all those years ago, not going to college and just riding and such. She asked me if my school would still take an application so you could join me in the fall."

"Yeah, whatever."

I'm debating what I will do with the poker winnings—save it or put it towards a new saddle? The ones I'm currently riding in came with Fortune and I don't think they fit him particularly well. Theoretically, a new dressage saddle might be a good idea, since dressage is what he is worst at. Some of it will just supplement my food and laundry fund, though. I need to find a way to play poker more often.

There's a knock on the door and when Sean gets up there is a girl on the other side, a blonde chick I recognize from a photo he sent me awhile back. She murmurs "hello" as he lets her in and then she sits down on a chair as if she owns the place.

"Natasha, this is my brother, Simon," says Sean. I know that the Russian is another one of the interns Sean is working with and he's sort of half-dating her in his way.

Sean goes into the bathroom, leaving me to entertain her. The conversation is hesitant at first, and mainly to amuse myself, I say, "I think it's very nice you're dating my brother despite his condition."

"Condition?" She has almost no visible eyelashes which makes her look even more startled.

"Oh, he hasn't told you," I say, sighing and looking at my hands.

"Shut up, Simon," says Sean as he returns quickly. "He always does that with my girlfriends, he's just kidding. I thought he'd out-grown that." When I was younger—okay, like a year or two ago—I'd love to perform my own intelligence test on Sean's dates by making veiled references to his "condition" or an "incident in his past" along with subtle hints about some made-up venereal disease, drug addiction, or terminal illness when I was alone with them. Then I'd leave them to pester him to tell them all about it. Personally, I thought he should have thanked me. Like I said, intelligence test as well as funny as hell.

Natasha glares at me a little bit from her creepy lashless blue eyes. "I'll come back tomorrow, I'm sure you have lots of catching up to do with your brother."

"Thanks, doll," he says, and kisses her.

"You didn't have to do that," I say. "I could have hung out with Heather while you spent time with her." Sean hands me one of the few beers that are left and shrugs.

"Nat'll be back, tomorrow," he says. Which I know is true because no matter how casually he treated his girlfriends in high school, they always came back—at least quite a few times—before leaving. A talent he inherited from somewhere that I didn't. Or maybe I did because the few friendships I did have with girls (like Heather) always tended to be more lasting than any of my relationships with boys. Maybe I just have less use of the talent than he does.

"Besides, Heather will be returning from whatever three-hour godawful art film she's seeing," he says.

"Isn't it weird to date someone when you're working together? What if you break up with her?" I think *when you break up with her* but say *if* because even I'm not that much of an asshole.

"We're interning together, that's not work. You know that expression 'they pretend to pay us and we pretend to work?' Well, it's kinda like that."

"Come back with me if you're tired of pretending to work."

"No thanks, it's nice not being kicked, stepped on, and bitten every day."

"That's just because the horses know you don't love them like I do."

"You're so weird."

Heather comes back. The three of us spend most of the night mocking high school. It's comforting, somehow, even though I didn't like high school when I was living it and I don't miss it one bit. I like Megan and even Cynthia alright but I don't feel like I can let my guard down with them the same way I can with Sean and Heather.

I'm not too worried about the upcoming event. It's just a schooling thing. I've been working on Fortune's turns for stadium and I'm also showing another one of the greener horses over lower fences at Novice level, a bigger, rangier mare than Trouble named Crackerjack who, despite her name, is fairly sane and probably destined for a quick sale to someone looking to finish off her quickly and move up the levels. Still, it is Fortune's first eventing competition with me and you never know how he will react. This is more of a critical pre-test to see if I can get the necessary qualifying results over the year to move up a level before my working studentship is done. I need my national qualifying results (NQRs) at Preliminary level to move up to the Intermediate level. I think Daniel at my age—many years ago—was actually at the same level where I am now, but people seem to move up much faster now.

I'm looking forward to competing again, of course, armed with all the knowledge Daniel has given me about approaching fences and a more secure leg and such. But beyond that, it's almost like I'm looking forward to a familiar country I can only access when I'm riding, specifically when I'm competing. Sometimes I feel like riding, especially when I'm very focused in a show situation, is the only place where I truly feel at home and right with the world. It's a mobile and shifting country, it doesn't matter where I am or where the show is or the horse I'm riding, but it's always there for me. Everywhere else I'm a foreigner without a guidebook or a translator.

As well as obsessively preparing for the event, the day before I spend an ungodly amount of time trying to restore my horse to his original color, vowing never again to buy a grey horse, and watching my fingers turn an interesting shade of bluish purple from the whitening shampoo. At least he likes the water and seems to watch me with a kind of bemused resignation as I scrub at his handiwork of encrusted mud and grass stains and he doesn't try to bite me. Megan has to work equally hard on Maggie (who is being ridden at Novice) although Maggie has considerably less surface area to dirty than Fortune.

Cynthia is also riding Blood at a lower level, at Daniel's insistence. I know she's upset, even though she's far too cool to show it, since she's jumped much higher fences in the hunters and in the eq. Daniel tells her that he's keeping her low (rather brusquely during a lesson, without apology) so she can work on her leg and upper body.

When my friend Heather calls me one evening when I'm doing night checks (making sure at 8 p.m. and then at 11 p.m. that all the horses are okay) I mention that to her in passing, and somewhat to my surprise she tries to find some ulterior, moral motives in Daniel's decision.

"Does he have all the girls riding at a lower level than you or something?"

"No, it's because Megan needs to work on her athleticism and Cynthia is just not reliable. Besides, Daniel's wife used to almost be as good a jumper as he was an eventer when she competed, many years ago." I know she passed away from something, I think cancer, and he has no children. The farm is like his baby, now, I guess.

Ever since she went to college, Heather is always trying to find reasons for people's motivations like that, I don't know why, and even if it was true, there would be no point in worrying about it anyway. Worry about the fences, not the other crap.

I have to hang up on Heather before I can explain all that because I must deal with Maggie and put her away. Maggie continues to let herself out from time to time but she never goes far or eats herself into a stupor on grass or in the grain room like some ponies (everything is secured and sealed in there, anyway). We've kind of begun to accept her meanderings at the farm. We treat her more like a large, lumbering dog than a pony, although sometimes I jokingly threaten to get on her if she's acting really naughty with Megan.

8

CAUGHT IN THE MOUTH

During one of our last schooling efforts over the little cross-country course set up at the farm, Cynthia (who has to practice with us when Daniel is around) suddenly is unable to jump any drops with her horse. Blood Money has always been pretty reluctant about jumping anything that doesn't look like a fence in general but the mare seems to be unusually silly and spooky today. I'm assuming it is rider error and nerves and the more Blood refuses, the shakier Cynthia becomes. This time, it's not even into scary water, just a relatively straightforward path from grass to grass. It's a practice question and mainly there to teach riders how to get off the horse's back and distribute their weight. Not brain surgery or even Badminton.

"Stop catching that mare in the mouth," barks Daniel. "You're sending mixed signals to her now." One of Cynthia's great faults as a rider, I've noticed, is that she has terrible trouble recovering from any setback. If things go perfectly well, she can look quite competent, even strong, but at the least unexpected detour her confidence starts to crumble. I've watched her school alone and she's markedly better solo than she is with us. It's just that Blood is used to jumping in arenas more than out in the open.

Eventually, Daniel tells Cynthia to get off. "At this point, you're training her NOT to go over it," he says. Slightly to my surprise, he tells me to get on.

Blood goes over it—reluctantly, but she does. There is a supple slinkiness that Blood has that I miss, that reminds me of the OTTB I used to ride, and for a second I don't want to get off of her.

Cynthia gets back on but can't replicate it. I kind of know that Daniel is subtly stoking the fires of competition among the three of us but knowing it doesn't make his strategy any less effective. If one of us is having a problem with one of the babies he'll put one of the other riders on the horse and usually the horse will behave just fine.

It takes practically the rest of the lesson to get Blood going, mainly because Cynthia is growing increasingly frustrated. Daniel tells Megan to pony Cynthia through the fence, using Maggie as a lead horse. But even having the brave little pony go first doesn't convince Blood that the ditch is any less scary. Eventually, Daniel asks two of the teenage barn rats watching to stand on either side of the ditch with lunge whips. Cynthia hand-walks Blood and the girls gently raise the whips, "persuading" Blood to go forward, which the mare does, sort of leapfrogging. We watch Blood go through several times until Cynthia gets on her again and can go over it without catching her horse in the mouth or communicating her expectation that Blood can and will refuse. I know next time we're out, she'll be fine, it's just Cynthia's mind is in the loop of failure that we all sometimes get in, which is hard to break if you're on the inside of the hamster wheel.

I take Fortune out that night after my chores are done, ignoring the carefully manicured cross-country schooling course and head straight to the trails. The moon is full and lights our path almost as brightly as the sun. There are potentially scary shadows in the darkness but Fortune doesn't question me when I ask him to head into what might be uncertain territory. He refuses me nothing although tonight I don't jump or go particularly fast since he worked hard during the day.

Already, since Daniel's not a fan of gadgets like draw reins (and neither am I), Fortune's neck has started to take its natural shape. He'll never be mistaken for an Arabian on a postcard but he does have a topline and he's begun to move better over fences, more rounded, less flat, and more responsive to me. He likes being outside more than anything. I think he's happy here.

Daniel has (along with how to take water and ditches) lectured us all about not rushing things and I don't just mean fences. Sometimes I feel I have all the time in the world and other times I feel as if I am running away from time itself and if I don't hurry things along I'll end up in the Box of an office, far away from horses in the end, after all is said and done. No matter what happens here, Cindy won't, so the stakes are much higher for me.

Megan doesn't bother to braid for our first show since it is a schooling show—she just combs out the burrs from Maggie's wild mane and tail. I wouldn't feel right if I didn't braid, however, and it helps keep me focused and gives my mind and my fingers something to do rather than worrying (not that there aren't other things around the barn that need doing). Plus, at my old barn, braiding was a way to pick up some extra cash and I'm reasonably good at it. Cynthia is pulling her horse's mane at the other end of the stable. I have a feeling she hasn't done it before, but I don't say anything.

Fortune's mane is wiry and tough but the pulling doesn't seem to bother him. He stamps and snorts at first and makes the motions of trying to bite and kick me for a bit, but not seriously, and then just sort of stands there, relaxed and resigned. I can see Blood dancing around on the crossties, however.

"I'm worried about hurting her," says Cynthia. I think Blood is just annoyed about being cross-tied for so long so I start the mare off, business-like as possible, which calms the horse down.

I go back to Fortune and periodically check on Cynthia so she doesn't end up with a bald horse. Eventually, I finish the mare off for her.

"Do you ever cut?"

"Sometimes as a last resort," I say. I do a little trimming, but nothing major. Unlike Fortune, Blood has a pretty easy mane—not too thick, not too thin. Then we start Blood's actual braiding.

"Does it always hurt your fingers so much?" Cindy whines.

"Use some athletic tape—or duct tape—until your skin toughens up. Or a surgical glove." I've done this for so many years I think my skin around my knuckles is probably even harder than tape. I root through the tack room's box of supplies, get some tape and show Cindy how to put it on the knuckle that bears the brunt of the pain on an uncalloused hand. Her hand lingers in my palm just a second too long and I pull away and start braiding Blood to show her how it's done.

"Wow, you're really good at this," she says, watching me do a sample braid or two.

"It's just like any skill; it just takes practice."

"Can you please, please help me? I'm afraid of screwing up."

"You'll never learn if you don't screw up," I say.

Cynthia puts Blood in a stall, watches me braid Fortune, and then we complete Blood's mane together. "Most little girls love to braid. My business came from older ammies who barely would find the time to ride, much less care for their horses."

"This isn't like braiding a Barbie doll," says Cynthia.

I roll my eyes because a childhood of braiding Barbie dolls' hair is just the kind of basic thing a basic girl like Cindy would like doing. "I'll take your word for that," I say. I pause and laugh. "My brother and I once got in trouble for setting the hair of my cousin's Barbie dolls on fire, but that was a long time ago and not quite the same thing."

"Were you a bad kid? I never would have pegged you for one," she says.

"Really? I guess you've just seen my more respectable side. Those things smelled godawful when they were lit."

"You're so quiet most of the time."

"Yes, well, sometimes I'm quiet, sometimes I'm not. It depends. Don't they always say that it's the quiet ones you have to worry about?"

"I can't figure you out," she says.

I'm not sure what that means so I just think comb, knot, loop, and pull. Over and over again. I tackle Blood's tail, which is much easier to braid than Fortune's tangled, wiry mess. And darker (no grass stains to be bleached away).

"Now I have to do Crackerjack," I say.

Crackerjack is sound and sane and her dark bay color reminds me of the last horse—a mare named Damsel in Distress—I owned even though she isn't nearly as brave (admittedly, Crackerjack has only been off the track for two years). At least not yet. She's more compliant than my old Damsel but also more reliant upon my urging her to go ahead. She really does have potential as a jumper (and I'm not just saying potential as a euphemism) although probably not as much as an eventer. Crappy record as a racehorse, though.

Cynthia continues to watch me. I kind of wish she would leave me alone although given that one time I yelled at her in the past I guess I should be glad there are no hard feelings.

"Cynthia, why are you here," I ask, after a time. "When you go back to where you came from, won't you have people to do this?" She won't have to clean a bridle, braid a horse, or certainly muck out a stall ever again.

"Because I know how much I don't know," she says, after a pause. "How am I ever going to get ahead if I don't start learning? I'll be stuck where I am and that's just not good enough. My father—my father always says I'm a black hole for his money."

That's what is so comforting about horse showing, no matter what the discipline. It's impossible to think any farther than the next six or ten minutes. At a show, nothing really bothers me about where I've been and where I might be going.

"Well, that's not just true of you, that's true of everyone with horses."

"Not everyone some—some people are successful. Surely you think about that? Where you will be after you leave here?" says Cynthia.

"I think about that all the time, but right now I'm thinking her mane needs to be pulled more." At least Cracker isn't like my previous horse, who I'm thinking of, who practically climbed up the walls or up into my lap to avoid the comb.

"It's a pity she doesn't have more chrome," drawls Cynthia.

"She's fancy enough. She's not crying out to be bought by a hunter princess like you," I mutter, coming as close as I do to smiling.

9

I'M SMILING LIKE I MEAN IT

The day breaks warm and humid, which seems to be inevitable with any midsummer event involving jackets. We have to be at the barn at 4:30 a.m. I get up before my alarm goes off and listen to my favorite song by the Killers, several times, as I've done before every horse show for as long as I can remember.

The dressage in the morning goes well enough. Fortune seems to be aware that people are watching and feels suppler and doesn't pull or mouth the bit.

Crackerjack and Fortune both jump clean cross-country with only time faults for Cracker. With Fortune, the competition is mine to lose in the showjumping phase. Poor Megan gets a refusal from Maggie riding at Novice level, so she won't place, although she handles it well. Or she just doesn't care enough.

Another nice thing about eventing is that unlike hunter-jumper shows there are also a decent number of guys here. One of them (not particularly cute, but a fellow male) stops to talk to me. "That table was wicked," he says.

Fortune didn't spook at the way it was decorated—with sculpted mushrooms all over it—but yeah, it was weird. "I'm not sure what they were going for with that one," I say. After all, theoretically a cross-country course is supposed to replicate what you might experience riding a horse out in the open.

"'Alice in Wonderland' theme, I think. Must have been smoking something interesting when they designed that," he adds and rides away.

This *is* Vermont, you know.

I also find in eventing, at least not at these levels, there isn't the general seething bitchiness that you pick up on when riding hunter-jumpers. No one cares what brands you're wearing or whatever. I attribute this to the lower ratio of women but it also just might be that we all know we're kind of crazy to be jumping weird shit out in the middle of a field on horses. We're collectively glad that no one gets hurt round after round because that means we're all going to be okay at the end of the day.

As for Cracker in general, well, I actually like Cracker but...it's hard to explain, I don't yet have that sensation of feeling the horse's mind like I do with Fortune. Of course, I'm still controlling Fortune when I ride him but at our best I feel that there is something going on before thought, that I'm not analyzing the questions posed by the course very consciously and deliberately in the same way I am for the other horses that I ride.

By the time I've changed back into my show clothes and am ready to do stadium with Fortune, in the warm-up ring I'm aware that I feel really odd. This is despite the fact that I am in show mode, which means that my mind is still in that comforting tunnel of knowing all it needs to do. No, I haven't been smoking whatever magic mushrooms the course designer was on. I think I might be hungry and then I realize that with all the braiding, schooling, and getting everyone else's horses ready, I haven't eaten anything since a cup of ramen and a Coke slurped down at lunchtime yesterday. It must have been more than twenty-four hours since I've ingested calories.

I see one of the little girls I teach, a nine-year-old named Melody who is in the Beginner Novice division. I know Fortune and I don't need any more practice, so I reach down, give Melody a five-dollar bill, and tell her to get me a slice of pizza. While everyone else is jumping, I drop my reins, take off my gloves and begin to eat, thinking that it would be a bad thing if I passed out at the end of what has been a successful day thus far.

"O'Shaughnessy? What the hell are you doing?" says Daniel, walking over from where he has been watching some of the other riders from the barn, the lower level teens. "What kind of pig eats in the warm-up ring?" I've gone this far so I just kind of finish as calmly and quickly as I can without burning my mouth and put my gloves back on. "If you don't win this, you're a dead man."

I knew that already. But we do win, which I also kind of knew we would. It felt easy, almost too easy. I should know by now not to get too confident with anything involving horses although right now I feel pretty much charmed. Even Crackerjack, despite her inexperience, comes in third.

In addition to our personal responsibilities, all of the working students are given three little Beginner Novice kids to coach. I am determined that Team Shaughnessy will surpass either Megan's or Cynthia's efforts. I know kids can get silly when they compete for the first time at eventing, regardless of the height of the fences, so I take all of them aside for a briefing. "I know all of your parents have probably told you that it doesn't matter how you do today as long as you stay safe and have fun." One of the little girls in braids nods solemnly. "But if we don't beat Cindy's and Meg's teams I swear, all of you are looking at no stirrups for a MONTH. Got it?"

Fortunately for my kids, Megan's group has one particularly amusing disaster. A little girl gets spooked by a jump coming up and circles her pony endlessly in front of it, saying "did not present," that is, did not present her horse to the jump. This goes on for ages. She gets the fat little gelding over it after a certain point but it's a major time penalty. Cynthia's kids have a few run-outs but the worst thing one of my kids does is jump one of the Novice fences by accident.

"Becky, are you COLOR BLIND!" I shout. "Was that a YELLOW BACKGROUND? I THINK NOT!" Fortunately, there is no penalty for an extra jump so Becky circles back, jumps the correct jump, and actually ends up with a good time.

Melody nearly falls off at the same jump (where I have stationed myself, knowing that although it is a simple coop, it is at a bit of a weird angle for their level). This would have been catastrophic. Elimination is automatic, even at the BN level, except for the odd chance of the kid landing on her feet. "YOU WILL NOT FALL OFF!" I shout at her. "No stirrups and no reins for a month if you fall off of that pony." She grabs the pony's neck, rights herself, and continues.

"Simon, you're awful," says Cindy after I finish.

"You're just jealous because your young ones came in last place." I buy all my kids ice cream. My mom used to buy ice cream for whoever—me or my brother—did better until I kept winning so regularly she just stopped getting it entirely, using the excuse it was bad for our teeth. I've never lost my taste for sugar like you're supposed to but thus far my teeth (and my skull) haven't been hurt, despite my bad habits.

A week or so after the show Daniel and I go for a wander around the property. He rides Trouble, who he is still trying to get used to new things, new sights, new people. He's taking it slowly with her over fences and hopefully she'll be sold as a jumper or at least a lower-level eventer once her brain is unscrambled from the track.

"You're ambitious," he observes. "And it frustrates you that you're not farther along."

"Yes, it does," I admit. Then I read off the list that has existed in my mind for so long of people my age or younger who are farther ahead than I am. My self-esteem tends to swing like a pendulum, with no in-between. Either I'm awesome like when I get an award or I'm going nowhere fast, just treading water. The sense of motionlessness is particularly strong when I read about someone my age winning an international event. This seems to confirm everyone's opinion that I'm making some sort of horrible mistake with my life. Of course, I tell myself that even if things don't work out, I can always teach riding or something like that. I actually like teaching even though I could do without the people factor outside of the riding ring for the most part.

Daniel says all the right things, that I shouldn't worry and the important thing is to get better and while it is great to be competitive (since it is all a competition and there is no masking that) there isn't much point about being paralyzed by what I can't change. He also says, "And don't get too attached to any one horse. Keep your mind on where you want to go."

I kind of read behind the lines: your horse sucks at a third of the skills needed to be a decent eventer and you don't yet have the money to buy one that is better. He looks at my face. "Well, we don't really know what we can expect of your horse—it might be rider education as well as the horse." I don't know if I should be relieved by that or angry, so I shrug.

"I'm not gonna lie to you and say horses are an easy business. It's possible to make a living at it, if you don't make it through the traditional routes but you have to work your ass off. And have some good luck."

Daniel doesn't say what those traditional routes are, but I remember another trainer back at my old barn being much more explicit, saying that you couldn't get into horses as a business unless you were, "Born to it, bought your way into it, or, if you're a woman, screwed your way into it. Kind of like royalty." He was crude and bitter and no one liked him much for that (yeah, Daniel can curse but his language doesn't have any edge of resentment like some horse people who aren't where they want to be and are going nowhere fast). Still, I've always remembered that phrase because, with my mom, I figure I get half a point for the first option, even though we don't have money or property anymore. But that's it.

I tell myself it doesn't really matter, that I don't have land or money or...or other attractive assets to get into the business. I am already sure that being inside a building for four years is not for me, an opinion solidified by recent experiences. If I'm sleeping on a cot near Fortune's stall in ten years, so be it. All I can do is keep my mind on my goal, regardless of whether I reach it.

Unless I'm moving at a very fast pace in the direction of something, my brain gets too distracted, unfocused, and bored. Like horse, like rider.

In the next few weeks, I'll be competing in my first truly competitive show—not a schooling show this time, a hunter-jumper show which I know Daniel is primarily using to orient the younger charges to tight, creative stadium courses but which has Open Jumper classes up to 1.45m. We start to talk about that for a little bit, how jumper shows are good preparation for both jumping eventing phases and how they keep your equitation sharper in some ways because you don't have to ride quite as defensively as you do cross-country.

"Sometimes it's good not to anticipate the worst with everything—with courses and even with people," says Daniel, as he slides off and begins to untack. "More people fail in this business because of a lack of people skills than horse skills because it's people that pay the bills."

Now I think he might be referring to my tendency to plug my iPod in my ears and pull up my hooded sweatshirt when I'm not riding or teaching but I don't say anything. Habits on horseback I can correct but that habit is too ingrained and I know deep down it's not going to die. I'll just have to make up for it when I ride.

I'm doing feed buckets first thing in the morning, scooping and pouring grain and throwing in the SmartPaks (iPod plugged in given what's playing on the barn radio) when Megan gets me. Her face is white and she looks terrified, which is unusual for Megan. "Oh my God, blood," she says. At first, I think she's just talking about the horse but then I realize that she is not only saying the name but Blood is, in fact, hurt. Somehow, in her stall the mare managed to gash her own eye. She can't even open it.

"How the hell did she manage that?" I mutter. It is really quite amazing how horses can creatively hurt themselves with no apparent means at their disposal. I get some gauze and tape and call the vet. Of course, all of us have every number for the vet—emergency number as well as standard hours number—ready at hand. Luckily, the doctor says he can come before he sets out on his regular rounds. It will be an additional charge since it's technically off regular hours but I figure Cynthia can and will be willing to pay for it. Blood has already gotten the eye dirty with shavings and muck and the eyelid seems to be hanging at a weird angle.

Dr. Max comes even before he said he would. He agrees that Blood is very clever. "Any horse can tear open its face outside, but in a stall with no sharp objects, that takes a bit more talent," he says, and begins to clean the wound.

Now that we can see it more clearly, without all the shavings concealing it, it's more obviously ripped apart.

Cynthia is finally up and hyperventilating by my side. Megan knew she would freak out, which is why she got me first. I notice Cynthia flinch as she sees the lid hanging off. Dr. Max has sedated Blood and the mare is awake but kind of dazed and loopy as she stands on the crossties. The Katy Perry song "Dark Horse" blasting on the barn radio seems singularly inappropriate at the moment and I turn it off.

I think I hear the doctor murmur, "Thank you," when I do. He stitches it up with bright pink thread, which is supposed to make it easier for Cynthia to see the wound and to clean it. Given that just about everything Cynthia owns has pink somewhere on it except her show tack, the corners of my mouth turn up just a little bit. But most of me feels bad even though I wish the vet could give Cynthia a tranquilizer as well as her horse.

"Will she look the same after you take the stitches out? We have our first real competitive show coming up!"

"You're actually lucky—she didn't tear open the tear duct. Wash her face at least twice a day. Cover the bandage with a fly mask and turn her out alone, in one of the small paddocks, always supervised. I'll give you some pain reliever and antibiotic to put on it. And obviously, don't let her get it dirty," says the vet. "Usually these things heal without scars or affecting the appearance of the horse." Dr. Max shows Cynthia the snaps on Blood's feed bucket in the stall—one has blood on it so it's possible that the mare was scratching against it a bit too enthusiastically. "It should heal in about three weeks."

I make mental plans about how to slot in Blood's aftercare into my chores and rotation of horses in the paddocks (since we will all be collectively responsible for it) and then start turning horses out while the vet calms Cynthia down.

It's so early it's still dim in the early morning light. I hear barking—clearly not a dog's—in the distance. Cynthia gasps as I walk by her. I have a horse in each of my hands (there are some horses that balk if they are taken out alone). But I'm not afraid.

"Don't worry, that's just a fox," I say. She looks suspicious of me, as if I'm lying and there is a monster that lives near the stables I've neglected to mention to her. "Their bark sounds a bit like a dog being strangled," I say, and imitate it. Dr. Max starts a bit then laughs at me. I'm not as good as imitating people as my brother but I can do a mean fox. Cynthia startles again, even though she knows I'm the source of the ugly sound. I feel relaxed. Things are back to normal again. The horses are used to my animal imitations and don't turn a hair.

Walking with more horses past the doctor's battered dark green SUV, at first I'm vaguely cognizant of the usual bumper stickers horse people have in the area like a show jumper clearing a fence and a USET sticker. But then I also register the words BATTLE BORN and SMILE LIKE YOU MEAN IT.

I know it's kind of dumb, but I sort of linger at the car to talk to the doctor after he is finished. "The Killers, best band ever," I say, pointing to the names of one of their albums and one of their best songs.

"I've seen them twice—once in Central Park and once in the UK."

"No way! I'm so jealous. I must have every version of their songs ever recorded and listened to them like, a million times, and watched all of their videos again and again. But I've never seen them live. That's one of my life goals."

"Well, they've been touring less consistently since Brandon started to do solo work."

"I really liked his solo album. Totally underrated and under-played. Their song from Hot Fuss 'All These Things That I've Done' is actually my psych-up song before every horse show. I always listen to it a couple of times when I'm getting ready."

The doctor takes off his glasses to clean them and grins. I don't say what is also true, which is that I particularly enjoy repeatedly watching the lead singer of said band Brandon Flowers in the video for said song take a shower. My brother, who still has an unfortunate and inexplicable fixation on country music, even after I tried to get him into the Killers and showed him the error of his ways, has only been willing to concede that the Asian chick in the video is really hot. Maybe who you fixate on in that video is some kind of a litmus test for your sexual orientation, I dunno.

I do note, "I love both the Killers' early stuff and their recent work. It kind of annoys me when people are like 'oh, I like 'Mr. Brightside' and the other songs from Hot Fuss, but not what they're doing now.' They've totally developed as a band—that's what I love about them, everything they do is amazing and different. They don't just recycle what worked in the past." Again, I also don't mention the fact that I like the eyeliner and flamboyant gestures of the earlier Killers/Brandon AND his current look, which tends to be more understated and involves cowboy hats and/or leather jackets. I did admittedly have hope when I first started watching their early videos because of Brandon's copious use of guyliner and his spectacular vests but even though I've acknowledged the lead singer's hopeless heterosexuality, I still enjoy the fantasy potential of all of it with his music. At least he's very comfortable with himself for a straight guy, which is also totally hot.

"I haven't been to a concert in years," says the doctor. "I love my work, but it does have its downsides. The last concert I went to was Duran Duran, actually. A blast from the past. Well, even I'm not old enough to remember them from when they were first popular. Neon Trees opened."

"I love them—both of those bands. Actually, I love pretty much everything from the early '80s or any band with a '80s sound. It's amazing how even the kind of cheesy, one-hit wonders from that decade were so good and then suddenly everything from the late '90s on, even the supposedly alternative stuff, suddenly became so bad." I find myself unable to look Dr. Max in his eyes and turn to scan the rest of his car. I tap another sticker I just noticed with my finger. "Another one of the best of all time. The Smiths."

"'There is a Light that Never Goes Out' is one of my favorite songs, I can't think of how many times I played that in my car, riding around in high school."

"I love the cover the Killers did of that song awhile back. Although I read in an interview that Brandon actually prefers Morrissey as a solo artist to the Smiths."

"That's odd. I can't say I agree."

"No, me either, but I totally think every genius should have at least one eccentric and totally unjustified opinion."

Dr. Max laughs. "So, what is yours? Your eccentric and totally unjustified opinion?"

"I didn't say I was a genius."

"Well, you do have quite a few opinions." I look over at the doctor, as he leans on his beat-up car. He's much fitter than even most of the college guys I've seen—actually pretty built. His hair is closely cropped in the back but it is thick and wiry and his bangs almost hang into his eyes; he's not losing his hair or anything so he can't be that old. He doesn't look old, even though he must be quite a bit older than me because he's a vet and obviously not a totally new vet. He has a refreshing lack of questionable tattoos and no odd and unsanitary body piercings. Again, my gaydar is pretty terrible but I swear I am getting signals and not just because I'm so goddamn desperate. Not anything that's said explicitly, for sure, but just in his level of interest and how near he stands and things like that.

My face is hot as hell, unfortunately. Hot Fuss indeed. "Sorry, didn't mean to sound like a know-it-all."

"No, I just don't meet that many people who like to talk about music on my rounds."

"I'll bet. It takes a lot of effort on my part to avoid listening to Katy Perry and Taylor Swift on the barn sound system all day."

He laughs and there is a pause as I wait and expect him to go.

"You know," the vet looks away from me a bit, "if you want to continue this discussion, we could meet up for dinner. If you're free. I know that they work you guys off your feet here."

Now, I think I am being asked on a date. But I'm not totally sure. It could be just friendly—hell, Daniel has asked Max once or twice to dinner, after a really bad or long appointment.

Either way, tomorrow I get to see the doctor at what passes for a restaurant in the town, kind of a greasy spoon diner that people go to after church on Sundays but weekdays is mostly populated by coffee-swilling college students and farmers who smell like hay and manure.

Walking back to the barn, I sing in my head: "All These Things That I've Done."

It's been awhile since I've been on a date—if this is, in fact, a date, and not simply a hallucination. Hell, I don't think I've ever been on an explicit date. Most of my sexual experimentation in high school was brief fumbling with high school guys so far in the closet they might as well have been in friggin' Narnia.

But for the first time I kind of regret that I haven't saved any of my clothes from getting chewed, spit on, and stained by horses. Before I am supposed to go out I carefully select my one pair of jeans without visible holes, only frays, and a polo shirt so dark you can't see too many grass stains. I won't have time between the end of work and tomorrow to do anything but shower (well, hopefully shower). I haven't even gotten my hair cut properly in weeks.

I knock on the girls' door since it seems like hair cutting is something Megan would know how to do.

"Why do you suddenly need it done now?" she says.

"It's okay if you can't," I say. I have the barn office scissors in my hand that I borrowed. They look sharp enough. "Hair's just bothering me, it's tickling my neck." I look across at the large mirror that Cynthia hung on the wall and see what I always see: light freckles, dirty blond dishwater hair that is not of any real describable color because it's irregularly faded with the sun, blue eyes that look equally faded. Somewhat more built and less skinny than how I was before I came here and maybe very slightly taller. My weird, irregularly shaped mouth and nose. None of this can be helped, unfortunately, but at least I can get my hair cut, even if I have to do it myself.

"Do you have a date or something?" says Megan as I sit down. She runs a wet comb through my hair. "I can see your neck turning red." Goddamn friggin' transparent skin, I think. "If you don't tell me who it is, I swear I'll cut it crooked." I stand up. "Oh, sit down, Simon, I'm just kidding. But really, you can be so, so—annoying. And you know I'm going to find out eventually."

As the hair falls, I say a little prayer to the God I talk to every now and then (usually on horseback, right before I'm ready go gallop at an event) that she doesn't. It has occurred to me that if I'm making a mistake it will be pretty awkward, since it's not like I can avoid the vet. Even if my own horse has been pretty healthy thus far, that's not something I can bank on. Health's the one area in which horses will disappoint you as much as people.

10

ALL GOOD THINGS COME TO THOSE WHO WAIT

When I go to the diner I've decided the fact that I don't look particularly dressed up is a good thing, in case I have been totally misreading Max's signals. The place is crowded but I'm still able to see him sitting in a corner. Now I feel sort of silly because he's obviously just come from his rounds and probably smells of horse as much as me. Again, I can't even detect the smell anymore but I can tell it is always there, based on the reaction of civilians. The diner is crowded and noisy and obviously the worst place for conversation.

All of this counts against it being a date but the slightly uncomfortable silence that passes between the two of us is clearly a point in favor of that estimation. I kind of have a win-loss column in my head right now.

"I'm sorry I am a bit late," I say. "Evening feed took longer than I thought it would."

"Oh, I understand. I'm sure Daniel gets his money's worth out of you."

"He's fair, but yeah, it gets tiring every now and then."

"He's very much the classic Yankee when it comes to a work ethic," says Max. "And probably knows just as much as I do, if not more, about veterinary medicine in some areas." Max has a kind of impassive, clinical way of discussing things that is oddly attractive, even when he is off the clock. He chooses his sentences carefully, as if organizing them before he speaks. "I wish I had enough time and money to lesson with him more than once a week."

"Most vets I've known don't even ride so I think that it is cool that you keep up with it."

"Yes, I know, it's kind of ironic—people become vets because they love horses and then don't have the time or financial resources to ride," says Max. "Where did you find your horse? Fortune, that's his name, right? The big grey?"

"Oh, he's someone's reject from my barn back home," I said. "But he's slowly become less rejected."

Max laughs and the tension between us softens. I've started thinking of the doctor as Max although it hasn't even been established what I should call him.

"Did you ever own your own horse?" I ask.

"Yes, before I went away to college. I was sort of your typical Pony Club nerd, though, always just as interested in the whole horsemanship aspect as much as riding. The highest I ever really jumped in competition was 1.2m but now I rarely venture above .90m and that's only if I'm feeling very brave. My younger sister actually got involved first and quickly lost interest but I stayed with it, even when I was the only guy, most years."

"I did show jumping, eventing, although my last barn was more of a typical hunter-jumper show barn. That's why I am here." Just as the conversation is beginning to flow, however, Max's cell phone rings.

"It's work, I have to answer it. I'm on call," he explains, apologetically. "Damn, Simon. There is a mare that is having trouble foaling. They think it is a breech. I have to go. I can drop you home on my way," he says.

"Could I come?" As soon as I blurt that out, I wonder if he was making some sort of an excuse, like Sean would ask me to call him on a first date to make sure that he had an escape route if things got really dire.

But I just have a feeling that Max isn't that sort of person and when he hesitates but then says, "Sure," I think he means it. "I should warn you, though, this might be a long evening."

The horse farm is located on a remote enough road that I've never seen it before. It looks like a riding barn, the way it is set up with a ring outdoors, but it's small. We're greeted by a heavyset teenage girl, who is hyperventilating and saying it's been almost an hour since the mare's water broke.

The girl's parents are standing by the stall. After putting on a surgical glove Max feels around inside the mare. She's small, just above a pony in size, a light strawberry roan who looks almost pink under the dim lights of the barn.

"I don't see why she had to wait until it was pitch black," mutters the father.

"DAD, they always do," says the girl. "So they can feel safe."

The father—a tall, lanky man who strikes me as being unhorsey—leans against the door of the stall and sighs.

"This is the second foaling on our property since we moved out here and bought the place. This is Lucy's first baby, though. We didn't have any trouble with the first one," says the mother, a small, nervous dark-haired woman with her hair in a tight bun.

Their daughter is about fourteen or fifteen, I'd guess. She's wearing pajama bottoms, a baggy T-shirt that isn't baggy enough to conceal the fact that she's obviously not wearing a bra, and fuzzy slippers. She appears to be more ready for a sleep-over than a foaling.

"The good news is that it's not a breech. The foal just seems to have its hock flexed so it is stopped in transit." Max looks through his equipment and takes out a thin rope that almost looks like something you'd find at a hardware store. He explains that he's going to put it around the foal's pastern and then someone needs to hold the rope so he can push the foal back in—this should straighten out the leg and the foal should slip out with very little effort. I can almost follow his line of thought as he looks at the girl's father (who is wrinkling his nose in disgust), the fragile mother, and the teary-eyed girl. I take the rope while Max cups his hand around the sharp foot and gently pushes the foal back into the canal. The mare is so exhausted she gives little resistance. She's tiny but the foal must be quite large, I'm guessing, based on the size of her belly.

Minutes later the entire foal emerges—he is huge, black, with an enormous, ungainly head. He just lies there and Max breaks the sac around him—I always thought that foals did it themselves but this one is just lying there, passive and still.

Max clears away the bubbles of mucus around the nostrils with a suction bulb but the foal still doesn't respond. I hear the girl murmuring, "Oh my God, oh my God, it's dead," but Max turns the colt upside down for a minute and more pus runs out, Max lets the colt down, slaps its rib cage, and it begins breathing on its own. As if we were all holding our breath with the animal, everyone watching exhales a sigh. Max cleans the foal's navel with antiseptic and the foal lurches across the stall and begins to suck. The mare has been lying there, seemingly, oblivious to all the drama until now, and starts cleaning the foal with her tongue.

"That wasn't as bad as I thought it would be. But as you can see, these were not very experienced people so they were pretty upset. I'm glad they called even though this wasn't quite the evening you were expecting, I assume," says Max when we leave.

I'm tempted to say that it was the best date ever but then again, there is still a small part of me that isn't even sure that it is a date.

"That was amazing," is all I can manage. I can't help thinking how incredibly cool it is for Max that something like that is all in a day's work. "I actually have never seen a foal born before—my family never bred horses and the two broodmares didn't take this year yet at Daniel's. As you know."

It's so late I know I have to go home. I have to be up early to feed and I know that Max still has his regular rounds the following morning. I want to see him again but I don't quite know what to say. I ask him to pull over and then before I can think too much, I kiss him, quickly.

Thank God he doesn't pull away. I'm vaguely conscious of putting my hand on his leg and moving closer to him. I can feel the muscles of his chest digging into mine. I'm tempted to go further but eventually, he says, softly, "If I don't go now, I probably won't go at all and that can't be good. I can't be late."

Unwillingly, I detach myself but I don't move too far away. "I guess not. I can't, either. When can I see you again?"

"Look, why don't you come over to my place for dinner tomorrow? It's not that far and it's not crawling with people and so noisy we can't hear ourselves think like the restaurant was tonight." I don't want to seem too excited so I just sort of look at my hands and nod. "You can just bring some beer or wine or whatever you like and I'll make something."

"Okay—but well, there is one problem. I can't buy beer."

"You don't drink?"

"Not exactly—too young."

Max raises an eyebrow. "How young *are* you?" He withdraws his arm.

I laugh and that relaxes me and I can look him in the eye, like I can breathe again, finally, just like when I was watching the foal. "I'm eighteen. I'm not that young."

"Eighteen is young."

"So how *old* are you?"

"Not eighteen." He hesitates.

"I told you how old I was."

"Thirty-four."

"Oh well, that's not that old."

"Thanks for the vote of confidence."

"Well, I kind of figured that out that you were older than me, being a vet and all. How old did you think I was?"

"Older than eighteen."

"Why? Do I look old, I mean, older than eighteen?"

"No, I guess it was just because of the music you said you liked. And I assumed because you were working at Daniel's. Most of his working students have gone through college at least, some are transitioning between careers, that kind of thing."

For one brief second I do feel a flicker of—regret—not at the fact I am here right now, working where I work but at the fact Max might think I'm stupid.

"I'm of age, in case that concerns you," I say, dryly. "And not everyone my age likes Katy Perry and One Direction."

"Okay and no, you don't look old. Any other surprises I should know about before we meet again?"

"Well, I once killed a man," I deadpan.

Max laughs and says nothing can surprise him now.

"I can bring soda. I hope that's an adequate replacement," I say.

11

WHAT DOES THE DRINKING
AGE MATTER, ANYWAY?

I never really understood what people meant when they said they could hear their hearts beating in their chests until now. I walk away from the car.

"What happened to you?" says Megan as she watches me lead the horses out for morning turnout. "Did whatever happen go well? Did my haircut get you laid?"

I still haven't recovered my sense of self-possession enough to crack a joke back so I just roll my eyes. Hopefully, none of the horses will need a vet between now and tomorrow night because that would be awkward.

"You look like you got laid in some hay," Megan says, "Your clothes are a mess." I realize I have shavings and multiple stains from various horse fluids all over the one pair of good pants and shirt I had.

The following night I ride my bike to Max's house, which is a kind of nondescript condominium in the midst of one of the developments that have slowly begun cropping up on the outskirts of town. I'm a bit surprised and I suppose it shows in my face. The living room has a kind of faceless, almost motel-like quality to it, with a cheap sofa, a small TV, and no decorations of any kind other than a coffee table with some papers thrown on it—a mix of what looks like scientific articles and information about new medications, work stuff.

"I've never really had the time to make the place look like much of a home," Max apologizes.

"With all the money I sunk at the vet's over the years with my OTTB, I always imagined you guys living in palaces with chandeliers and golden light fixtures."

Max laughs. "Sorry to rob you of your illusions. Maybe vets who own their own practices."

Max does appear to know how to cook (things other than ramen and Pop-Tarts like me, I mean). He makes these kind of weird, spicy lamb burger things in a pita, some hummus, and an oily salad. It's not the sort of thing that I usually like but I am completely and unattractively starving since I haven't eaten since breakfast. It's been one of those days at the barn where something happens every minute—false alarm about a lesson horse being off, a broken gate, and my needing to school another lesson horse after it acts up for a rider. I haven't had a chance to sit down until now. Which is good because it means I haven't had a chance to get nervous. Although, unlike the last time, I also haven't had a chance to make myself look presentable. My boots are still covered in mud and despite the fact that this is my first time here, just sensing from his look I've left them at the door. I'm also leaving a trail of hayseed from the cuffs of my pants but I hope he's kinda used to that, given that pretty much everyone who works with horses has hay in their clothes and hair, or somewhere on their person, at all times.

Despite the impersonal character of Max's setup, I notice a guitar hanging in the corner. "Do you play?" I ask.

"Yes. I was in a band in college, just like everyone, I guess. I try to keep it up. Kind of like my riding," he says, laughing. "Poorly."

"I've always wanted to learn the guitar but I never had the time. I was a pure barn rat in high school."

"I get it. I was pretty much, too. Like I said, I did Pony Club and kind of took over my sister's horse. "

"I've never understood that with girls. The two aren't mutually exclusive, boys and horses."

"No, although by the time I earned my B rating, I was the only guy in my Pony Club."

"I hear ya—the sacrifices we make for horses."

"Well, quite a few of my friends consider living here to be the greatest sacrifice of all, i.e., it means a pretty nonexistent social life for even any single heterosexual, much less a gay male. But I'm lucky to have a job to pay off my student loans. Quite a lot of my fellow vet school grads can't say the same. And I'm lucky as well to get a job working with horses, which is what I always wanted to do. Again, most people think I'm crazy in general to be working outdoors in sub-zero temperatures when I could be working in a temperature-controlled environment on cats and little dogs in the middle of a city somewhere."

"I like the weather here."

"That's because you've only been here during the summer so far. But I do actually like it all year 'round. Of course, I'm kind of a masochist about the cold, so it suits me."

"I grew up in Massachusetts, so it doesn't bother me either."

"That doesn't really count, trust me, you'll understand what I mean in a few months. Massachusetts isn't serious New England. You'd still be a flatlander—"

"Flatlander? I really do prefer Masshole—"

"—even if you hadn't spent time down south."

"New Jersey. I went to high school in New Jersey, not the south."

"That's down south in these parts."

I walk over and pick up the guitar and play the one or two chords I know, then I hand the instrument over to Max. He starts to strum it a bit as he talks and from the unconscious way in which he brings forth sound as he speaks I know that he really does know how to play. And sing—even just the note or two he hums has a kind of resonance in his chest that mine never does.

"Play something by the Killers," I tell him.

"You and your Killers," he says. But then he sings and plays from memory "All These Things That I've Done," which officially makes him amazing in my eyes. I tell him so and he laughs, sort of nervously again, and puts the guitar down.

I get a feeling that the uncomfortable tension in the room will hang there forever until one of the two of us acts so I reach over and kiss him again.

Max's bedroom is more relaxed and has more character (much like Max himself now) than the rest of his place. At least Max isn't speaking in perfect paragraphs like he tended to do before. I can practically hear him putting periods at the end of his sentences, sometimes. Although in a weird way I find that habit of his kind of charming.

My eyes get used to the dimness and I can see the walls are hung with these plastic pockets that have actual LPs in them that he has been collecting since high school. A lot of them are old—really old, like classic rock old, much older than Max himself.

For the first time in a long time I feel relaxed. It's nice not having any sense of furtiveness, awkwardness. Even though I've never quite felt it myself, tension has always been hanging in the air around most of the other guys I have been with and Max is obviously over all that. My right temple is pressed against his chest and I can feel his hand resting on my skull. I'm tired now and I have to remind myself not to fall completely asleep because no matter what I need to be up in the morning. As long as I'm awake for morning feed and not on duty, my time is my own, but those hours are very few and right now, very precious, although I have never cared about them much before.

I begin to focus on the hanging LPs, validating them for quality. Most of them pass my test.

"Are these organized alphabetically?" I ask, suddenly noticing a pattern in how they are arranged.

"Well, yes, how else would you organize them?" Max asks.

"If it were up to me, not at all," I say.

"Ha, you always struck me as very organized when I saw you in the barn."

"Sure, in the barn. Is that your version of a compliment, organized?"

"Organized and devastatingly good-looking I meant," he says, pulling me closer to him.

"Well, you don't have to overdo it," I say, glad that he can't see my face turn hot in the darkness. Once again, stupid, pale, hyperreactive skin always gives me away, burning like it's blistering in the sun whenever I feel anything too much.

I bike home even though Max offers to drive me because I know I have to shake off some of the nervous energy I have before I can face other people. I'm not sure I gave the right response when he asked, "When can I see you again?" and I told him tomorrow.

But hell, all next week I'll be on night watch. I remind myself that it's kind of pointless playing hard to get because probably it's not like he's taking anything very seriously between the two of us, the age difference and whatnot. The whole point of this year is just to take what I can from the experience in every sense of the word because in less than a year I'll be gone, somewhere, doing something else with horses. That is all that matters. Sex is a bonus.

I'm careful not to seem like I'm in too much of a good mood on the outside, so Megan doesn't tease me about getting laid again. But even though I have to teach a group of giggling eleven-year-old girls first thing in the morning with no sleep, I don't even feel tempted to lose my temper.

"Melody, I didn't hear you count the strides to that fence."

"Oh, um, yeah, I forgot."

"Now we're going to do the whole course. Can you remember it?"

"Trot over the red vertical, land at a canter, simple change at X, crossrail, oxer, blue vertical than halt."

"Easy-peasy, right?"

The next lesson is a bunch of teenagers, including one of the few guys who rides regularly at the barn—a high school kid named Jake who takes lessons with his girlfriend Sarah.

"Jake, are you seriously going to make me put this fence together again?" I say after he knocks down a rail on an easy vertical for the third time.

"Sorry." He's a tall, gawky guy with curly blonde hair whose brain hasn't quite caught up with his long legs but I like him anyway.

"Are you going to let Sarah chick you like that? She got it the first time."

"Chick?"

"That's what my brother says when a girl passes a guy running—she 'chicked' him."

"Simon, that's so sexist," says Sarah. "Besides, women are better riders than men."

"For that, I'm going to hike up the fences on your next combination."

"Go right ahead." I do and of course she clears three feet nicely. Sarah's a much better rider than her boyfriend and she should really be in a more advanced lesson but she likes to ride with him all the same. I just like busting her chops and Jake, well, he's pretty to look at (skinny, but a nice ass out of the saddle despite his lousy seat) and it gives me good exercise, having to reset his sorry-ass 2'3 jumps all the time.

So it's a good day and even during my own lesson I feel calm when Fortune refuses to counter-canter at all and instead gives me flying lead changes whenever I ask   Well, until Cynthia does it so easily on Blood and even Maggie, who has very little practice with the maneuver, manages to do so by the end of the session, proving that it's better to have no training rather than wrong or confusing training for a horse.

I show up at Max's after nightfall and he's obviously just showered. His shirt is clinging to his chest and despite the fact I've teased him about it, he really doesn't look that much older than me right now, in his wife-beater and jeans with his wet hair and his glasses slightly steamed up. He looks like some of the jocks I used to secretly have crushes on in high school, the ones I'd always make sure I out-threw or out-ran in gym class, just to prove that I could and so they'd notice me (not that any of them ever cared or did). But somehow Max has— noticed me, I mean, without my trying too hard.

I apologize for not cleaning up: I haven't put as much thought into my appearance as yesterday. I feel a little bit awkward since Max keeps everything in his apartment at right angles and everything even feels really, really clean, which I guess is kind of a good way to be if you are a vet.

I have a feeling that he knows I'm not very experienced at well, anything, based upon last night and part of me does feel young in a bad way—like an awkward little kid.

Max, after hesitating a moment, offers me a beer. I'm glad I don't drink much normally because I can use all the social lubricant I can handle and I hope that it relaxes me although alcohol really never does (possibly because I've never really drunk enough to make much of a difference, I guess). The glass has some Greek letters on it and I recognize them as being from some sort of fraternity, somewhere, which confirms my first impression that Max looks like kind of a nerdy, good-looking fraternity type. I hate fraternities, part of my never wanting to go to college, although I do kind of go for the buff, preppy, athletic look I have to admit.

"Were you out in college?" I ask him.

"Well, by the time I was a senior, sure."

"Did that bother anyone? My impression of frat guys is none too good, no offense."

"No, not really, by then they knew me pretty well."

"I've been out since my freshman year of high school."

He raises his eyebrow. "What, did you go to some sort of a progressive school or something?"

"Hell, no. Typical New Jersey high school."

"Really? That surprises me."

"Why?"

"Well, I don't know. I mean—"

"You mean I don't seem like I had to be out? Well, I was always the weird guy who rode horses and was into music everyone no one else liked so I guess they just assumed I would be weird in every other way," I say. It's a subject I hate: I've had people imply everything from obvious to not obvious and I know it's not something I should even have to think about. The best answer I've gotten is the one time I asked my friend Heather directly and after lots of hedging she said, "Oh, Simon, you just seem, very, I don't know, *Simon*, not one specific way or the other," whatever that means. "My freshman year someone called me a fag and a cocksucker and I punched him in the nose and it kind of spiraled from there," I explain.

"So it's not really true that you killed a man."

"No, just broke his nose and this definitely did not qualify as a man," I say. The guy's nose was always a little flat after that, like a boxer's nose. I felt kind of proud, even though he never bothered me afterward and the fight bought me at least a few weeks of peace. He changed schools at the end of the year and I never saw him again.

"Seriously, you broke a guy's nose when you were fourteen?"

"Yup."

"Well, thanks for warning me, I'll know to watch my back around you, killer."

"Don't be silly, I would never strike from the back. That would be dishonorable."

"Oh really?"

I realize he has one-upped me with his innuendo and laugh.

I guess it's kind of rude, but I've never been able to sit still. After I finish drinking, still waiting for dinner, I start wandering around. I notice that the spare room has a bunch of free weights in it and a treadmill. "My brother runs," I say. "A lot. Actually, he has a cross-country scholarship to Boston University."

"Well, I don't run as much as he does, probably, but in my line of work you have to stay in shape."

"I don't have time to do all that stuff. Running and lifting bores the hell out of me. I'd rather play a game."

"Well, you don't need to, you're on your feet all day and you're young. I didn't know you had a brother."

"One. Older. And one horse between us besides Fortune. Well, Cam is his horse, technically, but he hardly ever rides him. Riding isn't his thing although he rides okay. My mother used to ride professionally before she had us. She hates my current horse." And I find myself talking a little bit about Fortune, how he is a fine jumper but how I'm worried about moving up the levels in eventing given how bad he is at dressage.

I try not to seem bitter when I compare him to the hunter princess Cynthia's horse, but Max still smiles and says, "Well, that never
changes, barn drama. That makes me glad I'm no longer competing
except for the occasional schooling show."

"It's not a competition with her," I say. "Just annoying, especially
given that she's not that great a rider, at least over fences. I don't
mind being beaten by someone who is better than me." I'm worried
that he'll get bored as I start yakking about all of the problems I've
been having with Fortune and how I'm worried I won't get another
NQR at the next competition but Max listens patiently and actually
seems really interested.

"I'm sure you'll set Fortune right."

"I don't have much choice, we're stuck with each other. I can't
afford anything else and no one wants him. I've always trained the
horses I've ridden myself for worse or hopefully for better. So that was
my day."

"More exciting than mine. Just routine vaccinations and a PPE on
an unsound pony. Never a good day when you leave the kid and the
mother crying in the barn and looking at you like you're a monster
when you give them the bad news."

"I'm sorry."

"Oh, there are worse days. I'm still the low man on the totem
pole at the practice so I tend to get all of the assignments no
one else wants. Speaking of which, have you ever had your horse
checked out to see if his problem is physical? Have you gotten him
adjusted? I've done a little of that myself but I would recommend
a specialist."

"No one has ever found anything wrong." I pause. "I haven't been
able to afford a physical or a chiropractor yet but yes, Daniel has suggested that, too. Although he thinks it's probably the rider's fault, like
it usually is."

I feel a little bit dumb, now, and truthfully kind of ghetto, what with my bike and complaining about my riding problems and not even being able to afford what I should do to help my horse. I wander back into the living room, still looking for clues about who Max is (and he might be doing the same thing of me verbally, which makes me glad of the fact that we are technically on his territory rather than mine).

"Chess?" I say, pointing to a board set up in the crook of the shelf, next to a bunch of vet textbooks and a few bodybuilding books.

"You're really taking inventory of me, aren't you?"

"Nah, not really surprised that you're a nerd." He rolls his eyes at me.

Since dinner is ready by now (something chicken in an unpronounceable sauce that took forever but tastes pretty good because I'm starving by now) we play and eat. I beat him easily. I don't like chess as much as I like cards but with Max it's easier to focus on the pieces than on his face particularly since I do like looking at Max's face quite a lot.

"You're a tricky one, killer."

"What do you mean? That I'm not as dumb as I look?" I roll the white knight that I captured between my thumb and forefinger, staring at it, refusing to allow myself to smile. Max knows how to move the pieces but he obviously doesn't know very much strategy, like the fact I opened up with a classic Sicilian defense. I explain this to him after the fact.

"I thought everyone knew these openings," I say. I don't remember when and where I learned how to play chess. Not from Mom, she doesn't really know how. It's like I was born with the knowledge in my brain.

We play another game. Midway through, I say. "You don't want to do that."

"I don't?"

"Look, I can checkmate you easily in three moves if you go there."

It takes him a minute or two but he gets it. "I won't put the piece back, that would be cheating."

"I'm going to beat you anyway, but at least it makes the game fairer and more interesting for me if I can give you help," I say, not nastily, just stating the facts.

He gives me kind of a dirty look but resets his piece.

After I beat him a second time, since it seems Max is afraid to initiate anything too aggressive, I put my arms around his waist and kiss him. Max says he hasn't figured me out yet but I'm not sure I have Max figured out, either. Despite his careless chess, he seems so cautious in all other facets of his life.

12

IT'S NOT FAIR FOR GIRLS

O f course, I hardly get any sleep because it's the middle of the night by the time I get home. Still, I wake up well before my alarm. I'm aware of a strange sensation: shivering. At first, I think I'm sick even though I'm never sick (I think cleaning stalls for years with a piece of pizza in my hand has given me a pretty much cast-iron immune system to every microbe that could possibly exist). Then I realize that it's actually cold, even though it's still August.

"Forty-four friggin' degrees in August?" I say, looking at my phone's temperature. I throw on a heavy sweatshirt (my mother hasn't even sent my heavy winter clothes), slurp some soda and stuff a cold Pop-Tart down my throat in the hopes that the heat generated by the sugar high will keep me warm as I get to work.

Despite being ninety pounds soaking wet, Megan, having lived here all her life, is chirpy about the temperature, which she says is totally normal for this time of summer. Cynthia, being from the genuine south, is practically frozen in place.

"You'll feel better if you move around," I say. After doing feed, letting out horses, and mucking a few stalls I take pity on her and offer her my sweatshirt. She makes a face at the A for anarchy symbol on the back (I'm actually not sure what an anarchist is, but it seems like a punk thing, so I assume I am one) but puts it on.

We practice the stadium jumping phase in the cool, dewy morning on our horses since we have a few hours before we have our various other duties (clearing the cross- country field of debris, schooling babies, washing the windows of the indoors). Megan speeds Maggie over some of the lower fences. For a pony, Maggie can jump a pretty impressive height. I focus on Fortune's great weakness, which is, unsurprisingly, flexibility and turning. If I'm not careful, he will lean almost like a barrel-racer into a motorcycle turn. Once again, I am never quite sure what he was originally schooled to be—probably he passed through various hands over the years, so he is kind of a blur of different, inconsistent styles.

"You're hunching up on your horse's neck again, Cynthia," I say, watching her out of the corner of my eye. I expect her to snap back since I really don't have any business critiquing her without her request but she looks mournful instead.

"Darn it, I'm trying not to," she says, angry more at herself than me.

"Go with the horse, don't pose on the horse," I say, as I swing around again, actually doing a pretty nice, elegant, roll-back. "Green-and-white oxer," warning her where I am going. Normally, I don't critique other people's riding aloud outside of a lesson but today, maybe it's the lack of sleep or just the persistence of her fault, I can't help it.

When we are untacking, Cynthia says to me. "It's not fair for us girls, guys are so much stronger than we girls are."

I've been hearing that one for too many years and I say what I always say, "Even the strongest guy isn't as strong as the weakest horse. Even Maggie outweighs me."

"I meant in terms of holding my position."

"That's practice and balance as well as strength."

Pause.

"Simon, I've been meaning to ask you—this is my last day on nights—could you cover for me tonight? I'd like to leave early for the weekend." (This week, Cynthia has been on night watch while Megan and I get to play).

"You're leaving for another entire weekend?"

"It's—I'm going to see a guy back home." She smiles and puts her hand on my arm.

I can feel what Cynthia is trying to do—flirt with me to get her way –and that makes me even more annoyed. "No, I have plans."

"Plans doing what?"

"Plans." I consider saying to her, *it's about a guy*, and there is no reason that I shouldn't, but I don't. "I've covered for you before on Fridays but I can't anymore. It's not fair. I have one more day. And you really shouldn't be gone for the whole weekend anyway, Saturday is our busiest day."

She pouts. Suddenly, I regret offering her my sweatshirt, not because I'm physically cold but because I'm annoyed at her easy assumption that I have nothing better to do on the weekends, compared with herself. "It's important to me," she explains.

"Well, you can do whatever is important on Saturday evening if you leave on Saturday morning, since Saturday is when I go back to doing nights."

I can tell Cynthia is really pissed but I don't care.

"Besides, why do you ask me and not Megan?"

"Megs is seeing Ricky, you know that."

"Well, did it occur to you that I might have stuff I have to do outside of here? I could be a secret double agent, for all you know?"

"Simon, you're just being a jerk, now."

"I wasn't the one trying to get special treatment, don't call me a jerk."

Cynthia glares at me but says no more.

By mid-morning the temperature has risen to something approximating normal although not what any human being outside of New England would call summer weather. I'm okay with that, since it's cloudy, which is a good thing. Cindy gives my sweatshirt back, which no longer smells like me or a horse but her. I leave it on a hook in the tack room but even by the end of the day it still reeks of perfume and hand cream.

"I won't be able to see you next week," I explain to Max, lying beside him. "It's my turn to be on night duty—to keep an eye on the horses in case anything goes wrong." A week suddenly feels like a long time but of course I don't say that. Max puts his arm around me, pulling me closer to him.

"I understand," says Max. I think he sounds sad. Well, I'm feeling sad myself. "I might see you if I have to come to the farm. Come to think of it, I will probably be there later this week because I will have to remove the stitches on that little blonde girl's horse."

"Ugh. Little girl? Cynthia?" And I find myself going on about her praying mantis posing on her horse, the push-button horse that she still can't even push-button over a simple cross-country question, the pink everything, the monogramming everything that doesn't have a pulse. I try to be funny about it so I don't sound mean but I know I don't succeed.

"Remind me not to get on your bad side, killer. You really have it in for this girl."

"Spoiled rich hunter princesses—I've seen too many of them."

"Well, without them, I wouldn't be making a living."

"In that case, I guess I can learn to tolerate them. I promise to try to smile and play nice."

"It sounds like it was hate at first sight with Cynthia."

"More like contempt at first sight. I don't hate many things."

I know it's only a week but for me a week seems like a long time, so I want tonight to be special. I'm lying with my cheek on the pillow but Max tells me I'm too tense and although I don't consciously feel tense, objectively my muscles are. Like I am on edge, ready and waiting for something that could hurt me, even though I tell myself I feel safe and nothing can really harm me when it comes to Max. So we just do what we've been doing thus far (not that this is bad) and I leave when I usually leave, bleary-eyed and shivering in the cold. I will, ironically, get more sleep when I'm doing night checks than I have this entire week.

When Cynthia returns home from her weekend away she is unusually quiet for the next few days despite her excitement about 'the guy' beforehand. Neither Megan nor I ask why going home was so important and Cynthia doesn't volunteer. Besides, we have another show to prepare for this weekend, one with money at stake. The next competition is just a straight-up hunter-jumper show for practice. Much as I love the eventing I'm doing I'm kind of eager for the confidence booster, of performing something what I consider my trade, what I've been doing all my life, flying over those frangible, brightly-colored rails in the jumper ring.

13

We arrived at the show grounds early in the morning but there were already girls warming up for the pony and lower level equitation classes. A black horse bleating like a ram greeted us as we led our horses from the trailer to the temporary stables. Her rider was smoking a cigarette, the girl's boots dangling out of the stirrups while she was sitting on the horse's back.

The black horse had a kind of dishy Arabian face with a large, irregular white splotch on her forehead and looked amiable but the rider had obviously dyed black hair and a Roman nose. You see that sometimes—pretty horse, ugly rider. "Shut up," the rider said as the mare called out again and she slapped her horse's neck. The rider glared at Fortune, who the mare was clearly directing her come-hither whinnying to.

"My horse in season," she said, accusingly, as if that was my fault.

"Well, I don't let him date smokers," I said.

I'm riding some of the babies in the lower jumper divisions but the only class I really care about is the jumper classic. Total prize money is split between the winners, but it's still enough to mean something to me, not just financially, but also out of pride. I feel oddly calm yet excited as the time approaches, as if I know what the result will be, even while I am preparing to do all of the other various tasks I have to do, moment by moment.

There is a long pause before the buzzer goes off for the big chestnut before me. I think there was a loose dog or something like that near the arena and they had to stop everything until he was found. I canter Fortune slowly around the warm-up area with the other ten people left to go in my class. He's already pumped up. I'm mainly moving just to keep my mind from wandering.

It is funny how after eventing, a pure jumping class at a vanilla hunter-jumper show, even a class like this one, feels so relaxing. Also, I haven't had to ride in any hunter classes all day, just jumpers with the babies and that's a good thing since doing the hunters is just annoying, like moving in slow motion.

I hear the chestnut clip a fence and a rail fall and a visible gasp from the crowd. Even if I hadn't walked the course at all, I would have known that the sharp turn to the in-and-out would be a problem just by listening to the previous entries. Daniel walked the course with me, but he's over in one of the smaller rings now, helping some of the younger ammies with their classes. I can hear his critique in my head, telling me when to slow down, when to speed up.

Out of the corner of my eye, I see Cynthia cantering around. Blood, now shorn of all stitches, is antsy, prancing, and giving the occasional little buck. I can see Cindy is nervous by the way she is defensively sticking her feet out in front of herself and gripping the reins. I know Cindy can do this but she's clearly getting into her own head right now so I ignore her.

I'm still listening to the trip of the rider currently out there, counting the strides mentally, taking note of the tricky spots, more like chewing gum for my mind than real preparation.

From an almost-halt at the buzzer we spring to life: the first verti-cal, the early skinny, the oxer that gave so many people trouble. Focus, focus, don't get too confident until the end of the round. Fortune is clearing each fence with room to spare so there are no gasps from the crowd for any rattled rails. Daniel mentioned that some of the top rails are deliberately lighter than the lower ones, so don't get too confident. *I won't, I have this,* I can hear the words in my head, almost as if the horse is speaking to me in language I can understand. Clean and with the best time thus far, I leave the arena.

Only three of us make it to the jump-off. It was an unusually tricky course, so not totally surprising. Cynthia is not one of them. She clipped the skinny, knocking off the first rail, and the oxer was a complete disaster—she almost demolished it. I couldn't help laugh-ing a bit as I watched the jump crew sighing. From their perspective it doesn't matter who wins or loses, they just care how much they have to clean up and reassemble after every round.

I know this sounds arrogant, but even before I finish the jump-off, I know I'm going to win. I know it by the calm way I can observe things without emotion before I go—like the dog, finally caught and captive in his collar, barking by the fence. By the fact I can notice that one of the other horses in the jump-off is named Rubik, after the Cube, which I think is pretty cool. By the fact I can also take in the smell of smoke in the air from the concession stands, which has grown thicker throughout the day and the fact that I can hear but not be annoyed by the little pony kids watching me. They are singing the soundtrack from *Frozen* and eating cotton candy, wearing the ribbons they won earlier that day behind their ears. I can observe all these things and I can see the strides, know how my horse should feel going over the jumps, know I can sur-render yet control his motion, not get in his way but keep him from overpowering me. I feel very calm and emotionless and pleased even though Fortune has to be held back and controlled. He's enjoying himself almost more than me, in fact, a little too much, wanting to gulp the jumps like candy. Easy, easy, I tell him and make him collect before he surges forward.

After I do my victory lap, one of the little girls asks if she can pet Fortune. I'm about to tell her no because he's bitten people in the past but before I can say anything she starts stroking him. He doesn't flinch or respond, so I keep my mouth shut. The other little girls squirm to pet him as well. Fortune was so excited during the jump-off he practically bucked over every fence like a coiled spring set loose and I had to prevent him from rushing for half the ride. Now he's calmer, and he just looks at their sticky fingers with curiosity more than anything else. I'm still in my emotionless state of pure flow.

"You have a fan club," says Megan, who watched everything, having gotten a nice handful of blues and reds with both Maggie and a few of the sale ponies (mostly Welshes and Connemaras).

"The horse has the fan club, I don't," I say, patting Fortune. Truthfully, I can only give myself credit for spotting him in the field and giving him a chance, I think. We've only been together for a few months, there is a limit to how much credit I can take for his gifts.

Cynthia walks by, not looking at us. She's already dismounted and is carrying her saddle. Neither Megan nor I say anything but an uncomfortable silence settles over us, like we're in the presence of someone with a terminal illness and don't know what to say. But maybe in some ways that's what losing is, at least for me.

"She gets too nervous," I say, after Cindy is out of earshot. "Too bad they don't make calming supplements for riders, like that Perfect Prep all the hunter princesses use."

"They do make Perfect Prep for humans, Simon," says Megan. "It's called alcohol."

By the time we've driven back to the farm and gotten the horses settled, it is well after nightfall. Daniel drives the three of us to a kind of combination burger place and bar to unwind. Except for Cynthia, we all order burgers and fries and except for me (too young) they all order beer.

"Aren't you hungry?" I say to Cynthia as she slurps down her second lager. She just wrinkles her nose as I finish off Megan's fries. As usual, I don't remember the last time I ate, given the excitement of preparing for the show, and I'm making up for it now.

Since Megan doesn't have any night duties, Ricky picks her up from the bar after she texts him and it is just Daniel, Cynthia, and me on the ride home. The combination of alcohol, an empty stomach, and no body mass whatsoever means that after three beers Cynthia is more than slightly drunk. I have to steady her as she gets out of the car.

"Nice job," says Daniel to both of us. He makes eye contact with me and I can practically hear his thoughts—*make sure she makes it up the stairs without crashing into anything.*

"Yeah, right," I think I hear Cynthia mumble.

Cynthia stumbles before the narrow passageway up to our apartments and leans onto the nearby wall. I try to help her limp up a few steps and then I decide it's easier to carry her. She feels practically weightless. I cradle her like a baby even though she's a bit too tall for me to do so comfortably. I'm afraid if I put any pressure on her stomach she'll puke on me.

By the time I do make it up the flight of stairs, she's fully awake and can scramble out of my arms and rush to the bathroom. She's coherent enough to handle herself in there and I decide that hair-holding is not part of my officially-required duties as a gentleman. Then she comes in, flops on the bed, and falls asleep.

I've always hated the smell of alcohol on the breath even though I don't mind the occasional one or two beers. Cynthia reeks of it and her face is pink; her eyes already bloodshot. Her hair, perfectly coiffed in a net beneath her helmet before the show, is kinky and losing its straightness from the contact with her sweat. I feel sorry for her but I want to get away from her. I can't believe someone is that drunk off of three beers. Guess that's what comes from booze on an empty stomach. Drunkexia.

Before I go I decide to take off her muck books and this makes her startle awake. (Fortunately, she'd taken off her tall boots at the show because those would be damn near impossible to remove from a limp leg.) "Don't worry, I'm not taking advantage of you," I say.

"I don't care," she says, pulling herself up with effort. "You're so nice to me, even though I suck."

I flinch, thinking of all the times Megan and I made fun of her and all the times I've complained about her to Fortune when grooming him, as well as to Max.

"You don't suck, Cynthia. We all have bad shows. We just have to put them behind us."

"I know, but it's hard." She moves closer to me, very close. I feel one of her breasts against my arm. I take her hand, which is now almost on my leg, and put it aside.

"Good-night, Cindy," I say.

"Simon? Don't go," she says. Her voice is cracking. Suddenly, she is very close to my face. "Megan says you don't like girls but I have trouble believing you don't like girls at all."

"Cindy, I'm tired. So are you. You'll feel better in the morning." I say. Well, actually, she'll probably feel like hell tomorrow but I lie, rare as it is for me to do so.

Mainly as an excuse to get up quickly, I get her a glass of water. I ask her if she has any aspirin or something like that but she doesn't answer me.

Only as I take off my clothes do I take stock of the fact that less than three minutes of riding has earned me $1,500, my portion of the prize money. Discounting all of the preparation and money that went into that handful of minutes, I'd say it's not too bad a pay scale.

I set my alarm for an extra early time. I know I'm going to be shouldering most of the work tomorrow if Megan was with her boy-friend all night and Cynthia is as hung-over as I think she's going to be. I know it sounds mean but I kind of hope her head hurts enough that she doesn't remember anything of what she said.

14

SOME PEOPLE LOVE ME, DESPITE MYSELF

The day after the hunter-jumper show is cold and rainy, as if nature was holding back the storm until after my big class was over. It's a quiet Monday—there are only a few lessons scheduled since so many people are away on vacation this week. Cindy must be sufficiently in pain because she doesn't say anything to me about the night before which is more than fine with me.

The girls think I'm crazy but I ride Fortune in the rain for an hour or so, bareback so I don't ruin my saddle. Not really doing much, today is a rest day for him from jumping and galloping, we just go wandering around. But it isn't a hard rain so he seems to enjoy it. It's funny, I do agree that horses know when they're being judged in a competition and I'm convinced Fortune knows when he's done well—snorting and giving a little buck like he did yesterday—but they also don't seem remember victories or defeats like people, which is probably the best way to look at things. Fortune's just relaxed and curious on the trails and I give him a longish rein. He's used to being out in the rain so the wet doesn't faze him and even seems to make him more agreeable—no nipping or kicking when I use a sweat scraper and an old towel to clean him off, no ears back.

Both of us are soaking and muddy by the time we return and I put him in his stall to dry out and eat hay. Then I change into jeans and a sweatshirt and get a book to read, the first book in the series of *Game of Thrones*. I am probably the last person in the world to have just started reading the series. I was keeping up with the television show before I came here and lost contact with the rest of the world. Except for the occasional Sox game Daniel lets us see at his house for time to time and what television I see at Max's and on my phone, I'm pretty TV-deprived. I sit in a chair in the barn aisle, my iPod buds stuffed in my ears so I can listen to the Cure, which seems appropriate, given the weather. I stuff my nose in my book since I'm not really in the mood for conversation. I could read alone upstairs but I find the sound of Fortune's chomping oddly comforting. I'll turn him out in a bit so he can roll in the rain.

"Is something wrong?"

"Max?" I put my book down. "Why did you think something was wrong?"

"I don't know, you look so bedraggled, I thought you might be upset about something. I was on my rounds and—and I thought I'd stop to ask you how your class went, the one that was so important to you."

"I went riding in the rain. And the class—oh, I won."

"Oh, you won. You sound so casual about it."

"Well, it was over very fast." And I tell him about it—the structure and the money and how my horse was damn near perfect.

"Maybe that's his real talent."

"Showjumping? Yeah, well, maybe but the problem is that his rider likes eventing more." And I try to explain to Max that although I'm happy—happy especially because people now know what a good boy Fortune is, there is something that isn't quite the same as—as the release I feel from tearing around a field. And the fact that it felt almost easy.

"I didn't peg you for that much of a Puritan, that you only enjoy something if it's more difficult."

"No, I'm not like you, Max."

"So that's what I am? A Jewish Puritan?"

113

"Close enough."

"I can't stay long. If Daniel sees I'm here, he'll be terrified that I'm charging him for something."

I look over my shoulder to make sure no one is there, grab Max by the wrist, pull him into the tack room and kiss him. I know he has to leave so I let him go just as quickly as I seized him. I would need to do that anyway because I hear Cynthia and Megan's voices outside.

Cynthia hasn't been as useless as I expected today—I suppose she is more of a pro when it comes to recovering from drinking.

"How did the patient do yesterday?" asks Max. I'd almost forgotten about Blood and her injury.

"Her eye is all better," says Cynthia. "You'd never known there was anything wrong but I did really badly. Everyone else did well, though. Simon won the biggest money class at the end."

Max chats amiably with Cynthia and Megan. I'm afraid I'll give something away. I really don't want either of them to know about him and me, I don't want to deal with their giggling and possibly their sneers or think what would happen if Max and I broke up. So I go back to my book and my music. I wink at Max and pull the hood of my sweatshirt more securely around my face.

"Dr. Max is the nicest vet," says Cynthia. "Most of the vets I've known have been really old and it's nice to meet someone who is, like, our age, and really cares."

"He's easy on the eyes," says Megan. "Which never hurts."

"Yes, he's cute," agrees Cynthia. "Cute and a doctor. Ugh, I need more coffee. And Excedrin."

"Your pain is all self-inflicted, Cynthia," I say to her as she walks by me.

"Ignore Simon, he's just a self-righteous little shit," says Megan, sweetly.

"But some people love me anyway," I counter.

15

A LOT OF FUN CROSS-COUNTRY

Another difference with horses compared to the equipment used in other sports is that they will make you look like a fool even after a moment of great triumph. We go to a schooling event the following weekend with a bunch of the barn horses and Fortune actually manages to move sideways, away from my leg, right out of the white plastic confines of the dressage ring. The first time this has EVER happened to me, resulting in an automatic elimination. They allow me to finish my test for the sake of practice but he doesn't even redeem himself, he's ridiculously heavy and discombobulated throughout the rest of the test maneuvers. There aren't any useful comments on the test afterward, which reads: **I bet he's a lot of fun x-country! Neatly braided.** Right next to my lack of a score.

Great. I didn't realize they taught standup comedy as one of the components of USEA training. Again, they let me do the other phases because it is a schooling show but obviously no ribbons without a dressage score. Just to spite me, Fortune has great trips in both the cross-country and the stadium phases, without any faults.

The day after, I go over the dressage test again and again with Fortune, punishing myself (and I suppose him) with the repetition of the ring.

Daniel notices and I kind of hope he'll say something approving because I'm practicing what I least like to do on my own free time but instead he just says, "If I could get your horse drunk, I would, he looks so tense and miserable" and walks away. *Well, so is his rider.*

When Cynthia enters the ring with her horse, I flinch. It's one of those moments I wish I could be invisible, and I try to ignore her as Blood sails across the arena. Eventually, I force myself to say, "She's looking good; she's moving really nicely, Cynthia."

"Thanks," she says. Then, there is a pause. "Do you want to try her?"

"Sure," I say, surprised. "You want to switch?"

"Oh, no. I'll hold Fortune while you go."

"Fortune's not dangerous, seriously. He's nothing like the OTTB I used to have—not high-strung at all."

"But he's so strong."

Cynthia won't believe that Fortune won't try to kill her, so I just hop on Blood and try the mare out. It does feel different, more pleasurable, to have a horse that feels willing and responsive. For a few minutes I can relax my muscles and stop fighting.

"You look really good, Simon."

"Well, Blood Money makes me look good."

"She's always been very good to me. She's the best horse I've ever had."

No matter what you might say about Cynthia, I thought, at least she loves her horse, which is more than you can say for some. So when she asks, "Simon can you help me in the jumping ring with that exercise Daniel was telling us about the other day?" I agree.

"Traitor," says Megan, after watching us from a distance.

"Aw, Megs, if you wanted to practice with me, I'd be happy to as well, you know that. I've never turned you down."

"That wasn't practice; that was a lesson."

"Well, maybe it was, sort of, kind of. So what?" It made me feel better about the dressage debacle at the schooling show, if nothing else.

"Cynthia can afford her own private lessons."

"We're all in this together. This isn't a class war."

"Yes it is, Simon. When the top American riders of the world are the Jessica Springsteens, Georgina Bloombergs, and Cynthia Jacksons, it sure as hell is."

"Cynthia is far from a top rider. She's not remotely in the same class as Jessica or Georgina. She's a mediocre rider with her faults, just like all three of us. Jessica Springsteen and Georgina Bloomberg are great showjumpers. And besides, eventing's much friendlier to the non-millionaire."

"Simon, you're not a mediocre rider."

"When I qualify for Intermediate on Fortune, then maybe I will agree with you, not before. And by the way, Jessica Springsteen can do no wrong and her father has earned every penny he's put into her horses."

Deep down inside I know that although I qualify as poor by the standards of the horse world now, there is no way I could have had the childhood I did, growing up, if my dad hadn't had enough money to have property and horses. He might have indeed been the asshole Sean says he was, but there is that fact, despite the other bad stuff. There's always some bit of luck about getting into horses, it's never all talent or all money, always a bit of both.

"Oh, so you worship Springsteen, too? You're such a cliché, Simon, so friggin' New Jersey." I know Megan means this as a great insult. "I thought you just liked punk and New Wave and '80s music, anyway."

"No. I like good music and I hate bad music, that's all."

"Jesus, you really are impossible sometimes."

"Georgina Bloomberg rides a grey like I do, so she gets a free pass as well," I say, partially to irritate Megan.

It's funny, I never knew Megan was so angry about money stuff. Especially since she rides a pony, which means that she can never really be competitive on her own horse. Although some people might say the same thing of Fortune. He's big and he can jump a house but I'd be better off with a horse with a bit more finesse to really place well in all three phases. Realistically, if my only goal is to get enough qualifying scores to go Intermediate ASAP I would be better off with a horse who doesn't look like he's made of different bits and pieces randomly stuck together when he is under a dressage saddle even though he can jump more than five feet on his better days. But there is a part of me that says, what fun is that?

I see Max that night and complain to him since I've been holding back my thoughts around the girls. Times like these I'm so grateful to have a guy who actually understands what I'm talking about. Although there is supposedly a pretty high percentage of gay men in riding relative to other sports, once again, with my bad luck, I've always seemed to find myself in situations surrounded by a number of men who ride and are very nice, very attractive, and completely heterosexual. Most of the guys I'd hooked up with before (calling it dating would be a big stretch) were totally unhorsey. Max understands what I'm saying and because he finds Fortune's dressage ineptitude funny, I can as well even though before I was ready to burn the tests.

"Actually, the worst is when you get a comment like that and you haven't done anything to technically get you eliminated," he says. "For Pony Club, I remember getting back a test that just had three large question marks in the comments section. And the judges are supposed to be nicer at those events because it's kids."

We mess around for a little bit and then I whisper in Max's ear. Sometimes I've wondered if he's been upset at me if what we're doing isn't enough although he's never given any sign that he's unhappy.

The truth is, every now and then I do find Max hard to read. He's always been so nice and so patient with me, it's hard to know if he's contented or not.

He warns me that it might hurt me and then proceeds to apologize as much as possible through the act and afterwards. Like with so many other things it does hurt, more than I let on, but I've never much been bothered by physical pain. I think of all the times people made fun of me even before this happened so really it doesn't matter if I finally do it. Though I nap so heavily afterwards, Max has to shake me awake to get me home in time. He insists on driving me, even though I tell him it isn't necessary and uncharacteristically in the darkness before he lets me go he kisses me, without caring that someone might be passing by.

I'm exactly five minutes late and some of the horses are already kicking at their doors, letting me know that they are starving. Cindy was on duty overnight and must have slept through her alarm, despite the banging. I turn on my music and get to work.

"Oh, not them, again," she says stumbling down. I have the Killers' song "Human" blasting. "That song doesn't even make sense. I hate that song."

"What do you mean?" I say, slinging water into the buckets for the horses that need to have their feed moistened, pouring SmartPaks into grain tubs. "Saying stuff like that about the Killers' lyrics is why you and I will never see eye-to-eye, Cindy." I sigh.

"I liked the band you were playing yesterday better."

"Which band? I played several bands yesterday."

"The band with the songs...'Bizarre Love Triangle'? And that other one, 'Love Will Tear Us Apart? Was that their names?'"

I sigh. "Cynthia, those songs are not by the same band. 'Bizarre Love Triangle' is New Order. 'Love Will Tear Us Apart' is Joy Division."

"Well, they sound kind of alike, excuse me."

"That is because New Order was formed by the remaining members of the band Joy Division after the tragic suicide of the lead singer Ian Curtis, may he rest in peace. They have vaguely similar sounds, but are different bands. How is it you don't know this? This is culture, Cynthia. And you being a college graduate and all."

"Well, there you go, the lead singer of one of your favorite bands committed suicide. I told you your music was too depressing. You don't see Katy Perry or Taylor Swift throwing themselves off a building, hmm?"

"Ian Curtis didn't throw himself off a building, he hung himself. He had epilepsy. His wife found him."

"What, that's like, better or something than throwing yourself off a building? Just hearing that story makes me want to curl up and cry. I want music to make me happy, sue me."

I have no reply. I feel, however, that by mentioning Katy Perry, Taylor Swift, and Ian Curtis in the same breath, Cynthia will bring the wrath of the music angels upon her, so I better duck out of the conversation at this point. Besides, now that the horses are done eating, we need to do turnout. I hear one of the geldings start to kick at his stall and I know he'll take out a chunk of wood soon if I don't get the boys to the back field ASAP. I tell myself it's the same back at the barn, just the same, and that relaxes and comforts me even though I feel something has changed.

As I go, I overhear Cindy say to Megan, "He goes for days hardly saying anything and then he lectures me."

"Oh, he's just the barn radio Nazi, I ignore him when he gets like that."

"I can't figure him out," says Cynthia. "And I've never seen him smile, either, except when he's saying something sarcastic."

Megan laughs, not in a bad way, but not in a nice way either. "Oh, Simon's pretty easy to figure out, he's—" and then I can't hear what she says but I can guess at it by the slightly contemptuous and slightly triumphant tone of her voice. I don't need to hear the words. She thinks she knows me completely, Megan does, even though as far as I'm concerned our relationship merely skims the surface of things.

The horse at my side starts chafing and lunging because I'm walking more slowly than usual and I give a sharp jerk to the chain across his nose to let him know I'm still there, that I'm still in control.

16

NO STIRRUP DAY

Daniel is away, teaching a clinic, so I'm supposed to teach one of his usual adult lessons later that afternoon.

"I'm putting you in charge, Shaughnessy," Daniel said, before he left. "You're the one of my three stooges the least likely to screw things up."

"Thank you." I was genuinely flattered.

"I have a feeling I will live to regret this. Make sure the barn is still standing when I return. I'm not sure my insurance covers 'acts of crazy Irish kids.'"

When I see Max tacking up, we both give a little start.

"Daniel's away," I explain. The other riders—mostly middle-aged ladies who were competitive in their youth but now have so-called real jobs and kids—think I'm talking to everyone even though my focus is really on Max.

"Be easy on us, Simon," says one of them.

At the beginning of the lesson, while everyone is warming up, I watch Max with an objective eye. He has a nice leg and he doesn't slump like some of the riders who work at a desk 24-7. Although like many people who don't ride every day (especially men), he is a bit stiff and his leg slips back.

This isn't exclusive to Max, though, so I say, "Okay, back to basics. Official No Stirrup Day."

Two of the women groan openly while another says, "Oh goody, that way I don't have to go to the gym tomorrow. I can call you my Thigh Master, Simon."

I roll my eyes as I collect the leathers and irons. "Okay, let's not get crazy here."

Max is the last to hand his over and gives me a death stare. I really don't know why he is so upset, what with his weights and treadmill and books on body building and such. He's riding a half-Arabian, though, which might mean the horse doesn't have the most comfortable gaits. I've never ridden this gelding, so I wouldn't know.

While everyone warms up sitting trot, posting, two-point, and finally cantering both sides of the arena I set up a gymnastic, fairly low at first. I will go easy with them, since I don't really know what most of them are capable of. For their course later on, I set up mostly low verticals, and one oxer. The first rider does a pretty credible job, the second makes it through after landing on the wrong lead and correcting it. Max does pretty well, too. I'm not totally surprised. Most of them have forgotten what they can do, how strong the muscle memory is in their legs.

"Don't pinch with your knee," I say to Max, tapping his leg before he goes over the gymnastic a second time. A common habit when you're not used to riding without stirrups for long periods. He corrects his position but not before giving me another nasty look. The second time, I raise the jumps. Then I have the riders canter the full course.

"That was fun, in a sick kinda of way," says one of the women, after the lesson.

"You're lucky Daniel will be back next week," I say. "Otherwise, I'd take away your reins, too, in the next lesson."

"I can still walk, no thanks to you," says Max, greeting me at the door later that night. "With Daniel, we do ten minutes without stirrups at the most."

"I'm surprised Daniel is so easy on you guys. He must be getting soft in his old age," I say, strolling into the kitchen to see what he's cooking.

"Soft or wants to stay in business," says Max.

"Admit it, you and the old ladies you ride with loved it."

"Old ladies? They're my age, kiddo. When you're lucky to ride once a week, the riding muscles begin to atrophy."

"At my previous barn, they used to have no stirrup weeks for all of the lesson kids. It was like a barn holiday."

"Well, I'm not a kid, anymore."

"You ride well enough, doctor, to challenge yourself every now and then and if you didn't I would tell you."

"I'm sure you would, killer." Then he grabs me and slings me over his shoulder and I let him carry me that way into the living room, although I wouldn't let anyone else do that. He doesn't make it to the bedroom, just lets me down on the sofa. "Hopefully, I won't need any more Advil to make it through the night. I think I'm pretty much at the recommended limit for the week."

"Don't worry, I'll kiss it and make it better," I say.

Although I feel more comfortable with Max now, there is still very little I know about him, about his family, his friends, or former boy-friends. I know he used to live in this area as a kid, moved away to go to vet school and eventually came back to work here, which leaves lots of question marks in my mind for lots of years. I know I am much less mysterious to him, I feel he knows everything about me, that I am an open book. This bothers me, like he has an unfair advantage in a game. I even talk much more around him than I do other people, like there is a wall that has suddenly been removed and everything is spilling out all at once. Not just about riding and music like I do with the people at the barn, but about everything. It's like that Amy Winehouse song: "Love Is a Losing Game."

17

IT'S ALL IN THE CARDS

Sean goes back to school, taking a bunch of classes with names like Business Finance, and Derivatives Securities, and Calculus II for Finance Majors. Since the internship ended, his relationship with the Russian girl has faded. He bitches and moans about how he's going to die the first week because his classes are so hard and interfere with cross-country practice. I'm kind of glad he has something else to occupy his emotional consciousness—fear of failure and sexual frustration—when I drop the news I'm dating someone. I considered not telling him but I know he'll sense that something is up, just like I can always tell with him, so it's easier to rip off the bandage now than later.

"Really? You found a guy in the middle of cow country? That's kind of impressive. Student?"

"Nah, someone who rides at the stable."

"Really? There are guys who ride up there? English?"

"Of course, English, I wouldn't date someone who didn't know how to really ride."

Snorts. "Oh, of course not. What else? C'mon, tell me, this has to be good."

He senses I'm evading him and after dancing around the subject for a bit, I eventually admit, "He's the vet." I start to tell him normal things about Max but Sean is laughing too hard.

"Seriously? You're shitting me."

"What's so funny about that?"

"When you bought that horse, mom was like 'oh, what are you going to do if that horse gets sick, that'll bankrupt you,' but you're pretty clever."

"Fuck you."

"There is no limit to what you will do for affordable vet care, I like it, Bro."

"He's a young and good-looking vet," I protest. "Not like some of the vets they had at the old stable."

"Well, unless he's like Doogie frigging Howser or something, he's a lot older than you, I guess."

"Yeah, well, that's true," I say. "But for the record, all vet care is billed through the stable so even if I wanted to prostitute myself, that wouldn't work."

"You're so noble and pure, Simon."

"Fuck you again. You're just jealous because you're running so much you don't have the energy to get laid. Your balls will be shrunk to the size of tiny little raisins by the end of the semester with all the testosterone you'll be expending on all those stupid, useless miles."

He laughs. "You're just jealous because I'm faster than you and better at you at running. And have more endurance."

"Jealous that your most intimate sexual relationship right now is with a tube of Body Glide anti-chafing cream?" I don't mind sprinting but running and running and running and doing nothing but running with no purpose just seems so, I don't know, boring and self-flagellating and masturbatory all at once. Where is the risk, the danger, other than to the refrigerator given how hungry Sean'll be at the end?

Sean is more interested in telling me about his new running coach than hearing about Max. He says that the team will be running as many as a hundred miles some weeks at the peak of the season.

"This guy is the real deal. He's run ultras—fifty miles at a clip regularly. He's a machine. He's a beast."

"Fifty miles in a single race? Bad enough to run that in a week—or a month."

"Yeah and you'll like this. He's done this hundred mile race that actually began as a trail horse race endurance thing. The guy's horse came up lame and he didn't have enough time to get another horse so he completed the course by himself. Then it became a regular event for lots of people. Unreal."

"That's the stupidest thing I ever heard. If my horse goes lame, I'll borrow another horse, or wait for another event when my horse is sound again. I don't volunteer to complete the event MYSELF."

"I knew you wouldn't get it."

"Better you than me, is all I can say."

It's funny, but when we were little kids, I was actually better at soccer and baseball and all the other things Sean eventually played in high school. But I dropped out to focus on the horses—the coaches always said I was a talented but selfish player and a ball hog. And easily bored.

"I don't know how anyone can like running better than riding. At least when you played soccer that was something of a normal sport. Stuff actually happens during a game."

"Yeah, well, I wasn't good enough to get a soccer scholarship so I've learned to like what I am good in."

What Sean is saying—I guess—makes sense (if running your brains out makes sense). But I could never make myself like running or anything better than riding just because a school or even society as a whole threw me more bones for doing it, I just couldn't. I love what I love and that's that.

Sean has an ulterior motive in contacting me, so he doesn't bust my balls about Max for too long. I promise to help him with his Calculus

II homework (given that I helped him through Calculus I, he's already lost in the first week of class) and he shuts up. I ask to use Max's laptop when I see him that night so I can look at Sean's problem sets with a bit more room on the screen. I can usually do everything in my head but I try to type everything out in a Word document so theoretically Sean can kind of see how the problems were solved. In case he's asked about them in class, which is unlikely.

"What are you doing?" asks Max.

"My brother's calculus homework."

"Um, why isn't your brother doing your brother's calculus homework?"

"He's not a math major. Calculus is just something they require as part of what he's studying."

"Do you always do your brother's homework?"

"Just the math and any science that requires math." I shrug. Sean has always, always had my back and I've always had his and that's just the way it is. But Max doesn't have any brothers, just a younger sister, so I can see how he wouldn't understand.

"I sure hope you're brother's not going to be an engineer for any bridge I'm driving over soon."

"Nah, he's just studying finance, econ, whatever. Wants to work on Wall Street."

"Oh, well, that explains a lot. At least people will only lose their money, not their lives. Look, isn't that kind of unethical or something?"

"I'm not in school, I didn't sign any honor code or anything. I know Sean and there is no way he's getting through this stuff on his own brain power, trust me." Incidentally, I'm not saying my brother is dumb (although don't tell him I said that about his brains), I am just realistic about his limits. "And I try to help him through exams as best I can although that's harder—sometimes he'll text me or take a photo of an equation or whatever but they've kind of cracked down on that."

Max looks over my shoulder as I finish up. "So, you can do all that without even taking the class?"

"They made me take upper-level calculus in high school because of some scores I got on a stupid standardized test. This is actually pretty easy stuff compared to what I did back then." I save, close, attach, and press send, feeling slightly self-conscious for some reason.

"I'm not sure if even I remember all that stuff," Max says.

"Well, I bet you took calculus a long time ago, doctor," I grin. He playfully puts me in a headlock and I shake him off. "It's really not that impressive that I remember it from a year ago—it was just me and a bunch of Asian and Indian kids in the room all year so I suppose the class was supposed to be hard."

"Politically correct as always."

"Why? Why is that bad to say? It's true. That wasn't a bad thing. They always left me alone."

Max rolls his eyes. "Simon, seriously, why aren't you in college?"

"Oh, don't you start with the 'not living up to my potential thing." And I go on for a bit about my physics teacher, the standardized tests I took and my guidance counselor's reactions to them, and my loving but slightly hypocritical mother who didn't go to college and rode horses and teaches riding herself but who still reminds me now and again, ever so subtly, that although she is extremely proud of my eventing results, all my accomplishments are unlikely to translate into a financially sustainable future career.

"Well, it is kind of a waste," says Max. "Can you imagine what you could do in math or physics if you actually tried?" I put down the laptop, sit down on the couch beside him, put my arms around him and he pulls me closer. "Even the chess. You have quite a mind underneath there." He ruffles my hair.

Max couldn't have known this but chalk *waste* up as one of my least favorite words. I think of a conversation I overheard Cindy and Megan having while I was mucking out today. Blah-blah-blah. Girls-girls-giggle-giggle-giggle. "Now Simon, he's not cute but he's hot," Megan said. "What a waste." Blah-blah, then something unintelligible from Cindy before I turned up the music on the Killers to drown out the squealing as I heard her say something dumb like, "Oh, but it can be a challenge."

So although I flinch at the word *waste*, I continue on, talking very logically to Max: "Math is just like chess, it's a game and the only thing I've been good at all my life is games."

"Sometimes, just like with a game, having some structure is good. School can be a good structure."

"I have structure—the barn, what the horses need. That's structure with a point to it. School is just people's bullshit structure and that's why I hated school. You know me, I don't read anything except science fiction and horse books, and I hate being stuffed in a box of a classroom and having to sit on a chair and be called a faggot by the popular kids."

"Aw, killer, college isn't like that."

I shrug. "It's not doing what I like to do, either, and if I can do what I enjoy, what's the point of forcing myself to do otherwise? Why stuff myself in another box of a school so I can work in a box of a cubicle until the day I die? I guess my mom had to because she was supporting a bunch of kids after she left my dad but I don't. Besides, if I'd gone to college, I would never have met you."

Max laughs. "Well, I can't argue with you there, but just because one good thing comes of a decision, that still doesn't make it a good decision. And even the two of us, some might say, are questionably classified as a good thing."

"How else would you tell if a decision was good or bad, other than how things ended? I'm happy here." Which I am. I kiss him to shut him up.

The television has been humming on in the background; I reach over and turn it off with the remote. Then I grab Max and gently play-wrestle him down to the floor. I think, I've never known anybody so well, I know every bone in his body. I already have memorized every muscle on his stomach, even though we haven't known each other for long. I don't have to worry about my reactions with him, plan my responses, or hide and slip inside of myself like I do with other people. It's as close to relaxed and content as I've ever felt with another human being. We don't even bother to make it to the bed.

I haven't actually thought about the kids in high school for a long time. I suppose if they could see me now they'd say every name they called me was doubly, factually true, but I care even less now than I did back then. In a weird way I feel even more so that every punch, every fight I got into, large and small, even the ones for just not showing me respect was right. Because what is between Max and me shows how what they said about me had nothing to do with anything real at all.

18

PERFECT SHE'S NOT

I help Cynthia with her jumping a few times a week and she lets me ride Blood Money so I don't forget how to have soft hands and leg and can hopefully apply that to Fortune when he and I practice dressage together. He's never going to meld into me within the confines of the sandbox, but I am finally seeing some improvement. At least, there are no more eliminations and disasters and even Daniel proclaims us "less terrible" and "less ugly and painful to watch."

Megan has warmed a bit to Cynthia and the girls sometimes go drinking together, usually bringing beer or wine coolers back to their apartment so Megan can avoid spending money. Of course, I'm sure if Cynthia had her druthers she's be high-tailing it to the closest city to find a bar and be downing fancy, fruity cocktails, but she's stuck with us and our budgets. As I've said before, I'm not much of a drinker (especially when I have no cash) and they never bring back what I do like, which is Guinness. I often opt out of their alcohol-fests or just grab one of their horrible, watery-as-piss beers and pour half of it in a feed bucket for Fortune to keep his coat shiny.

"That's a waste of good alcohol," giggles Cynthia the first time she watches me do it, as my horse greedily slurps away. He was good today, he really deserves it more than any of us, I think.

Cynthia doesn't eat but will happily ingest liquid calories, glass after glass, but whatever.

Another reason I don't want to get drunk with them, though, is because Cindy tends to get very overly friendly with me when she's bombed. Nothing like the time after the show, but she'll put her arms around me or tickle me, which she would never do when sober. Megan thinks it's hysterical and I'm never sure if she is laughing at Cynthia or me or both of us. I'm not sure if Cindy is joking with me either or what she has to prove.

Megan is cool and all but sometimes it gets under my skin the way she talks. It's hard for me to put my finger on it but she'll ask me if I think a guy is hot in an annoying, leering way, or if she's complaining about "men" she'll say something like "oh, well, you don't count" so I know she's not complaining about me because she doesn't consider me part of the male species.

I know I could never have an open conversation with her about Max. I guess I mean that she doesn't take that part of me seriously or I know she would find it cute and funny in a way that her relationship with Ricky is not. I even hate the way she'll ask my opinion about what pair of breeches I think would look cute on her when she's thumbing through one of the old Dover catalogues laying around the barn or surfing SmartPak on her phone, like I'm her automatic asexual shopping buddy. I seriously would wear my Joy Division T-shirt to every show in every class if they'd let me, just don't fucking ask me about that stuff, okay?

Cynthia is around a lot more than she was in previous months. Whatever guy she was seeing back home and needed to see so badly that one day must be gone. She casually makes references to "that asshole I used to date" and says things like, "Why am I always attracted to unavailable assholes" and "Men are such assholes."

I vaguely gather that the "asshole guy" she is referring to her used to be her trainer and works for her father, which is pretty common from what I've heard, at least among some girls who ride. I guess when something is that available, it's hard for some guys not to take advantage of it (and maybe the girls are too busy to look elsewhere, which I kind of get). Although I think if I was working for some rich guy, I'd be pretty motivated not to spit in the same pot I was eating from, no matter how cute his son might be.

Pretty much every girl I've ever known says stuff like that about men being assholes (with the exception of my friend Heather, which is one reason why I like her so much). Often, once I get to know them better, that's usually followed by "but you're not like that, Simon." Translation: you're gay, Simon. Personally, I've never understood the unavailable asshole attraction thing. My life is complicated enough without trying to make it so. I'd much rather go for a ride to forget about things than have a guy take me on one. I always had very little patience for closet cases, about two weeks at the most.

Of course, it is possible that I'm the asshole and don't really know it. Anyway, I think Max likes me just the same. God help him.

The last time I saw him, Max said, "I've got something I've been wanting to show you, something I've had since my Pony Club days." When he came out with a copy of the book, I knew what he was going to say, what he was going to show me. It was the old version but the book has been reprinted a number of times since the '90s. It is a pretty common, basic book on horsemanship. Max opened up the book to a photo in the middle.

In the photo there was a slight, young blonde woman on a huge chestnut sailing over a fence. Her leg was in a perfect position, as if she was standing on the ground and her lithe gloved fingers were easing into an automatic release.

"Yeah, that's my mom," I said. The picture was taken during the height of her riding career as a junior. "That's Enigmatic." Enigmatic was a horse I never knew, I've only heard about him. He was her trainer's horse. Mom had a stallion when we were little kids and geldings after that but she wasn't competing as seriously then. Now she doesn't compete at all, just takes kids to shows as a trainer herself.

"She must have been seventeen when that picture was taken," I said. "About my age."

"She looks like you."

"I wish I was as advanced in my riding career as she was then."

"You still have plenty of time, Simon, riding's not like gymnastics," said Max. "Besides, didn't you say that your mom didn't go nearly as far as she'd have like to?"

"Yeah, she got married and there were—problems with my father. And she had kids and after the divorce it was more about working to support us."

"I guess that's a pretty familiar story for a lot of riders. Always comes down to money, I guess."

"It does. Now, if I had money, after working for Daniel, I would go to Europe and make myself the slave of some eventer over there for a year—preferably Germany, where they really know how to do dressage—so I could really sharpen up my skills. But I'm going to have to take something that pays close to a living wage as you can find in the industry instead. Still, better than working in a box of a cubicle or being stuck in a college dorm room, no matter what happens."

"I'm sure she's very proud of you."

"Nah, I told you, she just thinks I'm making the same mistakes she did, only there won't be a photo of me in any horse book any time soon."

I don't think there will be a photo of Cynthia in a horse book either, ever, at least not on Blood Money. When I'm talking jumping with Cynthia, I'll occasionally get on Blood and pop her around the course. Blood is beautiful and sweet and supple, sure, and she's reasonably athletic. But if you don't keep your leg on her and ask her for every jump with complete and total confidence, there is always the risk that she'll stop. The mare hasn't refused with me yet but every now and then I'll feel a slight hesitation, even when facing a relatively small stadium jump. Still, given that Cindy isn't that brave, in a way Blood is probably a good teacher for her, since she needs to learn to be brave for both of them.

I know Cynthia is crazy about her horse and the horse was crazy expensive, but every now and then she'll say things like, "My father is looking and such-and-such a horse in Europe." I know she has several back home she's ridden in competition but this one was supposed to be her best, her primary mount for this year and already she's thinking of changing.

I watch Cindy hosing Blood off on an unusually hot afternoon (technically it just turned fall but the frost in the morning on the grass is already appearing with greater and greater regularity) and as she raises the hose to hit Blood's back she splashes herself. Beneath the white of her T-shirt, on her stomach, I see several lines like cat scratches. I forget momentarily what I was going to say and instead ask, "What did you do to yourself there?"

"Oh." She blushes. "Those are old."

I've honestly never looked at Cynthia that closely in the light beyond her blondeness and the expensive clothes but as Cindy sweat-scrapes off Blood I also notice some less obvious fine lines on the soft part of her forearms and on the sides of her upper arms, which is a weird place for scratches to be. The scratches also have no real pattern or clear direction, like normal scratches from an injury usually do.

Cynthia sometimes will drift into my room after dinner the times I can't leave to go to Max's.

"Oh, you're here," she says. "Where do you go, anyway, when you're not required to be on night watch? When you first came here, you used to stay in your room regardless."

I'm annoyed she's prying so I just say. "Sometimes it's good to get away from wherever you are, no matter how much you like it."

"Aren't you tired, staying up most of the night?"

"I catch up on my sleep when I do stay here nights and I take a nap every now and then. Plus Mountain Dew and sugar. I've always been able to sleep wherever and whenever and stay awake, too, when needed. One of my gifts."

"Simon, this room is disgusting. Please let me clean it up." I'm so used to it, I don't really notice it. I guess she means the piles of dirty laundry in the corners (vaguely divided into dirty-but-still-possible-to-wear-one-or-two-times-more and beyond hope); the clean clothes flung on a chair (Max has been letting me use his washer so at least there is more in that pile than there was previously); plus the random sci-fi paperback books and candy and Pop-Tart wrappers on the floor. It's actually neater than my room at home used to be because at least I can leave the boots and tack I need to clean at the barn. "I don't understand how everything you touch is so spotless at the barn and you live like such a pig."

"Thanks, Cindy," I say, putting aside the book I was reading that Daniel lent me—*Reflections on Riding and Jumping* by Bill Steinkraus.

"Please let me at least fold up this stuff and put it in the closet," she says.

I find that statement pretty funny but I just stick my nose in my book again rather than laugh out loud. (The closet is, for the record, almost totally empty. As are the desk drawers.). When she moves to pick up some of the wrappers, though, I tell her to leave everything.

I'm not sure if there is anything I care about her finding but you never know when someone is nosy enough what they might discover. "I know my way around my own mess, Cindy, just let me be."

She sits down again. "I see you're studying the classics, just like Daniel told you to."

"It's worth a read. You know, it's amazing to me that at one point Steinkraus could only ride on weekends when he was working on Wall Street after college. He said he used to practice in his mind on his drive to the barn from the city." I know sure as hell I could never do that. My mind is just not that strong, I think, even though my legs might be. "And he served in the cavalry during World War II. How cool is that?" Cindy sits down next to me on my bed, takes the book away from me and closes it. Her thigh, pale despite all the time we spend outside, is right next to mine. She's wearing a pair of plaid men's boxers and a big, baggy men's college sweatshirt that says UVA. Just like I noticed on her arms, I see she has a couple of thin scratches on her legs as well.

"Cindy, were you in an accident a long time ago?" I ask, pointing at the spider web design. They look like they were made with a razor blade or a sharp piece of glass—did she fall through a window or smash into a mirror, I wonder? Fall into a bed of thorns?

"I told you, they're old," she says and stands. Suddenly, I experience a kind of flash of understanding deep in my brain. I've been worried about her prying about where I go at night (not that I'm ashamed but again, I think it would be weird if the people at the farm knew I was dating the vet), so I've been kind of dense about picking up on things.

"I'm sorry, it's really none of my business."

"No, Simon, I don't mind. They're from a long time ago, when I was a kid. I'm all over that now."

"I get it, Cindy."

"That was before I got Blood and really focused on my riding. I don't do such childish and adolescent things anymore, hurting other people."

"Well, it looks like you just hurt yourself."

"Sometimes hurting yourself hurts other people. Like my father. He was devastated when he found out. It was just very hard for him to understand."

"Honestly, it's hard for me to understand, too, Cynthia."

"Oh, Simon. Everything always comes so easily to you." I look at the book in her hands and gently take it away from her. That statement really, really, really fucks me off, but I literally bite my tongue to avoid responding. I'm not a monster.

"My friend Heather struggled with depression for a while but she's okay now," I say. "Well, they didn't call it depression they—called it by another name, but it doesn't matter. I guess all the names they call things like that are all the same in the end." Technically, I know that Heather is supposed to have high-functioning autism spectrum disorder or something like that but she always seemed normal enough to me, in some ways more normal than the stupid, normal giggling girls who used to tease me. She just got picked on a lot for being a nerd. If getting made fun of for not being the same as everyone else is a disease, then take a ticket, there's a lot of us in line for treatment.

"Did your friend Heather get help?"

"Heather's like me, she just throws herself into barn work whenever she feels bad. She's off at college—she rides there." Heather isn't a particularly good rider but she tries hard and she gets horses and that's the important thing.

It's hard for me to understand why Cynthia of all people would feel bad about herself, given all she has, but it's really not for me to judge. I say some things about how I'm glad Cindy feels better but Cynthia reroutes the conversation. "Was Heather your girlfriend?"

"God, no. Just a friend. She sort of dated my brother for a while."

"Did you have a girlfriend in high school?"

"Do you think I had a girlfriend in high school?"

"I honestly have no idea."

I take her question as fair, given that having a girlfriend is not really a reflection on a guy's sexual orientation. I messed around with plenty of guys who had girlfriends in high school and had some geeky guy friends whose every other thought was about girls even though they couldn't get laid if their lives depended on it, much less find a girlfriend. "No, Cynthia, no girlfriend. No prom, no nothing. I was *persona non grata*, as they say, in high school, in many ways. No boyfriend, really, either, back then. Anything else you'd like to ask?"

"No, just please don't tell Megan what we discussed tonight. I mean, I'm sure she's seen my scars but I don't want to talk about it with her."

"I won't." I page through the photos of the book as I wait for Cindy to go. In every picture, Steinkraus' leg is perfect beneath him, like he was standing on the ground, regardless of the size of the fence. Unperturbed and completely unflappable. Which is how I should strive to be.

"I'm going to check on the horses," I say, getting up. After all, that's why I am here tonight. Cynthia moves to follow me out, thinks better of it, and turns into her apartment.

Everything is fine, as I expected (although that is never a given with horses). I refill a few water buckets, scratch Fortune behind his ears. He doesn't try to nip at me anymore and for one brief second I swear he moves a bit closer to me, touching my arm with his muzzle as if seeking out affection. But then he pulls back. I give him a treat and he takes it as he always does, cautiously, savoring it as if it might be his last.

Blood gives a nervous whicker and I dig into my pocket, unwrap another peppermint and watch as she delicately plucks it from my fingers. It's hard for me to understand why a girl would hit on me, but then again there is always a part of me that never quite believed a guy would hit on me either. There's a tiny mirror hanging in the barn for adjusting your helmet before you walk out with your horse. I see my slightly odd, crooked lip reflected in it, looking almost symmetrical in the cracks, and a blur of pale, washed-out freckles.

I feel bad for Cynthia. Something I rarely feel—I don't know how I would describe it. Pity, maybe. I feel like she has a great, gaping wound that still isn't healed that she is looking for some guy to fill and I certainly can't (if any guy could, it certainly isn't me). It's hard for me to understand why anyone would hurt themselves because life has never had any problem hurting me first.

Of course, this isn't a girl thing, since my crazy brother right now is probably lying in bed after running until he pukes, so who can say what's normal after a certain point? *Hey Cindy, maybe try running fifty miles. That seems to work for my brother.* In contrast, Fortune, who has a habit of occasionally jumping things on his own which is really weird for a horse, would never deliberately try to injure himself to the point of pain; animals just accept what they feel, naturally, without question. They only hurt themselves by accident.

Maggie's let herself out again. I find her in the grain room, which fortunately has bins secured with padlocks. Still, she always has hopes that one day we'll forget and she'll find pony nirvana in an open bag of feed. "Trying to founder yourself, Maggie?" I ask her. Well, maybe ponies are different—they *do* seem to be on the lookout for trouble.

I put the pony back in her stall. In, out, in, out, a familiar pattern. We'll have a new lock on Maggie's stall door soon but she'll find a way to master it. It will only buy us time.

I have to admit, when I saw Cindy's marks, I suspected something different. When Sean and I were still really small, after the divorce but when we were staying at our grandmother's house, our mom would take us to a local swimming pool on hot summer days. Most of the time, I was too fixated on sneaking around so I could throw myself off the highest diving board reserved for the older kids. But once I remember asking Mom about the marks on her back and shoulders. She just shut down and didn't answer me. Sean took me aside later to explain. "They're cigarette burns," he said. "From him, you idiot, so don't mention them again." Even as dumb little boy, I didn't get mad at the force of Sean's grip or him calling me an idiot because I knew he wasn't mad at me.

The night after I saw the scars I remember sitting on Sean's bed (at our grandmother's we shared a room) and saying, "If I had caught our father doing that to her, I would have killed him."

And Sean said, "Yup, me too, and buried him in the backyard. And no one could blame us." We slapped each other's hands, like making a pact. I must have been what, ten, eleven when we had that conversation?

There is one more event before the season begins to taper off for the winter. I ask Max to come and watch it, or rather I tell him he has to see it. Besides just wanting him to see me, I'm curious what he will think of Fortune in action. Although he makes some noises about having to work ("is there any other vet who does any work besides you in the whole friggin' state of Vermont," I ask), he comes.

"Dr. Max," shouts Cynthia and waves to him when she sees him.

"It's nice to see all the horses when they're healthy," jokes Max, smiling and patting Blood. No one really questions his presence: Daniel makes a joke about how he hopes Max isn't charging him but then the two of them begin to talk about the breeding of one of the horses at the competition and do they think that gelding was started too soon over fences because although he's won a great deal he's had some soundness issues and what about the use of these new electrolytes during endurance racing and other such things.

I feel a bit bad pestering Max to come because I think that watching someone ride might be a bore, given that I tend to go into a kind of competitive trance whenever I ride and hardly notice who is around me. I do want to do well, though, when Max is watching. Thank God whatever nerves might be there beneath the surface get channeled into some kind of good nervous energy. Fortune actually feels pliable and yielding, although I struggle at the Novice level in dressage on yet another sale horse passing through the barn, Perfect She's Not.

Perfect is a hot little chestnut who I can barely get on because she dances around so much at the mounting block. She actually did very well on the track, which isn't necessarily a good sign regarding her adjustment to life outside. Even when I rode her at home she was very nervous and looky and of course now that she's in a new place she's even more uncertain. I can't so much as touch her with my legs without her crow-hopping or some other nonsense. But I like that far more than the opposite. Getting her through the dressage test is like trying to stuff a living snake in a bag, but we manage to look good even though I can see the mare's mind moving in overdrive as her ears spin around. I think the judge must like Thoroughbreds because she's kind to us.

Objectively speaking, the cross-country course doesn't look particularly challenging compared to what I've ridden at this level before. But in a specific area there appears to be a kind of ghost because one of the riders is unseated and several horses at various levels refuse different jumps. So it's not even a stupid jump, so I can't blame the course designer. It's probably the stupid shiny bush with glossy leaves sparkling in the sunlight that gives packers at the Beginner Novice level and Novice OTTBs alike a heart attack.

At least both of mine go clear. Perfect pushes through although we get time faults because she hesitates and slows down before the jump near the bush of doom. Still, not a refusal. Megan is one of the unfortunate riders who does suffer a refusal in that scary area. Cynthia makes it around and places third at Novice level.

With my own horse I have one of those trips where I know just when to pause and speed up before every fence. I'm always rotating the plane of the course in my mind with another part of my brain, preparing and setting up for things, with my eye on the clock in real time even though things have that thick, slowed-down quality that they always do when I'm competing.

Fortune and I are at the head of the leaderboard after cross-country at our level and stay there after stadium. And just getting through it all with Perfect is a victory, given how little experience she has, far less than the others at her level. It does help that Perfect was so perfectly scared of all the jumps during stadium she choose to leave the monsters up, over-jumping everything with inches to spare. After my victory lap on Fortune I take him back to our area to untack. One of the girls who came with us to help has already cooled down Perfect.

For the first time doing one of these events at this level, I feel a kind of security, as if I have a skill rather than am just muscling through on bravery and luck. It feels weirdly satisfying, not just because I've won. I know I haven't made any major mistakes, even at dressage. I have less of a sense of getting away with things and more of a sense of actually knowing what I'm doing.

As I graze Fortune a bit before we leave, I sense Max's presence behind me. I realize he's been watching me and I've been too absorbed in my own thoughts to notice he's there. He puts his arms around me, kisses me quickly, and then pats my horse.

"Where is the other horse you rode?"

"Perfect's in her stall in the trailer."

"Pretty girl."

"You want her? She's for sale. She's a fun ride."

"I bet—for you."

"It's true, I like the crazy mares."

"You do ride a lot of mares."

"They're sensitive. Unlike this guy."

"You'll be unsurprised to know that even when I was younger I always preferred geldings. I like to get on the same horse as the one I rode yesterday."

"They're not all that bad, but yeah, the chestnut is what you'd call mareish. She is flashy though, so I'm sure they'll move her before long. I bet the next time I ride her I can win something good." I put Fortune away with a pat, feeling a bit bad that I'm talking about another horse so approvingly and longingly when he went so well for me today. "He was a good boy," I say. "You should try getting on him, sometime."

"Oh, there's no way I could hold him back."

"I thought you said you didn't like mares."

"I said they were unpredictable. Fortune is predictably unstoppable which doesn't make me inclined to ride him, either."

"You underestimate yourself as a rider, doctor."

"You overestimate me, killer, but I'll take it."

So Fortune and I have yet another NQR, a national qualifying result that puts me one step closer to moving up to Intermediate: I can better see moving up a level in my very near future, even with winter looming on the horizon, which makes me happy. It's the best gift possible before the holidays. To thank him for his performance, I give Fortune another handful of treats, which he eats, as cautiously and slowly from my hand as ever, despite the fact he must be hungry from his efforts. Unlike me he's a slow eater and savors every bite.

He's good with me, I think, but he's still not a very affectionate horse. He doesn't seem to like many people and sometimes at home he'll put his ears back when one of the boarders walks by and will lunge at them with intention—or he'll raise his back hoof as a kind of a warning at the sight of a little kid who means no harm. He trusts me but trusts others only grudgingly—what's the point of trusting too many people for a horse, after all? All in all, I'm glad I bought him because I'm not entirely sure someone else would put up with him.

By the time I've begun to relax, someone from the show comes running over and asks if I know about the fun event they are staging for the spectators, a bareback puissance. I look at Fortune, check his breathing and think, hell, he has a few more jumps in him. I put on his bridle again and ride over.

Puissance is basically a high-jumping competition. The jump starts at an easy three foot and everyone keeps jumping it as they raise it higher and higher for each round, until only one person is left without a fault. This is a *shirtless* bareback puissance, which means that even if your horse knocks a rail you can buy your entry in one more round of jumping if you take off your shirt.

Obviously, this takes a bit more planning beforehand for the girls, but most of them are prepared with appropriate sports bras.

Cynthia is cowed by the whole thing but lends Blood Money to Megan, who of course *is* game. We only lose one horse at three feet but by the time we're above four feet or so, most of the girls are shirt-less. Megan has a tiny white bra on with a zipper going up the front that honestly looks slightly obscene. "What, does Ricky have trouble with hooks," I say as we wait. I still have my shirt on. "Maybe Velcro would be easier?"

"How the hell did you even know bras have hooks?" says Megan.

"I don't ride saddleseat but I understand the mechanics of the discipline," I say, grandly.

One horse goes over the jump, then the next horse, then the next, then we eliminate a shirtless rider, then the jump gets hiked up a notch. Stripping only buys you one extra round, so things go quickly.

Even the final jump of five feet, which Fortune clears—with me still in my shirt, incidentally—feels like nothing on the big horse, although by all rights he should be tired. I ignore the clapping and the catcalls and the girls saying stuff like, "I still think he should take the shirt off, to be a good sport." For a moment, it just feels easy and good and I am one with my horse. The other remaining competitor, a girl with her gut hanging out over her breeches and an ugly neon T-shirt bra, knocks down the jump and I've won.

One of the girls on the rail tries to yank off the T-shirt I'm wearing (I'm out of my stadium shirt and jacket) but I shake her off and go and accept the trophy and the hundred bucks they're offering for the spectacle.

The last puissance I read about, the winner jumped seven foot. We're a long way away from that. I'm not surprised he made it up to five feet at all. We've done as much schooling together, when I've worked him alone.

As I lead Fortune away, I hear someone say, "He's cute," and I'm not sure they mean me or the horse.

Her friend says, "Don't waste your time with that one," and for a second I'm still not sure if they're talking about the horse or me, since they said that about Fortune when I bought him. But then I register they're talking about me.

When we finally arrive home and I turn Fortune out, I spend a long time looking at him in the paddock. He's not the type of horse who likes to stay with the herd. My horse kind of stays on the margins, grazing, although he's not the low man on the totem pole of the paddock. The other horses just kind of acknowledge his presence and leave him alone (he will bare his teeth and fight and nip if they get in his way). Yes, we work well together, even though he's not overly race-y or fancy. I wouldn't mind having other horses (I would keep Perfect, if I could afford another, even though I know I really can't). But if I can only have one, he is the one that I want. It might be more sensible to have a horse that is better at dressage and more obedient to schooling but I'd feel like something was lacking in my life if I couldn't jump as high and fast as my heart's desire.

19

PERFECT HE IS?

Although that is the last event I ride at in Zone I (in eventing, the nation is cut up into various zones and New England is the first zone, i.e., the cold-as-a-witch's-tit-in-winter zone), Daniel teaches a clinic in Virginia and brings me along to demonstrate some of what he is saying but is too crippled to do anymore (his words, not mine). Personally, I think he rides pretty damn amazingly well for a busted up guy in his seventies but I certainly don't turn down the free trip. Also, there is a CCI (Concours Complet International) nearby which Daniel will attend, just to check in with his old friends. For me this is as exciting as going to a rock concert (more exciting, of course, depending on what band is playing).

During the clinic, Daniel says stuff like, "Look at how Simon's leg doesn't move. He's no praying mantis, see how he is out of the tack just enough rather than crawling up his horse's neck." And he counts my strides approvingly so I'm feeling pretty good about myself when it's all over. Of course, he's never that nice to me in my lessons and at the end of the clinic when they give me a little applause for demonstrating, I say that (the only time I speak the entire day) and everybody laughs.

The next day we go to the CCI and all of the confidence I've built up as the demo guy is completely sucked away within minutes, thanks to Frederick Whitechapel.

I've seen Whitechapel in my Facebook newsfeed for ages and watched him on YouTube. But I've never seen him in person before. He's not one of the elites like Buck Davidson or Boyd Martin—yet—but there are lots of people, Daniel included, who think Freddie's on his way. Whitechapel is half-British but moved to the United States to be with his wife Cheryl, a showjumper. Cheryl Whitechapel's at the event, watching, with the couple's three children. The kids are all tall and healthy-looking with bright blue eyes, like a Dover catalog photo, only they're real and smiling and very nice, even while the press pesters them with dumb questions. Like, the reporters ask Whitechapel if he's nervous and stuff like that. He says that his horse is still gaining experience at this level, so it's about the horse, not him, and no, he's not nervous.

Watching the dressage of all things, I suddenly become aware that however confident I might have felt at my previous barns, I'm so out of my league compared to the people riding here. It's easy for me to feel good about myself relative to my competition at home. But when you're up close and personal to someone who actually is good, and you still don't fully understand how to get that good, it's jarring.

Whitechapel's horse seems to have changed shape from when I saw it on the ground and it looks like the reins, his hands, the bit, and the horse's head are all part of the same animal. This is beyond just having decent hands. His horse is perfectly and equally engaged front and back when doing all of the movements, even though the gelding is still developing. When I watch Whitechapel cross-country later on, although I can see the set-up as he takes the tricky skinny and the water jump, even there I can sense an unconscious fluidity I haven't yet mastered. The horse trusts him completely.

As everyone applauds when he finishes the stadium phase, I notice that on top of it all Freddie (as Daniel calls him, since they are on a first-name basis) is completely gorgeous as well, one of those lean, sinewy riders who are thin without looking skinny. Off the horse, Freddie's got long dark lashes, blue eyes, tousled black hair, and sculpted cheekbones but he's also not effeminate in the way of some male eye candy at all. Of course, with the family in tow, I also note that he's hopelessly heterosexual in a really wholesome kind of way despite not being aggressively macho. This is, of course, another turn-on for me.

As an aside, with all of the British and European guys I've ever met as a rider, from the clinicians that used to come to my old barn to all of the cute guys at this CCI, I keep getting at first what I think are signals and I think, so, so possibly gay and then I realize, no, no so European and so totally not gay at all. There should be some kind of a Rosetta Stone translation dictionary for international gaydar because I sure as hell could use one. I have enough problems with the American as it is.

After the clinic and watching Freddie Whitechapel I do extra work all that week (not just on Fortune, but on a bunch of sale and lesson horses) until even my legs are shaky. I drill and drill in the ring and go over and over the obstacles on the practice cross-country course. I'm glad that I do because one day, without telling us all, Freddie stops by to look at Crackerjack. Daniel told him about her and for whatever reason he was intrigued.

"Put her through her paces, Simon," Daniel says, and I show off Cracker over a small showjumping course. Thank God, I get to ride rather than having to talk to Freddie. I know it sounds like I'm being disloyal to Max, but it's sort of a different feeling that I have, looking at the Brit. It's that weird place where wanting to be someone and wanting someone are all mixed up and it makes my hands shake a little when I'm looking at him except when I'm riding. Then I'm fine.

"She's a pretty girl," Freddie says of Cracker. "Of course, I'd have to change her name because Boyd already rides a Crackerjack."

When Freddie takes the reins and whip from my hands to try out the mare, the fingers of his gloves brush up against mine and I can't bear to look him in the eye.

The spacey horse is jittery at first with a new rider on her back but it is Freddie friggin' Whitechapel and he settles her down quickly. Still, when Freddie gets off of her, he says to Daniel, "She's a lovely girl but a bit greener than what I'm looking for right now. I have enough at that level as it is."

"I understand," says Daniel.

"I would never have thought her so green, looking at you ride her, though," he says to me.

"This is Simon, he's one of my working students," says Daniel. I nod and look at the ground.

"Nice. Well, if you're looking for the job at the end of your working studentship, I might have something. I need someone who can show off some of my own sale horses. I always hear good things about people who come through Daniel's program."

I'm terrified to sound too excited. I don't care what the salary is, what the money is, I just mumble something about how I will seek him out come June. Mr. Whitechapel—Freddie—shakes my hand. His fingers are cool beneath his gloves, despite the fact he was just riding.

"You're very lucky to have good training," Freddie says, as we walk back to the barn. "Daniel's all about the basics. He's like the Obi-Wan Kenobi and Yoda of the eventing world all wrapped up into one."

Freddie Whitechapel references Obi-Wan! And Yoda! I'm melting.

I'm feeling pretty full of myself for about a day but then the next morning after chores I notice something as Fortune relaxes while he's eating his grain. "Jesus, you look disgusting," I mutter to my horse. I've put it off for far too long. The day is warm so I get a bucket of water, some Ivory dish soap, plastic gloves and go to work.

"Damn, Simon, that's hot," smirks Megan. Cynthia walks by, appalled, her nose wrinkled in disgust. Somehow, I don't think Cindy's ever cleaned a sheath.

Megan stops and watches me try to extract the bean. "Eww, smegma city," she says.

The hardened bit of the smegma is lodged pretty snugly up there, but I get it, throw it at Megan, and begin cleaning. Megan shrieks. "Don't you want a souvenir?"

"Thank God I have a mare. I'll take being in heat over sheath-cleaning any day," says Megan.

"My last horse was a mare," I say, wryly. The girls usually leave this unenviable task to me on the rest of the horses, even the ones I don't own, anyway. Fortune snorts. "I hope this is as good for you as it is for me, buddy."

"He looks happier than you, that's for sure. When I had to clean the geldings at my last barn we'd use KY Jelly rather than pure soap and water."

"Good to know for next time. I'm learning so much about you Megs. Are you offering to loan me some because you're concerned I don't have any myself?"

"Hey, you know me, always there to help."

Now there is always in the back of my mind the question: Will Freddie remember his offer months from now? Whitechapel is based out of Maryland, which is perfect for me—not too hot and southern, but with enough nice riding weather year around. Closer to my family. But regarding Max, well, it is obviously farther than I would like but even then, not prohibitively far.

Max doesn't follow upper-level eventing like I do but when I tell him about the visit from Freddie, he's heard of Whitechapel and he's impressed. I'm kind of nervous telling Max about possibly getting a job away from here when my working studentship is over, fearing he'll be hurt. I want to tell him that I know I can make everything work out. I'm afraid to sound too intense, too soon and I cover up my feelings, like I usually do, with teasing him and messing around with him.

20

OPTIMUM TIME

I want Max to come home with me for Thanksgiving but he's already agreed to go to the house of a friend of his from vet school, two states away. At first I'm suspicious but he notes his friend has a wife and two children.

"That doesn't stop some guys," I joke.

There is a slight, uncomfortable pause that I want to ask Max about, and then he says, "Trust me, there is nothing to worry about, killer. No sexy freckles and blond hair." I look away—I always feel slightly uncomfortable when Max compliments me, especially my appearance, because I certainly don't see what he sees in my weird, irregularly shaped face.

"I wish you were coming home with me," I whine. "All those hours traveling alone."

"The truth is, I'm a little bit scared to come home with you."

"Why?" We usually don't do anything fancy for Thanksgiving. There is a local hunter pace we always ride in and then it's pretty much a preheated turkey from the supermarket and sides from a box, but I like it. It's all I've ever known and I kind of feel sorry for people who have Thanksgivings where they have to dress up and have nothing to do all day before they eat but talk to boring relatives. My grandma's dead, my mother alienated most of her other relatives when she married my father, and Sean and I kind of managed to scare away the rest. I refer way back to the incident of setting one of my cousin's entire Barbie collection on fire at a family get-together. (As usual, I had the idea and lit the actual fire although it was Sean who charmed one of the grown-ups into giving him a pack of matches).

Says Max, who I am sure has no such black marks in his own, youthful history, nice Jewish kid that he must have been, "I'm afraid if your mother meets me she'll attack me with a horsewhip rather than invite me in for dinner."

"I told you, with my mom, if there is something preoccupying her at the barn, there is a good chance she won't even notice you're there, even if it is Thanksgiving." The barn my mother operates out of might not be particularly fancy but she treats it like she's still competing on the international circuit. I may have outgrown her barn as a rider but I haven't outgrown her attitude, whatever you might say about Mom.

"She'll notice that I'm not eighteen and not I'm a girl, killer."

"Mom's known for forever."

"That doesn't always make it easier." I notice that although Max's parents are still alive and he has a sister, he's not going to see them for the holiday. True, his parents live in Florida now and that's kind of far. But he hardly ever talks about them and it's always in the past tense. I know there is quite a bit I don't know about Max, quite a bit that has been relegated to silence. As much as I have memorized every inch of his body in the present, bits and pieces of his past are still lost to me. I tell myself they don't matter, but I would still like to know.

I lay my head on his lap and feel his fingers in my hair, close my eyes, and tell myself to be happy with what I have.

Sean greets me at the train station. He looks like he's lost more weight and he's limping. "What the hell happened to you?" I say.

"Stress fracture in my metatarsal. Helluva thing—seriously, I was about to PR—my best time ever and then the last half mile my foot started to go. I still kicked ass and I still PR-ed but I'm going to have to lay off for a few weeks. The sports physician says six but I'm thinking two or three, max. At least I PR-ed when it counted and the season's pretty much over."

"This is what you get for running all those crazy miles with your lunatic running coach."

"I gotta say, this season has pushed me past my known limits to the best shape of my life."

"Yeah, except for the whole not walking thing, you look like you're in great shape. Would you like me to carry you back to the car?" One of my past horses, the dead one I still think of from time to time, was named Damsel in Distress and the name crosses my mind as I watch Sean struggle. I still respect her memory too much to joke about it and call my brother one. Even though he sure looks like he could use a helpful prince, given the way he's hopping.

Mom is going through paperwork for her job job (the one that pays the bills, as opposed to teaching riding) when I come home. I hug her and lift her off of her feet, slightly. "Simon, you look so grown up," she says. With all the added muscle from the farm I feel much larger in the narrow kitchen.

I've been away less than a year but even my own room feels smaller, more childish, with my kiddie horse books and my drawings tacked on the wall from high school. I look at all my old Black Stallion series books and remember how much I loved them, especially the novels about the Black Stallion's colt Satan and the Black Stallion's rival, the island stallion Flame. Daniel calls the series Uncle Walter's Kool-Aid because so many people have been motivated to buy unsuitable, wild horses after reading it.

Mom orders a pizza for dinner. Sean and I, both exhausted for different reasons, park ourselves in front of the television for a Quentin Tarantino marathon of *Reservoir Dogs*, *Pulp Fiction*, and *Kill Bill*. I've watched hardly any television since I left, except for a few bits and pieces on my phone or at Max's, so I'm as excited about this other, pre-Thanksgiving ritual of ours as I am about our turkey.

"I don't see how you boys can watch those violent things," says my mother. "And you know all the words already—what's the point of seeing the films over and over again?" She goes back to the kitchen.

Sean gets up for more pizza, hopping over to the box.

"You make a good gimp, brother." Sean expertly maneuvers back to the couch, barely skimming the ground with his busted foot.

"Fuck you," he says.

"Easy with the language, Tiny Tim, our mother is nearby."

I get up for thirds and Sean sticks his good leg out as I cross in front of him, tripping me into the coffee table as if he had deliberately set himself up to do so when he sat down.

"You're dead," I say, grabbing him and pinning him to the ground, putting his head in a lock. We used wrestle all the time as kids. We don't often anymore, but I'm feeling silly. I've been stronger than Sean for a long time but it's even easier than when I last fought him. "Jesus, what do you weigh, a hundred pounds?" I let him go.

"Tell me when the cutting off the ear scene is on so I know not to come in," says my mother.

"Wrong Tarantino film mom," says Sean. "That one's next."

"You do realize that normal people don't watch Quentin Tarantino films for the holidays, don't you? They watch, I don't know, *A Christmas Carol* or *Miracle on 34ᵗʰ Street*."

"I think the normal ship has already sailed in this family, Ma," says Sean.

"I realize that but I'm just trying to remind you of what other people consider normal," says Mom.

"Mr. Pink would make a great name for a show horse," I say. "Or Inglorious Bastard."

"Only your demented mind would think of that," says Sean. Then we shut up because the scene where Jules blows the guy away after saying a Bible verse is about to come on, which is one of our favorite parts. Both of us repeat the lines in unison along with Jules. I know it's weird because I'm not black or anything, but Jules is the character I most identify with.

"Get your ass out of my line of vision," says Sean, when I move to get more food for myself. "Uma's about to come on."

"You and Uma. Sick bag of bones."

"Still totally hot."

"Yeah, I know, that's why it's sick you're attracted to her. Fucking skeleton."

"What are you, Roger fucking Ebert?"

I'm tempted to point out that since the movie came out in 1994, Uma's old enough to be his mother now but then I think better of it, very quickly. "*Pulp Fiction* always makes me want a burger," I say instead, sitting back down with my slice. I only had a bag of M&Ms and chips and soda on the train the whole long ride, so I'm starving, plus the general hunger that always dogs me since I never have as much time as I'd like to eat while working.

"Well, tomorrow is the one time this year that I'm cooking and it's not burgers, so you'll eat it and like it," says my mom from inside, still avoiding the television room.

After the three films are over, I finish up the marathon with a documentary on wolves.

"I think I need a dog," I say as Sean gets up to get ready for bed.

Like my fascination with 'Shark Week,' Sean has always found my interest in wolves and my love of animal documentaries in general really weird and he tells me so as he leaves me there. I fall asleep in my clothes, too tired to move.

In the morning, when I'm getting dressed for the hunter pace, Sean says, "I'm not sure I should go. What about my toe?"

"What about it? You can still ride with a busted toe."

"The doctor said no pressure on it."

"You're not going to come because your toe hurts? What kind of a pussy are you?"

"Simon, language," says my mother, walking in. She looks younger and more beautiful when dressed to ride and like always, for the Thanksgiving hunter pace, she's wearing immaculate buff breeches, a velvet cap, navy coat, and a vest. A hunter pace is a pretty simple point-to-point race, with an award given for the closest optimal time rides over a bunch of obstacles and trails, but my mom treats it like a real hunt. I've brought my old tweed show coat back with me and cleaned my boots so I don't disgrace the family. With Sean, we're lucky if he doesn't ride in jeans and the Western saddle he prefers.

"You're calling me a pussy?" says my brother. "What the hell would you know about pussy?"

"Enough to know one when I see one. You and your stubbed friggin' toe."

"Stress fracture."

"You better come. Use your skinny ass for something useful for a change, to work some of the fat off of your horse."

Sean hasn't ridden Camera Shy for months but I know Cam'll be just like he always is—steady, with that Quarter Horse mentality, the same ride whether he's left to graze in a field for weeks or was worked like hell the day before.

Lauren, the barn owner, has promised me a horse to ride for the pace. She greets me with the usual hellos and comments about how much older and more mature I look and then says, "We just got a new girl in a week ago. When I heard you were coming in, I saved her for you."

That isn't a good sign. What Lauren means is, "No one else at the barn is crazy enough to get on this horse except you, Simon." But what the hell, I think. She asks me if I want to borrow a safety vest but I don't bother.

The mare is a gorgeous dark dapple grey—so silvery and slate-colored she's almost blue in the light—and her name is Blue Velvet. Blue isn't that bad. She bucks a couple of times and crow hops, throws her head around, but once I get her on the bit and propel her over a few jumps in the ring, she's fine. I'm a little disappointed. I was expecting something really crazy, given the way they were talking about her, but their fear was more grounded in anticipation than any real potential for danger from this mare. Maybe the barn girls have grown wimpy in my absence.

"I'll ride her in the pace," I say, eager to begin. We walk over as a group to the starting point rather than trailer over since the beginning of the race is only about a half-mile from the barn.

"How is your own horse?" asks Lauren.

"He's doing well. We won some nice money showjumping." Blue is spooking at every other tree, but I expected that.

"Heather!" I say and wave, because Heather is there at the starting line.

"I walked over early just to get him used to the surroundings," she said. Heather is riding a new horse from the barn—he looks dead calm and I doubt he needed to take a look-see but Heather has always been cautious to a fault, anticipating every possible mistake she or the horse might make. Despite this, she's become a pretty decent rider over the years. "She's so pretty," she says, nodding at the mare. "She suits you Simon." Heather's black hair is stuffed under a hair net and she's wearing buff breeches and a navy coat like my mom, like everyone else. I realize that Sean and I are the only guys. (Sean is wearing jeans and half-chaps, paddock boots, and a polo shirt over a thermal, refusing to get fully dressed up for anything that is less than a show. At least his hair isn't longish like it was in high school and doesn't stick out under his helmet.)

Heather has kept up her riding in college. Sean looks stiff and uncomfortable in his hips, I notice with my instructor's eye, even though I remember how easy and relaxed he was, especially when riding dressage, only a few years ago. Out of practice.

"Something to remember, everyone," says my mother. "The optimum time is much slower this year because there have been concerns about unsafe riding at the paces recently."

"What do you mean, a slower optimum time?" I say. "The Thanksgiving pace has always been one of the fastest courses in the area."

"I guess that's what they were afraid of, people taking too many chances," says Mom, looking at Blue as the unfamiliar mare snorts and paws. My mother pushes back her riding jacket, making sure she can see her stopwatch and keep her eye on it so she doesn't go too fast.

We start trotting as a group up the trail to the first fence. I'm disappointed because I feel confined and itchy in my skin after all the sitting on the train and the sitting watching movies last night. Suddenly, I'm like, "Optimum time? Fuck that." I squeeze Blue and she's off, careering to the first fence. She really doesn't know what she's doing, other than I want to go fast, but setting her up correctly has become so reflexive, after jumping so much out in the open in Vermont, we're fine. Unlike Fortune, she doesn't fight me if we have a dispute over how we're going to tackle this jump by jump. The land feels so flat and fast after all the up and down I've become accustomed to. I think in a flash that people have it easy here, too easy, another indication of how where I've been has changed me, at least as a rider.

"Simon—" I hear my mother say, because I know she wants someone from our family to win. But she's far away now, I give the mare her head, and we're flying away from the pack to the next brush jump. The mare might not have been worked much but her muscles feel solid and strong beneath me and I know I'm not asking too much of her. Perhaps I can have the worst time if not the best, then.

Heather wins and I'm ecstatic for her.

"Simon, I can't believe I beat you at anything horse-related," she says. "Granted the circumstances favored me more than you, but I admit I will take the boost in confidence. To have beat my riding teacher and idol even once is an honor."

I mock-salute her, like I do beginning and ending a dressage test.

As they give out Heather's award, the woman who is in charge of running the pace makes mention of me, noting that I deserve a special award for behaving most contrary to the occasion's new spirit of safety and decorum.

Blue is exhausted and walks quietly back and I know the experience was a good one for her, far better than fighting to contain her for some arbitrary set time.

As expected, Thanksgiving dinner is a precooked turkey from the supermarket, Stove Top, heated canned vegetables, rolls from dough popped out of a can, and instant potatoes from a box (heavily buttered and salted, which is all that matters). Followed by apple and pumpkin pie from the store. I like all of these things even though Sean makes noises and complains a bit. Mom heats what needs to be heated and won't let us touch anything cooking-wise because she knows we'll destroy it. I check my Facebook messages while I wait. I haven't hardly updated anything since I started working over the summer (no time) but I do check messages.

Enjoying your busman's holiday? Max has written me. I'm not sure what that is but I think he means he thinks it's weird I'm riding for fun when I ride as part of my job.

> *new mare* I type.
> *Should your horse be jealous?*
> *little but she can't come back with me not for sale.*
> *Did you win the race?*
> *no explain later*

God, I always hate the fact that not only does he sound like he's speaking with punctuation half the time, Max even uses punctuation on social media. He's used semicolons with me before, during some previous online conversations. I mean, seriously—semicolons on Facebook?

I can't help it, it annoys me so much that I write back.

> *using punctuation makes u sound angry*

Long pause.

> *Why does using correct grammar sound angry?*

Hopeless. I can't even begin to explain it.

> *its weird why bother*

I mean, does he think he's being graded or something? I don't know, maybe he does.

"Simon, put down the phone. It's Thanksgiving." I do, less to obey my mother than because Sean is looking over my shoulder and I know he's getting curious.

"I think he's writing something to the vet, Mom." He snickers.

"Why? Is something wrong with your troublesome horse, Simon?"

"No, he's fine. Everything is fine, Mother. Fortune is fine." Which it is. Which he is. I give Sean a death stare. So far as I know he's single right now so I can't even fire back with teasing on the subject of sex.

Mom lets us have some booze with dinner, like she usually does for special occasions. She pours red wine for herself and Sean and I have half a bottle of the Guinness she keeps in the fridge for the horses.

"Only you would choose that over Pinot," says my brother, the budding wine snob. But I don't really like the bitter taste of wine or really how wine makes me feel. Wine always gives me a headache and makes me sleepy and forget things and I prefer to be awake.

After dinner Sean and I toss a football back and forth to one another even though Sean prefers soccer and baseball as team sports go and I prefer basketball. With football, he doesn't need to move around that much. We just throw the ball back and forth and Sean stands poised on one leg half the time, like some kind of demented version of a lawn flamingo. Then we go back in and watch some college football to end the day.

By early morning, Mom has already left for some Black Friday tack store sales—some of the horses at the stable need new equipment and she's responsible for finding it. I still know what saddle I want to get Fortune and still need a little more money to do so. Other than that, for a guy, tack store shopping is always less interesting. Basically, my reasoning process is always:

1. Does it fit me and my horse?
2. Can I afford it?

If so, I must and will purchase it. But since ninety-nine percent (or so it seems) of riders are women and women like to shop more than men, I'm definitely not in the target market.

"I think Mom has already maxed out on the non-barn time she can spend with us," says Sean.

I laugh. "I don't blame her."

"If you spent more time around normal non-horse people, you'd know that the way she raised us is kind of weird and it's weird that when we're not at the barn she can't get away fast enough." By which Sean means basically letting us run wild (except when needed at the barn or when riding) until we did something wrong and smacking us when we did. But because we all ride we still spend a fair amount of time together, so I think that's good enough. Kind of like the stuffing from a box. It's what I've always known and I like it, so unlike Sean I never complain. I don't know where he gets his ideas about what's normal. I mean, it can't be movies because we've been watching the same Tarantino films together for ages.

"Mom just needs a lot of time to herself," I say. I guess to some extent you could say that Sean and I raised ourselves, which explains a lot, but I've never regretted it. She left us alone a lot as kids, long before I guess you're supposed to, because she was working or teaching but we turned out okay so I don't see why that's bad. I mean, we never set the house on fire even when we did stuff like experimenting with how long it took to explode various objects in the microwave.

Sean can't do much on one leg and the truck finally died so we have no car given that mom is gallivanting about. Heather picks us up later and we drive to the ocean where Sean can sort of walk in the sand (well, hobble) and we just spend time together, talking about nothing important. I grab Heather at one point and threaten to throw her into the freezing ocean and she shrieks. One of the things I like best about Heather is how easy it is to get a rise out of her, no matter how obvious to other people it might be that I'm joking.

"I think you've gained weight this year," I say, even though she doesn't really feel like she has. She hits me after I put her down and I laugh, pushing her away.

"She's such a nice girl," I say, after she drops us off. "Why did you break up with her? What was ever wrong with her?"

Sean says, "Sometimes, Simon, you can be so clueless." And for once, I'm not really sure what my brother means and he won't elaborate on that. Girls. Whatever.

21

KISS

On the ride back on the train I'm bored, so I sketch Fortune from memory. I took art all through high school, not just because it was a GPA-booster like I claimed but because I did love it. I haven't had time to draw at all, not so much as a doodle, since I began working on the farm but being back in my high school bedroom reminded me I used to be good at drawing. I draw Fortune jumping over a fence (jumping freestyle, because I never draw myself, not willingly, not even my own hand as an exercise). Then I draw the same picture upside down, then in reverse as if seen in a mirror. The journey is long so I do the same with other horses I know until I've covered several pages with rotated images. I think it looks kind of cool so I give it to Megan, who is the first person I see upon arriving.

"See? I drew Maggie," I say, pointing to a few of her pony.

"What the hell, Simon," she says and I know I've impressed her, which is pretty rare for Megan. I don't give it to Cynthia even though I've actually drawn more pictures of Blood Money because I know Cindy would take it the wrong way. It's not for anyone, not even myself, it's something I just enjoy doing to empty my head when I can't move around. And I don't give it to Max because, I don't know, like with the calculus and the chess, he might give me the not-living-up-to-my-potential speech again.

When I get back, it's like winter in Vermont. In New Jersey, my blood was already thicker than Sean's or Heather's so I didn't even need to wear long sleeves but the few days I've been gone, the New England weather has taken a turn for the worse.

Everyone moves slower in the morning, even Megan and Daniel, who are more used to this kind of cold than Cynthia. For the first time in my life I actually buckle and wear a long undershirt beneath my T-shirt and flannel, which I always resisted before as wussy.

"What music are you playing today, Simon? It's so depressing," says Cynthia as she strolls into the barn late one morning.

"Good morning, sleeping beauty," I mutter. I'm already halfway done with morning chores. Still, after our big conversation in my room that night, I've censored some of my more nasty jokes about being a hunter princess. That is as edgy as I get aloud nowadays. I'm not sure how much Cynthia can take; I don't trust my ability to read her moods.

"Can't you put on something happy?"

"Don't touch, I know you'll put on Taylor Swift."

"Who is on now?"

"Amy Winehouse, only one of the greatest singers ever to live and die."

"Wasn't she on drugs?"

"She left the world at age twenty-seven, like so many great musicians," I say, with exaggerated solemnity, carefully sifting the shavings with my pitchfork. Although I don't share Amy's vices, I've always found it really satisfying to listen to "You Know I'm No Good." Because I suspect I'm not.

"It's not fair that you always get to control the music, Simon."

"It's not fair that Amy is dead and Taylor Swift is still alive." I look out the tiny barn window as I pass Cindy with my wheelbarrow on my way to the manure pile. The glass has frosted over and I have to wait until I'm outdoors for an impromptu weather report. Yes, it's going to snow more today, I think, gazing at the slate grey sky. The sky matches my horse.

On my way back to the next stall, Cynthia blows her nose and glares at me but she doesn't touch my iPod plugged in to the barn's sound system. "What Do I Get" by the Buzzcocks is coming up next, I hurry so I'm there for the beginning of the song.

What I don't get, in all honesty is this—although I love Amy Winehouse and kind of get a rise from listening to songs like "Back to Black," I could never live with a guy who treated me like that for more than five minutes. Even the way that my brother has treated some of his girlfriends—I mean, he is my brother and I love him but if I had a conscience I'd hang a sign on his back for the women of the world to Proceed at Your Own Risk. But there is Cynthia, who has really lived all these things, and she'd listen to her bubble gum shit on a loop if I let her.

Max has remarked that my taste in music is pretty morbid. "Should I be scared, killer?" he asked when I asked if he knew how to play another my favorites by Florence and the Machine on his guitar, "A Kiss With a Fist."

"Nah, I just like the way it sounds," I say. I actually like the safe way I feel with Max even though how we are together doesn't really resonate with the songs about anger and violence and anarchy that I prefer. I guess that's weird but it makes sense to me. Max has such a great voice, too, and if he wasn't my boyfriend I'd be totally jealous of him. I love music so much but I can only carry a tune, nothing more.

I've been asking Max if I can follow him on some of his rounds. I know that some of the local high school kids help out the vets at the practice (they call it "shadowing"). I certainly have more knowledge than any of those students since my mom did as much of her vet care DIY as she could legally.

Most of it is that I want to see him more and sometimes he has to work when I have time off. Although there is another component to my desire that I don't want to admit to: I am kind of curious, just in case everyone is right and I am making a mistake with my life. I could see myself becoming a vet someday versus some guy in a cubicle, like everyone else wants me to become. I first run the shadowing idea by Daniel, about working with Max on my one day off every now and then, and he says okay.

But Max grouses about it for days and days and says he thinks it's unethical (yeah, he's always, "ethical this, ethical that"). Still after a number of kids don't show up when they're supposed to, he begins to cave. My impatience at missing time off with him comes to a breaking point when all of us at my barn have to stay on night watch for days when a couple of the horses are sick. I mean, at least I'd like to see Max during the day if I could. I stop by his boss and I'm all, "Gee, I am thinking of going to vet school and I could use the work on my resume." It's one of my better acting efforts, I guess because I can convince myself that what I'm saying is true, and the senior vet says okay.

The first Monday I'm formally working with him Max watches me warm my hands at the heater, shivering. "Don't you even have decent gloves, Simon? You really are a flatlander, I warned you it was going to get cold."

"Left them at the barn somewhere."

Max has a spare pair and gives them to me. "I'm sure you'll find a way to lose these in a day or two."

"Probably." The drive is long and for a bit we listen to the music—"Psycho Killer" by Talking Heads—in silence. When the next song comes up, I make a face and skip through it, then the next two until I find another Killers song. "The Grateful frigging Dead is on your playlist? I'm surprised and disappointed."

"They're classic rock."

"Classic stoner music. Classic rock is like Blondie and the Smiths. I don't approve."

"Well, I did get my undergraduate degree in Vermont. Let's leave it at that. You like some cheesy '80s music, admit it, killer."

"That's totally different. Those songs have like, beginnings and endings and a point to them."

"Broaden your horizons."

"I've already learned so much more about you, working with you for less than an hour. I never knew you smoked a lot of pot during your youth."

"Well, not by my college's standards, I didn't. Besides, you'll be pleased know it never really relaxed me, just made me hungry, so I gave it up around my sophomore or junior year."

"So that's your big drug confession, too uptight for pot? Well then, you have even less of an excuse for liking the Dead."

"Anything new to confess to me about yourself? I know that you said you killed a man once, but other than that, I mean."

"When it comes to drugs, that's the one area of my life in which I'm totally straight."

This the second time I've been called prejudiced in less than a week. Daniel was watching me work one of the babies and told me that I was getting sloppy again on the flat. He uses it as a springboard for one of his favorite subjects.

Ugh. Dressage again. "You think you can make up a bad score with the jumping phases. When I was competing you could, but now you can't. If I was riding competitively today, I'd spend six months studying in Germany at an eventing barn with some strong dressage instructors just to brush up my skills."

Well, I doubt I can afford that—after this year I'll have to get some kind of job job with horses. As long as I can make something of a living I don't even care that much anymore about all the other stuff I used to dream about. I'll let Cynthia blather on and on about endorsements and international sponsors and starred events. Again, I remind myself as long as I can avoid being in a box of an office, life is good even if it isn't fair.

Being around Max while he is working has given me a new kind of respect for him. After all, *he* seems to have managed to avoid the Box of working in an office. Even during the most routine vet visits in which he is just doing things like pre-purchase exams, I enjoy seeing the different farms and horses. Now and then, though, something unpleasant will happen. Like when we were called to check out a pony that a man had just bought for his daughter—shipped all the way from Florida—and Max asked, "Why didn't you tell me he'd had colic surgery before?"

"He hasn't had surgery."

"Oh yes, he has."

A flurry of discussion about the pony ensues, ending with the father sputtering, "The vet that did the PPE down there didn't say anything about that!"

"Well, I don't know about other vet. I can only report what I see," says Max.

Then the guy gets in Max's face, yelling at him like it's my boy-friend's fault. Max is very cool, stepping back a few paces and he says in a very dispassionate way how it's unfortunate. He notes some of the possible long-term problems associated with colic surgery. I can tell that the fact the father's been taken for a fast one is eating out the guy's heart and this asshole is taking it out at Max. Eventually, I can't contain myself and I step between the two of them.

"Look, it's not his fault," I say. I nearly say, "It's not his fault you got screwed over buying your dumb kid's pony," but I manage to swallow those last few words.

"What are you, his bodyguard?" says the father.

"Simon, please." Max's voice is cool, almost friendly, but the pressure of his hand on my arm as he moves me to the side says something different. He manages to calm the man down before we leave.

I feel sorry for the pony, a small chestnut that's been bought for a young girl to win ribbons. He looks very fancy and I can see how a pleading girl could make the parents rely more on feeling than sense to buy it.

"It always bothers me to see the work of an unethical colleague," says Max of the guy who vetted the pony as sound. "Simon, don't try to raise the stakes of an encounter like that."

"I was just mad."

"I know, killer, I could see your neck turning purple," says Max.

For the most part, though, everyone likes Max, which is something I also sort of envy about him. The last time he was over at the farm, he was giving Maggie her vaccinations and softly singing "Maggie May" by Rod Stewart (which Maggie is of course named after). Megan was giggling and flirting with him, saying Max has such a good voice (the vet at my old stable used to favor out-of-tune whistling when he was working).

After he left, Megan said to Cynthia. "He is *so* cute. Don't tell Ricky I said that. No harm in looking, right?"

Cynthia said, "Well, I never had a guy that didn't look at other girls." Then she looked over at me. "Do you have something bad to say about Rod Stewart?"

"Nah, he's not punk or New Wave or anything, but I'm actually okay with Rod," I said. Which I am. He is non-stoner classic rock I can actually handle.

When we get back to Max's house after working one day, like usual, I put on some (real) music—Blondie. He puts his arms around my waist and gently pulls me away from fiddling with the player.

It actually takes me a few long seconds to realize he is dancing with me and another few seconds to realize that I've never actually danced with a guy before. Or with many girls, either, since I always refused to go to stuff like horrible eighth-grade dances and prom. I say as much to Max, explaining why I'm so terrible. He laughs.

"You're taller than me so regardless of whether you know what you're doing or not you'll have to lead. As terrifying as that prospect may be for me."

"Okay, I'm used to leading, just not while dancing."

"I would have thought you knew how to dance, what with your obsession with music and all."

"Listening, not dancing. Besides, most of the music I like isn't exactly what they play to bump and grind to." I realize that Max actually knows how to dance—I mean, really dance, not just shuffle around.

"No prom?"

"God no, what girl would go with me?"

"I went."

"Did you have a girlfriend in high school?"

"Yeah, I did. I was also one of the only Jewish students at my tiny, tiny rural high school. I have to say that being Jewish and gay might have been more of a novelty than the rest of the student body could have processed."

"Everyone already knew about me."

"Not everyone is as brave as you, Simon."

"It wasn't bravery. I have no choice."

"I mean, it's not like—"

"I'm not obvious? Some people might disagree with you—obvious is in the eye of the beholder, I guess. I was just a weird kid and no one would have gone to any dance with me regardless. Not even you, apparently, in high school."

By the end of "The Tide Is High," I've sort of got the hang of this dancing thing but two songs in a row would just be too embarrassing, given my skill set, so I just give up and rest my head in the crook of Max's shoulder and kiss his neck. His cheek scratches my skin slightly—uncharacteristically for Max, he hasn't shaved in a day or two so he has stubble. I can feel my heart beating against him and for a brief second there is that stop-motion sense I also get when I'm going cross-country or something like that. Then I pick him up, drag him to the sofa and start play-wrestling with him like I always do—which is something that is familiar for me and somehow easier than just standing there. I pin him easily (years of practice, fighting my brother). For all of his weight-lifting and running and healthy living, I'm still stronger than Max. Only unlike when I'm trying to kick my brother's ass, then I release Max and let him pull himself on top of me. I feel the outline of his jeans press against mine and start undoing his belt buckle, which I can accomplish with one hand by now.

Sometimes I can't quite believe that Max is real, given how things were well, so *not* happening in high school. My brother lost his virginity when he was *fourteen*. That's four additional years he's had that I've not, being seriously sexually active. Not that I'm competitive or anything. So I need to make up for lost time.

My day off ends at 4 p.m.—I'm on night duty—and Max insists on driving me to the barn. Even though I've gotten more used to the cold, the darkness is unusually frigid. In the car, which is just beginning to warm up again, I don't look forward to the extra time I'll need to spend rotating the clipped horses' blankets to their very heaviest, or putting on an extra blanket in the case of the more fragile Thoroughbred and Arabian crosses. I especially don't look forward to the coldness of my under-heated apartment, even though I do have *A Clash of Kings* (from the *Game of Thrones* series) to read when I'm done. But when I enter the barn alone and smell the horses and hear them snorting I forget the warmth that I've left and their body heat warms my hands.

Fortune's head is hanging over the fence as he eagerly waits to be taken in for his nighttime grain. He practically charges me, he's so happy to see me, but I don't care because at least he's by the gate and didn't make me stomp through the frozen mud to get to him. The lights of the barn are dim, a very light snow is already falling (even though people have been saying all day it's too cold to snow) and night is falling fast, so I have to hurry.

22

I DON'T THINK IT'S PHYSICAL

Daniel is a great believer in the value of good breeding, so when he finds a six-year-old Morgan gelding with what he says has great bloodlines, he snaps him up immediately.

I know nothing about Morgans—I haven't ridden many purebred ones, only a few crosses, but I love the orangey tomato soup color of this guy.

"He's like Florence," I say. And I try to explain to Daniel about Florence and the Machine, one of the most awesome bands in the world, and tell him a little bit about my favorite song of theirs, "A Kiss With a Fist." I feel a little weird talking about music with Daniel but he seems to be cool about contemporary culture for an old guy. I talk about how Florence is known for her red hair as well as her stage presence.

"Well, we can't name him Florence," says Daniel. "Or 'A Kiss with a Fist.'"

The guy has been through quite a few names, apparently, as he's changed hands, so we decide to call him "Addicted to Love," (Ted for short) after another of Florence's famous songs, a cover of an old Robert Palmer tune.

"He bucks," says Daniel. "That's why he was so cheap. Morgans are very popular around here with riders at the lower levels. I can't resist a bargain, though, so I thought we could knock some sense into him. Of course, that sentiment is how I broke my arm when I was younger."

I get his meaning. "I'll get my helmet—and my safety vest."

Ted's reputation is not unjustified. Despite my lunging the hell out of him, he has some high-quality, serious bronco bucks in him when I get on his back. While he'll give me a decent walk, trot, canter, it's when he is going smoothly that he decides to give his best impression of a rodeo bronc. He's fast and when he's not trying to unseat me his color and his light build makes me feel like I'm riding a flame, all 15.2h of him, which is a much smaller mount than I usually prefer.

"When we get the PPE, we'll see if something physical is causing the bucking," says Daniel, "Although his last owner was honest with me and said they had him checked out. Anyway, he's on trial, so we'll see what we can do with him."

I don't think it's physical, either, since the bucking goes away after we give him something to keep his mind busy, like going over some low jumps. If he was hurting, his gaits and attitude should grow worse and not better. He's just ornery, I decide. I don't hold that against him, although when he tries to rub me off on the fence at one point, I do say, "Oh no the hell you don't, you little shit," making Daniel laugh.

I work Ted for about twenty minutes every day in the morning—not wanting to tax his brain too much but not wanting him to forget me, either. What's really bad and probably why his previous owners got rid of him is that he will, every now and then, give a little rear in protest. I know to lean forward fast to balance myself so I'm not too worried about getting flipped but I know we have a long ways to go until he's rideable by anyone other than myself. Ted gets better every time, less resistant and more willing to do what I'm asking him, which isn't really much.

Riding Ted takes all of my brainpower and I don't notice Daniel watching me until the end of our latest training session together.

"Max is here for the PPE," he says, and I look up, startled to see Max staring at me, looking even paler than usual.

Ted throws a buck but I stay on and I don't get off until he is somewhat mannerly.

"Careful, Simon," says Max, trying to force a laugh.

"Oh, don't worry about my working student, doc, he's eighteen and bounces, right Simon? Going to live forever?"

"Yup," I say, cheerfully, avoiding Max's eye.

The horse checks out sound and Max is even more cool and clinical than usual as he gives the rundown about the gelding. He says there is nothing physically wrong with Ted, just as we suspected.

"You scare me sometimes," says Max when we're alone together a few nights later.

"He was so much better today, so good, only a single buck or two," I explain. It actually is the most satisfying feeling in the world when I can see progress like that, even though I know Ted is decidedly a work-in-progress. "I like him. Can kind of relate to him. He reminds me of me when I was a kid."

"You're still a kid, Simon."

"A much younger kid, then. Max, this is what I do. Besides, he is a great horse. He's put together well and has great breeding and wouldn't you hate to see him left, probably sent someplace bad, because no one would train him properly? He's not mean, he's just been in bad—I mean, clueless—hands. The people were scared of him who had him before and let him get away with the crap he's pulling now."

I sound like Daniel—good breeding is all—again, sometimes I wonder if Daniel's knowledge of breeding and my mother's short but brilliant show career is why he's trusted me so much.

"I can't help but worry about you, Simon, it's my nature."

I start to kiss Max, because I've said as much as I want to say about this subject tonight. I pull him close to me. I slide my arms around his waist, which, for all of his complaining about his weight, feels tapered and muscular in my hands. But he resists.

"Look, Simon, I know you think you're immortal…"

That makes me impatient on a number of levels, physically for one, because I've waited all day to be here, but also because of what he is saying. "Max, I've been on a horse since before I could walk. I don't think I'm immortal and I'm not as stupid as you think I am. I watch Daniel hobble around all day on his hip. But then again, for a guy who's seventy-plus, there are plenty of them with busted hips from never having left their armchair and he's actually in pretty good shape. How many people his age do you know who regularly jump four feet? I'd rather be broken up, if I have to be, doing something I love, than doing nothing."

The truth is, right at this moment, I do kind of think that anything happening to me is impossible because I feel so strong, alive, and healthy but my mind does know differently as a kind of theoretical, intellectual possibility in the future. But I figure I've always landed on my feet up until this point, so I'm going to keep throwing the dice until I don't.

"Simon, I'm just asking you to promise me to be careful."

"Max, as soon as you start making promises like that, you're sunk as a rider," I say. "Do you understand? Besides, you could get hurt doing the work that you do, you could get kicked or worse. And it's not like you're playing golf or tennis on your off hours, there are plenty of people who would say you're dumb to even get on a horse and jump at all, the type of people who don't think horses should be ridden altogether and we should all just, I don't know, all be playing video games or something because those things are safe." Nothing seems more dangerously boring to me than to not ride at all.

Max is quiet for a bit. "I understand what you're saying, it just seems a question of proportional risk. I guess that's why I've never had much of a need to jump very high outside of an arena. To be brutally honest, those courses that they have above Preliminary level cross-country scare the hell out of me and seem excessive. For the horse as well as the rider."

"Max, this is something I *need* to do—I need to make Ted see sense, I need to qualify for Intermediate. And then, hopefully Advanced, and then…well, to go as far as I can with this."

"I see that, Simon, I just can't help liking your brains where they are, in your skull." And then he starts to kiss me, but I pull away.

"I've thought about this a lot Max, even though you don't think I have. But if I was ever hurt, the first thought I'd have—besides if my horse was okay—was when I could get back in the saddle again. Fortunately, I haven't been." I knock on the cheap wood of the dresser beside the bed. "I've always been lucky that way. But even if I was hurt, I could never hold it against the horse or riding. Even the worst, the very worst a horse could do to me is nothing as bad as what I've thought about doing to myself during my darkest times, like when it got really bad in high school. Horses and riding have saved my life already thousands and thousands of times, even horses like Ted, so whatever comes, I wouldn't and couldn't hold it against horses, they've already give me so much."

I literally don't remember the last time I cried and my eyes are dry now although my throat feels weird and tight. That was more than I intended to say and I'm sort of scared because it's the most serious thing I've said to Max, ever. I try to make a joke to cover up the emotion. "So, when you say to be safe, well, Max, to quote the title of the song of the great poet Meatloaf, 'I'd Do Anything for Love (But I Won't Do That.)'"

"Okay, Simon. I won't bring up the subject again," Max says. And the catch and the tightness in my chest and throat releases and I feel kind of a relaxation and rush of freedom that makes me realize how much hidden tension I still sometimes hold in my body, despite my best efforts to hide it even from myself.

I'm not sure Max understands everything I've said but at least he understands enough. I know I'm not supposed to think this way, but truthfully I think the only thing that matters in the world in the long run is horses and music and my own neck is a decided third place in that pecking order.

The next morning Ted bucks on the lunge line but not with me on him. A huge improvement. And not even a whisper of a rear. Daniel watches the end of our schooling session and as I take him over the last tiny vertical, he says, "I think we may have a horse underneath all that attitude. Nice work, Shaughnessy. That's what a lack of fear—and anger—can accomplish."

I feel very flattered.

"I remember when I used to have no fear," says Daniel.

"Well, I am afraid of some stuff," I say, dismounting. "Just not any horses."

23

IMMUNE

It's around that time of year that everyone gets sick at a barn. Not the horses (the colicking season is usually when the weather begins to change, not when it is coldest). The people. First, Megan catches a nasty cold from the grubby little brats that smear their mucus on her whenever she tightens their girths and adjusts their stirrups. Cynthia catches it from Megan. Daniel gets sick with the flu, probably from standing outside all day teaching. I do not, of course, get sick, since I never get sick. My mother swears that I never got sick or cried even as a baby; I was never troublesome then and very quiet but I've made up for it since.

Finally, even Max gets sick. He says he isn't until he can deny it no longer. "Jesus, Max, did you go to work like that?" I say when he greets me at the door.

Despite it all, I can smell that he's cooking something for my dinner and I feel horrifically guilty for my hunger—as well as the fact that I've brought laundry to do at his place. He says he's going to lie down. I follow him and lie down on top of him. "Simon, don't kiss me. You can't afford to miss work."

"I thought you've been insisting that you weren't sick for the past two days."

"I concede defeat. Don't—"

"I told you I never get sick, don't worry about it. Your forehead is hot." I vaguely feel as if I should do something to take care of him but I'm not sure what. Whenever Sean would get sick (which was rare) Mom would just tell him to stay in his room until he got better and douse him with ginger ale and toast, trying to avoid getting too close to him because she couldn't afford to catch anything. Like literally, not afford it financially, not just metaphorically. My usual method of dealing with my brother's sickness was strategic wisecracking and sarcasm to motivate him to get well as soon as possible so he could take his revenge out on me. A couple of times when he was knocked out from cough syrup when we were really little I drew on his face with permanent magic marker and he's never quite forgotten that.

I offer to take Max's temperature but he says he doesn't have a human thermometer, only one for horses in his truck because if he doesn't take his temperature and doesn't know what it is then he can't be sick. I can't argue with such brilliant logic. I throw a blanket over him. Even though he is sweaty, his hands feel cold. I rummage through the refrigerator to find something for him since he says he's felt too queasy to eat all day.

Of course everything in Max's refrigerator is neatly put away in containers and labeled with dates like specimens in a lab. I do find some chicken soup and manage to heat up some after ruining only one bowl because I don't check to see if the dish is microwave-safe. I also make some tea, which is pretty much the one thing I do know how to make versus nuke.

I sort of force-feed both to him and Max thanks me with unreasonable graciousness. I offer to make him some juice but he tells me not to bother.

"That machine cost four hundred dollars," he says. "I'm not sure I trust you with it."

"Gee, thanks. What the hell does a four hundred dollar blender do anyway? Levitate? Sexually service you when I'm not around? And people criticized me for spending four thousand bucks on a horse that couldn't allegedly do anything."

"I heard you explode something in the microwave."

"That is your fault for having fancy plates."

Max tells me to go and eat the chili he made for me because he's not going to be much fun tonight but I just put my arms around him, listening to his breathing. Eventually he relaxes into me. "What did I ever do to get so lucky? Sometimes I can't even believe you are real, ever since that first time I saw you...I thought just looking at you was enough, you were so beautiful."

"Max, you're not wearing your glasses," I say, kind of uncomfortable. I know he's not fully aware that he's talking aloud.

"Simon, I love you so much," he says, and pulls me closer to him.

Max is slightly delirious from the fever but I feel slightly cold yet sweaty in a way I know has nothing to do with illness. I've been telling myself all the while that I've been accumulating information this year for my riding career, not putting down roots, and keeping myself as unattached as possible so I can pull up and go where I need to go when the year has ended. But you know that when there is no place you'd rather be even when someone is lying sick beside you, that it's an awful lot like love.

I call Megan and tell her I'm going to be at the barn around 8 a.m., which is late for me. I want to stay late and leave when Max goes to work because I want to make sure he's okay.

Megan threatens to refuse to do anything until I tell her where and with whom I am staying, but I call her bluff and eventually she agrees.

I suppose it's kind of wrong and an invasion of privacy although I tell myself we're at the point of "what's mine is yours and yours is mine" in the relationship. But as Max sleeps, I snoop around some more. Max doesn't have any personal photographs on display (to be fair, neither do I in my hovel) but there is a Tupperware container of a few pictures, shoved in a corner of the bookcase, half-forgotten. I look through them.

A younger Max, evidently at a Pony Club rally, on what looks like a big Clydesdale cross. Max jumping on the same horse (nice release, leg slipped back somewhat but nothing terrible). Max playing guitar with some high school or college band. Max at some a fraternity gig in a t-shirt with Greek letters on it. He's heavier but not really fat like he said he was in college and has stubble. And the one that interests me the most, Max with his arm around the waist of some guy, a stocky blond guy with very short hair about the same height as Max. A similar fraternity brother-type. Based on the scenery in the background, though, I think it's from vet school. It's not exactly a romantic shot, but it's enough. No pictures of family, not even his younger sister.

The next morning, Max seems to only have a vague and fuzzy memory of the night before. He inspects the damage I did to the kitchen, throws away the broken bowl, cleans up the counter, carefully stores and labels the food I didn't eat last night and says he feels well enough to work. Then he makes me pancakes (I'm starving since I had no dinner) and whizzes up for himself one of those hideous green concoctions of spinach and kale and protein powder in his overpriced machine.

"You do look more human," I say.

"Would you like some more pancakes with that maple syrup and butter? How do you eat like that and stay so skinny, Simon?"

"What? Is that too much?"

"My heart and my teeth hurt just looking at it."

I shrug. "I've never been able to put on weight, I've always been that way."

"You're lucky you're cute to keep me from killing you when you say stuff like that."

"You're not fat. I like the way you look," I say.

"Yes, but I have to work at it." I offer Max a bite of my food. Initially, he refuses, and then he allows me to feed him some of it. "I'm a decent cook," he says, proclaiming it to be acceptable. "I think I will have to skip working out today."

"I'm shocked, doctor."

"I don't normally. Miss one day and the whole routine runs the risk of breaking down and descending into chaos. Like I said, you're lucky you don't have to work out like I do to stay in shape."

"I am lucky," I say. I don't use the other word that begins with an L from last night, though. Perhaps it was just his temperature talking, I think.

"Of course, you've been doing a pretty good job of breaking down my routine."

"I think I should say I'm sorry but I'm not. I'm not really bad, I'm more chaotic neutral than chaotic evil."

"Chaotic what?"

"You know, the alignment system from Dungeons & Dragons. I played it sometimes with the guys from the math and chess club."

"Now all of your secrets are revealed. You really were a dork in high school, despite all of your street brawling."

"You'd definitely be lawful good, Max." I roll my eyes.

"I never played that game but I have a feeling I would be, just from the way you say the phrase. Do they have a chaotic good category? Because despite how hard you try to be bad, Simon, I would place you more in that grouping."

They do, actually, but I just make a face at him. He kisses me and tells me I'm sweet, a word he usually doesn't use when talking about me. I'm not sure if he's still teasing me about all the sugar I've just ingested.

When I go out with Max on his rounds my next day off, the first farm we go to is a boarding barn. The call should be pretty routine, just some hock injections and a dental, but the atmosphere has a kind of frenzied chaos in the air that is anything but normal. Apparently, the barn owners left a few days ago, after the appointment was scheduled, without telling anyone—money troubles. Of course, given that the bankrupt owners were planning to skip town, there isn't enough food or hay or shavings left so everyone is pretty much making do the best they can before they can find somewhere else to go—not easy to do without notice. It's a nice barn, too, not exactly a show barn, but other than the emptiness of the grain room, it looks pretty well-kept.

"Thank goodness one of my friends with property is going to take my horses until I can find somewhere else," says an older lady with three (an off-the-track baby, a retired show jumper, and a big pony for her kid). "We're going to have to call animal control about the owners' horses, though." She nods at a handful of horses out in the field.

"That's a shame," says Max, because we all know that nothing good can come to horses that are older, haven't been worked for years, and aren't good for much more than eating hay. Aren't even particularly attractive from the looks of it.

"And the dog," she says. "The dog belonged to them, too—Jig."

Jig is a big black-and-white animal that kind of looks like a border collie. Well, border collie-ish. One of his ears seems to have been broken because he can't raise it—it's permanently cocked to one side. His blue eyes look crossed, which gives him a slightly demented appearance. But he seems friendly enough—he licks my hand when I pet him and just for that little bit of kindness on my part he starts following me around, nudging me in the calves.

"He likes me," I say.

"He's trying to herd you and keep you in line, Simon," says Max. "Good luck with that." I'm not sure if he's talking to the dog or to me.

"He's a nice dog," agrees the lady. "Friendly but ugly as sin. Like I said, a shame."

Since there is no paying work here, Max gets ready to go, first calling his boss to explain the situation.

"Simon?"

"Yes?"

"What is that dog doing in my car?"

"Max, you know no one will want an older dog with a broken ear like this. And he's a border collie, he belongs on a farm, not in some house with a bunch of brats, which is the best of what he'll get if he's adopted out by the humane society. And probably worse."

"Simon, that is not a border collie. That is a dog made up of some border collie spare parts."

"No one will notice if I take him to the farm. He'll blend in." I haven't had a dog since I was a kid and I have been kind of wanting to have one around for a while, so this seems like a good idea.

"Blend in with what? For a horse person, Daniel has shown a remark-ably restrained attitude in terms of collecting useless animals." It is true that there are no goats or minis or any of the other weird, unrideable livestock that we occasionally see at other barns. "Simon, you know as well as I do that Daniel will certainly notice and you can't pick up every stray animal and take all of them home with you. As you've seen, I don't have pets because I don't have the time or money for them."

"I'm not picking up every stray animal—I mean, it's not like I'm taking home the horses that have been left, I mean that *would* be crazy."

"Oh yes, *that* would be crazy."

Somehow, I manage to get home with the dog. I let Jig out and then take him up to my room to sleep for the first night to see how he is— he kind of runs around in circles for a bit at the newness of it all and then falls asleep on a rug by my bed. I get up early so I can keep an eye on him alone while doing chores but then I get distracted filling buckets.

Suddenly, I hear screaming. "Get away from my pony!"

I walk over and laugh. Jig apparently pinned Maggie to the wall as she was trying to make her way into the grain room. The grain is still secured in locked bins but I guess she was hoping to find some extra bits and pieces on the floor before we swept it. Clearly, whatever bits of Jig that are border collie have decided Maggie's behavior is unacceptable so he's standing there, barking, not letting her move a muscle.

I call him off, telling him "no," and he runs away, still barking. Maggie trots off into her open stall with a clear *oh shit, I have met my match* expression on her face.

"Simon, it's not funny," says Megan. But even Cynthia is laughing.

"Shaughnessy, what the hell is this dog doing on my property?" I hear Daniel's voice belting from the doorway. "I know this is your doing."

Despite the fact that he does look kind of crazy and askew, Jig seems to know enough to run away when you shout at him, so even though Daniel does chew me out, the dog kind of gets left on the farm to his own devices because he can't catch him. Fortunately, Jig seems to really like Daniel for some reason, and he follows Daniel around, barking, and occasionally lying down with his nose between his paws, watching my boss worshipfully. I get Jig his shots but he just kind of acts as our collective dog until the weather gets even colder, when Daniel starts taking him into his house at night. I think Daniel really likes the dog although he never admits it. Whenever the dog barks he mutters something about how he wouldn't trust me any farther than he could throw me. All in all, I consider it a pretty successful rescue, especially since Maggie is much more under control now—Jig seems to regard her as his special project to keep in line.

I try to teach the dog to go over some of the jumps since he seems athletic enough, but he's more interested in running around them than over them and only clears them accidentally, when they get in his way. When he bumps into one of the standards, Daniel says, "Dog training, Shaughnessy? Don't quit your day job."

I don't ask Max about the blond guy in the photograph right away. I bide my time until one night when he's making us dinner. It's some kind of beef thing, which he knows I like even though he refuses to keep ketchup in the house, which is what I normally slather on anything coming from a steer. ("Because putting ketchup on good meat is like stabbing me in the heart," he says, even though I protest that ketchup is like the universal condiment that makes just about everything better.)

"So who is the blond dude in that photo you kept," I say, stabbing meaty pieces in the skillet, ignoring him as he attempts to swat me away. I'm hungry. The meat burns my mouth but I don't care.

"What photograph?" When I tell him, Max's mouth tightens. "So you've been snooping around when I haven't been looking?"

"In a word, yes. You don't have to tell me, but I thought I'd ask." He's still so focused on his cooking, just to annoy him, I put my hands in his back pockets so he can really feel me grab his ass but he manages to shake me off.

He's silent for a few beats and says, "David's just my friend. That picture was taken years ago, killer, don't worry about it." Max turns off the flame and begins plating the food, giving me more of every-thing except the vegetables, which he knows I don't really eat.

"I'm not jealous, I'm just curious. It's not like I'm mad that you have more of a past than me. I expect it—I'm just curious."

"I told you about David, I visited him and his wife and kids over Thanksgiving."

"Well, I didn't know his name until now. Are you sure we're talking about the same person?" Max describes him well enough so I guess we are.

I eat while Max picks at his food a bit and finally he says, "We did have a relationship," and pours himself some wine.

"You said he was straight? Oh, he's one of those kinds of *straight* guys," I say, smirking.

"It's more complicated than that."

"I'm not a complicated person, Max, so to me it's very simple."

"It's been over for more than two years, so it's none of your business, Simon."

"Okay, fine," I say. "But you should have told me about that when you visited him over Thanksgiving."

"That was at his house, with his wife and kids there, Simon. Nothing happened."

"You don't have to defend yourself to me, Max."

Max puts his hand on my hand and sort of plays with my fingers. "Simon, I love you."

I look away, not wanting to say "I love you" back for the first time at this particular moment.

"I'm just not very proud of the fact that—well, that I had a relationship with a guy when he was married. It was an on and off-again thing for years. But it's been off for a while now. We were in different states so it hardly amounted to much of a relationship at all even when we were—sort of— together."

"Friends with benefits?" I say. I want to say, "A kind of a fuck buddy thing," because I have been there, even in high school, but I don't.

"If you want to put it that way."

"For how long?"

"Oh, I don't know. I guess five years."

"Five years? I couldn't even put up with that crap for five months."

"No, I don't suppose you could," says Max. "Simon, I should have told you before I visited him. Now it looks underhanded, but like I said I'm just not very proud of it. Not my finest moment. And I've never really spoken about it to anyone. I guess because I know his wife, she's very nice and anyway, like I said, not my finest moment. For five years."

"A moment that lasts five years?"

"You know me, killer, that's about as fast as I move. I'm not very good at leaving things, even bad things."

"I feel sorriest for her."

"For some people, things are more complicated than for you, Simon—"

"Oh, stop with the complicated, Max. 'Complicated' is what people say when they know they're doing something wrong and don't want to change it." I think of how sometimes people say that in a negative way about a horse. He's a complicated mount, usually means, "He's talented but I'm scared of him because I'm not a good enough rider to handle him."

"Whatever is going on now, it's between David and his wife, not me or you."

"I just hate how many stupid lies people tell," I say, pushing away my food because I'm no longer hungry. I go into the living room and turn on the television. Hockey's on and although Sean and I never followed it as closely as baseball, football, and basketball, we still always rooted for the Bruins and the violence of the game suits my mood right now. Max follows me and tells me he loves me a second time but I don't respond, even though I know by caring so much I'm telling him, kind of (at least in my mind) that I do. I trust him and I believe him but the situation still annoys me, even though it is past, and I tell myself I have to let it be.

I'm not jealous, I swear I'm not, it's just—kind of like the whole being-part-of-a-fraternity thing, it sometimes annoys me how much Max will take. Like, he says his frat in college tolerated him, sure, but I can just picture it was in a totally fake and self-congratulatory way, like, "Oh, we're so progressive, we have like, a gay guy who is a member." And that's also why I get so riled up when he's all, "You should be in college, you're wasting your potential." How much did Max waste, how much did he sacrifice of himself?

Max offers me a glass of wine. I still hate its taste, despite his best efforts to refine my palate. Besides, even though I really do want to forget it, I know that wine is not my way of forgetting and never will be.

24

THEY DON'T KILL THE FOX

The cold really starts to annoy me, not so much for how it makes me feel but because it makes the ground hard and limits how much we can ride. The sand in the indoor arena is soft and there are still places spongy enough to jump and gallop on the trails on warmer days—unusually, for Vermont there hasn't been a big snow yet—but it's cold enough most days to make the ground hard and unforgiving for serious cross-country work.

Cynthia says she needs to go home during the week—her father just bought a new horse that he wants her to look at. I'm a little bit surprised that Daniel lets her go but given the weather we haven't had much in the way of lessons. I can also kind of see things from his perspective: Blood Money isn't working out quite as well as Cynthia hoped and maybe this new horse will be more suitable.

For about five minutes I think about purchasing Blood Money but I know I don't have that kind of bank, even if Cynthia did offer me some sort of discount.

But then, Cynthia surprises me because she says, "Wanna come? I'd love to see what you think of the new horse. And my dad and I will be going foxhunting; it's the season down there while up here it is the season for nothing. I can't wait to get away from these horrible temperatures."

Hell, yes. I've done hunter paces and a drop-and-drag but I know that Cynthia has been full-on, real deal foxhunting with unplanned courses and foxes going to ground and everything. Virginia foxhunting is kind of famous for being traditional, versus what was available to me in my neck of the woods in Jersey.

I don't expect Daniel to let me go as well as Cindy but I think he can see the desperation in my eyes when I ask. He agrees, saying that some of the local kids can pick up the slack.

What does surprise me, however, is that when I mention this to Sean, instead of just kind of being all blasé or telling me that Cynthia is hot again as I expect, he turns kind of serious. "*Vernon Jackson* is her father? That guy on cable TV?"

"Yeah, he's some sort of political talking head or whatever."

"*You're* going to *his house*? Don't you watch the news?"

"From what Cindy has been saying, I don't think it's as much a house as a kinda mansion with a stable out back. I guess I'll find out."

"That guy is a bad dude." I don't know when Sean got so political. Every now and then since he's been going to college he'll get agitated about some issue although his passion usually dissipates just as quickly as it starts. But he tells me to look at some TV clips on YouTube on my phone of the guy before I go there, so I say, sure, whatever.

When I first flip through I see what I expect since I'm vaguely aware that Vernon Jackson is conservative. Negative stuff about abortion and immigration. Following link after link, I find what Sean really wants me to see. I have to give it to Cynthia's dad, this guy is pretty slick; it's not the usual wacko stuff about perversion and such that I almost find funny. He's youngish-looking for someone's father and he goes on about traditional values and religious freedom and the right of people of faith and is very polite and smiling and never raises his voice at all. But he even uses the word *sodomy*, at one point for Christ's sake. Who even says that word anymore? And AIDS of course, which is pretty funny to me because for all practical purposes until I came out here, I was the chastest person in my high school by a long shot.

I'm not surprised exactly. Although I do think it's pretty weird that given how long Cynthia has ridden it is pretty statistically improbable that she hasn't had at least one male trainer that's gay. I'm not counting myself and the little bit of help I've offered her, since I wouldn't really consider myself a trainer at this point of my career, you know what I mean.

Of course, what he says isn't anything I haven't heard before, just kind of what guys used to say about me, usually behind my back and occasionally to my face (which usually never ended well for either of us) only with the occasional five-dollar SAT words and rationalizations sprinkled in here and there. But it still pisses me off. Funny, someone once said that the older you get, the less you care about what people say but for me that sure as hell isn't true. For one thing, it isn't just about me anymore, it's also about Max, and I swear if anyone ever tried to say something about him, anything I've ever done to anyone to protect myself would look like nothing in comparison.

Sean says he doesn't think I should go. On one hand, I see his point. On the other hand, it seems pretty unfair to deny myself fox-hunting when I'm going as Cindy's friend. After all, Cindy has never done anything to hurt me, just annoy me. I'm not going to hold the odd Taylor Swift song she sings to herself as she works against her as a grudge.

As an argument I point out that if I only rode at the barns of people I agreed with one hundred percent I would still be at mom's barn, and even that is questionable. Sean says it's different and I agree but there is a tiny voice inside of me that says I will just ignore all the bullshit because I want to give real foxhunting a try and see what kind of a threat this new horse of Cindy's is to me in the future. I'm glad to have seen the clips so I know to steel myself and not let anything hurt me, just shut down as much as possible whenever necessary.

I've never flown first class before. For all of the superiority I've felt towards Cindy about the fact that she's never jumped as high and fast as me and never been to a horse show without a trainer, never even braided her own horse until she came to Daniel's, I know she's been all over the world. A car service picks us up and drops us at the airport. Cindy sits in the back, chirping on about how the hunting has been great this year and how much she's missed it and I wonder if I've misjudged her as a complete and total wuss. But then again, it's all what you're used to, I guess, in terms of what you're afraid of, more so than any real risk.

The whole thing feels really weird because Cindy is paying for everything and says, "Don't mention it," like it's pocket change. I know some of her friends have flown her to various places back and forth on their dime but there is part of me that still feels like it's wrong because I can't reciprocate (other than giving her jumping advice). When I told Megan I was going, she shrugged and said she didn't care because she and Ricky already had plans. But I knew, despite the fact that she's grown friendlier with Cynthia, that this gets me another check in her book as a class traitor in the horse world. Of course, Megan doesn't care about the other stuff, the political stuff; other than knowing who the president is, I don't think Megan thinks about politics at all.

Oddly enough, it was my mother who approved of the trip, saying, "If you really want a career in the business, you'll have to learn to accept gifts from rich people graciously, so this is a good time to start learning."

I don't have a fear of flying but the flight from the tiny airport is late and we still have to wait in the crowds of milling people. Cynthia tries to talk to me but I hate the crush and end up sitting on the carpeted floor, sweatshirt pulled over my ears, listening to the Killers and texting Max just to get away from the crowds. Max is working though, so I can't even communicate with him much here.

Another car—this time, sent from the farm where Cynthia lives—picks us up when we land and I spend most of the ride ignoring Cynthia as much as I can while still being polite. I have my nose pressed up against the glass; I'm looking at the rolling green hills. It's much warmer down here and I already feel excited to ride, less creaky in my joints despite being folded up in the plane. At Cindy's home, there is an elaborate security system with a watchful video camera eye and a code the driver has to punch in. Cynthia says, "My father has gotten death threats, soooo…" as a way of explanation of the armored look of the place on the outside. She sounds kind of proud.

The house is pretty much like every fantasy I've ever had about horses and riding. It's this huge, sprawling, white place that yeah, does look rather new or whatever, but is attached to a massive stable and courtyard like something out of Downton fucking Abbey which my friend Heather would sometimes force me to watch.

As we pull in, a man on horseback trots past us on a large, bay warmblood.

"Dad, you're not riding MY new HORSE?" screams Cynthia, giggling, rolling down the window, almost like she's flirting with him.

With a start, I recognize the guy from the YouTube clips I saw. It's really the first time I've ever seen a semi-major celebrity on television first and then in the flesh. "No, this is another new one. This one is mine."

"Good, I don't want you to mess up my new horse by riding it. This is my friend Simon. He can try out mine to see if it's worth what you paid. Simon's aiming to ride Intermediate level by the end of the year. He's a really good rider."

"As you can see, my daughter has a lot of confidence in me as a horseman. I just pay for everything." Objectively, I evaluate her father's seat. He seems to ride okay, for a middle-aged dude who isn't a professional rider. "You're coming hunting with us?" he asks me.

"Yes, I'm looking forward to it. I've just done drag hunts before," I say.

"That hardly counts, but if you're riding Preliminary you should be able to keep up."

"Dad, Simon's won tons of showjumping awards. He regularly jumps five feet on his own horse. He's the guy I told you about, the one who has been helping me."

Her father's gaze shifts to me. I kind of wish I could blend in with the upholstery, not because I'm afraid Cynthia has been overselling me as a rider but because of the fact that she's been talking about me at all to her father, which feels weird. I know I look kind of shabby and nondescript and I hope that's enough to make him ignore me. I'm glad it's too warm for my heavy anarchist hoodie here. I'm still not quite sure what being an anarchist means but I have a feeling he wouldn't like it.

The driver pulls away and we go in. Cynthia says she has to shower and change even though I immediately want to stretch my legs and go riding. She says I can walk around and look at things but first she calls the security people to warn them that I'll be milling about.

"Is that to make sure they don't let the dogs on me or something?" I joke.

"You're so silly, Simon."

I change into my breeches and (polished) boots quickly and one of the nice polo shirts that I've borrowed from Max. We're different sizes but it fits well enough.

There are dogs on the property, of course—hounds—and they're not let loose. They seem pretty friendly when I pass the kennels. I've always loved dogs but because money has been tight and always focused on our horses, I haven't had one since I was a kid. Although we have Jig at the farm, it hasn't worked out in a way that he's really mine. Even though I know I shouldn't, I stick my hand through the wire fence to pet them. They lick my hand. I kneel down for a long time, watching them until I feel kind of comforted and relaxed as they climb over one another to get at me. They're hoping I have food. I don't, just the candy I keep in my pockets for the horses.

The stables look nicer than any house I've ever lived in over the course of my whole life, including the not-too-shabby house I inhabited with my brother when my mom was still married to my rich asshole dad. The wood is new but carefully distressed to look old. The box stalls are huge and airy. Things smell more of grain and shavings than manure and dust unlike even the best barns I've been in before. All the horses have matching blankets and leather halters. Not only are there multiple tack rooms, a lounge, a climate-controlled indoor—there is a whole room just devoted to all the ribbons Cynthia and the string have won over the years, a whole room just for the blankets and another room lined with photographs from the past of winners. I see someone in the distance, I assume the trainer, working a chestnut mare. I vaguely recognize the horse from one of Cynthia's pictures as one she has ridden while hunting and I guess he's working out the kinks before she goes out tomorrow.

"You think she's a nice horse?" asks Cynthia, sneaking up behind me. Cynthia's wearing head-to-toe Ariat, which I know that when she is on the circuit is one of her sponsors. It always seems weird how rich people can get sponsors so easily when they don't need them. No one has ever offered to sponsor me. Daniel has warned me it would probably take years on a consistent mount and not to count on anything. Ever.

"I can't believe you have an entire tack room just devoted to Ariat."

"Ariat has been sooo good to me."

To be as honest as the voice in my head, the Ariat sponsorship seems especially odd because Cindy's not that good. I don't mean just compared with myself but also with lots of other riders in general. But without even asking I know it has something to do with being the child of someone famous and the fact that she is blonde, pretty, and rich, which must make for great advertising copy. I know Cynthia can't help any of this, though.

"Let's look at the new guy, let's look at Sam," she says.

The new guy is slightly smaller than Fortune but still powerfully built, a darker liver chestnut with chrome on his face and all four legs. His full show name is No Shenanigans. She looks a bit intimidated by him and tells me to get on first. A groom has already put a dressage saddle on him. I would have preferred to take him over fences after a short warm-up on the flat but it looks like that isn't happening. "My dad found him in Germany," says Cynthia, as if that makes him better.

As soon as I get on this horse, I'm suddenly aware of the fact that I am being regarded and watched in a way that I haven't before, not by people but by the horse; every shift of my seat, practically ever quiver of my skin. After warming up with some stretchy walking and lengthening at the trot, big circles at the canter, I start really riding him. There is virtually no effort involved. He gives me flying lead changes as if he can hear my thoughts.

I don't tell Cindy this as I'm riding but when she asks me what I think, I respond, "I think this horse is smarter than I am. Does he jump as well?"

"He does."

"Well, if he's not spooky or anything out of the ring, I'd say you got a pretty amazing deal."

"I love Blood but it's time I kicked things up another notch. Besides, I've worked hard with her for years but I don't see her getting any farther than she is right now up the levels. You know what I mean."

I think of Fortune and say, "Yes, I do." But I still like her mare.

"My father says it's time to move on. He's—he's not pleased with the way things are going." She sounds slightly scared.

"You don't have to justify yourself to me, Cindy."

"It's not just about me. If I do badly, it reflects on him, on his business. His brand."

If that's what you want to call it.

We play with Sammy a bit more. I'm kind of hoping Cindy will get out his jumping saddle but she just gives him to one of the grooms and shows me around the rest of the stable. She says we don't have time before dinner—we can't be late—and we'll have plenty of jumping tomorrow morning.

"You know about hunting, don't you, Simon? What to wear and everything?"

"I won't wear anything to disgrace you or your family, Cindy, I promise. No weird band T-shirts or anything."

"What you have on looks nice," she says, gesturing to Max's polo. "Where did you get it?" It's kind of an unusual white-and-blue geometric design that I can sort of appreciate as attractive, although more on Max than me since I'd really rather be wearing my Killers T-shirt right now in this alien place.

"Borrowed, not mine," I'm careful to say.

Cynthia gives me a rundown about greeting the huntsman and field master, about having to maintain pace and such, all of which I did know. She shows me the horse I'll be riding, a smallish gelding, a slightly darker blood bay than Cynthia's horse who she says was bought at the same time as Blood Money. "He's Blood's half-brother. I know he doesn't look like much but he loves his job. His name is Kissing Judas."

"Religious names?"

"Yeah, I know, kinda weird? One of my father's things, he likes to have sort of similar names for all of our horses. We just call him Jude, though." The horse looks pretty calm but I know not to be deceived by that; regardless, I'm just excited at the thought of getting out there. I'm actually glad we need to be up well before dawn because I know I'll hardly be able to sleep tonight with the excitement as well as the weirdness of sleeping in a strange place.

We enter the part of the barn that has the tack, feed, and other supplies.

"No Maggie wandering around here," I say.

I feel more comfortable in the barn than the house. Cindy's home is so clean I feel like I'm dirtying it up even after changing into my cleanest street shoes (well, basically work boots with the dirt brushed off). It looks more like a museum and I can see security cameras discretely hidden in odd places. There is even a hall that is purely made of glass windows and mirrors that looks like something from a movie. Cynthia is pretty blasé about all of it, though.

"I can see how transitioning from this to the apartment in Vermont you share with Megan was kind of a shock," I say.

Cindy laughs. "I'm more used to roughing it than you think. Remember I have fox-hunted for a long time. So has my father; we aren't total cream puffs."

I feel so wound-up I'd honestly prefer to skip dinner altogether but I know I'm not getting out of that one. I'm worried I'm not dressed up enough but there is nothing I can do but put on my second, borrowed, non-chewed-up shirt of Max's and hope to be asked as few questions as possible.

I get a better look at Cynthia's father at dinner, now that he's not wearing a helmet or in riding clothes. He doesn't look like most of the talking head politicians on TV: he's blond (losing his hair, but still has enough), tanned, and fit. In fact, his skin has a kind of a weird, taunt quality. His eyes are utterly flat and expressionless and seem to look right through me. I feel vaguely that I'm just in a "slot" of "Cindy's friend" in his eyes, which is comforting because he hardly seems to register my presence and mainly talks to her about the new horse and also a photoshoot connected to her Ariat sponsorship. This is fine because I can just imagine that I've disappeared and blended into the background, just like I used to do at school.

The food they serve is the sort of food I would like if I felt like eating but I just kind of pick at the steak and stuff because I feel so wound up. Of course, Cynthia drinks wine and cuts things up into tiny pieces without putting anything in her mouth. Even if I liked wine, I wouldn't drink right now since I think it's probably good I hold onto the few inhibitions I possess at the moment.

But then Cindy tries to drag me into the conversation, saying what a good rider I am and how much I've helped her. Mr. Jackson pries, politely, not out of any real interest and I talk a little bit about my background in a superficial manner.

Mr. Jackson says, "I saw your mother ride once, years ago. She was a great rider, so elegant despite her youth. She wasn't an eventer, though. She mostly did the hunters, some jumpers, correct?"

"She had us on ponies—my brother and me—practically before we could walk. I grew up on a horse."

"That's pretty rare today."

"Yes, it is. I'm very grateful. If I can ride well at all it is thanks to her," I say. I haven't much thought about it but as I say it, I know it's true.

"Simon can ride just about anything," says Cindy. "I'm sooo envious."

I don't know why she's selling my riding ability to her dad but I just shrug and say that I'm lucky to have a horse that has a big jump.

I get the sense that Mr. Jackson (which is what I've been calling him) does know horses, whatever else you might say of him, and that keeps the conversation alive through the meal. I just shut out the other stuff I know about him.

I check my phone when I return to my room. Sean has sent me a million texts, which is kind of funny because I really think he's not sure I'll still be alive by the end of the night. I respond:

havent let the dogs on me yet
funny asshole
iam ok rlly

I really just want to go out hunting and ignore the social aspects of this visit, as rude as that may be to Cynthia and no matter how I feel about her father. Still, I'm kind of glad that I was rather vague about who Cynthia's dad is when speaking to Max, to avoid having to field even more awkward messages over the course of the weekend that even I would have to answer in more than three words.

The sky is still a greyish purple in the morning. For all of the winter warmth here, it's still very dark. I don't have a special outfit to wear for foxhunting, other than my best stadium attire, but fortunately that's good enough and Cynthia says when she sees me I'll pass muster with the master of the hounds. Her father is in full hunting pinks; Cindy is just wearing a navy coat like myself but with fancy buttons to indicate she is a member of the hunt, too.

Mr. Jackson's hunting horse is a large, safe-looking but well-bred gelding. He doesn't have much chrome but he looks elegantly muscled and powerful. Cynthia sees me admiring him. "That's Filibuster, he was born on the farm, he's been around since I can remember. My father uses him just for hunting and says he's the best horse he's ever ridden."

"Nice. Wait, Filibuster?"

"All of the home-bred horses have kind of, political names rather than religious names. Like Tommy, my father's other horse I showed you yesterday on my little tour? His full name is Thomas Paine."

That makes me think of the Police song "King of Pain," I think, ruefully, which might be an even more appropriate name under the circumstances. I also say, "Seems kinda wrong to name a gelding 'Filly-buster.'" Cynthia giggles.

Other than the fact that the grooms have taken care of the trailering and the tack, it doesn't feel all that different from going to a hunter pace back home until we arrive. Then I see that the hunt is huge—I mean, really huge, to the point I can't even count the number of people involved.

"Holy crap," I whisper to Cynthia.

"Well, this is the height of the season," she says.

I watch the groom tacking up my horse. Like most of the staff, he is small and quick. I feel awkward and ridiculous standing there because I don't remember anyone having done this for me— ever—and I've done it for people countless times myself, back when I was working in high school for the owners with full training board. The tack is absolutely spotless, even the stirrups are immaculate despite the fact I'm about to stick my muddy-soled boots in them.

I look around and see a mix of trailers and various levels of self-care. One lady is actually riding sidesaddle. "Jesus, this is really is like fucking *Downton Abbey* on crack or whatever," I say to Cynthia.

Her father overhears me and laughs. "So I *can* tell you've never *really* hunted."

"Jersey drag hunts and hunter paces don't compare with this," I say, starting a bit inside that he overheard me in an unguarded moment.

"You'll enjoy it. Jude knows what to do. He'll take care of you."

"Oh, Simon doesn't need to be taken care of," says Cynthia. Her horse is a lean chestnut called Penny, bigger and leggier than Blood Money. Cynthia gets a leg up once Penny is tacked. I barely need to hop to get on Jude but I like the way the gelding feels supple and racy in my hands, so I approve even though I would feel more at home on a larger horse.

There is a guy who seems to be associated with the hunt coming around with a tray of silver cups filled with what I gather is booze. I take a glass to seem polite but I barely touch my lips to it. I want to remember what goes on rather than have a fuzzy head.

I notice that a number of the men in pinks have knives at their belts and Mr. Jackson follows my eyes: "That's for the fox, in case we catch one, to finish him off," he explains. "But don't worry, we've only killed a fox once in my lifetime and I've been doing this for many, many years. That was by accident before the hounds were called off in time."

"Yes, I've never seen a fox die, so don't worry, Simon," says Cynthia, cheerfully. "Simon's a real animal lover, as you can tell by the expression on his face."

I feel uncomfortably transparent right now, despite my best efforts.

"Oh, one of those," says her father. "Well, you'll fix him eventually."

I hear the call of the hunting horn—it really does sound like the movies or TV—and the field starts to assemble itself, like a mass of puzzle pieces coming together in moving order.

My horse is calm, having done this before, but I feel a kind of dizzy, ecstatic excitement, even more than I do when I'm galloping with Daniel or with one of my friends. Unlike even the most challenging course or trail there is no clear beginning and end to this; unlike even the most complex game of cards or chess there is no fixed strategy to rely upon. The smell of animal and leather in the air is lighting up something primal in the back of my brain that I don't feel even when I'm hacking out alone.

The first few fences are tall brush and despite his size, Jude clears them easily. He seems fit and I let him go into a full gallop. No worries about optimum time here, no constraints, no winners or losers, just running fast as we can go.

Jude's breathing is easy and regular and mine quickly matches his rhythm. I'm careful not to pass the master but I'm very close to the old lady riding sidesaddle who seems to know what she's doing on her large, slate grey horse. Her mount reminds me a little of Fortune, only darker and more Roman-nosed.

I haven't seen the fox yet but I can hear the joyful yelping of the hounds.

"You look like you've done this before," says the sidesaddle lady as we go over a longer pass which just requires galloping.

"Eventer," I identify myself. The fence in front of us is large but straightforward and Jude pounces over it as if on springs. I laugh. "For a little guy, he certainly can jump."

"Well, for one of Cynthia Jackson's boyfriends, you certainly can ride. Most of the time they're in the back, clutching on the pommel in fear. Even if they do have horses. I've never seen one in the first flight before. I guess they made an exception for you."

"Oh, I'm not her boyfriend," I say. I look around for Cynthia and see her going over the jump behind us. Every time we go over a very big fence she lets out a little squeal. It's actually kind of funny.

"Her last one threw up before—and after—we were done," says the old lady. "And that was only during cubbing season. He never came back. I think we scared him away."

"I'm not planning on puking," I respond.

After jumping a gate with a quick drop down a bank and splashing through water, we come to a wide ditch. The master's horse and Mr. Jackson's mount both refuse; I can see, despite the fact they try to laugh it off, that they're looking down at the rocks below the crevice and the drop must be easily five or six foot or more. It's not a difficult jump, just nasty if you miss it.

I give Jude a spur and he hops over. I'm not sure if this is a breach of etiquette but the old lady and a few of other members follow me so I guess we're okay. I wait on the other side. The lady says, "Young man, I must say I do think you're the right kind of crazy for this. I like you."

"Personally, I think you're crazier than me to be riding sidesaddle over a course like this, so I'll take that as a compliment."

"Every now and then, showing some respect for tradition is good for the soul."

"I've been told that, but I have no traditions to follow," I say, laughing.

"Oh, really? Everyone has traditions of some kind."

"I'm Irish, so maybe being slightly nutty when it comes to foxhunting is my tradition."

The field begins to thin out. It's been a long time since I've been galloping like this in free and unplanned territory. No course walk like at a horse trial; also, none of the weird, manmade fences that look like nothing you'd see in nature in eventing; none of the familiarity of Vermont or the need to slow down for steep hills and valleys. Despite the length of time we've been out, my horse doesn't seem to be tired at all but is fit, conditioned, and straining at the bit like me to go forward.

We stop, waiting for the hounds to pick up the scent again. Cynthia rides up to my side. "I knew you would love it," she says.

I grin. It's also cool to see people, even old ladies, going over these crazy jumps, like they have done so for years and years, like they regard the jumps as a natural part of the scenery—which of course the jumps are. For the first time I feel like I'm part of some kind of living, breathing organism of people, something larger than my own mind. I'm out in the wild, but still organized with some kind of common purpose. I feel like I belong to something, I don't know, a community of horses and riders and whatever.

I hear the sound of the horn, which signals that the hounds have found the scent again, and we're off once again at a full gallop. I know that if the fox goes to ground they'll leave it but our pace is pretty fast. We go over some brush, a fence or two, a few coops. Suddenly, out of the corner of my eye, I see a dart of red and white in the distance. The fox is far away but close enough for me to see his markings. For a second I'm surprised that he is real. Up to this point I've thought of the fox more as a moving bull's eye of a target or a prize, like a stuffed animal. Just like I did when I saw the knives at the men's belts, I feel a nervous, kind of a claustrophobic seize in my throat and then the thread of color vanishes like a needle in the sea of brown and green.

"He's gone to ground. So we'll leave him for another day," says Mr. Jackson, who has suddenly materialized beside me. He looks at me. "I told you, don't look so worried. The point is to have more sport in the future, not to kill the fox."

As we head back, I ride up near Cynthia's father to thank him. "That was amazing," is all I can manage.

"I've never seen Jude go so fast," observes Mr. Jackson. "My daughter was right—you can really ride." He sounds somewhat surprised.

"He's a great horse," I say. "I can tell he's had great training here." And for a moment I forget who I' m talking to, I'm on such a high from the speed. Not that I haven't gone fast and far before but I'm slightly drunk with pleasure and from soaking up the nervous energy of the other horses and riders around me.

Mr. Jackson gives me a rundown on Jude's pedigree and then asks me about my horse who I say, honestly, is a good jumper but is out of nothing by nothing (i.e., no idea).

It feels weird to give a horse to a groom before we trailer back. I'd actually like the time with the horse to decompress a bit from the experience but talking with Cindy and her father is good enough, better than I expected. Much better than the awarding of the prizes after some hunter pace, even though here the purpose of it all, as far as I can see, is to leave the prize be after the chase. I've always been called too competitive by nature but I'm more than okay with hunting not being a competition.

By the time we've gotten back to the house it's time for the mid-morning hunt breakfast. The meal is being served in a large room at the back. It's lined with mirrors and statues of foxes and things that at first I think are old and traditional but I eventually realize are new but made to look old. The doors are all open so people can come and go in their field boots.

I hardly recognize myself in the mirrors lining the room. It's not just that I'm spattered with mud or that I'm red from the excitement and the cold but for one brief moment I actually like what I see reflected. I can't stop smiling.

Most of the field comes for food after they have left their horses back at their barns. Some of them just trailer over and give the horses hay and feed in the trailers. The whole sight and experience is slightly surreal. I sit down on the steps of the house and watch them all before getting anything to eat myself, kind of gaping at the catering staff as they put out steaming trays.

"If I could do this every weekend," I say to Cindy, "I probably would never leave here. I can see why the British aristocracy never wanted to do anything useful but foxhunt all the time."

"You know you're always welcome, Simon," she says and reaches over to squeeze my fingers. Even with her gloves on, her hand still feels bony. "You know," she whispers, "There is going to be a job opening here soon—one of the trainers is going to be leaving." She blushes and looks at the ground.

I remember the trainer guy she mentioned and I know this is something more than an objective discussion of his decision to leave. "Well, I've made the commitment to Daniel for the year," I say.

"But after—it wouldn't be for a few months."

I'm somewhat taken aback. I have given some thought to my future after this year, of course, fantasizing about working for Freddie Whitechapel or finding some barn out in Europe to mortgage myself out to for no money at all (although I can't really afford to do that).

"Your dad doesn't know me, Cindy," I say.

"He knows I know you," she says.

This is all too much, so I go and get some food. I'm really starving. The booze is flowing freely but again, I decide that lowering my inhibitions would be a bad idea. I'm feeling loose enough as it is.

I kind of hide in the corner of the room so I can stuff myself with eggs, bacon, and toast, and hope that no one talks to me because this crowd is just way, way different than the people I'm used to dealing with, even from the show barn I used to work at. However, the old lady drifts over and begins chatting about her horses with me and I kind of relax a bit. She asks how I know Cynthia and I tell her about Daniel and such.

"Cindy's last boyfriend was your typical college boy who played with show hunters; you're an eventer, that explains why you weren't terrified," says the lady. I guess she doesn't know about Cindy's fling with her trainer.

"Oh, Cindy and I are just friends."

"That's what Cynthia always says," cackles the lady, shoving another piece of bacon down her throat. "You don't mind my being blunt? That's the nice thing about being old, no one cares what you say."

"I'm not Cynthia's boyfriend," I articulate again, more firmly and not laughing although not rudely either. Boyfriend seems to be the role people feel comfortable assigning me, regardless of what I say.

Then the old lady asks, "Do you have a girlfriend?"

"No," I say because I can't find a polite way to snap, "None of your business." My natural instinct is suddenly to look down but I don't. I just look into her eyes and speak normally. There is a moment between the two of us and she gives me that *oh, I've got you figured out* look and then walks away. I know that look well.

Cynthia comes over and grabs me by the jacket, introduces me to some of the people. Some are girls like herself (and one guy) who are still showing down here—all of them look healthy and athletic and rather bland and blond and generic. I recognize some of the names from various horse-related news websites. Others are friends of her father— neighbors, businessmen, local politicians. Those all blur into a collective jumble after a certain point. I'm starting to get a headache from all of the new humanity. I really just want to pull away but as brusque as I can be when I'm on my own turf, I know that I can't retreat into myself here.

"Hey, Cindy, who is that crazy old lady who rode sidesaddle?"

"Her? Oh, she must be as old as the hunt. She is really old money, owns her own farm—She breeds hounds and terriers. We've gotten a few nice bitches from her."

"She didn't think much of the riding of some of the guys you brought previously."

"Oh, yes, my previous boyfriend—he thought he could ride, sort of. Tennis and golf were more his speed. He was holding onto the pommel for dear life."

"You did fine."

"Well, I've been out here all my life. It's easier on a horse that is following everyone, to jump big fences, and these courses aren't so technical like all the ones in eventing that sort of freak me out."

"According to Daniel, that's how eventing used to be—more big jumping and less technical stuff."

"Yes, but you like the challenge."

"I do. I guess it's like figuring out a puzzle for me, with speed. But I like this too."

"I like challenges too, sometimes," says Cynthia, and I realize that she is beginning to flirt with me. Then I kind of shrug and pull away. I think again of the Amy Winehouse song, "Love Is A Losing Game." Maybe that isn't exactly true, it just depends on who you play it with.

I'm not really a tricky puzzle or riddle to figure out. Suddenly, I feel raw and exposed, and not in a good way.

There are some non-riders who come to the brunch later, people who I gather Cynthia's father has made some campaign donations to, members of the local media and such. I overhear words like "immigration reform" and "taxes" and "freedom" quite a bit with them, although her dad does talk horses with other guests. I will concede he knows something about horses, which means something—not enough to cancel the other things out, but something.

Afterward Cynthia and I go up to change into schooling clothes to play with Sammy once again. I stare at the electronic eye of the security system as we pass it in the hallway. Pulling on one of Max's shirts, it occurs to me that I should send a message to him and my brother. I write to Sean:

still alive

But of course he isn't up yet—it's early on a weekend and he's probably passed out next to some co-ed, or from playing poker with his buddies or something. Or getting in some extra running to flush out what he drank last night. To Max, I type:

foxhunting is awesome

He responds:

But does the fox agree?

I type back: *fox is fine.* Although I think of the knife Mr. Jackson and some of the other men were wearing.

Cynthia and I put Sam through his paces. He clears a 1.2m course easily with each of us and then I raise the jumps higher for me. Cynthia won't jump around at my chosen height, saying "I'm not confident enough yet, I don't want to mess him up." Sam does rollbacks and sharp turns like a cat; I feel like I'm riding an animal with a liquid spine. I don't know if it is training or breeding or both. I see the distance, the pace I need and he's already reading me and setting himself up.

Part of me thinks it would be nice to have such a horse. I know, just know, that I could easily rack up the NQRs I need to go Intermediate so easily. I can practically taste it. I bet I could be up to Advanced by, well, at least by the time I was twenty. Although it would be weird for me to do it on a horse that had been trained by someone else. I don't think it's cheating, exactly. Just weird, to me. I don't say any of this to Cindy.

I want to take Sam cross-country but she says that he is still so new they want to get him used to his surroundings here. We give him over to the grooms and hack out on two of the other horses in the stable.

The Virginia country is green and gentler than what I'm used to up north. Even with the big hunting fences we cleared earlier in the morning in the way, it's much less taxing to go at a full gallop. It's fun to ride here but I kind of miss the harsher ebb and flow of Vermont territory, as well as the views from on high. I can see that Cynthia is at home and she loves it here, though, and there is a relaxation to her riding I don't see back at Daniel's farm.

"Does your father really believe all the crap he says?" I blurt out.

Cynthia looks uncomfortable. "He doesn't say anything he doesn't believe. It's just the way he says things can be kind of harsh."

"Do you believe everything he says?"

"Some of it."

"Like what?"

"Like, being proud to be an American and protecting our way of life."

"Last time I checked, I was an American."

"Oh, *Simon*. Let's not talk about politics."

"I don't have any interest in politics, I just want to be left alone," I say and speed off, not so fast as to lose her but fast enough that I get some distance between the two of us.

It occurs to me that it doesn't really matter what Cynthia believes. Where would she be, after all, without her father and his money, and all this? My mother and my brother might think that trying to ride for a living is stupid but at least they support me, in their own ways. Without being dependent on a rich parent, I am, ironically, free enough to make my own decisions about what I do. I can afford not to care about the things people say I should care about, like being sensible and making money for the future rather than the here and now, because I have nothing.

I let Cynthia catch up with me. "Simon, Simon, you have to understand, my father loves me."

"I never said he didn't." But she sounds scared. Of what? Me? Him? God knows.

"I guess that's something. But I also know he doesn't like me."

"But he does, Simon—he said you were an awesome rider. He said, 'Where did you find this guy? He has no fear,' and he's never said that about any of the friends I've bought to ride here before."

"He wouldn't like me if he knew me better, not the real me."

"I don't think that's true."

Well, if what Cynthia says is true, then he's a big fat fucking hypocrite or she's lying or delusional, I think. That sounds too harsh to say to her when I am her guest. "Even if he thinks he likes me now, if he doesn't like how I love, he can't really like the real me," I say.

"Oh, Simon, maybe it's his generation."

"He's not that old."

"I understand—that it's not a choice and all, that you can't help it."

"You know Cynthia, that phrase kind of disgusts me too, like I'm diseased and I can't help being sick but I would choose to be otherwise if I could choose. You have no idea…" I want to say, you have no idea what Max and I have together because you've never remotely experienced anything in your life like love, but I know she wouldn't understand. "You don't have to justify yourself and what you are to me, why should I have to justify myself to you or to anyone else?"

"I'm confused Simon, isn't that the right thing to say, that it's not a choice?"

Our words clank up against each other, knocking together but not connecting, just like clichés do when people have a debate. We're saying nothing and meaning nothing. I wish I could be alone like I can be back at the farm when I ride out and then go lie in the grass and listen to Fortune eat, both of us calm and indifferent and silent. It's times like this I realize how truly stupid words are and how little of a connection they have to anything real at all—they don't even describe the skin of life properly. I want out of the marketplace of words entirely and the way words judge the value of things because everything everyone says sounds so wrong and so different from what I know in my heart to be true.

Once we return to the ring, we try out two other new prospects Cynthia's father purchased. They're greener horses but still willing and responsive. We take them over a course of low fences, first me, then Cindy.

When I'm sitting on one of horses, yet another grey named Chance (full name Take a Chance, the greys always seem to find me lately, although this one is dark and slate-colored because he's so young), one of the assistant trainers comes to the fence to watch Cynthia pop over some low combinations on her dun gelding. I start to talk to the trainer, asking him where Mr. Jackson got the new horses (Canada) and such and it immediately becomes clear to me that this guy is flamingly gay even though we just talk horseflesh. It would almost be funny, if it weren't funny. (It's also clear to me that this younger horse makes Cynthia look like a vastly better rider than she is—when she is slightly unbalanced, it corrects itself so she can sail over, pretty and unperturbed by the motion.)

"So, is he the trainer your father is replacing?" I ask Cynthia when he leaves.

"No, no, it's … another one," she says, blushing.

I ignore her embarrassment about the other trainer guy she dated because he doesn't interest me. "I assume you don't have a personal issue with Jeff, that's his name isn't it?"

"Oh—no," she says.

"Does your father?"

"Simon, you see, he doesn't care. Besides, you can't compare yourself to Jeff. You're different."

I sigh. "But Cynthia, what you don't understand is that I'm not. Honestly, Cynthia you can be so dense, sometimes."

She glares at me. "No, Simon, you're the one who is being dense. Do you agree with everything your father says?"

"I barely remember my father, I haven't seen him since I was a little, little kid."

"Oh, I'm sorry."

"I'm not. My older brother remembers him better and says he was a real dick, an abusive, alcoholic asshole."

"Simon, do you always have to be so—"

"Honest? I'm a shitty liar, Cindy, so I guess I do."

I'm angry now although I'm not sure if it is at Cynthia or myself. I'm also not sure in a way, who is dumber—Cynthia, her father, Jeff for working here, or me for coming at all. But I can't help it, there is also a part of me that wants to go out foxhunting tomorrow.

I give Chance a long rein. As we cool both babies out, I pat his neck.

"I like him," I say, changing the subject. "He likes his job. He's very willing."

"He's never refused anything. He's been brought along slowly, Jeff says."

"Well, that is the right way to do it, that way they're never afraid, isn't that so, boy?"

I see another guy riding in the dressage ring. He's tall, helmetless, wearing a polo shirt and has the horse in frame, easily, expertly. And honestly, he's really hot. Tanned. Muscular. And he carries himself like he knows it.

"Is he the other trainer, the one who is on the way out?"

"Yes," says Cynthia. "He's the one who is leaving soon." Pause. "He's the guy I said I needed to meet that time over the weekend."

We don't stop and talk to him.

I've heard that happening a lot between girls and their trainers and saw some of it at my old barn. Obviously, not where I am now, really.

I want to say, "I'm sorry" to Cynthia about the whole mess with the trainer. But there is a part of me that thinks it's kind of dumb, mixing business and pleasure like that. Although there are those who would say I have no business passing judgment on that issue, so I try not to.

After a certain point, I feel like I'm on Mars here, kind of like I always do when I go to really fancy barns—barns even fancier than Angel Heart. There was a girl I was sort of friends with when I was riding in rated shows back in New Jersey who asked me over to her private barn for a day. The horses almost felt incidental to the wealth around them, no matter how well-cared for they might be.

Sam is let loose in his paddock alone, still under quarantine because he's so new. He trots around nervously, back and forth, pacing and whinnying, wondering where the rest of his herd has gone. He looks confused, off-balance, out-of-sorts and I can't blame him.

I stand in the barn, looking at the dressage saddles, wondering if I could buy one of this kind or that kind, would it make a difference on Fortune's back. Then, suddenly, I sense Cynthia's *other* trainer is behind me. "You're Cindy's friend," he says. He has an accent. It takes me a second to place it. Men at Work? Australian, then?

"Yes." He looks uncomfortable.

"She's a nice girl." I think he may be thinking, she's your problem mate, not mine, connecting the dots wrong. I get a sense that he feels we're engaged in a masculine ritual of passing the torch or something.

This is just getting too complicated, way too complicated for a simple soul like myself.

Dinner is again a weird and uncomfortable event, although beautifully presented and all—they serve duck wrapped in bacon and some knobby potato things and other unidentified round substances, which I've never had before and by now I'm hungry enough to eat some of it even though my stomach feels knotted and closed as a piece of old rope. Cynthia, of course, just sips wine and picks at her salad. The house is warm but she's wearing long sleeves, which is not a good sign with Cynthia. I don't know what she has to be upset about, though, it's not like she had a horse show disaster or something since I last saw her.

"She lives on air," says her father, proudly nodding at his daughter as she deconstructs the food. "It's hard to believe she was fat as a little girl, but she was, wasn't she, Cindy?"

Cynthia blushes. "Have you told Simon about the position of trainer that will be opening up?" Her eyes cast downward and she mutters at her glass.

"My daughter thinks quite a bit of your riding and says you've helped her a great deal. It's important to me for a variety of reasons that she does well this year. Of course, we all want Cynthia to succeed and win as much as she is capable of winning, but as I'm sure she's told you, there is more at stake than just the horses in terms of the image we're trying to project. Several critical elections are coming up of candidates I support and if my daughter and my horses don't do well, that reflects poorly on me. It's never just about the horses here." Mr. Jackson gets up and puts his hand on his daughter's bare shoulder, squeezes it. It's meant to be loving, I guess, but because Cindy's so pale and bony it leaves a mark like a hickey on her skin.

"Naturally, I want Cindy to do well because we're all part of a team back at the farm, all of the working students. We're all working for Daniel and so we all help one another out, Mr. Jackson." I'm tempted to say "sir" for the first time in my life, but I don't. The impulse arises not out of respect, but from a desire to keep the distance between myself and him.

"Well, that kind of attitude is pretty rare in the horse show world."

"Not really. Eventers, at least at our level—I still need to qualify for Intermediate—we're all in this together. That's what I like so much about the sport. We're all a little bit crazy to do what we do and we're always rooting for one another, in a way." This is as close to an opinion as I've expressed all weekend. "We're all on the same level playing field of insanity."

"I understand you have a commitment to Daniel but after it ends, Cindy suggests you come here."

"I know. I talked to Cindy about it," I say. "It's very kind of you but I can't accept the offer."

I remind myself that it's likely that I could always stay on at Daniel's if I need a job. I know he can't pay me much, most likely, but given that my results have been pretty decent, I don't have to go begging for work.

Mr. Jackson casually names a salary that is roughly twice as much as I could expect from the other barns I've been looking at for future jobs, certainly more than I could get back in Vermont. I try to think about how to diplomatically refuse it when Cynthia interrupts. "Dad, Simon says he can't."

"Why not? Surely it's not—"

"Mr. Jackson, it's not the money, in fact I'm really not worth that much, to be honest, relative to my level of experience. Like I said, I've won some decent ribbons at showjumping and I'm still riding at Preliminary and it's only this year that I've really been seriously competitive at eventing with my own horse. I'm proud of what I've been learning and doing this year but I'm just being honest."

"So what is the problem?"

"I don't think I would be comfortable here. I don't think you would be comfortable with me," I say. I put down my fork.

I look him in the eye even though I notice Cynthia is looking away, as if I've said something embarrassing.

Mr. Jackson appears surprised at first and for one brief second I regret what I've said and feel bad and think he seems like a human being, not like the guy on TV. Then he understands what I mean, his eyes narrow and he shuts down completely. I think of all the things I heard in the clips I watched: *sodomy, mental illness, immorality, lifestyle,* and best of all *unnatural.* I shift my eyes to stare at the eye of the security monitoring system hovering just over his head. I just noticed its gaze. I stare it down, like I could make the machine avert its bulging pupil.

"A Kiss With a Fist" suddenly pops into my head. No, no, not for me. I like the song, I like how angry it sounds, but I'll take what I love without that kind of a beating in real life, thank you very much.

It seems kind of unfair that Mr. Jackson and I can't talk about, say, foxhunting and riding like normal horse people, as if what he does wasn't a factor in all this at all, but I remind myself that if it weren't for his TV persona then everything—the stable and the horses and even, in a way, Cynthia herself—wouldn't be here.

I remember what someone once said to me, a long time ago, that the only way to make a living in the horse business nowadays was to be born to it, buy your way into it, or, if you're a woman, screw your way into it. As much as that old cliché comes from a wellspring of bitterness, whoever said it first was sort of wrong about the last part, but also sort of right.

25

I'LL COME TO YOU BY MOONLIGHT... THOUGH HELL SHOULD BAR THE WAY

Cynthia and I arrive back at the farm late on Sunday, almost early Monday morning. There is an awkward moment when I turn away from her and we part. It's a relief finally to be alone and not have to hold things in but I know that it's pointless to try to sleep. I feel itchy and uncomfortable from sitting on the plane and in the car. I throw my bag on my bed, go down to the stable, bridle my horse, and swing my leg over him. There is still leftover snow on the ground, but it's not that cold. The really heavy stuff seems to be starting late this year and it's still rideable out there. I stuff a folding hoof pick in my pocket just in case.

Things are dark—dark dark in a way the trails never were back in Jersey, where there was always some kind of residual light from a nearby house or business. But there is enough light from the moon and the unclouded sky to find one of our favorite paths. I bet Fortune hasn't been ridden during the week and even with regular turnout he feels more antsy and anxious than usual. I give him his head and let him run when we hit open space. I know it's kind of not a good idea to ride half-blind in the night but I honestly can't move myself to care or worry enough. He knows his job, I think, although I sure as hell wonder about what mine is sometimes.

After a certain point, I realize that we're in a place I don't know very well. We're riding by someone's field. We pass some cows but Fortune isn't the type of horse who gets freaked out by the smell of farm animals. When the terrain starts to get rocky (I base my estimation on the sound and feel, not the sight, of things), I slow him down to a trot, then to a walk, for safety's sake. I know this is all aimless but it still feels necessary to release him from the pressure of doing nothing for so long. "It's your own fault, buddy," I tell him, "that no one likes to ride you but me." Of course, it's also to release me from whatever has been within me like a coiled spring all weekend, except during the few hours when I was hunting—hunting nothing, really, except motion itself because my feelings would have been very different if those knives some of the men had were used for more than show. I guess it's dumb to be sentimental about a fox—or wolves or sharks or even mares—but that's just how I feel about certain animals, I can't explain why

We're back on soft grass and I let him go again, barely touching his sides. I'd like to go even farther, to explore where I haven't gone before, but I know I need to be back for feeding and I don't want him to get so hot it takes too long for him to cool out. Instinctively, I find myself heading back—I may be a flatlander but my sense of direction works good enough here. I slow him from a gallop to a canter but he still spooks slightly (as do I) when I see Max at the gate of the barn.

"What are you doing here?" I say.

"You said you'd be back this morning for your usual routine," says Max.

"I am. I just couldn't sleep."

"God, you scared me for a second, I wasn't expecting that. You looked like a highwayman or something."

"I'm sorry if I startled you."

I slide off my horse and put my arms around Max before I head back to the barn. I'm sweaty from picking up on Fortune's body heat and for the first time I notice it's cold compared to what I was used to in Virginia even though the temperature is unusually warm for what it should be now in New England. Fortune rubs up his nose against me, reminding me that he's hungry and he's expecting the treats I don't have in my back pocket. I didn't dare give food to any of Cindy's horses, given the carefully balanced diets all of them had at that barn.

"I'm surprised you're back; from the sound of the messages you sent me, you wanted to stay. I thought I'd lost you."

"Aw, Max, don't say that, I'm glad I'm back."

And I tell him all about the hunt in a way I couldn't when I was just plucking out letters on my phone.

"So you like hunting—up to the point of finding the fox, and then you need to let it go," says Max.

"Why? Is that weird?"

"Not really, I guess. I suppose from the fox's point of view it's better than taking things to their logical conclusion."

"Have you ever hunted?"

"Foxhunting? No, just point-to-point stuff. I hunted deer when I was younger like a lot of kids do in this area."

"Really? I never would have thought that. I've eaten deer once or twice before but never hunted them. I can't say I liked the taste much."

"That was when I was in high school—younger, actually. I haven't in years."

"Our boy Morrissey would not approve."

"He wouldn't approve of the non-violent foxhunting, either. Or your leather saddle. Or my bad Jew's love of bacon. "

"I know. Sometimes I wonder if he'd be pissed off at both of us for liking his songs so much." The title of Max's favorite Smiths hit flashes in my mind: "There Is a Light that Never Goes Out." True, so true.

I've sobered up a bit from the high of riding at night. "I was thinking...I wouldn't mind working out there, down in the South, in foxhunting country—at another farm. When I leave here in June, I mean," I admit. I kind of feel uncomfortable bringing up the topic with Max, even though it is months away. It's something I've debated within myself as well—as much as I like it here, I'd rather live in a place where I know I can ride year-round without restrictions and although I've been lucky this winter, I'm sure that my days of serious hard galloping outdoors are numbered. However, I know that going south means leaving Max as well.

"Yes, I thought that was probably the case," he says, sounding very cool and logical about it, which means nothing in terms of how Max really feels. I walk Fortune around the property as he's still pretty sweaty even though I was riding bareback. I get off, sling a cooler over him, climb back on, and continue to circumnavigate the barn in lazy circles.

"Wait, why aren't you wearing a helmet?" says Max, suddenly noticing its absence.

"I almost always wear one. I wasn't jumping out there tonight."

"You almost always try to prevent traumatic brain injury?"

Oh, let's not go there, Max. To change the topic, I blurt out: "Cynthia's father offered me a job."

"Are you going to take it?"

"Hell no."

"Well, that sounds pretty definite."

"You do know who her father is? The guy on television? The cable network guy?"

"Wait a second—Vernon Jackson? That's her father? You do mean the little blonde girl I met who was crying about her horse? That's his daughter?"

"The family resemblance is more evident when you see them together," I say, "Well, physically, anyway. You sound surprised. He has money to burn, and he has a kid, so horses. It's a pretty common equation. Why should he be any different?"

Max seems hurt, as if, I don't know, Cynthia has betrayed her trust in him or lied to him. He stays around for a bit as I feed the horses alone. Megan is off-duty and even though the hunter princess should be helping me, Cindy's still asleep upstairs. Max tries to hash out his feelings about my revelation of Cindy's parentage aloud.

Max is actually pretty funny when he gets angry, since he tends to get progressively more rather than less articulate, unlike most people. He goes on, saying stuff like, "Well, if I'm *unnatural*, what does he call all of his horses that are the product of artificial insemination and years of careful breeding?" But I know it's useless since of course logic has nothing to do with why people stay stuff like that anyway. Given that whatever illogic Cynthia's dad has said has served him pretty well financially, I doubt he's going to stop; I know there really isn't any rationality in the reasons people believe what they believe or do what they do, or the logic of how so much hate could buy a man so many nice horses.

I also kind of feel bad because I get the sense that Max thinks I was being noble, refusing the job offer. The truth is, I was nothing of the kind. I was self-interested just as I always am, thinking, what point is it to leave the Box of high school, narrowly miss the Box of college and an annoying cubicle job like my poor brother, and then just make another Box for myself in the horse world? All I have in the world is my dumb confidence with animals and I know somewhere deep down that would be slowly stripped away, along with the rest of my sense of self, if I went to work for Vernon Jackson.

And then Max says something that really makes me feel kind of bad: "If you ever need anything, like a place to stay if you're looking for a job after this—or some, er, financial help if you find a situation that's good for you but doesn't pay, you know where to find me."

"Max, Max, you know that's just not my style. I couldn't."

"I really wouldn't mind. I know how hard it is to make it with horses as a rider, it's not like you should think less of yourself if—"

"That's true, but that's just not me, Max. I've been working to offset my horse's board since I was twelve, younger even. I'll figure something out."

I don't tell Sean or my mother that I turned down a job with Mr. Jackson. For whatever reason, I'm sick of hearing Sean go off on a rant just from what he's seen on TV and it's not like Jackson affects him in anything but a really kind of abstract and distanced way. I know my mother would want me to take the job and say something like I try to make life difficult for myself, just like she always does in such situations, just like she did when I decided not to apply to college. Even now she gives me a hard time about Vermont.

"I like it Ma, there's great cross-country up here."

"What, in the four months every year when it's not winter, yes."

"It's not that bad."

"Not yet this year, but just you wait."

Say what you will about Daniel, though, he still has the cred of his history even though he doesn't have a palace of a barn like Mr. Jackson. And his horses are free; they aren't shut up in stalls all day, left waiting to be used like someone's toy only to be put back again when finished.

26

BITTING UP

aniel gives his working students the week off for Christmas break so I get to leave "the frozen hellhole" (as my mother refers to it) while some local high school students (barn rats) pick up the slack. I wish one of them was a strong enough rider to work Fortune a bit, if only on the flat. But they're tiny girls, very nice, not even that confident handling him on the ground, much less in the saddle, and I don't want him to get in trouble for flinging one of them around like a piece of popcorn.

I casually ask Max on my day off before I leave if he'd like to go riding with me. I want to ride Fortune out of the ring, hard, before I go. I also want to spend some time with Max (a week feels like a long time, somehow) and this seems like the best way to combine those two desires.

"I can't just ride one of the horses without Daniel's permission outside of a lesson," Max says and shrugs. I know that he (and I frankly) wouldn't feel that comfortable asking.

"Ride my horse," I say, "He's mine and I can ride any of the others I want."

"Yours? I thought that Megan said he was unrideable."

"Ignore Megan. She's a nice girl but very prone to exaggeration."

I admit I kind of pressure Max into it, whining and pouting about missing him.

Although technically we don't need to sneak around, I am still relieved that neither Megan nor Cynthia in the barn when we go. It's freezing and night is already falling at 4 p.m. when Max gets off from work. I don't feel like explaining anything or making excuses.

Fortune likes the cold and I can tell by the way he's pulling as I lead him in that he wants out again.

Max notices that I'm changing the bit on his bridle in the tack room.

"You're bitting him up? That's not a good sign."

"Yeah ... might be a good idea, since it is your first ride on him and all."

"Well, it was nice knowing you, killer."

"Stop. You're just as bad as the girls. I thought you'd be happy I was taking precautions. Don't you trust me?"

"Yes, but I think you overestimate my abilities as a rider."

"I've seen you ride. Chill out."

"I've seen you ride and that's why I'm somewhat cautious."

"Don't worry, I'm always honest with you. I told you that you were a lousy chess player, remember? If you were bad like that at riding, I wouldn't have you ride my horse."

"Um, thanks?"

I saddle up Trouble for myself, thinking it will be good for her to get out and give her baby brain something to do. She's also a pretty good follower, so even if we're going into uncharted territory for her, she can always follow Fortune as the lead horse. Max tacks up Fortune fine, except for when he tightens the girth and Fortune tries to bite him. I smack my horse's flank and say, "You know better than that."

After we trot away from the barn I break into a canter and I hear Max gasp a little as Fortune grinds into motion. I look back and Max is moving with my horse well enough so I just let the two of them figure things out. Over the years, I've learned as a teacher that sometimes the best way to fix things is just to leave the rider alone with the horse.

The moonlight reflecting off the snow illuminates the world around us and Trouble is sufficiently delicate and stiff from the cold (she's from a racetrack down south originally, so she must really be wondering what the hell she did to deserve Vermont) that she slows down and Fortune matches her pace. I can still hear Max cursing a little bit—me or the horse, I'm not sure. Trouble spooks at the heavier snow that is pulling down the branches of the trees into strangely distorted, almost human shapes in the shadows. Fortune, as always, is unfazed. Even though Fortune's stride is huge, Max seems to be settling down and adjusting.

I want to take Max up to my favorite place on my mountain but there is a large, fallen tree on the path. I'm not sure if Trouble will refuse so I tell Max to take Fortune over it first.

"Maybe you should get on him and take him over."

"It's a tiny jump Max—it's nothing to a horse that size, it's like a crossrail for a pony. He won't refuse; he never has refused me."

Max circles Fortune around, gives him a kick and they go over, like I knew they would. I follow on Trouble. Max's face is red.

"I'm sorry, it's been awhile since I've been on a horse like this," he says.

"You're doing great; he's dumped both Cynthia and Megan over smaller fences," I say, brightly.

"I thought you said he wasn't a problem to ride," says Max.

"Well, you aren't having problems, are you?"

We go up to the top of the high hill where I can look across at the mountains in the distance. Without a full moon it would really be too dark to be safe but it's clear and cloudless and there isn't anything masking the stars. Either because he's tired or because we've slowed to a walk Max finally stops swearing and breathing hard and we sit there on our horses, taking in the view. There are enough flickers of light from the smatterings of civilization to see the outlines of things in a kind of purple and blue haze. We don't say anything for a long time, don't really speak until we've returned the way we came. I let Max go first over the log again and it's really deep night by the time we get back. I can sense the presence of something watching us at times—deer or maybe an owl—although nothing actually reveals itself to startle our horses.

"Back home, even on the trails, I'd never be able to see something like that," I say to Max as we untack and groom in the stillness of the barn. "When I've been around too many people and I'm feeling lonely, that's where I go to feel so not alone."

"Thanks for taking me there."

I haven't been conscious of the cold while riding but now my fingers have started to feel stiff and raw and the leather is unyielding against my fingers. "In New Jersey, there's no mountains and even if you were up high, you'd see strip malls in the distance right next to the trees. Sometimes I just can't deal with the rest of the human race."

"Even me?"

"Oh no, never you, you don't count as people, Max," I say. "Everyone else."

"That's an odd compliment but I guess I have to take it from you, since you mean it as one. I'm impressed how well you know your way around and you haven't even lived here for a year."

"I told you," I say, "I never get lost."

"You also said that your horse was no problem."

"Well, he wasn't, was he? He was good." I pat Fortune, then go to put Trouble back in her stall.

"It was a beautiful night and I didn't fall off so I suppose that qualifies as a yes."

We probably won't get a chance to spend another night together until after Christmas, I think. I know it's not that long—what, ten days from now, counting when I have to be on for nights as well as vacation—but it still makes me feel sad. I sort of wish I didn't have to leave, even though I miss my family, sometimes so much it hurts. "I wish you could come home with me," I blurt out, "even through I'm not sure you'd enjoy it, being with my family."

"Why do you say that?"

"I told you, they're kind of weird."

"Well, no offense, but after knowing you, I wouldn't be expecting anything normal." Max winks at me and slaps me on the ass, then goes back to currying Fortune.

"Take off and come home with me."

"I can't, Simon. I always work over Christmas. Someone always has to and since I'm the only one at the practice who doesn't celebrate the holiday, it seems the most fair."

"But isn't your holiday also over Christmas, kinda, this year?"

"That's not the same. Hanukkah is mostly for little kids; the only reason anyone who is Jewish makes a big deal about it is because it happens in December around Christmastime. It's would be kind of like people making a big deal about Groundhog Day because it's in February near Valentine's Day. For me December 25th is pretty much International Chinese Food and Movie Day, like it is for most Jews. I can celebrate that and still work."

"Doesn't sound so bad."

"Usually, it involves me making my own Chinese food because the places around here are so awful and watching *The Wall* by myself."

"I'm not as big a fan as you are but I'm okay with Pink Floyd. Pink Floyd is acceptable." Pause.

"I would have thought the lyrics from 'Another Brick in the Wall' would be your theme song."

"I never said I didn't need to be educated, I said I hate school and there's a difference. I'm learning more here than I would in college."

"True—in some respects."

"I got you something for Hanukkah."

"That wasn't necessary."

"Don't get all gushy, Max."

I walk up the steps to my room, grab the LP (which I haven't bothered to wrap) and hand it to him.

"This was missing from your collection."

"Hot Fuss?" he says, holding the blue record between his fingers. Uncomfortable for a second, I guess because to him the barn is like the office for most people, he puts his arms around me and kisses me. There is a noise which makes us both start but we soon realize it's just Maggie wandering around, nibbling bits of grain off the floor, and I put her back in her stall, shutting the door.

I do evening feed, giving the horses that worked a bit of extra grain, and we go back to Max's house. We only have a few hours before I have to be back and my time is no longer my own.

Max gives me my gift at his place, a pair of Doc Martins, which I've always wanted but could never quite justify getting over a new pair of horse-related boots. I immediately resolve to keep them (somewhat) clean, unlike the rest of my shoes, although Max tells me not to make any promises I can't keep.

"I thought you didn't believe in Christmas," I say.

"Well, you do."

"My family celebrates the holiday but in kind of a secular way."

"I always thought you were Catholic."

"Why?"

"Well, you're Irish, for one."

"My brother and I were raised devout Irish anti-Catholics."

"What does that mean?"

"That means my mom never baptized either of us or took us to church but every time there is news about some priest molesting a kid or the Catholic Church not supporting birth control, she gets all angry and starts shouting, 'Now that is why I left the Church. Liars! Hypocrites!' That type of thing."

"I thought you went to Catholic school for a year."

"Only as a little kid because the public school wanted to throw me into special ed because they said I had ADHD."

"You? Distractible and hyperactive? Never."

"I know, hard to believe. Anyway, we're all heathens but we just celebrate Christmas for the gifts and stuff. This is the best present I've ever gotten ever, though. I've always wanted a pair."

"I'm surprised you didn't have them before, what with you always trying to be so punk and all." Max smiles a bit as he says "punk."

"Tall boots come first, then Boggs, then work boots in my budget. But Docs are still sacred. And what do you mean *trying* to be punk?"

Sean has been home for weeks, of course, so he picks me up at the train station. "You'll be proud of me, I've actually been riding every day over winter break," he says.

"Cam must be in shock."

"Actually, he's being leased by one of the seniors while I'm away— she does speed—so he is in reasonably good shape. They sold that little mare you rode in the hunter pace, though, to a little girl."

"A little girl? That horse wasn't a kid's horse. People are always trying to make horses into something they aren't. Just because she's pretty."

"Yeah, since when did that stop anyone though? How's your guy? Still no brakes?"

For a second I'm not sure if he's referring to Fortune or Max. "Horse's getting better. I actually had someone else ride him and he did okay."

"Yeah, after they sent out a search party."

"Horse and rider both did fine. Horse is still crap at dressage, though."

"Since when did you care about dressage?"

"I told you, I have to be good at it, otherwise I'll never move up through the levels."

"Dude, you and your eventing levels. You say that he can jump big and has won at showjumping, why not just stick with that, what he's happiest at and what you're good at?"

"Because—I don't know, I don't like riding in a ring as much as I do cross-country. I just feel that eventing is the ultimate test of horse and rider and I want to be best at that instead."

I throw my bag in the back of our new (used) truck. It already looks almost like the old truck, minus some odd sounds and half-scratched off bumper stickers. Even the patterns of manure, hay, and dirt on the floor are the same as the old one.

"Now who's trying to make a horse into something he isn't?"

"That's not the same thing at all."

"Don't get *mad*, Jesus."

"He's the best at cross-country every time and usually stadium as well. It's just the stupid dressage."

"I actually always kind of liked dressage," says Sean.

"Yeah, you would. It's practically like Western riding to you."

Sean rolls his eyes. "Well then, it's obviously beneath you."

"No, I don't mean that." I pause. "Maybe you're right about me trying to change Fortune, but we're stuck with each other."

"Not really. Ride him in a bunch of those jumping events, sell him, and get another horse that can do what you want him to do."

I know that people do that all the time and what Sean is saying is actually kind of sensible.

"It's like buying and selling stock," says the future financial advisor.

I think of Cynthia's new horse that is about to replace Blood Money, a horse that you just have to think *suppleness* when you're on him and the horse falls into place like a piece of fabric slung over a chair or whatever metaphor they're using in dressage right now for harmony and such.

"But I like my horse."

"So that's the problem."

"This is why I need multiple horses."

"That would be your logic."

"Someday."

Deep down, I know that what Sean says is right. In fact, Daniel always tells the story about how he sold his first horse immediately (a hunter) when he decided he wanted to break into eventing because he fell in love with the sport literally at first sight. It never occurred to me that I might have to do the same with Fortune. I keep thinking there is some button I have to find and press inside of him to make everything all right. The frustrating thing is, I know he can be good at everything, it's just so rare that he is—clearly, it's something inside of me as well, not just him, as is often the case for horse and rider.

It's late, so when we get home there isn't much to do but watch TV. Sean sees me put up my feet. "Docs? Seriously, what century are you living in? You look like a fucking criminal."

I've used a razor to carefully carve a small skull and crossbones onto the top of one of the shoes and a large A for anarchy on the toe of the other.

"Christmas gift."

"Who would give you something like that?" I smile and Sean rolls his eyes.

"Jesus, he must have bad taste. Well, he's dating you."

"Nah, they aren't his style, actually, he just knows mine really well."

"Why can't I have a *normal* gay brother like everyone else, one who knows how to dress?"

I wake up at dawn because I'm used to it and I make enough noise to get Sean up so we can go to Mom's barn and ride together. He bitches at me but of course he comes because what other useful things are there for him to do? When I get there, I see Blue has a new name across her stall—Cinderella—and a bright pink halter, so I see she is in fact really sold.

"What's there for me to ride?" I ask Lauren. "Other than the usual suspects?"

"What about the rescue that's being fattened up?" says Sean.

"He's not broke to ride English," says Lauren.

What the hell, I think, why not.

The rescue is a big, black Appendix gelding with a Quarter Horse's powerful haunches who still has that kind of "oh shit" rescue look on his face that Fortune used to have. Like Fortune, he tries to bite me and kicks out at me on the ground—I'm prepared for that—but when I ease on him, he goes about his business like he knows his job.

I spend the rest of the morning racing barrels with my brother, which I haven't done in years.

For Christmas, I know the money is tight, what with my brother in school and all. His cross-country scholarship covers a lot but Mom's still supporting him and well, money has always been tight with us since the divorce. As far as I know, she never got child support or alimony or anything, even though my father's loaded. He was apparently very creative in hiding his wealth, even more so than he was making it on the stock market, kind of like some accounting three-card monte.

The point is, I'm shocked when I open up a box to discover the dressage saddle I've been talking about for ages. It's used, was advertised on a consignment tack website, but still expensive.

"Ma, that's too much. I really didn't want anything," I say. I got her a new down coat and gloves for when she teaches in the cold, a gift which now doesn't feel like nearly enough.

"I hope it fits the horse. You'll probably need to get it reflocked," she says. "It's for Fortune, not you, so don't thank me. I didn't really get you anything."

I know she's still not terribly fond of Fortune, since she doesn't see him every day and the progress he has made, and that makes me love her all the more. Sean gets new sneakers and running gear. I feel kind of bad since I know my gift is obviously more expensive than his, despite how overpriced running shoes can be. It's because it is for a horse, of course, but I'm not sure Sean totally gets that, even though he doesn't say anything.

He likes my gift, though—a complete remastered box set of every CD ever made by Johnny Cash, who is pretty much my brother's favorite singer ever, since Sean thinks of himself as a Southern New Jersey cowboy. In all honesty, I don't disapprove of Cash. I even kind of like some of his music, although I officially declared war on the entire genre of country music long, long ago. I mean, Cash covered Nine Inch Nails, so major bonus points for that, plus the whole Man in Black image. He's as badass as country can get.

Sean is happy and immediately takes off the old Christmas CD that's been playing "Silent Night" and puts on one of Cash's songs.

"'Cocaine Blues,'" says my mother, dryly. "Thanks, Simon, for giving your brother his gift, it's just what I like to hear on Christmas, a nice, traditional tune."

Sean gets me a blue-grey Irish wool sweater. Just a nice sweater. It's heavy and warm.

"It's when you need to be presentable," he says. Meaning, I guess, it isn't covered in horse hair and has no holes.

"Your brother works with horses. Other than show clothes, he never needs to look presentable," says my mother.

"What if he needs to look nice on a date?"

"Oh, don't be silly, Sean," says my mother. "Where would someone go on a date in the middle of frozen cow pats and sheep fields?"

We listen to Johnny Cash and stare at the same sad artificial tree we have put up every year since I was a little kid. Then we go over to my mom's barn and do all the chores ourselves since even Lauren, the barn owner, does normal person things on Christmas. We're used to that, though, part of the deal, and follow the work with hacking together over the fences on the trails. The ground is still soft and pliable here so we can jump. I take one of the lesson horses (not much choice, since Blue is sold) and although Caliban's kind of an old guy, I easily outpace my mother and brother. Soon I'm ahead of them, alone. I forget about everything for a while, even Fortune and Max.

Back home, my mother manages not to ruin the roast beef she got on sale, which she serves with the usual instant potatoes from a box, exploding biscuits from a cardboard cylinder, and apple and pumpkin pie from a supermarket. She makes herself some vegetables as a side but Sean and I don't bother with those. I don't have any wine, even though it's Christmas because I don't really feel like it. As I'm eating seconds and watching *A Christmas Story* like I always do with my brother, I text Max and send him a picture of my new used saddle.

Max is outside in the cold with a horse that's had a bad colic. He writes back that hopefully he'll be able to watch *The Wall* and make his Chinese food although the prognosis at this point is not great for celebrating International Chinese Food and Movie Day before midnight. He thinks the horse will be fine, though.

I want to write back that I want him here, where I am now, and I'm sure he would fit in perfectly, but I can't think of a way to condense that into a short enough text or Facebook message.

It snows the day after Christmas and when I meet up with Heather she's timid about riding without being able to see the ground through the snow on the trails behind the barn. The ground has hardened overnight, so I don't press it. We ride slowly, and I'm okay with that. The whiteness can make even the relatively tame and manicured trails here look interesting.

After we finish up, Heather makes a snowman in one of the fields. The horses don't spook at it, even though they give her weird looks as she rolls it. As do I.

"You're having entirely too much fun with this white stuff, Heather," I say. Snow is not exactly exciting to me anymore after living in Vermont.

Heather uses peppermints for eyes and a carrot for the snowman's nose. When she's done, I make a snowball and hit the carrot. I'm kind of surprised I have decent aim, since I don't remember the last time I threw a baseball. Heather throws a lame snowball back at me.

"Oh, so that's how it's going to be," I say. I lob one at her.

"Simon, that hurt," she squeals. I throw another one at her, she throws one at me, and eventually we end up wrestling in the snow together. I stick a handful of snow down the back of her shirt and she screams and hits me.

I don't know how other people define friendship or family, but for me, being able to be as jerky as I want with Sean and Heather is as close to perfection in those departments as I'll ever get.

I love that home seems never to change, every time I go back to it. My mom's not the type of mom that eradicates every sign of her kids in their rooms when they leave and even if she could, the horses are always here. No matter where we both go, Sean and I, no matter how far apart we stray from one another, there is always something unwavering and stable between us at a barn.

27

A SOUL, NOT A SOLDIER

When I get back to Vermont, Daniel's barn is still technically closed even though I have my duties regarding the schooling of the horses as well as the daily feeding, turnout, blanketing, and random scraping and shoveling of snow and ice.

Daniel suggested I take some dressage lessons, independent of himself, and now seems like a good time to do it. There is a lady, Daisy Knight, who has a barn within riding distance and that's attractive to me, since it means no messing with a trailer in the snow.

The dressage world, I know, is kind of a little bubble of its own and I'm familiar with the main trainer's pedigree and the list of USDF medals and awards she's won. I kind of don't expect her to take me, certainly not for a few lessons during a holiday week, but when I say Daniel's name and my last name (*wasn't your mother...*) she agrees. There was a part of me that hoped she wouldn't because I know it is going to be painful, but I go along with it, because I know I should.

The barn initially confirms every prejudice I've ever had about dressage riders. Ms. Knight is elderly and short and looks kind of frail. And I kind of feel that I confirm every prejudice she's ever had about event riders. My last exposure to the dressage world was at a show I went to as a high schooler when my barn's trailer was next to a dressage barn's. It was one of those schooling shows where they have a bunch of different events all running together. The DQs (dressage queens) chewed us (okay, me) out because the music playing was "disturbing the horses while they were resting." I mean, seriously, you're actually dressed up like the Panic! At the Disco music video for "I Write Songs, Not Tragedies" and you're gonna object to that song being played at a reasonable volume?

At my first barn I saw a couple of lower-level dressage lessons where the ladies (all of the riders were ladies) spent more time in the ring discussing the movements than actually doing them. It seemed like the worst high school class ever, only they were subjecting the horses to it as well as themselves.

Most of what Daisy and I go over is pretty basic about getting the horse on the bit and the whole dressage pyramid business that I know about rhythm, relaxation, connection, impulsion, and straightness. Oh, and collection. That too.

My mind feels fried after the lesson in a way that it doesn't after doing other types of riding, even though I'm pleased to find that Fortune does have a nice shoulder-in and even a reliable collected canter. I just don't find the sense of release and continuous flow that I do outside of a ring so I don't feel the same sense of accomplishment after practicing a dressage test, although I should. I still kind of feel that putting so much weight score-wise on dressage was deliberately done to subvert me, somehow. I mean, what I like about riding is that it gets me out of my head but it seems like dressage does just the opposite although it is possible I'm just doing it all wrong.

Daisy is still a trip and I get a kick out of how she calls me "young man." By the end of the lesson, she says that I didn't do too badly for an eventer.

"Thanks, I think."

"Still, you need to understand that being accomplished at riding is more than being able to do everything bigger and faster."

"It is?" I say, and laugh. At least she didn't put me on the lunge line for the whole damn lesson, which I was kind of afraid she would.

"Ah, let me guess, you're one of those men who thinks what they call ballet on horseback is dull. My son was that way at first but now he and his wife are both USDF bronze medalists and he's working his way towards his silver. I wish he was around so you could see him ride. Perhaps you'd be persuaded otherwise."

"I doubt it," I say, "I've been trying to like dressage for years but, you know, different horses for different courses and it's just really not for me. It's a testimony to how much I love going cross-country for eventing that I'm here at all."

Daisy tells me to get off Fortune because she wants to show me something. I'm kind of afraid she's going to break a hip or whatever even just getting on him. I hesitate but I also sort of know she's not the type of woman you disobey even though she looks about eighty, what with her white braid in a bun and her weather-beaten face.

With Daisy on his back, despite the fact that my new saddle is far too large for her, Fortune seems to change shape before my eyes. She trots him around and he's shifting gaits like I've never seen him do before, then cantering and counter-cantering with visibly different speeds. She ends with some lateral work and finishes it off with what looks like a semi-credible stab at a piaffe, which I didn't even know Fortune had as part of his skill set.

"Who taught him that?" I ask.

"He's very, very rusty," she proclaims, getting off and giving him back to me to cool out. "And certainly not a natural, the way he's put together. But he does have the capability of learning, if his rider believes he can." She winks at me.

I get back on and my horse feels slightly different even from that short ride, in a way he never has with me on his back, even after my longest dressage schooling session with him.

"He has the capability of jumping five foot with ease," I say, not sure if I am defending Fortune or myself.

"Oh, I'm sure he does, with you," she says, still sounding bemused. "But I love how you eventers are always so proud about how your horses are bad at dressage, even though you claim you love to win. *Eventers*," she says, like someone else might say 'children.'

"Oh trust me, I am trying," I say. "It's not like I can import a warmblood on a whim to replace him."

"You'll have to convince yourself that it doesn't make you less of a man to be sensitive enough to ride dressage."

I laugh at that, self-consciously, because obviously she's clueless.

But riding back, slowly because it's a cold day and the ground is frozen, my mind begins to wander and I half-wonder if I'm the clueless one, not her.

When he was seriously riding, Sean was always better at dressage than me. That was when we were still in our early teens, before we moved to New Jersey and my mom was still getting us trainers and stuff, trying to keep us riding in the style we had been accustomed to before the divorce. That didn't last for long, money-wise, and always made mom feel bad although I often spent more time arguing with the trainers than listening to them. I was a stubborn little kid.

I remember riding with Sean and the trainer complimenting him on his horse's lateral work as we warmed up for jumping (Sean never seemed to like jumping in particular, even back then). The trainer said, "Maybe the elder Mr. O'Shaughnessy's real talent is in dressage."

And some girl said, "That's one way to meet girls, because no guys I know specialize in dressage."

"Or not to meet girls," said the trainer, and everyone laughed.

I was still bored with dressage, back then, particularly since I was so restless—even without the sniggers and innuendos, I didn't take to it like I did jumping. Still, the contempt in their voices didn't exactly make me long for praise at it, either.

I take another dressage lesson and I do try to school Fortune a bit more within the confines of that lettered ring. And he does get better. The new saddle, the lessons do help. I try to remember the feeling he had after Daisy was on him in my mind. I try to let myself love that a little bit, too. Daisy gives me the whole spiel about how dressage was originally a way to condition military horses to be effective in battle. I guess she's trying to convince me it's manly but I know I'd make a terrible soldier. I've never been a good team player.

I just prefer to have the focus of fences as an objective, I explain to her, I'm not actively resisting anything.

"Your horse thinks otherwise," she says.

I don't eliminate the long rides outside the ring, since that is what both of us really look forward to out here. Fortune now has special shoes to give him added grip on the ice although some days it's so slick we can't do much more than trot most of the way. I love seeing other riders too, even though I ride outside to be alone. I like to pass my fellow equestrians on the road, nod in solidarity, and then head on my way.

One day, I'm riding Fortune on a country road and this SUV speeds by me. I could forgive that, given that I know people don't really know how to drive around horses anymore (although they should with all the farms in the area). But then the guy starts honking and kind of weaves into me, like he thinks he's being funny. I don't know what his deal is.

I ignore him at first but then he slows down in front of me, waits, and kind of swerves into me, again, blaring his horn and blasting his music. Even Fortune, who normally wouldn't spook if a rustling paper bag climbed up his butt, shies away. I hear a string of Quentin Tarantino -worthy curse words come out of my mouth.

All I can think is, thank Christ that I'm riding a brave horse and not one of the Thoroughbred babies with scrambled eggs for brains, otherwise you'd be scraping me off a tree. And what if a rider like Cynthia or Megan was out riding by this road instead? Or God help them, Sean or Heather? The sound and the motion of the car scared even me for a second.

The guy pulls the car in front of Fortune after he hears me cussing at him and then grabs my horse's bridle. "What did you call me, you fucking asshole?" he says.

Oh. So it's going to be like that?

I swing down off of my horse. The guy (he's this skinny kid, maybe a little older than me, more head than body) threw the first punch, sort of, with his car, so I feel totally justified when I turn on him. It's been a long time since I've been in a fight. The worst fight I was in before this was when I was a freshman in high school. There were a few scuffles after that but they were usually broken up before they got as bad as the one during which I broke the guy's nose. But there are no principals out here, no lunch monitors.

Fighting is like riding a bike. You don't forget how, and I know this guy doesn't really know what he's doing. I feel his nose and cheek-bones against my fists, I duck and swerve to avoid whatever he has for me, and suddenly I have him up against his shiny red SUV. I want to keep going at him but I move away just enough so he can duck back in his car and then speed away.

The whole thing is kind of a blur but there is a little bit of blood on my knuckles (I hit his nose, didn't break anything) so I

253

know I got him good enough so he felt something, even if it's just a bad nosebleed. I don't feel any pain at all. I escaped completely untouched except for the beating sound of my heart against my ribs. Fortune stood there through the whole thing, quietly, just watching me. Like I said, thank goodness I wasn't riding one of the young Thoroughbreds.

I would have bit and kicked him, ineffective human, I imagine Fortune say in my mind. *That would have finished him off.* I laugh a little as I haul myself up in the saddle and pat him. I feel relaxed, weightless.

I know it's not right but there is a part of me that enjoys fighting. I've never started a fight in my life but I've never walked away from one, either. Besides, in high school, the only time the other kids respected me even slightly was when they saw me go at some bigger guy and beat the hell out of him. Riding meant nothing to most of them.

The main casualty of the fight by the road hits me by the time I get to the barn: The warm gloves Max gave me must have fallen out of the pockets of my jacket at some point, because they aren't there anymore. I look for them the next time I ride by the road but by then there is more freshly fallen snow plus some mud, slush, and salt all over the place, too. I'll never find them again.

I don't tell Max about the fight, of course, and I let him think I just lost the gloves in the barn or something. I get some new ones from the general store in town, since I need them pretty badly in the morning—I'm not a wuss about the cold like Cindy but I don't have the impenetrable reptile-like skin Megan seems to have. Although the new gloves aren't nearly as good as the ones I used to have, I don't know where Max got them.

The next time I'm out riding with Max, he gets a call from the practice, directing him to a farm that's on his way. It's an emergency. When we get there, the owner is practically incoherent with fear and

I can see why when he takes us to the field because the horse looks so bad.

The fences at the farm aren't barbed wire, thank God, but somehow, maybe it blew in or was stuck in some hay—who knows— there is a coil of metal twisted around the gelding's leg. He's kicking out and trying to free himself but of course the wire just gets more deeply embedded.

The owner says he tried to put on the animal's halter but couldn't get over to the horse. "Josh couldn't either," he says, indicating his son, a teenager standing behind him.

Max tells me to wait by the side of the paddock. I want to go in with him, I almost do, but he says, "If we crowd the horse, it will just scare him more."

Stay still, I think, as if I could mentally will the horse not to move, as if the animal could hear my thoughts, even though of course every logical fiber of his equine brain is telling him to take flight from whatever is trying to kill him, from that wire snake.

I can't hear what Max is saying, but it must be soft and soothing.

Every time the horse moves, the wire twists deeper into his leg. Then Max is holding the animal's halter and gradually, slowly, the horse's motion stills. Max puts the halter on and injects the gelding, I assume with a tranquilizer.

The owner fortunately has had the sense to bring wire cutters, and now I do slowly make my way into the paddock. Max holds the animal as I snap at the evil, twisting barbs.

For the first time in a long time someone speaks. "Suturing barbed wire cuts can be tricky," breathes Max. "Too jagged." He looks over the cut, though, and decides that the irregular gash isn't so bad and he can still do it.

It feels like hours as he slowly, painstakingly stitches. The animal seems to sense now that Max is trying to help him and stands, dopey from the drug. We manage to get him back to his stall and Max gives instructions about keeping the wound clean. The horse is dazed but at least he doesn't look like he's dying anymore.

It's times like this, despite all the years I've been around horses, that I feel slightly helpless. That I want to kind of give everything up, and go back to school, and be like Max. I envy his calm, steadying patience so much, even the patience to wade through all those years of study. Max does seem to have his life down to a system, I think, more so than he even fully realizes himself.

It's hard for me to explain even to Max but it is at moments like this when I love him the most, far more than for anything he's ever done for me, even though he has literally given me the shirt off his back and would do so again if I asked him for it.

28

DENSE

Later in January, Cindy and I go down to Florida with Daniel, where he's teaching a clinic at a pretty ritzy stable of a friend and where we are supposed to ride the horses of the barn's owner during said clinic. We're also bringing Fortune down for me to ride in a nearby event.

Megan doesn't go, which floors me. She's getting married to Ricky in June and says she needs to "work on stuff" for the wedding. I tell her she's crazy and missing the opportunity of a lifetime. I need one more NQR to go Intermediate and this is it. I need it now like oxygen.

So it's just me and Cindy. I've ridden in Florida before on the winter circuit. I'm familiar with the weird sights of palm trees next to jumps in arenas. What with the cold back home, at this point I'll take galloping around in swampy heat, even if I have to slather on the sunblock. Daniel laughs at the fact Cindy and I complain so much about the ice and snow; he says our blood isn't thick enough and we're not broke to winter yet.

Once we're there, when Cindy and I are practicing on the demo horses for the clinic, I'm almost reconsidering my pronouncement about the cold—I'm so used to trying to keep warm all the time, I'm revoltingly sweaty after very little effort. Even Cynthia is dabbing her neck with a (monogrammed) handkerchief.

I'm riding a big mare named Eazy and Cindy has been given a smaller mare named Fly (officially Fly Me to the Moon). Given that my adult sexual history has been boringly monogamous for the most part and Cindy, based upon my extensive viewing of early '80s rap videos, is probably the least fly person I know, these names seem very inappropriate. But I like my big chestnut girl—she seems willing and uncomplicated as a finely-tuned machine, although slightly stupid. After riding Fortune so much, I'm lured into a sense of complacency.

The small cross-country course at the barn is serviceable (it hits all the necessary high notes, there is even a very welcome little splash so we can try the horses out over water) but by the time we've finished, the heat his pretty oppressive. We decide to do a little dressage just to cool off and call it a day.

Cynthia says, "I'm sick of this, it's just dressage," and takes off her helmet. I've ridden helmetless before, more out of convenience than design, like when I need to get back from a far field, I'll hop on a horse's back when I don't feel like walking. And the last time I rode Western with my brother I didn't bother because he no longer wears a helmet, now that he's not a junior and wearing helmets is merely encouraged rather than required for the Western classes he rides in. So it doesn't seem like a terrible idea. Until I'm cantering past C.

The wind has picked up ever so slightly, just enough for me to be grateful for a breeze, and my mind is still fuzzy from all the traveling, the heat, and the disruption to my routine so I don't really see the candy wrapper flitting in the breeze. But Eazy sure does and spooks huge just when I am mentally preparing to ask for a downward transition. Suddenly, there is no horse beneath me and for the first time in years—years, I tell you—I'm on the ground rather than on my feet, like I usually land. I feel the smooth plastic of the dressage fence against my collarbone and part of my skull.

"Oh my God, Simon, are you all right?"

I'm embarrassed as hell that it's me, not Cindy that ate dirt, so my immediate instinct is to laugh. "Foiled by a Snickers bar," I say, "but okay."

I think of the famous saying of George Morris, "Hospital or on." You bet. I get on Eazy and I'm very careful not to take the fact I'm pissed off at the world out on her. She's an easier ride than Fortune and I shouldn't have fallen. By God, come hell, high water, or every goddamned candy wrapper in the universe, I'm going to be an Intermediate-level rider by the end of my trip here, not be told by some doctor to sit on my ass.

I think I'm okay, and all of the adrenaline in me carries me through the rest of our practice, but by the time we're back at the hotel my collarbone is throbbing in time to the beat of the muzak being pumped through the lobby. I don't even have any Advil with me so I have to buy some at a convenience store. I don't know why I feel secretive about getting dumped. Okay, well I do, something is wrong but it's nothing that can't be patched up after all this is over, I tell myself.

I don't even remember the fall that well, to be honest. My head feels thick and fuzzy but I am aware that some other part of me, located in the body, was able to get me through the rest of the ride with Cindy so I'll be okay at the clinic and better than okay when I ride Fortune at the event.

The clinic (what I can remember of it) is uneventful and I just do what Daniel tells me to do; most of it is spent focused on the paying people's riders and their horses.

At the event there are no blowing candy wrappers on any parts of the course and it's not particularly tricky, which is a good thing because honestly, I'm not thinking all that well. I know there is a thick, opaque pane between me and the world and I'm sort of going through the motions. My hands and my legs remember how to do things and we get the best cross-country time, perfect optimum time. I find myself enjoying the sense of flight but not as much, I am dimly aware of the fact, as I would be if my head were screwed on correctly. Banks, coops, drops, water, logs, oh my, oh my, rinse, wash, and repeat. We also go clear in show jumping and by the end of the day I do get that much-coveted NQR.

Daniel says, "Well, you should be proud of yourself, O'Shaughnessy. No more bellyaching from you about how you aren't progressing."

I grin. I do feel happy and even the feeling in my collarbone doesn't seem so bad. The drum of its throbbing matched my horse's hoof beats as we rode. The fuzzy feeling isn't visible to the outside world, thank goodness, and I'll be damned if I'll be kept from celebrating this moment by something that can't be seen, smelled, or touched and doesn't need to even be taped, much less put in a sling. *Don't be a pussy*, like I said to my brother when he was whining about his toe and his stupid running injury. I just wish I could enjoy things a little more and didn't feel so queasy and achy. Why do I feel nauseated even though I hurt my head and collarbone?

I try not to think about things too much, which is easy since thinking is a bit challenging, and by the time I get home, the fog has begun to lift. The achievement becomes clearer and sharper, as does my sense of happiness. I don't get to see Max for a day as we settle back into the routine of the farm. Megan has done a pretty good job of keeping things up, though, despite preparing for her dumb wedding.

Of course, the first thing Max does is embrace me in congratulations. But I know suddenly that things are still wrong since this is too much, this is the first time someone has touched my shoulder since it happened, and I yelp involuntarily and pull back.

"What's wrong?" he asks.

"Leave it," I say. I don't want to but I'm too tired and my brain is still righting itself so rather than stonewalling I just tell him the truth.

Max is pretty pissed off, which I kind of expected. "What were you thinking? What were you not thinking, I mean?"

"Max, it was a dumb thing to ride without a helmet on a horse I didn't know but what could I do? It was NQR or perish," I explain.

"You know you might have a broken collarbone."

"If it was broken, I would be in more pain." Max puts his fingers to my temple. I didn't tell him about my throbbing head but he notices the slight shadow of a bruise.

"We're going to the ER to get you checked out," he says.

"Max, I'm not going to the ER. There is nothing they can do."

"They can give you an X-ray. And check to see if you have a concussion."

"All they'll do is tell me I can't ride."

"Do you want your collarbone to heal broken? Then you'll be really screwed. If it's not broken, then fine, but at least get it checked out."

Max keeps going on about how I should have told Daniel and gotten it looked at and then I snap, "Well, it's obviously not a clean break and you know small fractures don't even show up on X-rays before they begin to heal. My brother's stress fracture didn't when he first got it and then two weeks after, then they saw the crack."

"What, now you have the medical degree?"

"You're being a real dick and you know what I'm saying is the truth. I might not have a degree but I sure as hell know the science of getting hurt." I can't believe he's throwing the whole college thing up at me at a time like this. I realize he's sort of mad because he's worried but I feel that if it's my neck I risked, not his, he should just back off.

"Do you have health insurance? With you, I guess I shouldn't be so sure."

"Of course, I have health insurance through my mom, I'm still a kid, remember," I say, glad that I can bring up the age thing to him in response and make him feel at least bad enough to shut up.

Even if I did have a concussion—which I don't, of course, but if I did—it is clearing and (based on my brother's experiences playing soccer) it seems pretty mild. I know I'm lucky even though I'm mad at Max right now. All of the anger I felt at myself for making such a dumb mistake is turned against him.

The doctor first looks at my shoulder. "Nope, no break or fracture and it would have shown up by now," he says. "Just bruising and swelling."

"See?" I say to Max. "*By now*—I told you that it takes a while to show up."

"You're just lucky you're not some little old lady, with that kind of a fall. Your bones must be pretty dense," says the doctor.

"Oh, he's dense all right," says Max. "He hurt his head, too. You can see the bruise."

"Yeah, now I do."

Shut up, Max. I think the thought so hard I am sure Max can hear me, even though I don't say anything or raise my eyes. The doctor looks bored and clearly wants to get us out of there and I want to get me out of here, too.

The doctor is young, younger than Max, but he's got a gut, is pasty as hell, and is already losing his hair. Now he needs to run all sorts of questions by me to see if I got a concussion. Did I lose consciousness? Did I have any confusion? Any double vision? Any sense of time moving slower? Irritability?

No, no, no, no. "And I'm always irritable," I say.

I know all of these questions, and I know the right answers because of Sean and soccer and even the brief time I spent playing team sports. It's not just standardized tests with fill-in-the-bubbles that have obvious true-false answers.

It seems to me that if you can't honestly state that you don't have a concussion, the next best thing is being able to fake not having a concussion reasonably well. I mean, being able to fake wellness is a pretty good sign that whatever you have isn't that bad at all.

No, no, no sense of confusion. No loss of memory. No delayed reaction times, I say. "I mean, I placed at the last event I rode in after the fall, and I wouldn't have been able to do that with a concussion."

I can feel Max getting angrier.

"He's clear to go back to work," says the doctor. "What do you do again?"

"I'm a trainer. I ride and work with horses," I remind him. "Stuff like this happens all the time. You just get back on."

"Sure, okay," says the doctor, his voice flat and I swear a bit smirky.

"Look, you don't know him. Of course, he's going to say he's fine, that's the mentality of a rider," says Max.

"Max, seriously," I say. "Drop it." I use the same tone as I would on Jig if he picked up a dead rat or something.

"What is your relationship again? You're his brother?" I vaguely note that the tone of the doctor is well, different than the tone of the doctor when mom dragged Sean in to our pediatrician after he got whacked on the head, but I'm too fixated on the door to care. Nothing busted, nothing broken, out the door we go.

"I'm his friend," says Max. "Shouldn't he lay off the riding, even if the symptoms of the concussion have abated?"

"I don't have a concussion, didn't have a concussion," I say.

"Stop it, Simon," says Max.

"You heard him," says the doctor, already walking out the door. The guy's mind is on the next case.

Max is fuming and I know he's cursing me out in his own, all-too-clear head as we go to check out of the ER. It takes a long time, it seems, to get out of there and as we wait, I overhear the doctor that saw me saying to some nurse, "Yeah, it's been a night. I just saw these two gay guys. One of them probably beating the other one up just to get his kicks." She giggles.

I think that's when I fully admit to myself that my mind is working pretty slowly because suddenly I hear a silent "click" in terms of the doctor's sniggering and lack of concern for me.

I look at Max but he's talking to the person at the front desk, (I've given him my health insurance card to settle the paperwork.) We walk out together to where we've parked the car a million miles away in the crowded lot when suddenly I say, "Can you meet me at the door?"

Max thinks I'm not feeling well, I guess, so he says sure and doesn't ask any questions, thank God. I stride back in the hospital and wait for a second, wait until the doctor stops flirting with the stupid nurse and is in the hall alone. I walk up behind him, look around to make sure no one is watching, get him by the wrists, cross them, and shove his face into the wall. The corner hides both of us and I don't see a security camera in this tiny, miserable hospital out in batshit nowhere so I think I'm okay.

"I heard what you said. Listen, asshole, if you had any brains in your head and a fucking medical degree from anywhere else than from a fucking cereal box you would know that I got busted up from riding."

"Jesus," he says, and I know he's scared. It feels like pressing into a pillow, his arms are so flabby and soft.

"Call security, if you like, I have no problem telling them what a homophobic fucking asshole you are," I say. "I'm not going to hurt you though, just know that I could twist your goddamn arms out of their sockets if I wanted to."

"Simon?" I let the doctor go at the sound of Max's voice.

"Max, he said—"

"Simon, I heard what he said."

"And you didn't even react? Max, you're not even human."

"Simon, are you out of your mind? You're lucky you didn't get arrested."

"A guy with that attitude shouldn't be practicing medicine."

"What am I going to do with you?" Max takes off his glasses and wipes his eyes. "Simon, you can't *do* things like that." I know he's acting horrified and all but I think a tiny portion of him wants to laugh although I'm not sure if it is nervous laughter. "One of these days you're going to cross paths with someone with a gun or a knife and the fact that you're stronger than him won't do you any good."

"Well, until then, until then, I will—" I can't finish the sentence, so I leave it hanging like a threat to, I don't know, some nameless guy in the future.

"I thought that was the reason he didn't give you any painkillers," says Max, starting the road before us as if he is angry with it.

"Oh, I don't care about them, I wouldn't have taken them. Can't be doped up at work with the horses," I say. "And I know you, Max. You would feel the same way if it happened to you."

Max sighs and keeps his eyes on the road for black ice. "Some nights, there just isn't enough wine in the world. What would you have done if your horse had pulled up lame? Would you have still kept going then?"

"Of course not." I'm confused. What the hell does my having a (non)concussion have to do with the fact I'd never do anything to hurt my horse for the sake of winning? Seriously, Max, and this isn't my rattled head talking, but that's the dumbest comparison I've never heard. It's just not the same thing at all.

Want to know the funny thing? After all that nonsense at the ER, I feel much better—the bruise over the bone doesn't feel like anything, I don't feel the slightest touch of pain and the last bits of fog from the concussion (which of course was not a concussion) seem to lift. So in a weird way, the visit to the doctor worked. I suppose he was a kind of angel of mercy in disguise.

I think about what Max said, that one day some guy is going to have a gun or a knife or whatever, if I'm too quick to fight. It happened a long time ago but I still remember that easy first fight I had in school, how the guy's nose felt so satisfying, flattening against my fist, after all the crap I had taken that year. And for some time afterward, people respected me, said I was cool. And then in a month it all started up again, as if things had never changed, which they hadn't. Cocksucker. Faggot. Ass jokes. The kiddie equivalent of all the crap Cindy's father says on TV.

I wish I could take whatever makes people say the things they do and flatten it, crush it, cut it down to size, rip it out. Like cancer or like the heart of something evil in a science fiction book. But if it makes me feel good to hit back, even if it's ineffectual, even if one day I lose (which I haven't yet), I think it's better than lying down and taking it, no matter what Max says.

I also feel thoroughly justified in my decision to ride, regardless of what may be technically correct according to a medical textbook. The doctor's behavior clearly shows that some members of his professions are idiots. I got the result I needed and I've even proven to myself that I can make it around a course with my brain beaten up a bit. Hell, for something I really need to win, I bet could do it with my brain oozing out of my fucking ears. Just let the muscle memory take over.

29

TWENTY POINTS FOR A... (REVISITED)

I'm so excited I wake up even earlier than my alarm on our day off. Megan and I have made plans to drive to the Indian casino in Maine, with Ricky and Cindy in tow. I know I'll end up doing the morning barn chores, just by virtue of being around, even though the high school kids that volunteer are supposed to handle them all today.

It's been awhile since I've played cards and when Megan asked me to go, suddenly I realized how much I missed gambling. I missed the slick feeling of the cards between my fingers, the calm focus that comes from staring at hearts, diamonds, clubs, and spades, and the strange sense of knowingness and anticipation that comes from those types of games. It's not the same love that I feel for riding but I love it all the same. No one here at the farm likes to play games much—certainly not Megan or Cynthia, they aren't even big sports fans. Megan likes shooting but mainly as a way of messing around. There's no purpose to it. Daniel doesn't play anything, although every now and then he's let me watch a Sox, Celtics, or (most recently) Pats game on the TV at his house.

I nuke myself a Hot Pocket, grab a Mountain Dew and sit outside in the early morning darkness, watching Jig half-run, half-stagger in circles as he jogs around. He barks and I tell him to hush because it's not quite feeding time yet. I throw a stick to distract him and watch how he makes a black and white trail in the frozen whiteness. Then I grab a lead rope and we play tug-of-war for a little bit. It's so slippery, even with my work boots, I can't gain much traction and he almost wins. I know you're not supposed to play tug-of-war with dogs, it teaches them bad habits—to bite and pull and not let go— but according to Max, Jig doesn't have many teeth left, and none of them are good, so I figure there isn't much damage he can do.

As I walk back to the barn, I notice a red-tailed hawk fly over us, slowly, circling and circling. I stand there watching it, slightly hypnotized. It feels like a good omen. Then I hear the horses kicking and I see the high school kids' ride pull up and I snap back to reality.

It's a rare day off that I don't spend with Max. I begged him to come with us, I'm sure the girls would get a kick out of the vet being there, I tease him.

"I'm working. Besides, I don't gamble, I work too hard for my money. The house always wins, they say."

"Well, that's why I'm going, I need the money."

"How can you be so sure you'll win? What do you do, count cards? Oh, I should have known. Of course you count cards. That would be something you know how to do."

"I'm okay at it but probably a little rusty. I know I'll win something. I won't let the house beat me, I'll quit when I'm ahead. What, I thought you admired my math skills?"

Ricky's Mustang chugs uncertainly over the icy streets. We start by playing his iPod in the sound system he's built into the souped-up old vehicle ("Yup, that's what he fixes first, not anything else in this junk heap," observes Megan) but I quickly grow tired of the heavy metal and ask Megan to plug in my own.

Cynthia groans. "Oh, no, Simon, what do you have for us now?"

"What do you mean?" I ask.

"What is *this*?" says Cindy.

"Don't tell me you haven't heard the cover of 'I Fought the Law' by the Clash?"

"If I have, I don't remember it."

Kind of just to piss Cindy off, I start drumming along with the song on the back of Megan's seat. Megan just laughs and even Cynthia begins to kind of sway along in time and I actually put my arm around her so we can bob together to the beat.

When the song is over, I say, "Seriously, that's the first time you've ever heard that before?"

"Seriously, I'd never even heard of the Clash," says Cynthia.

How can someone live so long without listening to the Clash? I don't get it. I remember everyone asking if Cynthia and I were dating when I went hunting and I think, even sex aside, I could never love someone who liked Taylor Swift better than Brandon Flowers. To paraphrase a great science fiction series: *Trust no one, unless they have your taste in music.*

Cynthia isn't bothered by my disdain, though. "Let me guess, Simon, there is some sort of morbid backstory with this band, like some member got so depressed by his music he killed himself or something, like with all of the bands you listen to..."

"Yes, Cynthia, there is a tragedy—the lead singer of the Clash, the legendary Joe Strummer, tragically died of an undiagnosed heart defect. But I don't see what that has to do with knowing or not knowing one of the greatest songs by one of the greatest bands ever. This is not a depressing song. It's like, life-affirming or whatever. Now, the next song coming up, the 'Guns of Brixton,' is depressing, but still, one of their best."

"And really angry, I bet, from the sound of that title," she says, giggling. "So who is the band on your T-shirt? I have never seen you wear that."

I don't know what she means at first; all of my band T-shirts are dirty with manure and horse drool and I won't be able to do laundry at Max's this week. I'm in a free The Hungry Puppy T-shirt, a pair of bleached and faded jeans that are so worn they have a nap to them like velvet, my anarchist hoodie, Doc Martins, and Carhartt jacket. And of course the Sox cap.

"The Hungry Puppy isn't a band, it's a feed store from back in New Jersey. What, are you thinking of Skinny Puppy?"

"So here I was thinking, Simon is going to be all, what, you haven't heard of Hungry Puppy? Its lead singer tragically killed himself years ago, its lead guitarist had a horrible disease, its drummer had a bad heroin addiction, and and…"

"The lead female singer had a terrible eating disorder and was coked up all the time," offers Megan.

"Don't forget getting arrested," adds Ricky.

"Whatever," I say. "Life is often very cruel to great artists. Besides, you know my favorite band is the Killers and they haven't done any of that stuff. Everyone in that band has had pretty normal lives. They're on the playlist too, followed by Queen."

"I know Queen," says Cynthia. "They used to play Queen at football games all the time at my high school."

Of course they did, they just played, "We are the Champions." Just scratching the surface, which is all most people know about Queen, surface meanings. I roll my eyes and stuff my hands deeper in the pockets of my Carhartt and refrain from giving everyone my Freddie Mercury lecture. I'll save that for next time.

I'm wondering if I should have gotten more dressed up. Cynthia is wearing tons of makeup, her hair is even straighter than usual and she has on a white wool peacoat and a plaid scarf that Megan says is Burberry and worth probably more than I make in a month. Oh well, as long as they let me in the casino to play dressed as I am, I don't care. I'm not here to impress anyone. Megan and Ricky aren't quite so dressed up but neither of them are in jeans.

The casino is so sad and miserable inside, I almost want to turn back. Lots of old people at the slots—people who look like they can hardly move without a walker but can still pull the levers with arthritic glee. But the blackjack tables look more promising and there are even people who still look somewhat alive there, albeit kind of plastered. We're here in Maine because the legal age to gamble is eighteen, unlike some other states (I checked beforehand). I still can't drink of course but I think that is going to give me an additional advantage.

Megan, Ricky, and Cynthia go off to play the slots and presumably drink some of the pretty cocktails I see floating around in people's hands. I park myself at a green, soft, plush table. It feels like a tennis ball beneath my fingers. I don't pick a relatively high-stakes one to start at. For all of my bravado, I'm no savant at this. To my left is a guy with a bad comb-over who has already had one too many. I eventually glean he is a professor at a local university. Then there's a pudgy, ghoulish dude whose skin takes on the appearance of alternating shades of green and yellow under the casino lights; a guy who looks like he used to play football or something in high school by the sheer size of his neck; and an elderly bald man and his equally old but mysteriously red-haired wife.

I signal for the dealer to hit me and I'm off.

As my pile of winnings increases, some of the other players start to make little comments. The woman dealer, who has a bad perm and frosted lipstick, barely bats a heavily mascaraed eye at me, but the other guys, especially the plastered professor, start saying stuff as they get annoyed. Like, "You couldn't have dressed the part of a rube better, what are you hiding?" I guess they mean the feed store T-shirt and the Carhartt jacket. I just shrug and kind of grunt because I've got nothing to say to them and split my next hand. There is no one I feel like talking to here and I only expose my personality to strangers I like.

Cynthia comes over to check on me at one point. She's drinking something with an umbrella, which I gather is a signal that there is something very strong in the glass. "Wow, Simon," she slurs and giggles.

Shut up, I think, and look away as if I don't know her. She gets my drift and sort of staggers away. Underneath her peacoat I now see was some sort of a strappy shirt thing that looks more like a bra than a shirt (whatever those things are called) and I feel idly concerned about her as she circles around, but then again, she has Megan and Ricky to look after her. It doesn't matter if she wins or loses playing the slots, she has money to waste and I do not.

The professor's wife comes over to collect him. "I think you've had enough," she says, meaning his multiple gimlets, the cards, or both.

"Just another hand," he says. "Look at the kid," he adds, jealously, nodding at my pile.

"That's nice for him, but you promised we'd be home by now. I've soaked up enough second-hand alcohol fumes to last me for the rest of the year. You've had your fill of your little taste of Sin City."

"The cynic Diogenes said when caught in a house of ill-repute, 'does not the sun pass through the privy walls but is not defiled,'" says the professor, grandly, clinging to the table like it was a life preserver in an ocean. His wife manages to drag him away.

I take this as yet another sign of the rightness of my not being in college. That guy's a professor and been in school for, well, for fuck-ever long it takes to become a teacher, and he's the shittiest player at the table.

The fat, yellowish man frowns at me as I win again. I don't like the look neckless dude is giving me either, so I move to a different table.

There, the people don't talk or glare at all. They are also drinking less because they've come to play. It's all men at this one, including two guys who look like extras from *Goodfellas*, although I'm going to hope that is just the impression they project.

I walked into the casino with $200 and I'm at $2,000 now. That's still less than I could have won riding at some shows, I think, and play on. I'm not really greedy but I want to make this worth my time, I'm not here for pleasure.

So $2,000. Then $5,000. At first Ricky and Megan get restless (Cynthia is too drunk to care). Come $6,000 they shut up and just start to watch. "What are you doing?" whispers Megan. I tell her to shut up and wait by the slots and I'll meet everyone when I'm through.

At $7,500 or so I start to feel as if the casino staff is passing by the table a bit more. I'm honestly a little scared myself. I've never wagered this much before. But the pile of chips, with all of its strange, brightly-colored glory, feels completely detached from the money I came in with, so I play on. There is also a part of me that knows I'm riding something which, while partly due to my skill, also has an element of luck involved. Not just with the cards but the ability I've found to shut everything out and just flow. Kind of like with riding, it's as if all I've learned this year has sharpened my ability to abandon myself to the present. I've forgotten everything, even the reason why I am doing this (the need for a better saddle, entry fees, and for the future I will have when I'm gone).

Around $9,000 the presence of the casino security guards is even more palpable and I know that my run will be over shortly, not because of luck but because of the men.

So I cash everything in at around ten grand. My friends watch the casino staff watch me from the distance.

I leave with a brown paper bag in my Carhartt, my anarchist hoodie drawn up around my face, and my heart beating against the brown paper like a small wild animal stuffed in my coat. Oh yeah, and an IRS form so apparently I shouldn't get too crazy about thinking of spending what I've won in total.

"Holy shit, Simon, that was amazing," says Ricky. He's sobered up and so has Megan. Even the buzz has been taken off Cynthia's drunkenness, since she's been watching me rather than drinking for quite a while. She still slips and nearly falls in the icy parking lot. Ricky insists on driving, maybe because he thinks I'm drunk from my winnings although I'm the only hundred percent sober person, physically speaking, of all four of us.

"Did you know that would happen?" asks Megan.

"Not exactly," I say.

"Do you always win that much money when you gamble?" asks Ricky, as if he still doesn't believe that what I was doing wasn't witchcraft.

"In two words: Fuck. And no."

"Do you—count cards?" asks Cynthia.

"Why do people gamble without counting?" I ask, laughing. "I'm okay at it, not great, I've never won this much before."

We're all starving and dazed. We stop at a steak house on the ride home. I buy Ricky, Megan, and myself three sirloins. Cynthia gets a shrimp cocktail with six shrimp, chased down with a glass of white wine.

"She doesn't eat," I say, explaining to the waiter, when ordering for the four of us.

"Simon, that isn't cool to say," says Megan, when Cynthia goes to the bathroom.

"Why? It's true," I say. Megan of all people isn't going to lecture me on etiquette.

I ask for ketchup with my steak and fries and ignore the waiter's disapproving look.

We hit the road again and the rocking rhythm of the car soothes and comforts me and soon I'm falling asleep. I can still feel the weight of my winnings in my jacket pressing up against my heart. Cynthia is dozing off next to me too and even that doesn't bother me. I love the roaring sound of the heat in the car which, unlike the rest of the car itself, works incredibly well.

And then suddenly the light of the headlights momentarily grows brighter as it shines not just against the white of the snow and ice before us but the flank of a great big buck. Ricky, despite being half-hypnotized by the unending slickness of the road, swerves to avoid it—not much, but enough that it can scamper free. Another car might have continued on, unperturbed, but it is too much for the Mustang and what with the tires that should be replaced suddenly the car is slipping off the road, down the embankment and smashing into a tree in a nearby ditch.

Cynthia is awake now. "Oh my God! The one time in my life I'm not wearing a seatbelt and the car gets driven into a ditch!" she gasps.

I think that is pretty funny so I start to laugh. Ricky is so tired he starts to giggle too. Megan begins to hit him. "I told you not to buy this stupid car, you idiot. I knew this would happen." Ricky can't hit back, of course, he's a big guy and Megan is like a little wisp smacking him with her tiny fists, although she is strong for her size. I find both of them hilarious, the picture they create looks like a tiny bumblebee trying to kick a hippopotamus' ass in one of those science documentaries I love.

I take out my cellphone to give a call for help—kind of hoping Ricky has AAA or something, because I know whoever comes to tow us out is going to charge us a ridiculous amount of money, having to come through the snow and all and because we are so desperate. But then... "Um, guys, does anyone else have service on their cell phone? Because I sure don't."

Everyone checks. There is a long wait as we all scuttle out of the car. We don't even look at the Mustang at first because we need to get out of the depression and hopefully the more elevated road will give us a better place to get a signal.

Nothing. Nope. No signal at all. It's a pocket of deadness, which is not unusual in this remote area.

"Oh noooo," says Cynthia. Megan starts cursing Ricky out and hitting him again. I look back at the car. The front of the powder blue Mustang is now a powder blue accordion.

"That's tragic," I say, looking at the car.

For the first time, Ricky fully internalizes what has happened. "My poor car is dead."

"Good riddance," says Megan.

I clear my throat. "I will say the last rites. Dearly beloved, we are gathered here today on this sad and solemn occasion." I'm trying to remember the words from movies and television shows I've seen. "The Mustang was a good and noble car. It served Ricky well in his time of need."

"Shut the fuck up Simon," says Megan. "What are we going to do?"

"We're doomed, doomed, I tell you!" I say. I'm obviously not happy about this but it is kind of funny, or rather, I find the reactions of everyone else pretty funny. I guess I'm a bit punchy, too from all the gambling.

Cynthia, on the other hand, is like, hyperventilating or some-thing. She hasn't said much but she looks so white and terrified she can hardly talk. More seriously, I add, "We'll just have to walk back. We know the way. We're lucky it happened close to the barn." Well, relatively close, and not in bumblefuck Maine.

"It must be more than five miles!" says Ricky.

"Do you have a better idea? Walking is better than standing here and freezing and we might get a signal—or a ride, or something, if we keep moving. Five miles is like a nothing run for my brother." I'm wearing my heaviest work boots and I actually wonder how far I could run in the snow. I have never really run more than three miles but if I was alone I'd try as best I could—maybe run three, walk one, then walk the last one and change. That would keep me warm and be easier than hiking the whole damn distance. But I look at Ricky's gut and tiny little Megan, and Cynthia who is already as blue as the dead car and I know that there is no way they're even running a step. "Okay, onward march!" I say.

"But they say if you're lost you should stay in the same place," says Megan.

"We're not lost. We have a dead car but we're not lost," I say. "We're better off walking on the road than we are standing here, waiting for someone to come along who probably won't come along. And if a car comes by we can flag it down. We'll just walk along the same road that we were going to drive on. We're not lost."

They can't argue with my logic, I know, even though they hate me for it. I still feel slightly cheerful and energized by the thousands I've won and the dizzying delights of the reflected snow and the crispness of the cold around me. "Hup two, three, four," I say and they slowly follow me.

Even for the first mile, they walk pretty slowly. I have to keep turning around and wait for them to catch up.

"Cheer up Cindy," I say. I see she is really struggling and isn't just sore and pissed off like Ricky and Megan. "If we have to do a Donner Party, Ricky and I have more meat on us so we'll be the first to go."

"I'd be the first they'd pick," says Ricky. "You'd be too lean and gamey, Simon. Like venison."

Gamey and lean like a fox, I think, kind of randomly. "C'mon guys, pick up the pace. The faster you walk, the warmer you feel."

"Still no signal on my phone," says Megan, who keeps checking.

"We're going to die and no one will find us until spring," moans Cynthia. Actually, she does look pretty bad. I backtrack so I can walk beside her. With all this back and forth, I'm going to end up walking way more than five stupid miles. Take that, Sean, I bet your skinny, freezing cross-country ass couldn't cover that in the snow.

I can't resist so I start humming the dueling banjo song from *Deliverance*, which I remember seeing with Heather ages ago. "Deedle-dee-dee-dee-dee-dum."

"Shut up, Simon," says Megan again.

"Simon, are you trying to tell me something?" asks Ricky, laughing, who I guess has seen the movie.

"Nah, I wouldn't worry about me, if I were you, Ricky, I'd worry more about Megan killing me since they won't find the body until June in these parts."

Two miles more, I estimate. Cynthia is really fading fast. I realize that she's slowing us all down so I stop and basically sling her into my arms, like I'm carrying a baby. "Hang onto my neck, hunter princess," I say and speed up to warm up. She feels icy next to my neck, like I'm carrying a snow sculpture.

"Simon," she says, "you can't carry me the whole way."

"I'll do my best. If Blood Money can do it, so can I."

I sense a shortcut. I remember riding near here with Fortune during the summer. "Follow me," I say. Yes, I know, just through these trees and we'll get to the back of Daniel's house and the farm.

"Simon, are you out of your mind?" says Megan.

"Trust me." As long as they can navigate the snow and branches, we'll be okay. Under other circumstances I might not take them through this way but I'm worried about Cynthia. In fact, I think I'm going to stop at Daniel's, who has a better heating system in his house, so Cindy can warm up more quickly.

"What the hell?" Daniel says. I know I look weird standing there on the doorstep, holding Cynthia. Like I'm a villain from a silent film about to tie the beautiful maiden to the train tracks. Or some guy from one of those period films Heather likes so much, saving the heroine from peril after she's twisted an ankle.

"Ricky's car got busted in an accident. We walked back," I say. "Can we come in to warm Cynthia up?"

Daniel gets Cynthia some coffee and a shot of whisky, which I'm sure she appreciates and Megan and Ricky follow suit. I refuse both so Daniel heats up a can of chicken soup from his pantry. Everything floating on top of the broth is plain and square and symmetrical— the chicken, the potatoes and carrots—and it tastes like metal, like I imagine a bit must taste. But it's what my mother used to make when she made me soup, so it's very, very comforting.

"You don't make a bad hero, Shaughnessy," says Daniel, as he spoons soup into a mug and gives it to me. "I don't think those other yahoos would have made it back alone."

"Well, if it wasn't for me, we wouldn't have stayed so long at the casino," I say.

"Probably not, you crazy Irish bastard. But I bet they still would have gotten into some mess going home, no matter what the hour of night. Are you sure you don't want anything? What kind of an Irishman doesn't drink?"

"I drink a little," I say. "But I feel like staying sober."

As we sit and get warm, Daniel hooks up his ancient VHS to show us some footage from one of the Olympics in which he competed—the 1976 at Bromont. I can't help it, but I'm laughing at all the people who fall off and get right back on again, wearing no vests and thin helmets that look like they're made of cardboard. "Wow, you guys had balls then," I say approvingly. This was before falling off was an automatic elimination at the Advanced level, I know.

"Balls and no brains."

Daniel has said not-so-nice things about the current short format of eventing, how it's more technical and not the big, rolling, galloping courses of the former long format. It's true, in this Bromont video there are no weird jumps in bright neon colors, no magic mushrooms, teddy bears, or tiny fences that a normal rider would go around on a real hunt. But it's still not a pretty little show hunter course, by any stretch of the imagination. I don't say this to Daniel, of course. Just a different kind of dangerous, one which I would have loved to have used to test my mettle.

All of us fall asleep in various places in Daniel's living room: couch, sofa, and in my case, the floor with a pillow at my head and Jig snoring at my feet. I'm warm enough to take off my jacket now, but I cradle it (and the money inside) in my arms as I snooze.

In the morning I take out the money, count it again at the kitchen table, and take a photo of it with my phone.

"I think I need to take you to the bank first thing," Daniel says.

On the ride over, he says, "Don't spend it all in one place, Shaughnessy."

"I'm not," I say. "This is for entry fees and such. And for the future, whatever that is going to be." And other practical things.

I show Max the picture, in case he doesn't believe me. "I'm considering going pro as a gambler," I joke.

"That wasn't all luck," he says.

"No, it wasn't, although to be honest, some luck was involved. I've never won so much before. The stars aligned. Maybe you should take me to a casino and we can try to pay off some of your student loans."

Max says he'll think about it.

The next day at the barn we order lunch from this new organic place that makes fancy sandwiches. The food comes with long explanations about where the ingredients come from, there's something like a poem about the long, happy life of the turkey and pigs involved in making my club sandwich on its wrapper. But the food's good and discounted since the place is new. Cynthia orders a diet drink and some fruit salad.

"Look Cindy," I say, stuffing down a quarter of the sandwich and some potato chips I've slathered with ketchup (organic of course and no GMOs or whatever). "You gotta eat." She looks with disgust at the chips.

"Ketchup on potato chips?"

"It's a potato, so ketchup, right? You want some? There are a few that aren't smothered."

"No, no thank you."

"Here, have half of my sandwich," I say. You can see the outline of Cynthia's jaw bone beneath her skin, like a living skeleton, so I feel bad stuffing my face. It truly kills me to give up what is my favorite kind of sandwich but I can't help myself. She shakes her head and kind of leans back.

Jig is circling me, barking. "Crazy dog, I'll give you a biscuit when I'm done but this stuff is way too good for you, you can't appreciate it," I say. I give him a piece or two of bacon all the same.

"Cynthia, I can't end up carrying you everywhere, every time you pass out."

"Oh Simon, the only times that happened were under very extraordinary circumstances."

"But you don't eat. You'll never get stronger, no matter how much you practice, if you don't eat."

"I don't want to get too fat for my horse."

"I ride your horse no problem and I weigh a helluva lot more than you do."

"I don't know about that. You're so skinny, Simon."

"My skeleton alone probably weighs more than you."

"Oh, Simon, it's complicated…" Ugh. That word again. I wish they would just eliminate that word from the world's vocabulary.

Eating is not complicated, I think. But I say, "I'm sure it is, but sometimes with complicated stuff it's best to just simplify things and go with the sandwich, you know? Like sometimes when a horse is having issues you're better off giving him a good gallop. Even if it doesn't solve everything, it gets his head on straight and he feels better."

Cynthia takes a bite or two of a quarter of the sandwich. "You make everything seem so easy, Simon, but it's not for me," she says.

I don't want to upset her more but as always when people tell me I make things seem easy it really pisses me off. It's taken me a lot of hard work to make things seem easy this year.

"That sandwich is expensive, so finish what I gave you," I say. She asks if I know how many calories are in it. I say I don't know but she finishes it anyway.

"You know, once the snow clears, Blood is going home," she says. "To Virginia."

"What?"

"I'm going to be using Sam to compete for the rest of the year."

"But why would you do that? Sam's already a made horse."

"I know. But my partnership with Blood Money has been—inconsistent—in the words of my father."

"I get it, but weren't you here to learn? You have all of next year to win on Sammy."

"I don't really have much say in the matter," she says.

Of course, Cynthia is an adult, I think, but she can't object. It's funny how if your parents are rich enough, it's like you'll always be a child…I think about all the decisions I've made that no one but myself would approve of and suddenly I feel a stab of relief that I'm (relatively) poor and free.

"I'm not like some of those girls…with rich fathers but who can do it on their own because they have enough sponsors and support… because they're naturally good," says Cynthia, wistfully.

"Well, maybe someday, you will be," I say. "And no one is naturally good."

"I'm sorry, Simon."

"Don't be sorry, they are your horses."

"I know how much—how much you like Blood Money. I like her too," says Cynthia.

When we school the next day, Cynthia lets me ride Blood. Blood Money isn't gone yet, so I savor the experience of all of her quivering, vibrant, and flexible silliness. I miss a horse that is so responsive to me, that is a bundle of nervous energy, even though I know it doesn't always work in my favor. I've heard such horses compared to sports cars, and they say such creatures have a tendency to crash and break down, spin off the road into infinity and leave you in pieces in the process, although the ride is fun. Of course in my world, I think of sports cars as nervous animals, reversing the analogy. I consider the death of Ricky's Mustang the result of a big spook.

30

BETTER THAN NOTHING

February is so cold I can hardly get out of bed every morning. After her last adventure, Cynthia is actually eating a little bit more so she is looking less wan and ghostlike. I still have to help her with her stalls and buckets because even with heavy gloves on she can barely move her fingers. "No problem, hunter princess," I mutter as she looks at me with her big blue eyes, but now I'm more pretending to be upset than I am actually contemptuous.

Blood is still there, there is just too much ice and snow on the road to risk moving her. After several snowstorms, Fortune and I are mostly walking and trotting when we go out (and he has special shoes, which cost extra). We spend most of the time schooling in the indoor. I clip him and blanket the hell out of him so his coat doesn't grow so much and so he can't get too sweaty and we can still work. I tell myself that this is good, we can work on our dressage more, and we do, along with stadium. Even in the relatively small confines of the dusty arena, he will still jump the moon if I ask him.

A few days before Valentine's Day (which falls on a Friday), Cindy tells me she's going to Charleston for a cousin's holiday wedding.

"But Megan and Ricky are going out to eat," I say. "It's my weekend off as well."

"Do you need it?" she asks.

"Yes, I do."

"Why?"

"I just do."

"I couldn't miss this wedding, even if I wanted to."

It may be sub-zero degrees but I feel hot as hell right now.

"I just thought…."

"You didn't think at all, clearly." I know she means that I'm not seeing anyone but she still should have said something.

For a brief minute, I think of complaining to Daniel. But that would be weird. Anyway, from his perspective, I'm sure the wedding has priority, followed by Megan with her fiancée and then me.

Fuck you. Fuck you because it is the first fucking Valentine's Day when I actually have something to do besides work. Or watch violent movies with Heather.

There is another part of me that stoically says just suck it up and deal, it's a cheesy, stupid Hallmark of a holiday about chocolate and cards and girls and stuff I don't care about. But still a principle is being violated, I feel, even though no one else at the barn is aware of it.

All of the little girls I teach wear pink and red sweaters, scarves, or neck warmers to the barn. Two of the girls actually give me Valentines, the little teacher cards you get with those boxes of little cardboard Valentines people buy for their elementary school classes. Melody writes "I will work on my two-point" on hers and it is attached to a little box of chocolates.

"Thanks sweetheart," I say, genuinely kind of touched, and I kiss her on her cheek. She blushes as red as her Keep Calm and Canter On sweatshirt.

I also teach my high school couple, Sarah and Jake, that day. Sarah walks in with the enormous teddy bear, box of chocolate-covered cherries, and balloons Jake sent to her during school.

"No expensive jewelry?" I say. "I would break up with him, Sarah. He's gotta step it up."

Jake looks at the ground, blushes and mutters something.

"Well, Jake, we're on the flat today because the ground is so frozen, even in the indoor, that's my Valentine's gift to you," I say. So you don't look ridiculous like you usually do in front of your girlfriend, I think but don't say.

Max tells me he understands I can't go to his place tonight but slightly to my surprise (given his anti-holiday Hanukkah rant), he says he's kind of bummed because it's his first Valentine's Day with someone in years. He says he'll work late as well, though, might as well save his time off.

When I'm checking the water buckets, I jump at the sound of a noise. The monotony of the wind battering the shingles of the barn has lulled me into a kind of stupor.

"You didn't need to come," I say. It's nearly 9 p.m. and truly, truly wicked cold now that it has been dark for several hours. Even Max, who seems to never feel the cold and who always feels warm to my touch, looks chilled from working outside all day.

"I had to stop by."

"Why? No point in us both being miserable." I check water buckets (we have a heated automatic waterer, thank God, unlike my mom's old stable, which required an ice pick on days like this) and I throw a few flakes of hay in Fortune's stall. I scratch my horse behind his ears and pat his shoulder. He's still holding his weight despite the bitterness outside. That's one advantage to not having a Thoroughbred.

My last horse seemed to be able to lose weight by sheer force of will, especially in the cold.

"I wanted to take you out to dinner but we'll just do that another time."

"Come up to my room with me," I say. "You'll be horrified. I haven't cleaned it at all and it's cold as a witch's tit."

I go in the tack room (which is warmer than my room) to unfreeze my fingers. I don't want to even go out to walk up the stairs. I linger a bit amongst the smell of leather, which I love. Max follows me.

"Sometimes I think about sleeping here for the warmth," I say, ruefully, rubbing my fingers, which are so frosty I don't want to touch him with them.

Max takes a small box out of his pocket and gives it to me.

"Aw, Max." I have never worn jewelry in my life so I'm not sure what it could be. I open the box and it's a stopwatch, the kind specially made for equestrians that has a really big face that's easy to see when you're going fast cross-country. (And a setting for optimum time, of course). "Thanks, mine was getting ready to give up its ghost."

Earlier in the day, I sent Max his gift (since I didn't know I would be seeing him tonight), a download of the Killers' concert at the Royal Albert Hall, one of their best. I've carefully researched a number of different concerts and the Killers blow just about any other band out of the water today. I mean, I think another sign of a great artist is sounding even better live than in a studio. Not like the bands today that are auto-tuned like hell, to the point that they can barely sing happy birthday when you shove a microphone in their face when they have to sing at an award ceremony or something like that.

Max leans over and kisses me, ever so slightly, and then I, who have not really been paying attention to the sounds outside (one of the horses is kicking her stall to annoy her neighbor), am suddenly aware of Jig barking at the door. Max and I turn around and see Daniel standing there.

"Is something wrong?" he asks Max.

Oh, Jesus. There is a long pause, I have no idea what to say.

"No, I stopped by on my own accord," says Max, firmly, although somehow I can feel him dying inside. "Don't worry, Daniel, this visit won't cost you anything. See you, Simon." I'm not sure how much Daniel saw, and he doesn't say anything.

I tell Daniel everything is all right, I mention which horses' blankets I changed to a heavier weight and such, and basically act as if everything is normal. My face is red and suddenly I don't feel the cold at all.

After Daniel goes, I slink back to my room. Stupid, stupid, holiday, I think.

For once, Max texts me without correct punctuation.

fucking awkward

Fucking awkward indeed.

The next day, things are normal between myself and Daniel, pretty much, we just go through the motions like we normally do, even though there are a few moments of discomfort at the beginning. I can't really read what he thinks, to be honest. But he still treats me the same and that's good enough to get me through most of the day. I try to be especially careful doing the typical winter chores, plus I hurry extra fast to mend some fence sections that have come down between two of the fields. I go running hard through the snow even though it sucks at my ankles.

I volunteer to ride Ted—he's still here and that will focus my mind, although he hasn't been naughty at all in weeks. I muscle him through a dressage workout, kind of ugly, but keep him in frame the entire time. I'm sure he's kind of thinking, *what the hell did you eat for breakfast, Simon, I'm the one that's supposed to be the more pissed off of the two of us.* I see Daniel at the door, watching us for a bit, as we breeze through a shoulder-in. "Nice, you'd never know that was the same horse that came here a coupla months ago," he says. I know that there is nothing particularly special we're doing today, though.

When I'm doing evening feed, I feel a tap on my shoulder and I see Daniel behind me. He asks me if I'm okay. I'm not sure what he means by that so I say, "No different than usual." The whole truth is, "No different than usual, other than the weird gnawing in the pit of my stomach," which I'm not sure is fear, humiliation, or both. I don't really have a father or grandfather but I guess if I did, that's how I would feel if he surprised me.

"I'm fine," I add.

"Good, that's what I thought, Simon," says Daniel, calling me by my first name, which he hardly ever does except when he's introducing me to demonstrate something at a clinic. He gives my shoulder an extra squeeze and then goes on with the usual notes about what horses might need an extra blanket tonight.

A few weeks later, Max does really, truly take me out. He shows up in his car to pick me up and takes one look at me. "Simon?"

"What?"

"The anarchist shirt?"

Everyone hates the anarchist hoodie for some reason.

"This is a *nice* restaurant," he says.

"Probably too nice for me," I pout.

"Besides, you're not an anarchist. I've told you."

"Anarchy is a punk thing, you wouldn't understand."

"You're not punk, either, Simon. Downloading the Clash and the Sex Pistols does not make you punk."

Some people even say the Clash aren't technically punk, so I consider this a common failure of judgment.

"You're so wrong, Max."

"The punk movement was at its height during the 1970s. The anarchist movement was from, oh, I don't know, the early twentieth century, right before World War I. Both of which happened before you were born."

"What is this, Wikipedia or a date?"

"Please change, Simon."

I remember the sweater Sean got me. I go inside, exchange it for the sweatshirt and put on a slightly nicer pair of jeans. I'm still wearing my Docs, which are the only shoes I own other than my show boots that are not encrusted in manure. I also leave the Red Sox cap at home.

"I'm sorry, Simon, but is it too much to ask that for once, I can be seen in public with a really good-looking boyfriend? I know that you hide it all beneath the sweatshirt and that awful hat, but every now and then I like other people to see your face. Even if you never do smile, it's still a nice face."

I can't believe that *both* Max and Cynthia complain that I don't smile. What the hell is up with that? I'm sure I do smile sometimes, I guess I just don't very often or time it correctly when other people can see me. And the Sox comment is a low blow. "Awful hat? What kind of a fan are you? That was from 2004. It passed from my brother to me." I can still remember when Sean got it; it practically covered his whole head at the time.

"What, it's some kind of a superstition or something? Well, it didn't help them this year, so maybe it's time to retire it."

I brush my hair out of my face. It's getting long and I'll have to get Megan to cut it again, as she does every few weeks in exchange for me doing some of the worst, really early chores on the coldest mornings.

Max drives me to a restaurant an hour away. "I wish," he says, "I had enough time to take you somewhere where we could relax more and just be ourselves." It occurs to me that we haven't gone out much at all, certainly not like most couples that have been dating as long as we have—since August, and it's almost March now. But neither of us feels like talking above the din of a bar anyway.

On the ride over, I talk about entering Fortune in an upcoming jumper show. "Daniel thinks I should get him out there as much as possible, not just for the experience, but in case I'm thinking of selling him in the future," I say, "In case I want a horse with a broader skill set to compete at the upper levels now that I'm qualified."

I expect Max will support this decision but he looks sad. "Oh no."

"Why 'oh no?'"

"Well, truthfully, I kind of like riding him."

I laugh. "I thought he terrified everyone but me."

"I know I look kind of white-knuckled when I'm up there but I'm getting used to him, like I'm getting used to you."

"Oh, I'm terrifying, then?"

"In a different kind of way."

At the restaurant, I want to hold hands with Max across the table every now and then, like some of the other couples, but I don't. The waiter doesn't seem to notice or care what our relationship is, and after he takes our order, I just kind of look at the fancy plate in front of me that they have there for show and thank Max for everything. Even if we could hold hands I doubt I could look him in the eye and tell him that I love him so directly, though. I'm glad for the candlelight that makes everything look dim and dreamlike and shadowy.

Like I usually do in a nice restaurant—the few nice restaurants I've been in, in my life—I order a steak and fries (which is what steak frites is, even though they dress up the name slightly). I still remain indifferent to good food and booze (which I can't order anyway, in public, still). And clothes and stuff like that. Which I know annoys Max. I feel, however, that when it comes to important things, like music and horses and Max himself, I know what is good.

"You look slightly less like jailbait in normal clothes," says Max, pushing the bread away from himself over to me. I take some.

"I've never been jailbait to you," I say.

"I know. But I still think I'm ignoring my better judgment."

"True, you are by dating me, but that has nothing to do with age."

And although it's even worse, in a way, than saying I love him, I blurt out what I've often thought, "Well, the older we both get, the less it will matter." Which means, of course, that I've been planning and thinking about what life for us will be like, not just months from now, but years.

And he says, "I've been hoping that, too," and I relax, let my guard down a bit more, and squeeze his hand beneath the table, very briefly, in the rising darkness.

I don't say, however, that I have always felt old to myself, even when I was much younger. Objectively, I have never felt particularly young, which I know sounds kind of dumb. I can look back at some of the things I said and did as a kid and think they're stupid, but by virtue of that comparison I feel wise and old right now even though people tell me I'm not.

31

RAISED BY WOLVES

The snow begins to melt in March, an early thaw, and my mother asks me to visit. I tell Max that it's time he should meet my family over a weekend and somewhat to my surprise, he agrees. I mean, he agrees with the level of enthusiasm he had when riding my horse for the first time, but at least he does agree. (And he's getting better at riding Fortune, too. There's much less pulling and fighting between the two of them now).

As we get closer to my house, it feels weird to be driving next to Max, his hand on my knee. I keep thinking of the phrase "worlds collide," and not in a good way, but he needs to meet my family at some point so why not sooner? My heart sinks a bit and I begin to doubt my judgment when I see a bunch of cars in the driveway. "Uh-oh. It looks like a horse show this weekend."

"Why do you say that?"

"Lots of times the little girls will sleep over at the house the night before if they have to leave really early. The house is going to be a friggin' zoo." Or a friggin' henhouse, that is.

My brother, home from college on break, is leaning on one of the trucks, back in suburban cowboy mode in a wife-beater and Western shirt, jeans and boots. I guess he's enjoying the attentions of the adoring female barn public. He's talking to a tall, slightly heavyset redhead holding a dry-cleaned Western show shirt in plastic slung over her shoulder. My brother's always had kind of a thing for red-headed girls I've never quite understood.

"Look at my brother, chatting up the ginger rodeo queen," I say.

"That's your BROTHER?"

I smack Max on the shoulder. "What do you mean by that?"

"Nothing, he just looks nothing like you."

"Ew, that's disgusting. He's my brother."

"I didn't mean it that way." Max is blushing and looks really embarrassed but I'm not letting him off the hook.

"It's fine, I'm used to being emotionally scarred by rejection because my brother is so much better-looking than me. I'm sorry you're stuck with the ugly one."

"Simon. I said different-looking, not better-looking."

I guess I'll let Max out of that one but I seriously don't get it. I suppose it's Sean's dark hair and blue eyes that fool everyone into making them think he's so charming, or the curly hair. I don't know but whatever it is, it's the genes I wasn't dealt. Oh well, gotta play the hand you have, not the hand you want, right?

We park on the street and I lead Max in through the back door. I'd like to greet Sean but I want to introduce him to Max properly when we're alone.

However, that alone thing clearly isn't going to happen. Inside, the dining and living rooms are filled with girls of varying ages. They're cleaning tack and boots; eating junk food and squealing about their weight and how they'll look in their breeches and jods; looking over the old riding books, catalogues, and magazines that always lie in piles on the floor; or if silent, they're in a text war with someone. There are unrolled sleeping bags too, so some are clearly going to crash here the night before the show.

One girl, who has grown up so much I hardly recognize her, shrieks and throws her arms around me as soon as I walk in. "Simon!" She blurts out that she's finally graduated to the .90m jumpers after riding in the 2'6 hunter ring for ages and begins to tell me about her new horse. I don't even get a chance to find mom at first, kid's babbling so much. Even then, when I catch my mom's eye she's on the phone.

"Simon, for some reason, I thought you were coming the week after this one. It's total insanity here, as you can see, and will be until tomorrow night."

"Sorry mom," I say.

"That's all right, you can make yourself useful and come to the schooling show tomorrow, can't you? I have girls in both rings at the same time and some of them are riding new horses I don't trust."

"Ms. O'Shaughnessy, you don't mean my horse?" says one of the teenage girls with braces.

"Some of the girls are moving up a division or are on greenies," my mom clarifies. "And Jenny—the little girl who bought the mare you rode at the hunter pace at Thanksgiving—needs someone to ride out the kinks before her trip."

"I'll be there," I say. "Mom, this is Max."

"Hi, Max," says my mother absentmindedly. "What are you doing to that saddle?" she says to one of the girls. "You'll ruin the leather!"

It's past 8 p.m., which is late for me in terms of dinnertime and I want to show Max upstairs but I take the saddle away from the little girl, sit at the dining room table where one of the portable trees are spread out and begin cleaning. The dining room table has various leather cleaners and conditioners, sponges, and cloths all over it.

"This new stuff smells good," I said, looking at the bottle. "What's in it?"

"It's rosemary and ginger and orange," says my mother. "The company sent me some free samples."

"Almost smells like someone is cooking," says Sean, drifting in.

"Don't get too excited. I sent one of the girls out to get McDonald's," says my mother. "There should be enough extra for you, Simon."

"If Simon's going to be there tomorrow can I leave after the Western classes in the morning? That way I can get my long run in during the afternoon," says Sean. Great, the Western classes. So it's one of those awful schooling shows with a mess of everything, not even a decent English show.

"Your brother is running a marathon in a month," says my mother. "Apparently, the mileage he does for track at school isn't challenging enough for him."

"Hi, Max," says my brother, reaching over to shake his hand with somewhat exaggerated politeness. Max is sitting next to me, clearly uncomfortable. I think he prepared himself for some kind of confrontation with my mother but this chaos is somehow even more nerve-wracking.

"Knowing you," I say to Sean, "you're running a marathon just to get out of staying at the show."

"As always, it's about testing my limits, but I know you don't get that."

"Max is a runner," I say, nodding in his direction. "He's run a marathon already."

"That was several years ago. And very slowly," says Max, as he casts his eyes down to Sean's ropy, bulging calf muscles, which look even thicker because the rest of Sean is now so skinny. This is more than Max has said the entire time we've been in the house.

There is a weird, ear-piercing shriek of laughter and the girls start singing along to the new Taylor Swift song—I think they're watching the video on one of the kids' iPads.

"I should turn in," says Sean, clearly wanting to duck out before mom gives him tack to clean or more duties for tomorrow. "I need to save myself for tomorrow's run. It's my first twenty miler ever."

"Save yourself for a run? What, like you're talking about your virginity or something? Is busting your twenty-mile cherry some kind of a big milestone?" I say

"Good luck, Max," says Sean, winks at him, and heads up the stairs.

By this time I'm seriously considering eating the saddle leather. Finally, someone comes with food. The girls, after a long day of braiding and cleaning and schooling, head to the white bags like ravening hordes but I manage to squirrel away two Quarter Pounders with cheese, large fries, and a strawberry shake. I offer one to Max but he just shakes his head. I'm not sure what he is more grossed out by, the fast food or the kid picking out Chicken Nuggets from her plastic blue braces next to him.

"There probably isn't much food in the refrigerator," I say.

Max looks and returns with some apples and a carrot.

"Those are for the horses."

"Of course. The horses, I should have realized that."

"Simon, do you think I'm going to have trouble in the eq division? It's my first time and I'm terrified," says blue braces girl.

"Do a mental check to make sure you don't fall into your bad hunter-world habits—body upright, don't fall on your horse's neck." I think of the famous praying mantis fucking a tree branch metaphor but decide not to use that on a thirteen-year-old.

"Simon, I don't see why you have it in for the hunters," says a girl named Susan from across the room, the owner of the iPad which is playing Taylor Swift nonstop. "I know you used to compete in them way back when."

"Only when they were trying to unload one for sale, never out of choice," I point out. "You can have your eight fences, Suzy Q, knock yourself out if that's your thing." Just don't think you're a good rider if you knock him out with Perfect Prep and some worse stuff beforehand, I think but don't say.

"Susan, don't listen to him, my younger son's only interested in something if there is obvious speed and danger involved," says my mother. "Although it's only because I rode the hunters and ingrained in him the value of a good position and an eye for distances at a young age that he's been able to get himself out of all sorts of scrapes as a rider over the years. He likes to forget that if I don't remind him often enough."

It's after midnight before Max and I head up to my old childhood room. "See, I told you she wouldn't even notice you were here," I say to him.

Max lies down on my single bed. "I think I'm going to fall asleep right now," he says. "That was exhausting."

Suddenly, I realize I'm just as tired myself and do the same. I pull off my jeans and Docs and flop down beside him.

I manage to wake up early enough to talk to Sean alone, however. I go over to his room and poke him awake. "Asshole, we still have a half hour," he grunts.

"Look, I'm leaving Max to sleep in. When you return to do your run, I need a favor from you. Ask Max to come with you and amuse him, so he isn't left here by himself all day. I'd take him with us to the horseshow but that would qualify as cruel and unusual punishment, I think."

"Take him running? I don't want to be slowed down by an old guy," he grins.

I punch Sean. Hard.

"Okay, I guess that will give me a chance to see if his intentions are honorable. As your older brother, I have that responsibility."

"Play nice, and take him out for some real food afterward, because he won't have eaten all day. He doesn't eat that crap Mom keeps."

"So you'd like me to exercise and then feed him? Wouldn't lunging and grazing be more appropriate than running and going to a diner?"

"Thanks, Sean," I say.

"Oh, okay, he's just lucky it's a distance day and I won't be going too fast."

"I'm the lucky one of all three of us. I'm not running anywhere."

I inform Max that he can sleep in (it's 4 a.m. when I wake him) and tell him that Sean will be back around 11 a.m. to take him for running and food while I play traffic cop and trainer with the kids. "Uh, I think I'll annoy your brother since I really haven't been training much," mutters Max, looking for his glasses. "My long runs are ten at the most. I've been focusing more on lifting because of the weather."

"You'll be fine," I say. Ten, twenty miles, it's all the same to me. Weirdly, I'm looking forward to the horse show now. I know it's just a crappy little schooling show but I guess I have enough of my mom's blood inside me that it doesn't matter, I always get excited by one, even though my main duty will be riding the freshness out of the quicker ones for the girls who are over-horsed.

We arrive at the show grounds early and don't even head to the normal warm-up rings; there is a big, green field where we can take the horses to run. First thing, I ride the horse formerly known as

Blue Velvet (now Cinderella) around. She's lost some of the supple, elastic wildness that made me love her so much when I rode her back during Thanksgiving break. But I still say to my mom (who is lunging a balky pony), "I love this horse. She's too nice to be ridden over just a 2'3 course. And she's really no hunter."

"Why not ride her in one of the jumper classes today? Her owner has a crush on you, like all of my little girls. I'm sure she'd let you."

"Ma, you know they only have eyes for Sean. Think Blue's fit enough?"

"I don't know, what do you think? I haven't gotten on that mare recently. The girl's got to learn to ride her own horse herself but I admit I am concerned about her nerves affecting the horse during their first show."

I take Blue over the one jump set in the field, a simple vertical less than a meter high.

"Yes," I say. "I think so." I'm not wearing my show clothes but I have on clean breeches, boots, and one of Max's shirts to look respectable enough as a trainer, not a hooligan (as my mother sometimes calls me), so I think I'm okay for the jumpers.

Sean arrives later, when our girls are in the real warm-up ring. Mom and I stand in the English ring, directing our riders and barking orders to them, while Sean goes to coach his one or two riders around the barrels. "Vertical, then oxer, Janie!" I say.

"Vertical," says one of my riders, warning the others to get the hell out of her way as she careens over the fence.

"Half-halt, half-halt—I said, half-halt! Okay, maybe next time! Try again. And you, Desiree, don't you dare let that pony trot over! Next time, I want to see him at the canter."

The girl sort of pouts. "It says that trotting won't be penalized."

"Maybe the judge won't penalize you, but I'll kick your—butt—if you trot because I know you can canter that course blindfolded on Rocky, if only you try. MORE LEG!"

The girls don't disgrace themselves in the morning and even Sean's riders pick up a handful of respectably-colored ribbons. He waves to me as he leaves but I'm too busy going over a 2'6 course with a new rider to really notice. Hopefully, Max will survive.

My class isn't until after lunch and Mom and I do finally get to sit down for a bit. I stuff a cheeseburger and fries down my throat while Mom eats a hot dog. Like Jig, she never quite relaxes, even when eating. She has one eye on her food, one eye on all the girls to make sure none of them do anything stupid under her watch.

"Your kids look good," I compliment her. "You always do a nice job preparing your riders. They've been working hard."

"Thanks. I was worried after Daniel you'd be much harsher in your critique."

I find that funny and kind of touching that my mom is intimidated by me, of all people. "Daniel teaches ammies as well as people aspiring to go pro and he's got me teaching riders of all levels and ages. My friend Max is one of his students."

"I was going to ask you about him. Is he—?"

"Yes, Mom, he's my boyfriend."

"I'm sorry Simon, I haven't had a chance to think or breathe the last forty-eight hours."

"Oh, I totally get it, mom. So does Max. Max is a vet, so he understands; he's in the industry."

"Well, I suppose I should have known that you wouldn't be like your brother and date a civilian who hated horses."

"I never could. You'll get to meet him properly tomorrow, when you relax from all this."

"I never relax, Simon. I haven't since I was twenty. I have two crazy sons and riders to manage."

"You'll like him, Mom. I love him," I blurt out. Then my face flushes and I can't help looking away. To break the tension I feel, I collect our garbage from lunch and throw it in the trash can. I see a girl on a little chestnut pony in the warm-up ring taking advantage of the sparser traffic during lunchtime. Cute, I think, he's really on automatic pilot while she's just sitting there. None of our horses take care of our riders that way; they're all cheap and defective for the most part, given the average level of income at Mom's barn, but our riders are better for it in the end.

I know Mom and I don't have much more time to talk and that's kind of a good thing although my mother looks neither pleased nor displeased with my admission about Max. "Of course you think you love him. I thought I loved your father when I wasn't much older than you."

I didn't expect her to fully understand. "Once you talk to him, you'll see what I mean. That is," I try to joke to diffuse the tension, "if there is anything left of him to like after Sean finishes with him—my brother's taking him running this afternoon, twenty miles."

"Twenty miles? Only Sean would rather run twenty miles than be at a horse show." Maybe not only Sean, but I certainly don't get it. "Simon, I just don't want to see you making more of the same mistakes that I made—he's a much older man if he's a vet like you say he is, and I am concerned," my mother says.

My first thought is to joke, "Don't worry, Mom, I won't get knocked up," but of course I don't say it. But my mother knows me so well she can see the joke in my eyes and her eyes narrow. "At times like this, I thank God that I have sons. They say sons are easier than daughters and I've always questioned that but I suppose in regards to this they are. Well, I guess Sean could theoretically get a girl in trouble but at least he's always had very strong self-preservation instincts. I hope you use protection—"

"Ma!" I can feel myself turning red and looking away from her. "I can't discuss that stuff with you."

"Well, I'm a mother and I'm concerned and I have to ask."

"I don't take dumb risks. And I'm working twelve hours a day, some days. It's a miracle I found one guy, it's not like I'm having some wild and crazy life up in rural Vermont. Don't worry about that, I'm not stupid."

"Simon, I've never worried about *you* being stupid, but you are willful. Oh, I know, you'll do what you want. You've always done whatever you want, no matter what I've said, ever since you were a very little boy. I mean, both you and Sean were wild but at least I can usually stay one step ahead of what he's thinking. With you I never can. I could never read you, even though you are my son."

I don't know if she means that as an insult or a weird compliment but hearing her say that makes me feel lonely, somehow.

I have to get ready for my class, so I leave my mother and start schooling Blue. I can't help thinking of the mare as Blue, as if she were mine, even though she is officially named after a Disney character now. I didn't see the division she rode in with her owner but it was apparently a disaster because the owner was in tears and Blue was sweaty and fretting.

I get on the mare, gallop her in the wide openness of the green field outside the show, and eventually Blue settles and I can trot her back to the warm-up ring. I school her over a few fences and once again, I am in love with the fluid springiness of her jumps. Even compared to the OTTBs I've ridden back at Daniel's, she has an extra liquidity to her step, so different than Fortune's. The truth is, she reminds me of the old horse I used to have as a kid, the one who busted herself up and died.

Some things never change. I even recognize some of the people from when I used to do these shows years ago, when I was riding for Mom's barn. There's one fat girl who used to own a horse named Amigo who now has a kid and a husband. (I see the husband with the baby on his knee, both of them are the same pudgy shape as the mother.) She's on another warmblood this time—even bigger and probably dumber than her last one. I can't imagine having a kid at my age or being married. But like my mom said, when she wasn't much older than me she got pregnant with Sean.

If the fat girl hadn't been so nasty to me when we were competing against one another (she was always one of those girls who would say things behind my back) and if Blue had even a lick of proper training, I'd feel bad beating her after competing at a much higher level eventing, but I don't. The course is 1.2m and so simply laid out it looks easy to me. Despite Blue's wanting to rush the fences we go clean—an ugly clean round, but free and clear all the same.

I hear someone say, "It's like a different horse." The girl evidently watched Blue with the new owner, earlier in the show. Only two other horses go clear and I easily beat them both in the jump-off. Slowing Blue down is the problem, but that's fine by me.

"I want her," I say to my mother. "She's not right for the kid. I'm going to buy her." I still have the money I won gambling and I know I can talk the owner (or rather her parents) down.

Mom is busy directing a gaggle of eq girls to the ring, so she doesn't hear me.

When I return, Sean is in the kitchen, drinking a glass of orange juice.

"How did things go?"

"Well, I had to go slower, thanks to—"

"I don't care about your running. What did you think of Max?"

"Actually, for an old guy, he's pretty fast. But I guess you knew that."

"You're such a dick. What did you tell him about my childhood? What lies? I deny everything."

"Well, first we covered your history—all true incidentally, unlike you I don't have to make shit up about my brother to get you in trouble—and when that didn't warn him off we talked about the Red Sox, college sports, and music history. He likes Johnny Cash, surprisingly, so he's not a totally prejudiced idiot against good country music like you are."

It sounds like it went reasonably well, so I go to find Max after punching my brother—gently.

"As I often find myself saying lately, I hope that the warning label on the maximum dose for Advil isn't meant to be taken seriously."

"Shut up. Sean said that you did fine."

"I didn't appear to injure anything, so I guess that's a good report. Whether I will be able to walk in the morning is still an open question."

"Sean has very high standards with running, although nothing else in life."

"I guess that's a compliment. How did you do at the show?"

"I've decided I need a second horse. No, I'm not kidding. Seriously, this mare has potential—not just jumping, but with dressage. I think I can handle two prospects. And she was a beast cross-country during the hunter pace at Thanksgiving. Her talents are wasted with a timid young teenager. I'm going to make an offer. Would you do the PPE?"

"But won't it be hard to take two horses to wherever you're going after Daniel's?"

"No harder than one. Look, I was thinking—when we ride together, you can ride Fortune, he likes you so much, and I can ride this mare."

"But you'll be leaving in a few months."

I tackle him and kind of pin him to the bed with a hug. "Stop saying that. You're going to visit me all the time, wherever I end up. And don't say that you have to work every minute of the day. I won't allow it." He pushes me off.

"Anyway, I made arrangements to meet the girl's parents at the barn—they weren't crazy about the horse's performance the last couple of shows, which is fine by me."

"You know, your brother is a remarkably tolerant guy," says Max. "He's very open-minded."

"What, Sean? I guess so. Everybody likes him." Well, except teachers, but that's different.

"Not everyone is like that. Not my family."

"Do you mean he tolerates me?"

"Well, more that he tolerated me, actually."

"He knows he's stuck with you because he knows he's stuck with me and he's not passing any of his math classes without me."

The next morning, I wake up, suddenly conscious of someone's presence in the room.

"What the hell are you doing up so early?" I say to Sean, who is standing at the door. "Privacy, asshole?"

The lock on my room has been busted for ages. It never really mattered until now.

"Mom woke me up to wake you two up, don't blame me," says Sean. "She wants to see the two of you before she goes to work. I'm going back to bed."

"I don't know why Mom needed you as a messenger to say that. What, you're not going to run five million miles this morning?"

"Hell, no. Rest day today."

Max is hiding as much as it is possible to hide in a single bed. After Sean leaves, he says, "I was kind of hoping to talk to your mother after a shower and two cups of coffee, but I guess that's not going to happen. Stay in bed, Simon, I'm going to hobble down alone."

"Max—"

"Just let me be, Simon."

I listen to the voices downstairs as I lie there, not able to go back to sleep, although I realize I'm so tired I can barely get out of bed. I have to be up in an hour if I'm going to make it to the barn on time, so eventually I shower. I still want to go downstairs. At least the voices aren't raised. The door slams as my mother goes to her office job, as she has done every weekday, year after year after year without complaining, even though I know she hates it.

Max is sitting there at the kitchen table, still in his bathrobe. "So what did she say?" I ask him.

"She says that you're young and she pointed out that she and I are closer in age than you and me." Yeah, I've done that math before, I think. "She said that you're very impulsive." Max has his coffee now and is looking at the empty cup rather than into my eyes. "And I said I didn't know at first how young you were and things kind of snowballed from there."

"Well, I hope you also told her to butt out of my business."

"I also said I could understand that if our situations were reversed, I would feel the same way."

"Max, why do you always have to be so goddamned fair all the time," I snap.

He shrugged. "She also said you are an adult and there is nothing she can do but it makes her uncomfortable."

"Mom can be very conventional about some things even though she doesn't give a shit about some other stuff."

"She said she wasn't going to ask me to leave or anything but just to remember that, like I said, you were very young."

I'm totally pissed off in so many ways I can't even articulate it. "Well, what she thinks shouldn't change anything. My father was much older than Mom when she married him. She had Sean when she wasn't much older than me."

"And what a horrible mistake that was," says my brother, entering the kitchen. "And worse yet, she made it twice."

I look at the time and grab a Coke from the refrigerator. "I have to be at the barn soon, we need to go," I say to Max. "You're coming with us? We'll find you something to ride, I just need to talk to Blue's owner first."

Although I say it isn't necessary, after he makes a face at the refrigerator Max fries up omelets for breakfast before we head out. All three are perfect, unbroken symmetrical spheres as organized and balanced as his speech and thoughts.

The parents of Blue's owner are there but when I see the girl grazing Blue and holding onto the pink lead rope with a death grip, I know that the news isn't good.

"We've talked it over and we can't sell," says the father. I can kind of hear in his voice the "I think my daughter is crazy but I am not going to confront her" vibe.

The kid looks at me like I'm a monster for asking to buy her Cinderella: I'm sure she hasn't forgiven me for winning on her horse when she did not. She's braiding a wild daisy she found somewhere in Blue's mane.

I nod and smile and say the right, nice things and wish everyone well but I can't take my eyes off the horse. Even stuffing her face with grass Blue's muscles are tense and she keeps looking over her shoulder for ghosts that might be lurking in the daylight. The bright pink halter looks garish against her slate grey color and I just can't help saying to myself *what a waste,* even though I know that it's silly, that horses don't know their full potential or what they are missing, not like humans. Or at least, that's what people tell me. Still, I am convinced that this is waste in a way, a real way, not the way that the girls at the stable said "waste" about me behind my back. Is "waste" in the eye of the beholder, more than what's beautiful, because no one could deny that the mare is beautiful but it's not like that beauty is buying her what I consider a real, free life for an animal?

Max, Sean, and I go riding. Nothing intense, just a trail ride on some of the lesson horses and Cam. It's not the same riding out in the open like it is back in Vermont, but Sean doesn't know that and he seems relaxed and happy. Now that he's eighteen, he doesn't have to ride with a helmet and goes bareheaded but Max is here so I sure as hell have to wear one. We don't go that fast because the two of them are still sore from running yesterday.

Max insists on going to the supermarket afterward and picks up what he calls real food although I tell him a million times it's not necessary and my mom won't appreciate it. "Are you trying to buy my mom's approval? It won't work."

Max tells Sean to get some stuff from the produce aisle while we head over to the meat counter.

"Damn, lamb's expensive. I guess that's why we never eat it," I say.

"I feel that the least I can do is cook dinner."

"A sacrificial lamb? For her second-born son? That sounds so Biblical or something."

"Please Simon, this weekend has been hard enough as it is. I think wine is also in order, even though I know you don't drink it."

"Do you drink red or white with lamb?"

"In the specific case of this weekend, both, I think."

There's a guy checking out the prices on the chicken behind us who I swear looks sort of familiar from the back. It takes me a minute or two but I begin to place the balding head in my mind.

"Mr. Shackleton," I say. "My old physics teacher," I explain to Max and head over.

"Hey, Mr. Shackleton, remember me?"

Old Shackleton looks taken aback for a second but then his face softens. "Oh, they still talk about you and your brother in the faculty room from time to time. No, Simon, I couldn't forget you. What have you been doing with yourself? I assume not college, since you never asked me for a recommendation."

"No, I've been working and riding and learning. It's been going really well—I bought this horse, and well, he's amazing. He can jump anything." I can't explain eventing in a way that Shackleton will understand, so I leave it at that.

"Well, if you ever do tire of playing with your ponies, you know where to find me if you need advice," he says.

I suddenly feel sorry for Shackleton, in his ugly, dated clothes, scrimping and saving on his teacher's salary with coupons in hand, always reading about things flying through the cosmos but never knowing what it's like to travel fast and free of gravity himself. Although I kind of get the feeling that he feels sorry for me, that he thinks there is something more important I don't understand about the alignment of time and space. In his eyes, I should see nothing but atoms or the law of gravity, I guess, when I watch a horse over a fence. But I don't, I just can't see the world that way. I couldn't ever, so I don't let it trouble me.

We talk science a bit—I'm still dorky enough to keep up on some science news like the space program and stuff—before he heads off to buy the rest of whatever he's cooking for himself that night.

Max gives me a meaningful glance. "Shackleton?" I say. "No way."

"Oh, come on, Simon. I mean, I hate to say it, but it's so obvious. You really had him as a teacher for an entire year and never even thought—"

"Shackleton is asexual; he's an amoeba."

"Simon, this is why you have such bad gaydar—rule number one, just because you're *not* attracted to a guy doesn't mean he's straight."

"Amoeba, Max, he's a total amoeba. Scientific fact. Asexual organism."

At home, Max browns the lamb in a pan, squinting against the steam, and then puts everything in the oven with a bunch of cut-up vegetables and potatoes. I know he's exhausted from the running and the argument with Mom and the riding but he doesn't complain or even act cranky like I would. While part of me is irritated by this there is another part of me that is in awe of him and knows I could never be that way.

I'm still angry Max feels guilty as hell and that Mom made him feel bad. Hypocrisy always enrages me, but like I've said before, people just don't make sense and there is no point in arguing with people, they'll just make up rationalizations for doing what they feel. All Max and I can do is ignore what we don't like about what my mother says. Eventually she'll break down, just like she did about my not going to college this year.

Max hums to himself a bit as he cooks and I recognize it's my—maybe I should say our—favorite Killers song, "All These Things That I've

Done." It makes me feel kind of warm in my heart, even though I don't say anything about the tune aloud.

Well, not at first, that is, until even my brother recognizes it, not because Sean understands the Killers, of course (despite my educational efforts over the years), but because he's heard me playing it so much. "I got toast but I'm not a toaster," my brother says, taking out the bread because he presumably can't last until dinner without starving to death. "I got ham but I'm not a hamster." He gets out mayo and ham to make himself a sandwich on said toast.

"Don't profane the lyrics of the song," I tell him, annoyed, but Max starts to relax and actually laughs out loud in an easy way, which he seldom does, even with me.

We watch a Sox game Sean DVR-ed until my mom comes home. I put my arm around the back of Max's seat on the couch. I don't touch him, I'm just beyond the edge of what might be appropriate if he were indeed just a friend sitting beside me.

When my mother arrives home from work and teaching her own riders at her barn, she looks annoyed about something beyond me. She gives Max a look that I recognize. The *are you still here* look. The same kind of look that she gave to most of my brother's girlfriends in high school because she hated them for other reasons—too preppy, too suburban, not horsey enough and generally too wimpy and girly to tolerate. She accepted Heather because she knew her before she dated Sean but perhaps my mother's approval, however grudging, was why Sean lost interest so quickly.

"What's that smell?" she asks.

"Max cooked dinner," I say, hopefully.

"No wonder I had trouble recognizing it, I'm surprised he could find the oven."

I think laziness about cooking wins out because my mother does sit down to eat with all of us. The three of them drink and I don't because I still hate the taste of red wine (which Max finally settled on). I'm starving though, and the food is the kind of food that I like—meat and potatoes—so I eat it.

The conversation is halting and stilted at first. My mother makes a joke that Max certainly didn't learn to cook from me. But then I ask her about her riders and if their parents were pleased about the kids' performances at the show and that relaxes her a little bit.

"Yes, they were for the most part. Of course, Cinderella had a few run-outs but at least you showed the owner that she can perform well if ridden properly. I talked to the father, incidentally, and he says they aren't interested in selling her. The little girl is totally in love with her horse, regardless of whether Cinderella is suitable or not. Oh well, perhaps they'll make it work eventually."

"I know."

"Simon, you still pout like a twelve-year-old. So, you're a vet," she says to Max, switching focus. And then begins to grill him about whether one of her adult riders should buy a horse despite finding a floating bone chip during the PPE since the woman's not going to jump him very high, what to do about colic since the change of season is coming, and about one of the lesson horses prone to navicular flare-ups. Max survives her initial interrogation and she seems to soften.

"Max used to do Pony Club. One of his old books has a picture of you in it, the one of you on Enigmatic," I offer, hopefully.

"Oh, that was a million years ago," says my mother, shrugging and carelessly smashing down one of Max's carefully cubed roasted potatoes with her fork. "Before I had these animals," she notes, gesturing and nodding to Sean and me. Her eyes go to the fireplace, which supposedly can be lit to make a real fire, although none of us have ever bothered to find out. "The only old photo we have displayed in here is the one on the mantle of the two boys with their first ponies." I know the one she is talking about—me on a white Welsh cross named Siobhán and Sean on an all-black drafty thing named Scout. Mom clearly had a thing with s-names at one point.

"That pony was such an asshole," says Sean. "It's amazing I survived."

"She was very good to you when you rode her properly," I say. "When you weren't cowboying her around the field."

"I wasn't the one who used to see what weird crap I could find to jump a pony over; mom nearly beat you senseless when you were trying to jump picnic tables."

"We used to live on our own farm when the boys were very small and there was plenty of space for them to ride safely—well, safely as they chose—alone out back. It's not like that in many places anymore."

"It is where we—where I am—now," I say.

"Both boys can ride very well, even though Sean tries to hide it, because I've never believed in push-button horses," says my mother.

"Scout would buck like hell if you tightened her girth even a hole too much," says Sean. "And if I wasn't careful, every time we went to a show, before I went in the ring, Simon would always hike it up a few notches. The times I didn't check it, I'd always end up last because she'd have a bucking fit. Or I'd be flung head-first like a lawn dart right in front of the judge."

"Yes, I remember that," says my mother. "It really is remarkable that you've made it this far, alive, with Simon as your brother. Simon, after that incident I was tempted to leave you on the show grounds and disown you."

"Repeatedly, Ma, Simon did that to me and Scout on *several occasions*. Even after you practically twisted his arm off in the car ride home and smacked him a few good ones."

"Well, it taught you to check your girth," I say. "Any punishment I had to suffer was worth it, though, given the look on your face. I only feel bad if it caused Scout some discomfort."

"Then, after the divorce, they shared a pony for a bit, but Sean switched to Western and we bought Cam, who you've met, and Damsel, Simon's first real horse. And that's our history, all you really need to know," she says, firmly, as if the history of our horses is the history of us, which it kind of is, although that is an abridged version.

"Max got a B-rating in Pony Club when he was growing up and did the Tet rally," I offer, since I know he won't say anything.

"Well, you must be able to ride, then," Mom concedes. "And that explains the running."

"I don't ride as much as I'd like, given my schedule," says Max.

"Knowing Simon, he wouldn't be interested in anyone who couldn't keep up with him well enough on a horse," says my mother, shrugging. She collects the plates. "Since you cooked, I'll do the washing up. Simon, I need to talk to you in the kitchen. It's nothing about you, Max," she says, understanding that his mind is still working in overdrive. Still, I know it must be bad because she pours herself another glass of wine and Mom's not much of a drinker. "I'll come out with dessert, shortly."

In the kitchen, I immediately attack my mother. "He's nice, isn't he?"

"Well, he is obviously a real vet, he does ride, and he can cook," says Mom.

"Did you have any doubt that he was a vet?"

"Oh, Simon, I don't know where you found him, so I wouldn't have been satisfied until I talked with him. But this isn't about Max. Simon, it's about your father."

"Who?"

"Your father—he contacted me. Or rather, someone on behalf of him contacted me. He's in hospice."

"Hospice?"

"Simon, stop echoing what I'm saying, it's very annoying. Yes, hospice. He apparently has cancer. They say he's dying, although he used that excuse before to avoid paying me what he owed me and kept on living. But since it's the hospice who contacted me, he might be telling the truth this time. He wants to see us—the three of us."

In addition to cooking lamb, vegetables, and potatoes, Max also whipped up a batch of chocolate chip cookies, which I've been arranging on a plate while stuffing one or two in my mouth while she talks. But now I stop, swallow, and kind of gape at her.

"Simon, I know I should forgive and forget, but I can't go to him. The hospice is in some suburb near Philadelphia. I don't even want to take off from work. He's hurt me enough. I've put that behind me, I just can't. Is that awful?"

I hug her. "No, mother, no, you should do what you want to do. But Sean and I should go see him, I guess."

"Simon, I feel bad that things weren't—better when the two of you were young. I really did try."

"What do you mean? I had a great pony. I didn't think mine was an asshole like Sean's Scout. Not that many kids have that much freedom growing up, not nowadays."

"Simon, if you don't watch your language you'll start to talk that way around everyone, not just your brother. I meant all the fighting between your father and me and all the violence."

"Sean remembers more of it than I do."

"I guess you were always out with the horses."

"Yes, I guess I was."

I remember my father in broken bits and pieces, and always unwillingly. There was the smell of alcohol on his breath when he'd come home with my mother; the smell of cigarettes when he'd smoke when we would go on long trips with the car windows rolled up against the speed of the highway. The fighting that would come up about stupid stuff, like what television channel to watch and what to eat for dinner, and not-so-stupid stuff like how much time Mom spent riding or with the horses. Or just all the animals around the house in general. Mom used to breed dogs back then and there were cats hanging around the place, too. Mom just rode when we were little and gave some lessons to people at their own, private barns as a trainer. We had a small barn out back; I know we were pretty well off then. No indoor, though, but that was fine for Sean and me because that way we had an excuse to ride in all weather.

Not that this fancy set-up mattered to us after the divorce. So far as I know Mom never got any child support out of Dad, thanks to his creative accounting and lawyering and the fact he got married twice after he married her and claimed poverty or something I guess, for various reasons.

Sean lazes into the kitchen, wondering what's been keeping us, shoves a cookie in his mouth, grins, then we bring him up to speed. Then he gets quiet.

"I'm not going," he says, immediately.

"You don't have to," says my mother.

My brother remembers more and like myself, most of it is not good. I kinda remember the final fight between my parents but Sean saw the whole thing, the night of the epic screaming match that ended with my father running over my mother's favorite dog with his car on purpose. Well, my father said by accident later, but I don't believe him in retrospect any more than my mother believed him at the time. She left soon afterward, Sean says, because the one thing you don't mess with is Mom's animals and also, I kind of wonder, if she was worried that one of us or her would be next.

"Just because the bastard is dying doesn't make him anything less of an asshole," says Sean. "Even assholes die eventually although they take longer to do it."

"I know but…I feel that I should go," I say.

"He might be making the whole thing up," mutters Sean.

"I don't think they let you fake it through hospice."

It's hard to explain but—I don't know, I haven't known many dying people, only a few dying animals and if it is true, that he wants to see us, I just can't deny him that. Besides, I am curious. I haven't seen him for more than ten years.

But I never saw the dog dead, and Sean did, so maybe that makes all the difference in the world. Sean leaves the kitchen in disgust.

Max, left outside all this time, cautiously ventures into the room as Sean exits. At first, I wonder if Mom will say anything but she does give a sort of sanitized version of recent events.

"I can drive you," Max says, but I won't let him.

"You've taken enough time off of work. Besides, I think I should do this alone." It's going to be awful, I know, and I don't want to pollute what Max and I have together with whatever goes on—I certainly don't want Max to meet my father. No point in that.

"I can't let you have the car, Simon, I need it for work and you can't get there by bus or train," says mom.

"I'll borrow Heather's car, she should be home for break."

"You take advantage of that girl," says my mother.

"She's my friend, Mom."

"Yes, she's a friend to you," says my mother.

"What's the deal with Heather?" asks Max, as he drives me over to her house.

"She's Sean's former girlfriend and we're still friends with her—she was my best friend all throughout high school." She was an even bigger dork than I was, I almost add but think better of it.

Heather doesn't live far away and we actually see her in the driveway with her car holding a vacuum, her jeaned butt sticking out of the vehicle as she is cleaning it. There are books, plastic containers, and riding boots lying beside the beat-up puke green ancient Golf.

"Simon," Heather says, jerking her head out in surprise.

Heather always looks so normal to me—jeans, Uggs, a big baggy college sweatshirt with the logo of her IHSA team on it. I guess that's how I should want to be, even though I don't. But just seeing her makes me feel comforted, like a blast from the past, good part of high school, so I hug her before I explain what I need.

I tell her everything—well, almost everything, everything except what I can't quite articulate myself. Which is why I'm going even though I've never thought much of my father morally or much of him period since the day my mother left him. That I'm also thinking of the horse that caught his leg in the barbed wire, the fox that almost got caught, and even and perhaps especially the mare that had to be put down when I was a kid. It just feels wrong to leave any creature sick or dying alone. I can't do it and live with myself.

"Simon, of course you can drive my car, but"—I can see just a little check of thought constipating Heather's generosity—"it's old, it can't go very fast." Translation: Don't drive like you usually drive.

"I'll be gentle with it, I promise," I say.

Max stands by his car, as if he doesn't want to get involved for some reason.

"That's Max," I say, gesturing to him because I can see she is looking at him, curious. "Don't bother to clean the car out, it won't be worth it if I'm using it."

Heather takes off her baggy sweatshirt—she's wearing a tank top beneath it—and pulls her tangled hair back in a bun like she's trying to look presentable. I don't know why she cares.

Max drives me home so I can pick up some stuff. I have the directions on my phone. Heather's beat-up car certainly doesn't have GPS. Max will drive home alone so he can make it back in time for work. I can just train it back to Vermont.

"That girl must trust you quite a bit," he says, "I presume she's driven with you."

"I'm not a bad driver, just fast."

Heather has a lot of books and papers in the passenger seat of the car. Basically, if a book has a painting of some guy in a ruffled shirt or a lady in a long gown on the cover or it was written a million years ago, Heather is reading it. I briefly glance at the titles—*Pride and Prejudice, Wuthering Heights, Maurice, Lolita*—and then I look away, bored and disinterested, shifting my eyes back to the road. Like all old books, they have nothing to do with me.

I drive all night. I plug my iPod into the sound system. At least that part of the car works pretty well. Heather has replaced the original radio since music is just as important to her as it is to me. She listens to a lot of Broadway, though, which I can only handle in small doses.

The hospital is located in some suburb that is as godforsaken in its own way as the farm in Vermont. When I get into the hospital, the directions to get to the hospice wing are very complicated. It's on its own floor, like they want to segment those who don't have hope away from those who do. The hospice nurses, unlike most nurses I've encountered, are very pleasant and kind. I'm suspicious of this, as though they must be trained to conceal something, but they seem sincere enough.

"You're his son?" asks one. "He said he had two."

"I'm the only one who is coming." Pause. "What is he like?"

She thinks, understandably, that I'm just asking about how sick he is. "His pain is being managed. It's small cell carcinoma, the kind that is most typical with smokers." She explains that small cell is very difficult to treat because the cancer is like dust, like being shot with buckshot to the chest and the little bits of cancer take hold and grow and spread and there is no way to cut them out. They've tried all the usual therapies and some experimental ones too, to contain it. That works for some, but not for him. It's all due to fortune and fate who responds and who doesn't. So he is here.

I admit I'm terrified to see him, more terrified than I've ever been in my life. Waiting to go on course or being on the back of a bucking horse doesn't even compare. I'm wearing my Joy Division T-shirt as a talisman, damn it all to hell if it isn't appropriate. This is my armor and I need the protection.

It's weird but—because I have the same coloring as my mom, I assumed my dad would look like Sean. And yeah, he has dark hair and no freckles but I recognize my off-center nose and curving mouth in his face. I see myself in him as he lies there. But what he really looks like in that white hospital bed—excuse me, hospice bed—is death. He's so thin I can see the skeleton behind his skin and that gives him a kind of generic appearance, as if I am looking at a mirror of not only what I am but what I and everyone else will become. For the first time in my life I can feel the skeleton behind my own face. I'm not worrying if some guy will find me attractive or figuring out how to scowl and crunch my mouth up to keep someone I don't trust away.

"Simon?" my father says. "They told me you were here." His voice is low and sounds very correct. Not British exactly, but I don't know, proper and educated and not sounding from anywhere, certainly not New Jersey or New England or any of the accents I'm used to on a daily basis. His voice doesn't sound like mine at all, which is kind of a relief. It does take me aback that he is sucking on a lollypop. He follows my gaze and train of thought somehow.

"It's a fentanyl lollypop," he explains. "It's for the pain, especially when I'm having trouble swallowing. Makes heroin look like sugar water, they tell me, but it's not helping that much."

"Dad, I'm sorry."

"Don't be—I smoked. Only quit a few years ago. You play, you pay, they say. Well, not in so many words but—there are those who get this who don't smoke, the poor bastards, but not me." Pause. "Where is your mother? Where is your brother?"

Silence.

"I guess they aren't coming. I was going to contact them before this. Here is the irony—I was in AA and you're supposed to get in touch with the people you hurt in the past as part of the recovery process. I was getting around to it and then this, after being totally alcohol and drug free…" He gestures with the lollypop to the machine next to him, which I gather is pumping some kind of a pain relief drug in him. "Then this diagnosis. Life is full of ironies."

I sit down by his bed. "I'm here now." The room is hot and close. He's not in a private suite, he's behind a wall of sheets designed to separate him from the other patient's bed in the room. It's to give us privacy, but like cubicles in an office, I can still hear and smell the other patient who is moaning on the other side. The odor of urine from bedpans hangs heavy in the air. It's like everyone is part of the same, dying organism here. The health evident in my muscles, the outside dirt on the Docs that Max bought me, the nibbles from horses on my shirt, even the dirt under my fingernails that never quite gets scrubbed away, it is all being mocked by the death around me, somehow.

"I'm sorry, Dad," is all I can say, although I hardly remember or recognize him as my father. I recall only bits and pieces. Smells.

Shouting. The closed windows of the car when he drove, the odor
of nicotine burning my sinuses. The boozy scent and the fights that
always ended our dinners. Going to the barn out back afterward and
sitting there with the horses and the dog.

Another memory: the dinner table, left empty mid-meal because
they were fighting. Sean and me just sitting there. Wine in both of
my parents' glasses. We filled both of them up to the top with the
bottle that was still on the table. Sean managed to slug his down but I
spit mine out, I'd never tasted anything so terrible. Leaving a pattern
of red droplets across the white tablecloth like blood.

"I wouldn't have recognized you, Simon, if the nurse hadn't told me."

"Well, I've changed a bit since I was eight, ya know!" I laugh, suddenly feeling silly.

"You look good, Simon."

"Thank you, Dad."

"I hope you don't smoke."

"I don't. Never even tried it."

"Not that I could lecture you if I you did, or about anything. I keep
thinking of that line from a play—what is that line…a play I saw with
your mother. It's also a quote from a poem." He really seems bothered
he can't remember. I know Mom and him went to the theater a lot
when I was a little kid. It was part of his attempt to teach her about real
culture she said, since most of her childhood (like mine) was occupied
with horses.

"I couldn't help you with that, Dad. I don't think I've ever been to
more than two plays in my life. And I certainly don't read poetry. Ever."

"Ashes to ashes, dust to dust, if women don't get you, then the whisky must.
Something like that."

"I'm not much of a drinker, to be perfectly honest."

"Well, I guess the apple does fall far from the tree, but then again,
neither was your mother. You look like her."

"That's what they say."

"Does she still have horses?"

"She is still a trainer, doesn't ride competitively anymore. I do. I work with horses. Sean doesn't. He's in school. We both turned out okay, Dad," I add, firmly, and suddenly I realize that is what I came here to say. "We're not robbing 7-11s or anything. I have a job and Sean will have a good one when he graduates from college. We're doing really, really well and anything bad in the past doesn't matter, just forget about it now."

"Thank you Simon," says my father and puts the lollypop back in his mouth, sucking it so hard it kind of looks like a cigarette.

"Can I get you anything?" He doesn't respond so I just sit there for what feels like a long time. I don't have my iPod plugged into my ears but I run songs through my head on a loop.

I think all addictions—all addictions that involve putting something in your body, at least, not like being addicted to a person or to doing something—are all kind of the same because my father starts to tell me stories about his youth, when he was my age, and although they are amusing at first, the tales all blend into one. He also tells me about some fancy places he's visited through his work, one or two famous people he's met I've never heard of. Eventually, he drifts to sleep.

I know from my Mom that my father (unlike her) came from money and used that money to make more money, which is why we had the farm and the ponies when we were growing up. All his talk of deals confirms my impression that Wall Street is just a kind of glorified form of gambling. But I also know, deep down, that if it hadn't existed I never would have become the rider I am now, that I was lucky to start so young, with such freedom. I still believe, no matter what Max might say, that sometimes things with bad beginnings can have good ends. It's weird to think how all of his money and the hell that my mother went through bought me so much, in ways they didn't even recognize and probably never will.

I look around the room. It's kind of sad and impersonal but beneath the television there is a bookcase with a bunch of games, mostly for little kids who are visiting their relatives I assume. Candy Land. Monopoly. Life. Connect Four. But also chess, albeit kind of an awful, tacky set. I take out the box. I look, out of idle curiosity, to see if all the pieces are there.

"You taught me this," I say when he wakes, suddenly remembering, connecting things like dots in my brain.

"You still play?" he asks. I set up the board.

"I remember one of our first games. I was actually beating you but then I lost because I wasn't willing to sacrifice my knight. Because it was a horse. And after you won, you flicked me on the ear so hard it stung, telling me to never be sentimental during a game. To win."

"Do you sacrifice your knight now?"

"If I have to."

"You play white. It's only fitting."

"I usually play black."

"You're white against me." My father watches me as I set up and open. "The queen's gambit. I prefer the king's Indian attack when playing white." Yes, him teaching me that, it's all coming back. I shrug. I know I've made the right decision.

My father's hand is so shaky he can barely move the pieces but we wage the longest and most difficult battle I've had in years. Far harder than anything I've played against Max or even against the geeky, brainy boys in my math and science classes I used to challenge every now and then with the old chess sets in some of the classrooms, when we had a substitute and were running wild all period. But I win, I beat him.

"You always had a good brain, Simon, although you were a weird little kid. Did you do well in school?"

"Terrible. It's just not the kind of brain that's good for jumping through those types of hoops, the kind that schoolteachers set up. You see, I told you I should play black."

"I don't remember you as a bad kid, Simon. Another game?"

"Sure."

We play several games. I'm ahead, three games to two. I don't back down, even though he's dying. I know he doesn't want me to. To be honest, I wouldn't even if he did want me to lose.

I leave the room once he is asleep and stop one of the nurses in the hall. "He keeps tugging and pawing at the blankets with his hands. Does that mean he needs something?"

"That's normal," she says.

"I know they say he has lung cancer but his breathing isn't that bad."

"The cancer started in the lungs but then quickly spread elsewhere. It's not typical that his breathing isn't as affected as some people's but not unusual, either."

The nurse comes to check on him. I'm starting to feel sick. I can spend all day cleaning out the worst, urine-soaked stalls or sit up all night with a colicking horse but the smell of human piss and shit and the weird, stilled atmosphere from all the people on the pain medications makes me feel ill. At least in a stable there's always a couple of healthy horses there to give you hope.

"Come back later. He's exhausted," says the nurse. "You're the only visitor he's ever had."

"He said he's been married several times, in addition to my mother—what about his other wives?"

"I couldn't say. Wait, I have something for you."

The nurse comes back with a bunch of pamphlets and flyers. She explains that they will tell me about the stages I will go through and things like that, like grief is proceeding through the levels Novice, Preliminary, Intermediate and so forth. She's very nice but a quick look over the cartoons and the bolded headers tell me that this stuff will be as useless to me as all the textbooks in high school were in helping me to understand myself. They tell people how to mourn a relationship, while my father and I never had such a thing. They tell you about being sad that something that is passing, not about what never existed. And they also say that death is natural, which I know, but not that it can't still seem pretty horrible, which it clearly can. I think of the bones in own my face reflected in the skeleton of what's left of my father lying there.

"He has such strength of will," says the nurse. "I've never known someone so sick to fight so hard."

I thank her as if that is a compliment, since she means it that way. But going over all the boozing in my mind, the first thing that pops into my head is, well, of course he won't let go yet, given that he lived an essentially unlived life. I keep thinking of all the sameness of all the stories of bar and after bar after glass after deal after deal after deal after glass after glass after getting screwed over on a deal and screwing someone back in return to even out the score.

I stuff the pamphlets in a garbage can on my way out. I kick the can with the toe of my Docs, hard. The razor-drawn skull on the toe makes a satisfying, smacking sound against the tin. It doesn't hurt me but it's not enough. I want to kick and punch something. I want to fight someone and hurt him good but there is no one around I can justify making bleed for this, not even myself.

I look around the town. I know, thanks to my phone, that there is a university nearby, one of the few historic landmarks in the area.

The weather is beautiful. It's sunny, cool but not cold, with a blowing breeze. All the students are milling around, some of them throwing Frisbees (but no Nietzsche Factor Frisbees). Others are lying on the grass and reading, others are eating lunch. There is a college tour snaking through the grounds and I kind of follow it, not sure where else to go.

The kid leading the tour is a cute Indian guy who is really good at walking backwards. He says he's a double major in neuroscience and French. We go around to all the buildings and I see kids sitting in a massive biology class learning about animal cells; a little seminar of kids holding Heather-type books meeting in a circle at a big round table; and dormitories plastered with posters advertising upcoming dances and study break sessions. The dorm walls are also filled with posters of movies and sitcoms that must have been released while I was away from civilization because their names are so unfamiliar. Well, there is one poster that makes me smile—the one with a picture of Gandalf from the *Lord of the Rings* movies that says ORGANIC CHEMISTRY: YOU SHALL NOT PASS. And some stickers of rain-bow-colored triangles. But that's about it, in terms of the jokes and references I get.

I talk to some of the kids on the tour and they seem nice. To blend in, I blather on a little bit about the physics projects I worked on a year ago and go on about my calculus class and that buys me their respect. I could be one of these nerdy kids, I think, in a parallel universe. The tour ends at the school's cafeteria and we all eat—me, the kids, and the few parents tagging along. Almost to my surprise, I feel hungry and fully capable of vacuuming up my usual three slices of cheese pizza as I talk about school and annoying teachers and people in high school. When they ask me about my background and why I didn't apply to college as a senior I say, "I took a year off after high school. My father has cancer." These facts are true and make a more understandable story to these civilian outsiders than the reality of horses. I feel kind of guilty for my sins of omission when one of the parents insists on buying ice cream for me and her kid. I can tell she feels sorry for me and says stuff like what a terrible disease cancer is and how her mother died from breast cancer.

With the ice cream and the pizza and the balloons and signs in the cafeteria advertising some fraternity event, it's like some kind of a party, in a weird way. I feel especially guilty since I still possess the welling urge to hurt something and have nowhere to vent my rage. I can't even drive fast because I have Heather's car, not my own.

I walk past the bookstore as I leave. Damn, those calculus and animal biology and organic chemistry textbooks are expensive. Yet I know, despite the Gandalf poster on the wall, I could pass those things. It would be so easy to walk into this world, especially after this past year at Daniel's. I think of the faces of all the students, so stressed because of some stupid test that isn't life or death at all. It's nothing like going over an obstacle on a horse or nursing a horse through a difficult night. It's too easy, I think, for me. I mean, I know that it could lead to becoming a vet or some job where I wasn't necessarily trapped in a cubicle all day. But still those confines of dorm rooms and the little circles the students sit in…I wouldn't last, not the seven gabillion years it takes to get to vet school. I just don't have Max's patience.

I would get bored, dangerously bored. God knows what I would do without the boundaries of my sport to test me. I close the book on animal physiology. It smells plastic and fake with its newness.

I think about my father's bragging about how much he drank and smoked. All the AA in all the world isn't going to take away the sense of pride he feels in the boozing. Like drinking hard was his greatest accomplishment, a worthless risk. Anyone can shove a drink down his throat.

I haven't been away that long but already I know I need to ride my horse. I miss him. I need Fortune.

I go back to the hospital. My father is awake. He can barely eat (again, the nurses tell me this is normal). I help feed him some applesauce. The nurse says that sometimes the act of eating can provide them (by "them" she means the dying) with some comfort. Then, although it kind of grosses me out, I help my father with his bedpan because I feel I should, not a strange nurse.

"Do you want me to come back tomorrow?" I ask. Visiting hours are almost at an end.

"Simon, let's leave it like this." I know what he means. He wants me to remember him while he's still coherent enough. "Simon, I'm sorry for everything."

"Dad, I can't forgive you on behalf of my mother." I consider saying that she still has the scars but I don't. "Or Sean. But for me, there is nothing to be sorry about, I'm doing just fine. I was always out with my pony during all the bad stuff. And I'll never be sorry about the horses we had. I'm still grateful for the horses."

"Your mother loved her animals more than she loved me." There is a kind of accusatory tone in his voice that the drugs haven't weakened. I can hear it even through the lollypop in his mouth.

"She loves animals more than Sean and me, as well, probably, so don't take it personally," I say. "Truthfully, there are only two, three, people I love even as much as animals, so I'm not any better."

For a minute, I think of that comment of my father's in regards to myself. I can't separate it all, what I feel for my mother and Sean and Max and all of the animals I've cared for and known. It all seems bound up equally in the same kind of love and there is no way to break it down. It seems weird to feel jealous of animals.

I call Sean before I drive home. "He's really dying. He's in his final days, they say."

Sean is silent for a long time, so long, I think I've lost the connection.

"I can't, Simon, I just can't."

"Okay, well, I'm coming home now."

I show up late at Heather's to drop off the car. I ask if I can crash because I don't want to disturb my mother who has to get up early for work. Heather insists I sleep in her bed while she sleeps on the couch. I say the couch would be fine for me and I don't say honestly, we could both share the same bed since she is as close to a sister as I'll ever have, but I'm too tired to fight or explain.

"How is your father?" she asks, as she follows me up to her room.

"He's dying, Heather."

Somehow, I sleep very soundly. I don't even hear Heather's mom getting ready for her job and when I come down, it's just Heather, sitting there in her pajamas with her hair in a sloppy bun, drinking coffee and reading a novel. I know she said that she's going to be working at mom's barn over the summer but I guess she's taking one day off because she just got home from college. We eat strawberry Pop-Tarts from the freezer and Heather gets me some orange soda. I know Heather doesn't eat that stuff much anymore (she's gone all healthy since college) but she must have bought junk food knowing I'd be back. She remembers the type of stuff I used to inhale when we'd hang out at her place all night after riding at a show, unable to go to sleep. Then I'd crash at school and doze all day at my desk and be bright and chipper to muck stalls and ride until dark. Heather makes herself some more coffee.

I still haven't processed what has happened. The "I'm sorries" the nurses and the parents on the tour said continue to annoy me and the desire to punch stuff remains strong. I know "I'm sorry" is what you're supposed to say when someone's father dies and I guess that is what bugs me. They think I feel sad in some generic way for the end of life and time passing and the loss of a parent they assume I must love. But I just feel empty and disgusted and sick. Kind of like the time I got the concussion only worse. What a waste, I think. I think of the times people have said "waste" about me. Well, I know what real waste is now.

Max left a message on my phone telling me he is sorry as well but I can't even respond to it, my hands are feeling all shaky and want to be balled into fists.

I tell Heather about the school tour I crashed to pass the time. She knows a bit about the college. It's apparently a good one. "But not for me," I say.

"I think they have an equestrian team."

"I don't play nice on teams, Heather. Anyway, no place to gallop around. Too many books with questions at the end of chapters I don't think are worth answering."

"You know, they do have an animal science major at my school that's pretty highly rated."

"I'm sure it is but I would still have to do Shakespeare and all that *Romeo and Juliet* and *Hamlet* crap, right?"

"Well, you have to do stuff you don't like to do even now, like dressage. Besides, isn't your horse still named after *Romeo and Juliet?*"

"I'm slowly making my peace with dressage," I say.

"That's better than me. I still haven't made my peace with math. Fortunately, I'm studying literature so I don't have to take much of it. If you don't think college is right for you, Simon, don't go. It's not like I'll think any less of you."

"It's not the people thinking less of me, it's the money I'll make that seems to bother my family. Or the lack thereof."

"I'm not going to be buying a fancy warmblood from Europe on my salary when I graduate, either, not with my English major," laughs Heather. "So count me in the 'stupidly doing whatever the hell I want club,' too. At least you won't have student loans."

Heather and I play a game of Scrabble. I'm not ready to go yet and leave the bubble of Heather's warmth. Scrabble is Heather's favorite game and she's pretty good at it but I still beat her. Heather loves words but I know where to place the letters better to get the most points. Or I just want to win more at games and take them more seriously than she does. Maybe it's a mixture of both.

"Heather, I should go. I've already taken more time off than I should. Thank you so much for letting me use your car."

Time is short so Heather drives me home, where I pick up the rest of my things and say goodbye to Sean. I'm too tired to even joke much with him and he sees that. Even though I've slept, I still feel beat up inside and out. Sean gives me a one-armed hug and kind of ruffles my hair like he used to when I was a kid and much shorter than him.

I doodle on a piece of paper all the way up to Vermont. Not animals like I usually do, just geometric shapes piling up on one another. When the page is full I doze a bit more.

It's night when I arrive—the train is slow—and no one is there to meet me at the station because I've told no one I'm coming. I haven't felt like answering Max and forgot to call Daniel. It's well after evening feed by the time I've walked the couple of miles back but the walking feels good so I don't mind, despite all the clumps of snow and refrozen ice and mud all over the place. I sit by Fortune's stall and watch him eat. He has no idea of what has happened to me, how much I've changed just over the weekend since I've been away.

"Shaughnessy?" I turn around to see Daniel.

"I just got in. Thank you for giving me the extra time off."

"Don't even thank me. How's your father?" I remember that Daniel's wife died of cancer. I don't know what kind. It doesn't matter. Cancer is cancer is cancer.

"I think—I don't think I'll see him alive again," I say, flatly. I can't say all the complicated feelings I have, which might be why I long to be alone so much. People will likely say the types of things they say to someone who has lost someone they love and that's not what I lost.

A long silence. "I'm sure he's glad he saw you," says Daniel.

"Yes, I think he was," I say.

More silence. "Um, Max called." My head jerks up. "He said he had called you and left you messages but you didn't answer. He wanted to make sure you were okay."

"I just haven't felt like talking to anyone," I admit. This feels really weird, like—I don't know, like talking to my father about my boyfriend, but actually not my real father, actually much worse than my father. I also know that Max must have been worried beyond all hell to have called Daniel. I really do feel like the asshole in the relationship, right now.

"Well, I think you should probably tell him you're okay," says Daniel, clearly just as uncomfortable as I am.

"I'm not going to sleep tonight, so I'll bike over and be back for morning feed tomorrow."

"It's okay if you need another day off, Shaughnessy."

"I won't. I need to work Fortune again before he forgets me." I want to ride now so badly—much more than I want to talk to anyone, even to Max—but it's a bad cold snap up here. I know the ground is too hard and icy slick to ride out on in any meaningful way, even with Fortune's special shoes. And I'm not going to practice dressage in an arena, not the way I feel right now. Tomorrow I'll put up some practice jumps.

"Where the hell have you been?"

"Jesus, Max, you knew where I was. Cut me a break. Why did you have to call Daniel? That was really weird."

"Couldn't you have at least left me a message? With the way you drive, I thought you might have been in an accident or something."

"I just didn't want to talk about it. Is that so hard to understand? I've never been in an accident, anyways, not as the driver."

"Simon, sometimes you can be as infuriating as hell. There's a limit to how much I can take of being dragged around and beaten up inside like this."

"I'm not beating up anyone. I just needed to be alone." I vaguely can hear how selfish that might sound to Max but there is a part of me that is too cold right now to care. "Anyway, I'm okay. Do you want me to go?"

"Fine, go." I turn to leave.

"Is your father—?"

"Not yet. Close to it." I'm standing at the closed door, but I haven't opened it yet. I'm fingering the doorknob in my hand just like my father obsessively fingered the blankets when he was lying there in hospice. I think I want to leave, now that I've told Max I'm alive and my father is dying, but I don't. I want to slam a door but I don't want to go.

"I'm sorry."

I blurt out what I've been thinking but couldn't say to the nurses or to Heather or Daniel. "Well, I'm sorry that they can't put a person down like a horse or a dog, that's what I'm sorry about. It would be the kinder thing to do."

I don't look at his face but I think of all the horses Max has had to put down in his career. I'd much rather have that, I think, not all the sweet nurses and all the drug-filled candy at hospice.

He walks over to me and puts his lips on my forehead. I can feel Max's anger start to ebb away. I realize I kind of knew it would.

"If I got cancer, I wouldn't go through all that, I'd just find a horse that would throw me down dead and get it all over with," I mutter.

"Damn it Simon, that's a pretty grisly thing to say. You're scaring the hell out of me."

"Sorry, *doctor*, but it's how I feel."

"I guess he was pretty bad."

"Yes, I guess he was. Cancer and all."

I sit with Max on the couch for a long time in his arms. The urge to punch something slowly, slowly dissipates within me. Like an animal being tranquilized. Eventually I can unball my hands, which have been bent slightly into fists, and hold one of Max's hands. I don't want to think too much but the thought crosses my brain how strange it is that the body can be so cruel, so cruel it can even kill itself. But I can't hate it because it is also the only thing that has ever provided me with any real and lasting comfort. Other than horses, of course.

I don't know if it is wrong or right but I find myself kissing Max. The muscles of his chest and his thighs feel very alive and hard against my own in a way that seems right like nothing in the hospital ever did or ever could. At least for a little while I can pretend that I'm so healthy I can never possibly die, ever.

Then I have to go back and feed and everything returns to normal as if what I saw never happened, although of course it did, otherwise I wouldn't be here.

32

THE TRICKY COFFIN

Our first event of the season is several hours away. Finally, the snow has melted enough for us to travel. It's me, Cynthia on her new horse Sam, and Megan on Niles (one of the new, large sale ponies). Megan still hasn't sold Maggie. Unlike Cynthia and me, Megan doesn't see herself becoming a professional rider in the future, she merely aspires to teach riding, so she hasn't been that motivated to sell her precious pony. What with the plans for the wedding and all she seems more content to get better at a slow and steady pace, with no particular competitive aim in mind. On one hand, I'm kind of glad because I like Maggie and I'm amused to watch Jig and her spar together every now and then, as he tries to herd her into her stall (which he's figured out is her place). On the other hand, it still seems kind of weird to want to ride yet not push the envelope and see how far you can go.

Cindy's Sam seems nonplussed by the new, rougher surroundings. I guess he's changed hands enough in his life it doesn't bother him.

This will be my first event at Intermediate level, so I won't be competing against Cynthia. She says she's relieved but to be honest, I'm not feeling as confident as I have in the past.

I took a lesson with Daisy before coming here, though, and (without her having to hop on him), Fortune was more supple and giving than he has been in a long time. I was worried that the winter chill still in the air would make him inflexible at his lateral work and too fresh to have more than one speed (fast) but he surprised me. "The two of you look more comfortable with yourselves," she said.

The stabling area is rough but nice enough and I graze Fortune a bit before putting him in his stall. I keep a blanket on him all the time to protect his carefully washed, unspoiled greyness. Of course, I'm in my muddy Killers T-shirt, jeans, and anarchist sweatshirt.

The place is crawling with spectators and press. I see representatives of all the magazines I've been reading since I was a kid conducting interviews with the big names. One of the reporters even stopped to talk to me.

"I bought him for four grand," I tell the woman. "He's out of, well, nobody. Around nine-ish, I gather." No one cares what I have to say, though, since I'm nobody as well, despite the presence of Daniel.

"This is a tricky coffin," Daniel tells me, as we do a course walk. Since this is my first time at this level we go over things very slowly and meticulously. He warns me about some of the difficult questions and for the first time since forever, I'm nervous. Nervous enough to want to ride now; I can't hardly wait to get in the start box and hear the buzzer.

Max said he might drive by to see the showjumping tomorrow. It's a long drive for just a day but I still hope he does, selfishly, although I know I'll probably be too absorbed to talk to him.

Megan looks the most relaxed of all of us, talking and laughing with some of the other competitors. She knows that just as long as she makes it through the course on the newbie, her objective will have been realized. I guess the same is true for me as well. Making it to the end is always the primary goal.

After it is all over, I graze Fortune, leaning against him slightly, watching him eat. It's been a long slog for him. I suppose from his perspective he's mysteriously propelled through a series of peculiar moves, then gets to run and have fun over jumps, then gets to do more jumping, then gets a reward.

"You looked really good," says Max, who only watched my stadium.

"Well, not good enough."

"Fourth for your first Intermediate is excellent."

"I know," I say. "I'm just getting used to the difference in competition."

"I heard some people say it was one of the hardest courses they've ridden in a long time."

"We shouldn't have lost that rail at the end."

"I didn't see your cross-country but you did well at that."

"So why didn't you watch what we're best at," I say, laughing.

"Because it makes me nervous," says Max.

"I'm the one riding it." I don't say, "I'll be riding even more difficult courses in the future, most likely, you'll have to watch them."

Max shrugs. Weirdly, it never occurred to me that Max might not want to watch me ride because he might be afraid for me or something—then I remember his reaction to my riding Ted. But now Ted is good enough he can even be ridden by some of the better teenage riders without incident. I thought I had proved my point. I guess not, or maybe there was no point to prove. Fear is just dumb because it's never the things you're afraid of that catch you in the end, but I can't convince Max of that.

I leave Fortune with Max and go to get something to eat. On my way, a guy stops me—obviously not a rider, but a dad-type—and compliments me on my ride. Then he introduces himself as the father of one of the guys riding Novice. He says stuff about his son, that the kid is almost fourteen, a good rider, blah blah and looking to move up to Training.

He asks me a bit more about Fortune—is he spooky, does he buck or bite, would he be suitable for a young rider and so forth. "He's got quite a jump in him," he says, approvingly. "My son does the jumpers, too." Out of pride I go over Fortune's record showjumping, including the puissance class he won topping out at five foot.

Then the guy asks if Fortune is for sale. I'm kind of taken aback.

"Well, every horse is for sale," I say. I kind of laugh nervously. But I know he expects me to make an offer so I say the first thing that pops in my head. "Oh well, I wouldn't let him go for less than $40,000."

So the guy gets out his checkbook and suddenly I realize that he's serious although I'm not sure that I am.

"But I still need to think about it," I say.

He's annoyed and I can tell he thinks I'm jerking him around. We exchange contact numbers, though. I say I'll have to sleep on it. I know that I didn't come off as particularly professional or whatever. I can practically hear my mother's voice in my head: "You're making $36,000 over what you spent on that horse, get rid of him now, Simon, don't be an idiot." I mean, yes, he was good today, but I know he's certainly not a good enough mover in dressage to take me far. But as impulsive as I was when I bought him, I can't throw him away with the same lack of care.

By way of explanation to the dad, I say, "Things have been hectic for my family—my father is dying of cancer," and then the guy is all apologetic for trying to rush me. It's true but it's a lie, too, because my father has nothing to do with the reason I don't want to let Fortune go just yet, even though I know I have to. I can force myself to lie to others but not to myself.

Back at the barn, while I'm putting stuff away, I check my phone. There is a message from my mother which I at first assume is just congratulations but then, when I open it, it just says to call her immediately.

"Fourth," is the first thing I say to Mom.

"You sound disappointed. Did you expect to win your first Intermediate event?"

"No, I didn't, but it never feels good to say 'fourth,' regardless."

"Simon, your father is dead."

Pause.

I feel I should say I'm sorry, but to whom? Certainly not to Mom. To myself? But once again, what I feel is more of an absence and a hollowness, not really sadness. I can't explain it. I really don't want to talk about it with anyone. My mother continues, "Anyway, he apparently left you something."

"Left me what?"

"The lawyer didn't say, he needs to speak to you directly."

"I thought he said he didn't have anything anymore—money or whatever." Property. Investments. All the same to me.

"Simon, do I know anything about your father? Just call the lawyer. But I also think you need to visit the lawyer yourself; he said he would like to talk to you personally."

I ask Daniel to let me borrow the barn's truck to drive to the lawyer's office.

I hate asking Daniel for transportation since he's been so nice to me in other ways and also because it brings up the c-word again. I worry that it will make him think of his own wife. But I ask all the same, painfully, looking at the ground, speaking in halting, slow bursts of sound. Rather brusquely, Daniel says, "Sure." He hands me the keys without lots of "I'm sorry," which is exactly what I need right now, at this time.

Daniel is one of the few people I've met whose ability to know what you should do to help horses translates to how he acts around people. There usually isn't that much cross-over.

"You're his son?" the lawyer greets me with a question, as if he is surprised.

I can feel him taking stock of my flannel shirt, feed store T-shirt, barn boots, even my build and dirty fingernails that never quite come clean. There's some hay I didn't notice caught in the rolled up cuff of my jeans. "I work with horses," I say, somewhat apologetically, to explain why I'm leaving hayseed and manure on the clean carpet. I stare at the toe of my boot, which is shedding dried mud.

"I can't imagine Mr. Wright working with horses, no offense," he says. For a second, I have no idea who he is talking about and then I remember it's my father's last name, which neither my mother, brother, nor I have used in ages.

"I didn't know him well," I say. "My parents got divorced when I was a kid. I only saw him once after he got really sick."

The lawyer obviously looks uncomfortable with all of this emotional and psychological talk and shifts back to what he does know, which is money and the law. He goes over a bunch of stuff, like my father's assets, debts, and such. I interrupt him once, mid-sentence, saying, "I thought my father said he didn't have any money, he never paid any child support to my mother as far as I know." I vaguely understand the lawyer's explanation of all the smoke and mirrors behind how my father hid stuff. Then I just let the lawyer continue until he says, "Your father left the remainder of his estate to you."

"What?" I ask, stupidly, I can even feel my mouth hanging open, slightly.

"To you," he says, and he names the figure. I stare at him.

"Shit," I say. I've actually never had an extended conversation with a lawyer in my life and I kind of know that isn't an appropriate thing to say after it leaves my mouth but he's not offended or anything. "What about Sean and our mom?"

"He changed his will, after…"

"After I visited him? Did he leave something to them before that?"

"No, not even then, though. Before, he left it to charity. The amount will probably be around three million dollars after taxes." He looks at me, critically. "You might want to get a financial advisor."

"Uh, what?"

"Of course, probate takes time and you won't get it immediately."

"I guess this means I won't need to sell my horse."

"What?"

"Well, I was thinking I would need to sell my current horse to move up the levels but I guess now I can afford more than one."

"You definitely need to talk to a financial advisor. I can give you a few names."

33

DON'T LOOK AT THE GROUND, THERE'S NO MONEY THERE

I drive home to New Jersey and wait for Mom to come home. I call her beforehand while she is still at work so I don't give her a heart attack when she finds me sitting at the kitchen counter.

"Simon, what are you doing here?"

"I went to the lawyer. I have to talk to you."

"Simon, when you called me I thought something—terrible—had happened."

"Well, my father is dead."

"I know that."

"After all the legal stuff is taken care of, his estate will have more than three million dollars left in it."

"That bastard. I knew it all these years. How did he hide it?" My mother rants on a bit and I try to reconstruct what the lawyer told me. And then I hit her with the news.

"He left it to me, the remainder of his estate."

"To you?"

"Yes, to me, not to Sean. Not to anyone else."

My mother, who has just come back from the barn and has been pacing the kitchen floor, leaving mud and manure all over it, suddenly stops and sits down. She looks at me from her chair, blinks, she's speechless in a way I've never seen her before. Then she laughs.

"So, Simon, I suppose you did make the right decision to see him that day."

"What's that they say about a stopped clock? That it's right at least two times a day? I suppose I can always say that I was right once. I mean, I don't know about morally right, but right enough for all intents and purposes." Pause. "I talked to the lawyer and I'm going to split it three ways."

"What?"

"Did you think I was just going to hold onto the money like that? I'm dividing it. You, me, Sean."

"I don't want it."

"Mother, don't be ridiculous."

"You're young and you think a million dollars is so much. It's not today, it's not going to set you up for life in the horse world or anything like that."

"If I expected three million to do that, I'd be an idiot as well. Look, this way you can do some of the stuff you've wanted to—get a younger horse, take some clinics, maybe do some showing yourself. Take time off work or find a job you actually don't hate. I mean, I know you like teaching, but the job job at the office that sucks."

"If you give it to me, I will only hold it for when you do need it. This is a gift, not from your father but—oh, I don't know what I believe in Simon, but fate or the universe. I should have known that with all the talent you had riding, it wouldn't go to waste. At least you can get a real horse now and study with a trainer who isn't off in the middle of nowhere, someone with more secure financial backing..."

"Fortune is a real horse, Mom. But yes, another horse as well, probably. I think maybe—maybe from Europe. But I need to go and study there first. Everyone says that you need to study the way the Germans ride and now I have enough of a financial base without being dependent on you or anyone to go there and train. I know some things but after this year I see I don't have half of the knowledge or experience or technique of some other people my age to compete like I want to compete."

"So what about your horse then?"

"Daniel will keep him for me. And Max can ride him."

"Max can't ride your horse."

"Oh, he has, on a number of occasions."

"I suppose I underestimated him."

"That's okay, Mom. People often do."

"Does Max know this?"

"Not yet."

"Simon, what about your brother? Are you sure you want to give him that much money? Why not just offer him some if he needs it?"

"Mom, I'd be no good being some rich guy dispensing money every now and then when I thought someone needed what I had. I can barely control my own life properly, I can't control someone else's like that. I think it's wrong." I think of Cindy, sitting on Sam for a moment, and the horrible and uncomfortably elegant dinner I had with her father that night.

"Yes, but knowing Sean he'll quit college or something if he doesn't think he has to work."

"I'm sure you'll convince him that isn't a good idea if he does want to; he's not like me, Mom, he actually does listen to other people from time to time. He helped us with the horses all those years even when he'd rather have been playing soccer or baseball or running. He'll make good use of it, I'm sure, he'll do—something. People like him, he has charm, unlike me."

"You could have more people like you if you tried, Simon."

"Nah, not really, Mom, either you like me or you don't. That's just my way. I think that's what my father wanted, you know, to break us up as a family. It was the one thing he couldn't do with his money."

"What do you mean?"

"I don't know, for the two of you to like, hate me or something for getting all the money."

"Yes, that would be like him." And my mother talks a bit about the times when he tried to do things like that, turn her against her own family, her friends, isolating her.

I don't know if my father was as bad or evil as she says but I can at least refuse to play this game, fold my hand on this one.

"I'm going to stop and see Sean on the drive back to Vermont," I say. "I still have to finish the year out with Daniel. Daniel will tell me where I should go to train in Europe. He'll know."

"Simon, before you tell Sean, just remember, even in the Bible the youngest son always keeps his inheritance and doesn't divide it and give part of it back to the eldest that's lost it. You don't have to do this, I want you to know."

"I don't know anything about the Bible, Ma, the only thing I know is what you taught me, which is stuff like being kind to animals and always leave the horse in a better state after you get off of him than he was when you got on. Sean will be fine."

"He's so lazy, I worry about him, or that he'll go through the money like he does through his girlfriends."

"Even if he does, it's on him, then, not on me."

"And like I said, Simon, I'm not quitting my job or selling the house to buy a mini-mansion. What's mine is yours so far as the riding goes."

"I know, Mom, I know."

"Are you willing to leave your horse and your boyfriend to go over there? You can't take both of them with you."

"It will only be for a year or so, Mother. But yes, that's the hard part. Not dividing it all. But I do sort of feel that the stars are aligning and I can't say no to the universe. It's the only thing I've really ever wanted. God knows I don't have expensive tastes otherwise," I say, looking down at my jeans and work boots.

My mother kisses me on the forehead, which she hasn't done since I was a child and I hug her for a long time, which we also don't do very often.

Sean is surprised, to say the least, when I show up at his school unannounced. I can't get into his dorm room without an ID so I text him asking when would be a good time to meet him in front of the building. I see him walking over, wearing his running clothes: shorts, but with neon compression tights beneath them; a baggy technical shirt; gloves; and his school backpack. It's somewhat chilly and damp and he looks like he's in his own climate zone, especially since he's topped it off with a knit hat. He looks like a well-dressed homeless person, truthfully, carrying everything valuable with him, wherever he goes.

"What the hell are you doing here?" he asks, cheerfully. "Stir crazy up there or something?"

"Nah, I have to talk to you." I follow him up the steps of the dorm room. The building is really nice and new, more like an apartment, but his place still looks as messy as mine, maybe worse, because he's sharing it with two other guys and their junk is piled all over the place. It kind of smells too, and not like horse. Like beer and sweat and some other stuff I'd rather not think about. But we're alone and that's all that matters.

I sit down. "You know that Dad died."

Sean puts his backpack down, throws some clothes onto the floor and takes a seat on the couch. "Yeah, Mom told me."

"You know he left me—something—and not you."

"She told me that, too," he said, clearly uncomfortable. "I guess that's to be expected. It doesn't matter to me."

"But it does," I say, laughing weirdly. And then I tell him how much.

Pause.

"Well, the bastard said all those years he had no money."

"He managed to hide it somewhere I guess."

"I'm surprised he didn't leave it to a dog or something, just to spite us all. I guess he liked you or something. Well...you came and saw him..."

"I'm not sure the visit was worth three million dollars," I say. "That's what the lawyer thinks it will be, roughly, after taxes, fees, and that kind of stuff. I figure—after we split it three ways, it will be about a million for each of us."

"Wait, seriously you..."

"I'm not sure how long it will take to settle. Maybe you understand the legal rules behind all of this better than I do, depending on how much you paid attention in all the financial classes you took that don't require math," I say. I look at the textbooks stacked up beside me, which are being used as a kind of a table for the remnants of the party that was clearly there last night—there are empty glass beer mugs and a half-eaten bag of potato chips piled on top of *Introduction to Financial Accounting*.

"Simon, seriously, you—I don't know what to say."

My brother and I hardly ever address one another by our first names (we usually prefer "asshole") so I almost feel like he's talking to someone else. He sits down beside me. I feel uncomfortable so I look at the ground. There's an open box of pizza with a half-eaten slice hanging out of it. I never look at the ground when I'm riding, I realize; I often look at the ground when I'm not. I think how I say to the kids when they are jumping, "Don't look down, there's no money there." Well, maybe I'm wrong. There's a handful of pennies and dimes next to the pizza box, probably strewn there when the drunk guys were fiddling to pay the deliveryman.

I also think, as different as they all are, just looking at this place would give Max, Cindy, and Daniel the dry heaves.

"Look, Bro, it's not like you have to do this, I know—I know what the horses mean to you. I'm okay."

"Well, of course Mom said she's not spending most of her portion and will help me out if I need it, when I'm ready to buy my own property or something like that. Look, one million, three million, it goes fast with horses if you don't have the talent to make something from nothing. I'm going to Germany, that's what I'm going to do, to study more and maybe find myself another horse. Then see what I can do from there. And you can do with your portion what you want Sean. Mom says she doesn't want you to leave college though."

"I won't."

"I knew you wouldn't."

"She wasn't so sure?"

"You know how she is," I say.

"Yeah, she doesn't trust me. She trusts you, though," says Sean.

"Not really. She just thinks I'm dumber than you and has less control over me, so she's clinging to the little she has over you," I laugh.

"Not dumber. Braver, maybe."

Who else called me that? Max? I don't know why. "Look, it doesn't matter. I just want you to know where it stands with the money. That's all." Sean hugs me and starts to thank me. I stiffen up because it's awkward. "Don't thank me. I don't want to think about how it got divided this way ever again. We'll always help one another out."

I stand and say we need to get something to eat because I'm starving. We wander around and eventually find a place that serves cheap bar snacks. We watch the Celtics game on the bar's television (although I guess we could spring for some fancy place to celebrate, somehow we don't because that feels foreign). That way we have something else to talk about and because we need to know the outcome of the game. It's satisfying to know that something still has clear winners and losers.

34

FORTUNE'S FOOL

I don't talk about what I've learned about my future fortune to anyone at the farm for about a week. For one thing, the thing isn't real at this point. Nothing has actually changed. I'm kind of suspended in limbo. But then Daniel takes me aside to ask if I've thought about what I'm going to be doing in June, when my working studentship ends. I mention what he's talked about before, about needing to learn more from people beyond just this single year.

"Are you still thinking about working for Freddie?"

"Yeah, I'm sure I will apply to his barn after a year, after…after I take more time to study. I'm thinking of doing another year as a working student…Germany, I'm looking into going to Germany. Do you think you could, um, give me the name of someone there?"

Daniel looks at me. "I could, but not someone who would pay you. You'd have to prove yourself all over again there and the system is pretty rigid."

"That's okay."

"What can you learn in Europe that you can't here, exactly? It's not worth mortgaging yourself, you know there is nothing you can count on in the horse world."

"Oh, I know that—but I won't be mortgaging myself." And I tell him everything—well, not about splitting the money three ways, but about the money.

He doesn't seem surprised, exactly, although he does kind of laugh and say, "Well, Shaughnessy, poor little rich boy, hiding your secret from us all this time."

"My father hid this from my mother, somehow, so I didn't know either. Actually, the lawyer thought I would be upset that there wasn't more."

"Still, I stand by my contention that you don't need to go to Europe to learn to ride."

"Maybe so. But I'm restless. Even if it is the same over there, I need to find out for myself that it's the same. And I know me—well, you know me, too. If it doesn't kind of kick my ass and scare me slightly, I'll get bored." Daniel laughs and that makes me relax enough to ask him if he'll take Fortune for a year while I'm away. "He's less bad about pulling his riders, I'm sure some of the better teens can pilot him around the indoor at least, over some low fences during lessons. And Max can ride him," I say.

Daniel pauses for a second, as if hesitating to ask then says, "Have you told Max about this plan?"

"I haven't even told him that I'm going yet. But he knew I was going... somewhere."

"You're very talented, O'Shaughnessy, and you know that. But you're still rough around the edges and you haven't been pushed enough as a rider. You've gone as far as you can with the horses here and you're still pretty young and dumb and brave. You still think you bounce." I think this is Daniel's version of giving me his blessing and I thank him, looking him in the eye, gratefully, rather than looking at the ground.

35

ICH LIEBE DICH

I walk through the door to Max's and for a change I remember to take off my work boots at the door before I throw myself onto the sofa and stretch out. I say, casually, "So, you were in Pony Club, Max, you might know this. Do they have like a Rosetta Stone or whatever for horse German? Like, I don't really need German for asking to please pass the Bratwurst or whatever but I do need to learn the words for collection and on the bit and such."

Max sits beside me and kind of cocks his head, confused.

"Other phrases I'd like to learn include 'I hope you don't put me on the lunge line for six months without reins or stirrups like you guys supposedly sometimes do,' and 'just because I'm an American doesn't mean I can't ride,' and 'so, how fast can you really drive on the Autobahn?'"

"Does this mean that you're going to Germany for—?"

"For a year," I say. "I would have told you sooner but I didn't find out until today."

It's been more than a week since I've learned about the money. I thought it would be best to tell Max everything all at once, rather than break it to him in stages.

"So now I have the funds to become slave labor and take a bit longer to really learn how to ride. One year here just isn't enough.

And I can buy a second horse over there as well as have some time after to make a name for myself. It's a start."

"I'm still kind of taking this all in."

"I do realize that a sane person would probably invest it or something. I don't intend to spend all of it but I take this as a kind of a gift from the universe enabling me to see if I really am as good as I claim myself to be. I don't want to go to any college but you have been right all this time, I see now. I do need some structure. I do need to learn more, a lot more. I was on my own for a long time as a rider and there are still huge gaps in my knowledge. I'm getting to the point where I can't fake anything, not the slightest bit, and even if I could, I wouldn't want to—"

"A gift from the universe, you say? Your father, more specifically. I guess he wasn't such a bad guy after all."

"Oh, he was. This doesn't mean that there are no scars—if he was a really good guy he wouldn't have left it all to me." Max, I'm sure, thinks I'm referring to metaphorical scars but I'm referring to real ones.

"I don't follow."

"He wouldn't have tried to set me against my brother and my mother, leaving all the money to me."

"But you were the only one who came to him when he was dying. Maybe he didn't realize how close you were to your family."

"Maybe, or he did and didn't like it. Anyway, that's settled. Everything is settled, now, except you and me." I mean, I know I'm going to Germany but I don't know where that leaves me and Max, exactly. "I wish you could come with me."

"Being a vet is not the most mobile of occupations."

"No. And I'll only be over there for a year. A year isn't forever."

"Simon, you're still very young. Are you sure you want to be tied down?"

Pause.

"Does that mean you don't want to be tied down?"

"I think I've always made it pretty obvious what I want. But I sowed my wild oats a long time ago, Simon. You're still a kid."

"What is it that you want? Not to get hurt? Or me not to get hurt? You don't have to choose."

Max has been slowly turning his head away from me over the course of our conversation. I put my arms around him and pull him closer, so I can look him in the eye.

"You know this doesn't mean I don't love you. But this is something I have to do. I might fail at it, but I have to see how far I can go as a rider. Please Max—" I try to think of some way to say this without sounding corny. "As long as we love each other we won't really be parted." I kiss him. "You know when I want something, I take it, and you're not getting rid of me that easily."

We spend the night together. We wake up early. Max has work and I am still responsible for morning chores and will be until the morning I leave on the plane. It's only over breakfast that Max asks me what I'm going to do about Fortune.

"I'm keeping him now, of course."

"Are you taking him over to Germany?"

"No. For one, I'll have too many horses to ride over there, and I want to learn as much as I can from the Germans. And for two, he's really gone as far as he wants to go up the levels. I'll always ride him, of course, but it's not fair to expect him to be an Intermediate-level horse when he's not. Plus, he's already been moved around so much, all of his life. So he's staying at Daniel's. I told Daniel you'd ride him."

"What?"

"Don't you want your own horse, like you had when you were in Pony Club as a kid? Think of it as a free, free lease."

"Won't I mess him up?"

"If I thought you'd mess him up, I wouldn't be giving him to you. Now you know you can't get rid of me because if you have any problems with him, you'll have to ask me about them, since I know him best."

"I'm not sure if I should thank you for this or not but I seem to have no choice but to accept," says Max. He makes a face at whatever green concoction he's made for himself this morning in his blender while I shovel down my eggs.

"You do know, after me, he loves you best," I say, grinning.

"I'm not sure I can survive all this love, but I'm trying," says Max.

There is one more thing, an awkward conversation I'm not sure how to broach. "Max, if you need any help with your student loans…"

"Simon, wait until you see what you need to do in Germany. I offered you help, if you remember, all those months ago, and you said it wasn't your style. It's not mine either."

"What's yours is mine."

"In a year; see how you feel in a year, Simon."

There is part of me that wonders what I would have said if Max had told me, "Don't go." But I realize somewhere, deep down inside, that is what he's saying. As I lay beside him last night he wrapped his arms around me tightly, half asleep, almost to the point I could barely move and I swear I could hear him mutter, "Don't go," even though he would never say that to me now, in the harsh light of the kitchen. But the fact that I know that he knows I need to be free and still loves me anyway, no matter how much it might hurt him at times, binds me to him even more. There is even a little part of myself that thinks, just as I want to try harder to be a better rider and learn more about horses while I'm still young and hungry, I also want to be a better man for him, someone who is worthy of the respect of Max, before I settle down. I doubt that will happen in a year but it's a start.

36

IT'S A KISS THAT'S BETTER THAN NONE

J ust like she arrived late, Cindy is leaving early. Her horse will
be shipped in a few days; Cindy is taking a plane to "detox" in
Europe, visiting a friend who summers in France. Her friend
has horses there, and Cindy says, "The detoxing will be riding on the
beach, not worrying about being judged." I think the friend is a guy
she reconnected with at the wedding she attended a couple months
ago, and the way Cindy talks the rides on the beach may be only
part of the detoxification program. Then it's back to training Sam,
though, and back to showing for her father's stable.

Cindy has gotten better over the year. There is no question her
riding has improved, and while she isn't perfect, neither am I. There
is a part of me that feels bad about how harshly I criticized her.

I tell her I'm going to Germany because I've inherited some
money.

Unlike Max, Cindy is totally blasé because that happens in her
world all the time. To her, the million after taxes and everything
is probably pocket change. Still, she says she's happy for me all the
same. "That's what you wanted, isn't it Simon, to really immerse yourself as a rider in learning? Much better than just reading Steinkraus
at night under the covers!"

"It is, Cindy, it is exactly what I wanted. Although I will still read Steinkraus under the covers in Germany to inspire me. I only wish I could take Fortune with me. But it wouldn't be fair to him; he'll be happier here."

"Who will ride him?"

"Max will."

"Simon, is Dr. Max...?"

"Yes, Cindy, he's my boyfriend."

"Has he been for a long time?"

"Almost as long as I've been here."

"I'm so dumb, Simon, I should have spotted it. Is that why he doesn't like me anymore?"

"No, Cindy, that isn't it." I want to say the real reason why he turned so cold to her but there isn't much point in doing so, not now. And I know that Cindy is still tied to her father and his money, no matter what she feels about everything he says.

"Simon, I wanted to thank you for all you've done for me this year. The extra training, dragging me out of the snow, and listening to me. The sandwich. Covering for me when I didn't know what I was doing. All that. I couldn't have survived without you."

"Part of my job description, hunter princess," I say.

Cindy's luggage is in the back of the car waiting to take her to the airport. Still pink and still flowery, still monogrammed. It angers me less than it did, though, when I saw it all those months ago. Practically a lifetime, it seems.

I watch Fortune in the distance. Another thing that hasn't changed: He's still alone, still keeping his distance from the other horses and baring his teeth when they try to get at his hay. He's tolerated here by the other horses and he tolerates them, but I still wouldn't say he's made friends, exactly. He canters around restlessly. I know I'll have to take him out riding later to settle him.

Cindy follow my gaze. "I'm sorry he wasn't the Intermediate—or better—horse you wanted, Simon."

"I'm not. They thought he was useless before and clearly he wasn't that. He's still accomplished many things, more than anyone thought possible when he was sold. And he has a home now, for good. I'm never getting rid of him. He's been too good to me and is too much fun to ride."

Cindy laughs. "You're more sentimental than I thought you were, Simon."

"It's not sentiment. I still like him even though I am going to be moving on."

"I'm going to miss you, Simon."

"Oh, I'm sure we'll see each other around as competitors, Cindy, before long!"

"As friendly adversaries, of course."

"Would we be anything else?"

"I meant my father—"

"You can't control what your father does, only what you do, Cindy," I say, not wanting to end everything here sour. "That's true of all of us."

"I wish it was different, but there is nothing I can do."

Cindy still looks pretty fragile, as if a strong wind could blow her to the ground. She's in her civilian clothes: a tasteful plaid mini-skirt, brown boots that could never be worn riding, and a long-sleeved pink cardigan and blouse. It's as if she's trying to shield her arms from my view or it's just because it's still cool here today. Her hair is pulled back tightly and I can see her face clearly. Even getting ready for a plane ride home is still a production, maybe because her father will see her when she arrives and she needs to look perfect, maybe because Cindy always needs to look perfect for Cindy.

I smile a bit. "There are some people who would say I've made a series of bad choices, not going to college, for example, and buying my horse, and—" visiting my father, I think, but don't say— "not doing anything sensible and it's all worked out in the end. Given how I am as a person, I couldn't see myself doing otherwise. I knew I'd never make it in college and like working in a box of a cubicle and I was right." This is the first time I've ever mentioned the Box to Cynthia, but she seems to kinda get it.

"You're a very passionate person, Simon, that's why, you follow your heart." She looks away, uncomfortable, and then takes out a mirror to check her makeup. I haven't seen her wearing a full face since the night I carried her home, the snowy night of the Mustang's demise. "Most people question themselves, I know I do. You're very brave. That's why all the horses trust you so much."

Max has called me brave as well. "I've never gotten along with people that well, only horses, so it has nothing to do with being brave at all. Nothing else for me to do."

Cynthia is about to go and she takes my hand as if to shake it but suddenly she's kissing me. I don't pull back but I don't respond, either. "I'll miss you, Simon," she whispers in my ear, like she's telling me she loves me. "I wish you were coming to work for us but I understand why you can't."

As the car taking her to the airport pulls away it strikes me that its black squareness is a kind of box itself.

Fortune gets excited as the car speeds by his paddock and while the other horses stand and eat he starts running around, trying to race the vehicle. He really needs to be exercised; he really needs to jump something big today, I decide. I know Max will work up to it but until then, I'd best ride Fortune hard as I can, as often as I can, until I leave, imprinting what it feels like to be with my horse on my memory over and over again for as long as possible.

THE END

ACKNOWLEDGEMENTS

Many, many thanks to everyone who encouraged me during the writing of this book and its predecessor—but to my friends Rob and Melissa in particular. Also, my former teachers Virginia Blasi, Beverly Muldoon, and Judith Chaiet.

Many more thanks to my riding instructor/trainer Nancy Bloom of Best Chance Farm for putting up with a middle-aged rider without either the talent or the confidence of the protagonist of this novel.

And, of course, to all the horses that I rode before, during, and after writing this novel.

ABOUT THE AUTHOR

Mary Pagones is a New Jersey-based writer and editor. An enthusiastic reader of all things pony-and horse-related throughout her life, she took up riding seriously as an adult. This is her second novel.

Mary has a slight (*cough*) Internet addiction and loves to interact with her fans (or any people who love horses and reading). Please feel free to "friend" and "follow" her on Facebook, Twitter, and Instagram. And if you liked this book or any of her other novels, please let fellow readers know and leave a review on Amazon, Goodreads, or both!

Cover image Credit:
©iStock.com/ Somogyvari

41694340R00208

Made in the USA
Middletown, DE
21 March 2017